A Tr      nunity

D1579523

# A Thousand Splendid Suns

## Khaled Hosseini

W F HOWES LTD

This large print edition published in 2007 by
W F Howes Ltd
Unit 4, Rearsby Business Park, Gaddesby Lane,
Rearsby, Leicester LE7 4YH

1  3  5  7  9  10  8  6  4  2

First published in the United Kingdom in 2007
by Bloomsbury
Translation of the Poem 'Kabul' by
Josephine Barry Davis

A CIP catalogue record for this book is available
from the British Library

ISBN 978 1 40740 544 5

Typeset by Palimpsest Book Production Limited,
Grangemouth, Stirlingshire
Printed and bound in Great Britain
by the MPG Books Group

This book is dedicated to Haris and Farah, both the *noor* of my eyes, and to the women of Afghanistan.

# PART I

# CHAPTER 1

Mariam was five years old the first time she heard the word *harami*.

It happened on a Thursday. It must have, because Mariam remembered that she had been restless and preoccupied that day, the way she was only on Thursdays, the day when Jalil visited her at the *kolba*. To pass the time until the moment that she would see him at last, crossing the knee-high grass in the clearing and waving, Mariam had climbed a chair and taken down her mother's Chinese tea set. The tea set was the sole relic that Mariam's mother, Nana, had of her own mother, who had died when Nana was two. Nana cherished each blue-and-white porcelain piece, the graceful curve of the pot's spout, the hand-painted finches and chrysanthemums, the dragon on the sugar bowl, meant to ward off evil.

It was this last piece that slipped from Mariam's fingers, that fell to the wooden floorboards of the *kolba* and shattered.

When Nana saw the bowl, her face flushed red and her upper lip shivered, and her eyes, both the lazy one and the good, settled on Mariam in a flat, unblinking way. Nana looked so mad that Mariam feared the *jinn* would enter her mother's body again. But the *jinn* didn't come, not that time. Instead, Nana grabbed Mariam by the wrists, pulled her close, and, through gritted teeth, said, 'You are a clumsy little *harami*. This is my reward for everything I've endured. An heirloom-breaking, clumsy little *harami*.'

At the time, Mariam did not understand. She did not know what this word *harami* – bastard – meant. Nor was she old enough to appreciate the injustice, to see that it is the creators of the *harami* who are culpable, not the *harami*, whose only sin is being born. Mariam *did* surmise, by the way Nana said the word, that it was an ugly, loathsome thing to be a *harami*, like an insect, like the scurrying cockroaches Nana was always cursing and sweeping out of the *kolba*.

Later, when she was older, Mariam did understand. It was the way Nana uttered the word – not so much saying it as spitting it at her – that made Mariam feel the full sting of it. She understood then what Nana meant, that a *harami* was an unwanted thing; that she, Mariam, was an illegitimate person who would never have legitimate claim to the things other people had, things such as love, family, home, acceptance.

Jalil never called Mariam this name. Jalil said she was his little flower. He was fond of sitting her on his lap and telling her stories, like the time he told her that Herat, the city where Mariam was

4

born, in 1959, had once been the cradle of Persian culture, the home of writers, painters, and Sufis.

'You couldn't stretch a leg here without poking a poet in the ass,' he laughed.

Jalil told her the story of Queen Gauhar Shad, who had raised the famous minarets as her loving ode to Herat back in the fifteenth century. He described to her the green wheat fields of Herat, the orchards, the vines pregnant with plump grapes, the city's crowded, vaulted bazaars.

'There is a pistachio tree,' Jalil said one day, 'and beneath it, Mariam jo, is buried none other than the great poet Jami.' He leaned in and whispered, 'Jami lived over five hundred years ago. He did. I took you there once, to the tree. You were little. You wouldn't remember.'

It was true. Mariam didn't remember. And though she would live the first fifteen years of her life within walking distance of Herat, Mariam would never see this storied tree. She would never see the famous minarets up close, and she would never pick fruit from Herat's orchards or stroll in its fields of wheat. But whenever Jalil talked like this, Mariam would listen with enchantment. She would admire Jalil for his vast and worldly knowledge. She would quiver with pride to have a father who knew such things.

'What rich lies!' Nana said after Jalil left. 'Rich man telling rich lies. He never took you to any tree. And don't let him charm you. He betrayed us, your beloved father. He cast us out. He cast us out of his big fancy house like we were nothing to him. He did it happily.'

Mariam would listen dutifully to this. She never dared say to Nana how much she disliked her talking this way about Jalil. The truth was that around Jalil, Mariam did not feel at all like a *harami*. For an hour or two every Thursday, when Jalil came to see her, all smiles and gifts and endearments, Mariam felt deserving of all the beauty and bounty that life had to give. And, for this, Mariam loved Jalil.

Even if she had to share him.

Jalil had three wives and nine children, nine legitimate children, all of whom were strangers to Mariam. He was one of Herat's wealthiest men. He owned a cinema, which Mariam had never seen, but at her insistence Jalil had described it to her, and so she knew that the façade was made of blue-and-tan terra-cotta tiles, that it had private balcony seats and a trellised ceiling. Double swinging doors opened into a tiled lobby, where posters of Hindi films were encased in glass displays. On Tuesdays, Jalil said one day, kids got free ice cream at the concession stand.

Nana smiled demurely when he said this. She waited until he had left the *kolba*, before snickering and saying, 'The children of strangers get ice cream. What do you get, Mariam? Stories of ice cream.'

In addition to the cinema, Jalil owned land in

Karokh, land in Farah, three carpet stores, a clothing shop, and a black 1956 Buick Roadmaster. He was one of Herat's best-connected men, friend of the mayor and the provincial governor. He had a cook, a driver, and three housekeepers.

Nana had been one of the housekeepers. Until her belly began to swell.

When that happened, Nana said, the collective gasp of Jalil's family sucked the air out of Herat. His in-laws swore blood would flow. The wives demanded that he throw her out. Nana's own father, who was a lowly stone carver in the nearby village of Gul Daman, disowned her. Disgraced, he packed his things and boarded a bus to Iran, never to be seen or heard from again.

'Sometimes,' Nana said early one morning, as she was feeding the chickens outside the *kolba*, 'I wish my father had had the stomach to sharpen one of his knives and do the honorable thing. It might have been better for me.' She tossed another handful of seeds into the coop, paused, and looked at Mariam. 'Better for you too, maybe. It would have spared you the grief of knowing that you are what you are. But he was a coward, my father. He didn't have the *dil*, the heart, for it.'

Jalil didn't have the *dil* either, Nana said, to do the honorable thing. To stand up to his family, to his wives and in-laws, and accept responsibility for what he had done. Instead, behind closed doors, a face-saving deal had quickly been struck. The next day, he had made her gather her few things from the servants' quarters, where she'd been living, and sent her off.

'You know what he told his wives by way of defense? That I *forced* myself on him. That it was my fault. *Didi?* You see? This is what it means to be a woman in this world.'

Nana put down the bowl of chicken feed. She lifted Mariam's chin with a finger.

'Look at me, Mariam.'

Reluctantly, Mariam did.

Nana said, 'Learn this now and learn it well, my daughter: Like a compass needle that points north, a man's accusing finger always finds a woman. Always. You remember that, Mariam.'

# CHAPTER 2

To Jalil and his wives, I was a pokeroot. A mugwort. You too. And you weren't even born yet.'

'What's a mugwort?' Mariam asked.

'A weed,' Nana said. 'Something you rip out and toss aside.'

Mariam frowned internally. Jalil didn't treat her as a weed. He never had. But Mariam thought it wise to suppress this protest.

'Unlike weeds, I had to be replanted, you see, given food and water. On account of you. That was the deal Jalil made with his family.'

Nana said she had refused to live in Herat.

'For what? To watch him drive his *kinchini* wives around town all day?'

She said she wouldn't live in her father's empty house either, in the village of Gul Daman, which sat on a steep hill two kilometers north of Herat. She said she wanted to live somewhere removed, detached, where neighbors wouldn't stare at her belly, point at her, snicker, or, worse yet, assault her with insincere kindnesses.

'And, believe me,' Nana said, 'it was a relief to

9

your father having me out of sight. It suited him just fine.'

It was Muhsin, Jalil's eldest son by his first wife, Khadija, who suggested the clearing. It was on the outskirts of Gul Daman. To get to it, one took a rutted, uphill dirt track that branched off the main road between Herat and Gul Daman. The track was flanked on either side by knee-high grass and speckles of white and bright yellow flowers. The track snaked uphill and led to a flat field where poplars and cottonwoods soared and wild bushes grew in clusters. From up there, one could make out the tips of the rusted blades of Gul Daman's windmill, on the left, and, on the right, all of Herat spread below. The path ended perpendicular to a wide, trout-filled stream, which rolled down from the Safid-koh mountains surrounding Gul Daman. Two hundred yards upstream, toward the mountains, there was a circular grove of weeping willow trees. In the center, in the shade of the willows, was the clearing.

Jalil went there to have a look. When he came back, Nana said, he sounded like a warden bragging about the clean walls and shiny floors of his prison.

'And so, your father built us this rathole.'

Nana had almost married once, when she was fifteen. The suitor had been a boy from Shindand, a young parakeet seller. Mariam knew the story from Nana herself, and, though Nana dismissed

10

the episode, Mariam could tell by the wistful light in her eyes that she had been happy. Perhaps for the only time in her life, during those days leading up to her wedding, Nana had been genuinely happy.

As Nana told the story, Mariam sat on her lap and pictured her mother being fitted for a wedding dress. She imagined her on horseback, smiling shyly behind a veiled green gown, her palms painted red with henna, her hair parted with silver dust, the braids held together by tree sap. She saw musicians blowing the *shahnai* flute and banging on *dohol* drums, street children hooting and giving chase.

Then, a week before the wedding date, a *jinn* had entered Nana's body. This required no description to Mariam. She had witnessed it enough times with her own eyes: Nana collapsing suddenly, her body tightening, becoming rigid, her eyes rolling back, her arms and legs shaking as if something were throttling her from the inside, the froth at the corners of her mouth, white, sometimes pink with blood. Then the drowsiness, the frightening dis-orientation, the incoherent mumbling.

When the news reached Shindand, the parakeet seller's family called off the wedding.

'They got spooked' was how Nana put it.

The wedding dress was stashed away. After that, there were no more suitors.

In the clearing, Jalil and two of his sons, Farhad and Muhsin, built the small *kolba* where Mariam would live the first fifteen years of her life. They raised it with sun-dried bricks and plastered it with mud and handfuls of straw. It had two sleeping cots, a wooden table, two straight-backed chairs, a window, and shelves nailed to the walls where Nana placed clay pots and her beloved Chinese tea set. Jalil put in a new cast-iron stove for the winter and stacked logs of chopped wood behind the *kolba*. He added a tandoor outside for making bread and a chicken coop with a fence around it. He brought a few sheep, built them a feeding trough. He had Farhad and Muhsin dig a deep hole a hundred yards outside the circle of willows and built an outhouse over it.

Jalil could have hired laborers to build the *kolba*, Nana said, but he didn't.

'His idea of penance.'

In Nana's account of the day that she gave birth to Mariam, no one came to help. It happened on a damp, overcast day in the spring of 1959, she said, the twenty-sixth year of King Zahir Shah's mostly uneventful forty-year reign. She said that Jalil hadn't bothered to summon a doctor, or even a midwife, even though he knew that the *jinn* might enter her body and cause her to have one of her fits in the act of delivering. She lay all alone on the *kolba*'s floor, a knife by her side, sweat drenching her body.

'When the pain got bad, I'd bite on a pillow and scream into it until I was hoarse. And still no one came to wipe my face or give me a drink of water.

12

And you, Mariam jo, you were in no rush. Almost two days you made me lay on that cold, hard floor. I didn't eat or sleep, all I did was push and pray that you would come out.'

'I'm sorry, Nana.'

'I cut the cord between us myself. That's why I had a knife.'

'I'm sorry.'

Nana always gave a slow, burdened smile here, one of lingering recrimination or reluctant forgiveness, Mariam could never tell. It did not occur to young Mariam to ponder the unfairness of apologizing for the manner of her own birth.

By the time it *did* occur to her, around the time she turned ten, Mariam no longer believed this story of her birth. She believed Jalil's version, that though he'd been away he'd arranged for Nana to be taken to a hospital in Herat where she had been tended to by a doctor. She had lain on a clean, proper bed in a well-lit room. Jalil shook his head with sadness when Mariam told him about the knife.

Mariam also came to doubt that she had made her mother suffer for two full days.

'They told me it was all over within under an hour,' Jalil said. 'You were a good daughter, Mariam jo. Even in birth you were a good daughter.'

'He wasn't even there!' Nana spat. 'He was in Takht-e-Safar, horseback riding with his precious friends.'

When they informed him that he had a new daughter, Nana said, Jalil had shrugged, kept brushing his horse's mane, and stayed in Takht-e-Safar another two weeks.

'The truth is, he didn't even hold you until you were a month old. And then only to look down once, comment on your longish face, and hand you back to me.'

Mariam came to disbelieve this part of the story as well. Yes, Jalil admitted, he had been horseback riding in Takht-e-Safar, but, when they gave him the news, he had not shrugged. He had hopped on the saddle and ridden back to Herat. He had bounced her in his arms, run his thumb over her flaky eyebrows, and hummed a lullaby. Mariam did not picture Jalil saying that her face was long, though it was true that it was long.

Nana said she was the one who'd picked the name Mariam because it had been the name of her mother. Jalil said he chose the name because Mariam, the tuberose, was a lovely flower.

'Your favorite?' Mariam asked.

'Well, one of,' he said and smiled.

# CHAPTER 3

O ne of Mariam's earliest memories was the sound of a wheelbarrow's squeaky iron wheels bouncing over rocks. The wheelbarrow came once a month, filled with rice, flour, tea, sugar, cooking oil, soap, toothpaste. It was pushed by two of Mariam's half brothers, usually Muhsin and Ramin, sometimes Ramin and Farhad. Up the dirt track, over rocks and pebbles, around holes and bushes, the boys took turns pushing until they reached the stream. There, the wheelbarrow had to be emptied and the items hand-carried across the water. Then the boys would transfer the wheelbarrow across the stream and load it up again. Another two hundred yards of pushing followed, this time through tall, dense grass and around thickets of shrubs. Frogs leaped out of their way. The brothers waved mosquitoes from their sweaty faces.

'He has servants,' Mariam said. 'He could send a servant.'

'His idea of penance,' Nana said.

The sound of the wheelbarrow drew Mariam and Nana outside. Mariam would always remember

Nana the way she looked on Ration Day: a tall, bony, barefoot woman leaning in the doorway, her lazy eye narrowed to a slit, arms crossed in a defiant and mocking way. Her short-cropped, sunlit hair would be uncovered and uncombed. She would wear an ill-fitting gray shirt buttoned to the throat. The pockets were filled with walnut-sized rocks.

The boys sat by the stream and waited as Mariam and Nana transferred the rations to the *kolha*. They knew better than to get any closer than thirty yards, even though Nana's aim was poor and most of the rocks landed well short of their targets. Nana yelled at the boys as she carried bags of rice inside, and called them names Mariam didn't understand. She cursed their mothers, made hateful faces at them. The boys never returned the insults.

Mariam felt sorry for the boys. How tired their arms and legs must be, she thought pityingly, pushing that heavy load. She wished she were allowed to offer them water. But she said nothing, and if they waved at her she didn't wave back. Once, to please Nana, Mariam even yelled at Muhsin, told him he had a mouth shaped like a lizard's ass – and was consumed later with guilt, shame, and fear that they would tell Jalil. Nana, though, laughed so hard, her rotting front tooth in full display, that Mariam thought she would lapse into one of her fits. She looked at Mariam when she was done and said, 'You're a good daughter.'

When the barrow was empty, the boys scuffled back and pushed it away. Mariam would wait and

watch them disappear into the tall grass and flowering weeds.

'Are you coming?'
'Yes, Nana.'
'They laugh at you. They do. I hear them.'
'I'm coming.'
'You don't believe me?'
'Here I am.'
'You know I love you, Mariam jo.'

In the mornings, they awoke to the distant bleating
of sheep and the high-pitched toot of a flute as
Gul Daman's shepherds led their flock to graze
on the grassy hillside. Mariam and Nana milked
the goats, fed the hens, and collected eggs. They
made bread together. Nana showed her how to
knead dough, how to kindle the tandoor and slap
the flattened dough onto its inner walls. Nana
taught her to sew too, and to cook rice and all
the different toppings: *shalqam* stew with turnip,
spinach *sabzi*, cauliflower with ginger.

Nana made no secret of her dislike for visitors
– and, in fact, people in general – but she made
exceptions for a select few. And so there was Gul
Daman's leader, the village *arbab*, Habib Khan, a
small-headed, bearded man with a large belly who
came by once a month or so, tailed by a servant,
who carried a chicken, sometimes a pot of *kichiri*
rice, or a basket of dyed eggs, for Mariam.

Then there was a rotund, old woman that Nana
called Bibi jo, whose late husband had been a

17

stone carver and friends with Nana's father. Bibi jo was invariably accompanied by one of her six brides and a grandchild or two. She limped and huffed her way across the clearing and made a great show of rubbing her hip and lowering herself, with a pained sigh, onto the chair that Nana pulled up for her. Bibi jo too always brought Mariam something, a box of *dishlemeh* candy, a basket of quinces. For Nana, she first brought complaints about her failing health, and then gossip from Herat and Gul Daman, delivered at length and with gusto, as her daughter-in-law sat listening quietly and dutifully behind her.

But Mariam's favorite, other than Jalil of course, was Mullah Faizullah, the elderly village Koran tutor, its *akhund*. He came by once or twice a week from Gul Daman to teach Mariam the five daily *namaz* prayers and tutor her in Koran recitation, just as he had taught Nana when she'd been a little girl. It was Mullah Faizullah who had taught Mariam to read, who had patiently looked over her shoulder as her lips worked the words soundlessly, her index finger lingering beneath each word, pressing until the nail bed went white, as though she could squeeze the meaning out of the symbols. It was Mullah Faizullah who had held her hand, guided the pencil in it along the rise of each *alef*, the curve of each *beh*, the three dots of each *seh*.

He was a gaunt, stooping old man with a toothless smile and a white beard that dropped to his

18

navel. Usually, he came alone to the *kolba*, though sometimes with his russet-haired son Hamza, who was a few years older than Mariam. When he showed up at the *kolba*, Mariam kissed Mullah Faizullah's hand – which felt like kissing a set of twigs covered with a thin layer of skin – and he kissed the top of her brow before they sat inside for the day's lesson. After, the two of them sat outside the *kolba*, ate pine nuts and sipped green tea, watched the bulbul birds darting from tree to tree. Sometimes they went for walks among the bronze fallen leaves and alder bushes, along the stream and toward the mountains. Mullah Faizullah twirled the beads of his *tasbeh* rosary as they strolled, and, in his quivering voice, told Mariam stories of all the things he'd seen in his youth, like the two-headed snake he'd found in Iran, on Isfahan's Thirty-three Arch Bridge, or the watermelon he had split once outside the Blue Mosque in Mazar, to find the seeds forming the words *Allah* on one half, *Akbar* on the other.

Mullah Faizullah admitted to Mariam that, at times, he did not understand the meaning of the Koran's words. But he said he liked the enchanting sounds the Arabic words made as they rolled off his tongue. He said they comforted him, eased his heart.

'They'll comfort you too, Mariam jo,' he said. 'You can summon them in your time of need, and they won't fail you. God's words will never betray you, my girl.'

Mullah Faizullah listened to stories as well as he told them. When Mariam spoke, his attention never wavered. He nodded slowly and smiled with a look of gratitude, as if he had been granted a coveted privilege. It was easy to tell Mullah Faizullah things that Mariam didn't dare tell Nana.

One day, as they were walking, Mariam told him that she wished she would be allowed to go to school.

'I mean a real school, *akhund* sahib. Like in a classroom. Like my father's other kids.'

Mullah Faizullah stopped.

The week before, Bibi jo had brought news that Jalil's daughters Saideh and Naheed were going to the Mehri School for girls in Herat. Since then, thoughts of classrooms and teachers had rattled around Mariam's head, images of notebooks with lined pages, columns of numbers, and pens that made dark, heavy marks. She pictured herself in a classroom with other girls her age. Mariam longed to place a ruler on a page and draw important-looking lines.

'Is that what you want?' Mullah Faizullah said, looking at her with his soft, watery eyes, his hands behind his stooping back, the shadow of his turban falling on a patch of bristling buttercups.

'Yes.'

'And you want to me ask your mother for permission.'

Mariam smiled. Other than Jalil, she thought there was no one in the world who understood her better than her old tutor.

'Then what can I do? God, in His wisdom, has given us each weaknesses, and foremost among my many is that I am powerless to refuse you, Mariam jo,' he said, tapping her cheek with one arthritic finger.

But later, when he broached Nana, she dropped the knife with which she was slicing onions. 'What for?'

'If the girl wants to learn, let her, my dear. Let the girl have an education.'

'Learn? Learn what, Mullah sahib?' Nana said sharply. 'What is there to learn?' She snapped her eyes toward Mariam.

Mariam looked down at her hands.

'What's the sense schooling a girl like you? It's like shining a spittoon. And you'll learn nothing of value in those schools. There is only one, only one skill a woman like you and me needs in life, and they don't teach it in school. Look at me.'

'You should not speak like this to her, my child,' Mullah Faizullah said.

'Look at me.'

Mariam did.

'Only one skill. And it's this: *tahamul*. Endure.'

'Endure what, Nana?'

'Oh, don't you fret about *that*,' Nana said. 'There won't be any shortage of things.'

She went on to say how Jalil's wives had called her an ugly, lowly stone carver's daughter. How they'd made her wash laundry outside in the cold until her face went numb and her fingertips burned.

21

'It's our lot in life, Mariam. Women like us. We endure. It's all we have. Do you understand? Besides, they'll laugh at you in school. They will. They'll call you *harami*. They'll say the most terrible things about you. I won't have it.'

Mariam nodded.

'And no more talk about school. You're all I have. I won't lose you to them. Look at me. No more talk about school.'

'Be reasonable. Come now. If the girl wants—' Mullah Faizullah began.

'And you, *akhund* sahib, with all due respect, you should know better than to encourage these foolish ideas of hers. If you really care about her, then you make her see that she belongs here at home with her mother. There is nothing out there for her. Nothing but rejection and heartache. I know, *akhund* sahib. I *know*.'

# CHAPTER 4

Mariam loved having visitors at the *kolba*. The village *arbab* and his gifts, Bibi jo and her aching hip and endless gossiping, and, of course, Mullah Faizullah. But there was no one, no one, that Mariam longed to see more than Jalil.

The anxiety set in on Tuesday nights. Mariam would sleep poorly, fretting that some business entanglement would prevent Jalil from coming on Thursday, that she would have to wait a whole other week to see him. On Wednesdays, she paced outside, around the *kolba*, tossed chicken feed absentmindedly into the coop. She went for aimless walks, picking petals from flowers and batting at the mosquitoes nibbling on her arms. Finally, on Thursdays, all she could do was sit against a wall, eyes glued to the stream, and wait. If Jalil was running late, a terrible dread filled her bit by bit. Her knees would weaken, and she would have to go somewhere and lie down.

Then Nana would call, 'And there he is, your father. In all his glory.'

Mariam would leap to her feet when she spotted

him hopping stones across the stream, all smiles and hearty waves. Mariam knew that Nana was watching her, gauging her reaction, and it always took effort to stay in the doorway, to wait, to watch him slowly make his way to her, to not run to him. She restrained herself, patiently watched him walk through the tall grass, his suit jacket slung over his shoulder, the breeze lifting his red necktie.

When Jalil entered the clearing, he would throw his jacket on the tandoor and open his arms. Mariam would walk, then finally run, to him, and he would catch her under the arms and toss her up high. Mariam would squeal.

Suspended in the air, Mariam would see Jalil's upturned face below her, his wide, crooked smile, his widow's peak, his cleft chin – a perfect pocket for the tip of her pinkie – his teeth, the whitest in a town of rotting molars. She liked his trimmed mustache, and she liked that no matter the weather he always wore a suit on his visits – dark brown, his favorite color, with the white triangle of a handkerchief in the breast pocket – and cuff links too, and a tie, usually red, which he left loosened. Mariam could see herself too, reflected in the brown of Jalil's eyes: her hair billowing, her face blazing with excitement, the sky behind her.

Nana said that one of these days he would miss, that she, Mariam, would slip through his fingers, hit the ground, and break a bone. But Mariam did not believe that Jalil would drop her. She believed that she would always land safely into her father's clean, well-manicured hands.

They sat outside the *kolba*, in the shade, and Nana served them tea. Jalil and she acknowledged each other with an uneasy smile and a nod. Jalil never brought up Nana's rock throwing or her cursing.

Despite her rants against him when he wasn't around, Nana was subdued and mannerly when Jalil visited. Her hair was always washed. She brushed her teeth, wore her best *hijab* for him. She sat quietly on a chair across from him, hands folded on her lap. She did not look at him directly and never used coarse language around him. When she laughed, she covered her mouth with a fist to hide the bad tooth.

Nana asked about his businesses. And his wives too. When she told him that she had heard, through Bibi jo, that his youngest wife, Nargis, was expecting her third child, Jalil smiled courteously and nodded.

'Well. You must be happy,' Nana said. 'How many is that for you, now? Ten, is it, *mashallah?* Ten?'

Jalil said yes, ten.

'Eleven, if you count Mariam, of course.'

Later, after Jalil went home, Mariam and Nana had a small fight about this. Mariam said she had tricked him.

After tea with Nana, Mariam and Jalil always went fishing in the stream. He showed her how to cast her line, how to reel in the trout. He taught her the proper way to gut a trout, to clean it, to lift the meat off the bone in one motion. He drew pictures for her as they waited for a strike, showed her how to draw an elephant in one stroke without ever lifting the pen off the paper. He taught her rhymes. Together they sang:

*Lili lili birdbath,*
*Sitting on a dirt path,*
*Minnow sat on the rim and drank,*
*Slipped, and in the water she sank.*

Jalil brought clippings from Herat's newspaper, *Ittifaq-i Islam*, and read from them to her. He was Mariam's link, her proof that there existed a world at large, beyond the *kolba*, beyond Gul Daman and Herat too, a world of presidents with unpronounceable names, and trains and museums and soccer, and rockets that orbited the earth and landed on the moon, and, every Thursday, Jalil brought a piece of that world with him to the *kolba*.

He was the one who told her in the summer of 1973, when Mariam was fourteen, that King Zahir Shah, who had ruled from Kabul for forty years, had been overthrown in a bloodless coup.

'His cousin Daoud Khan did it while the king was in Italy getting medical treatment. You remember Daoud Khan, right? I told you about him. He was prime minister in Kabul when you were born. Anyway, Afghanistan is no longer a monarchy, Mariam. You see, it's a republic now, and Daoud Khan is the president. There are rumors that the socialists in Kabul helped him take power. Not that he's a socialist himself, mind you, but that they helped him. That's the rumor anyway.'

Mariam asked him what a socialist was and Jalil began to explain, but Mariam barely heard him.

'Are you listening?'

'I am.'

He saw her looking at the bulge in his coat's side pocket. 'Ah. Of course. Well. Here, then. Without further ado . . .'

He fished a small box from his pocket and gave it to her. He did this from time to time, bring her small presents. A carnelian bracelet cuff one time, a choker with lapis lazuli beads another. That day, Mariam opened the box and found a leaf-shaped pendant, tiny coins etched with moons and stars hanging from it.

'Try it on, Mariam jo.'

She did. 'What do you think?'

Jalil beamed. 'I think you look like a queen.'

After he left, Nana saw the pendant around Mariam's neck.

'Nomad jewelry,' she said. 'I've seen them make it. They melt the coins people throw at them and make jewelry. Let's see him bring you gold next time, your precious father. Let's see him.'

When it was time for Jalil to leave, Mariam

always stood in the doorway and watched him exit the clearing, deflated at the thought of the week that stood, like an immense, immovable object, between her and his next visit. Mariam always held her breath as she watched him go. She held her breath and, in her head, counted seconds. She pretended that for each second that she didn't breathe, God would grant her another day with Jalil.

At night, Mariam lay in her cot and wondered what his house in Herat was like. She wondered what it would be like to live with him, to see him every day. She pictured herself handing him a towel as he shaved, telling him when he nicked himself. She would brew tea for him. She would sew on his missing buttons. They would take walks in Herat together, in the vaulted bazaar where Jalil said you could find anything you wanted. They would ride in his car, and people would point and say, 'There goes Jalil Khan with his daughter.' He would show her the famed tree that had a poet buried beneath it.

One day soon, Mariam decided, she would tell Jalil these things. And when he heard, when he saw how much she missed him when he was gone, he would surely take her with him. He would bring her to Herat, to live in his house, just like his other children.

# CHAPTER 5

I know what I want,' Mariam said to Jalil.

It was the spring of 1974, the year Mariam turned fifteen. The three of them were sitting outside the *kolba*, in a patch of shade thrown by the willows, on folding chairs arranged in a triangle.

'For my birthday . . . I know what I want.'

'You do?' said Jalil, smiling encouragingly.

Two weeks before, at Mariam's prodding, Jalil had let on that an American film was playing at his cinema. It was a special kind of film, what he'd called a cartoon. The entire film was a series of drawings, he said, thousands of them, so that when they were made into a film and projected onto a screen you had the illusion that the drawings were moving. Jalil said the film told the story of an old, childless toy-maker who is lonely and desperately wants a son. So he carves a puppet, a boy, who magically comes to life. Mariam had asked him to tell her more, and Jalil said that the old man and his puppet had all sorts of adventures, that there was a place called Pleasure Island, and bad boys who turned into donkeys. They even got swallowed

29

by a whale at the end, the puppet and his father. Mariam had told Mullah Faizullah all about this film.

'I want you to take me to your cinema,' Mariam said now. 'I want to see the cartoon. I want to see the puppet boy.'

With this, Mariam sensed a shift in the atmosphere. Her parents stirred in their seats. Mariam could feel them exchanging looks.

'That's not a good idea,' said Nana. Her voice was calm, had the controlled, polite tone she used around Jalil, but Mariam could feel her hard, accusing glare.

Jalil shifted on his chair. He coughed, cleared his throat.

'You know,' he said, 'the picture quality isn't that good. Neither is the sound. And the projector's been malfunctioning recently. Maybe your mother is right. Maybe you can think of another present, Mariam jo.'

'*Aneh*,' Nana said. 'You see? Your father agrees.'

But later, at the stream, Mariam said, 'Take me.'

'I'll tell you what,' Jalil said. 'I'll send someone to pick you up and take you. I'll make sure they get you a good seat and all the candy you want.'

'*Nay*. I want *you* to take me.'

'Mariam jo—'

'And I want you to invite my brothers and sisters too. I want to meet them. I want us all to go, together. It's what I want.'

30

Jalil sighed. He was looking away, toward the mountains.

Mariam remembered him telling her that on the screen a human face looked as big as a house, that when a car crashed up there you felt the metal twisting in your bones. She pictured herself sitting in the private balcony seats, lapping at ice cream, alongside her siblings and Jalil. 'It's what I want,' she said.

Jalil looked at her with a forlorn expression.

'Tomorrow. At noon. I'll meet you at this very spot. All right? Tomorrow?'

'Come here,' he said. He hunkered down, pulled her to him, and held her for a long, long time.

At first, Nana paced around the *kolba*, clenching and unclenching her fists.

'Of all the daughters I could have had, why did God give me an ungrateful one like you? Everything I endured for you! How dare you! How dare you abandon me like this, you treacherous little *harami*!'

Then she mocked.

'What a stupid girl you are! You think you matter to him, that you're wanted in his house? You think you're a daughter to him? That he's going to take you in? Let me tell you something. A man's heart is a wretched, wretched thing, Mariam. It isn't like a mother's womb. It won't bleed, it won't stretch to make room for you. I'm the only one who loves you. I'm all you have in this world,

31

Mariam, and when I'm gone you'll have nothing. You'll have nothing. You *are* nothing!'

Then she tried guilt.

'I'll die if you go. The *jinn* will come, and I'll have one of my fits. You'll see, I'll swallow my tongue and die. Don't leave me, Mariam jo. Please stay. I'll die if you go.'

Mariam said nothing.

'You know I love you, Mariam jo.'

Mariam said she was going for a walk.

She feared she might say hurtful things if she stayed: that she knew the *jinn* was a lie, that Jalil had told her that what Nana had was a disease with a name and that pills could make it better. She might have asked Nana why she refused to see Jalil's doctors, as he had insisted she do, why she wouldn't take the pills he'd bought for her. If she could articulate it, she might have said to Nana that she was tired of being an instrument, of being lied to, laid claim to, used. That she was sick of Nana twisting the truths of their life and making her, Mariam, another of her grievances against the world.

*You're afraid, Nana,* she might have said. *You're afraid that I might find the happiness you never had. And you don't want me to be happy. You don't want a good life for me. You're the one with the wretched heart.*

There was a lookout, on the edge of the clearing, where Mariam liked to go. She sat there now, on dry, warm grass. Herat was visible from here, spread below her like a child's board game: the Women's Garden to the north of the city, Char-suq Bazaar and the ruins of Alexander the Great's old citadel to the south. She could make out the minarets in the distance, like the dusty fingers of giants, and the streets that she imagined were milling with people, carts, mules. She saw swallows swooping and circling overhead. She was envious of these birds. They had been to Herat. They had flown over its mosques, its bazaars. Maybe they had landed on the walls of Jalil's home, on the front steps of his cinema.

She picked up ten pebbles and arranged them vertically, in three columns. This was a game that she played privately from time to time when Nana wasn't looking. She put four pebbles in the first column, for Khadija's children, three for Afsoon's, and three in the third column for Nargis's children. Then she added a fourth column. A solitary, eleventh pebble.

The next morning, Mariam wore a cream-colored dress that fell to her knees, cotton trousers, and a green *hijab* over her hair. She agonized a bit over the *hijab*, its being green and not matching the dress, but it would have to do – moths had eaten holes into her white one.

She checked the clock. It was an old hand-wound clock with black numbers on a mint green face, a present from Mullah Faizullah. It was nine o'clock. She wondered where Nana was. She thought about going outside and looking for her, but she dreaded the confrontation, the aggrieved looks. Nana would accuse her of betrayal. She would mock her for her mistaken ambitions.

Mariam sat down. She tried to make time pass by drawing an elephant in one stroke, the way Jalil had shown her, over and over. She became stiff from all the sitting but wouldn't lie down for fear that her dress would wrinkle.

When the hands finally showed eleven-thirty, Mariam pocketed the eleven pebbles and went outside. On her way to the stream, she saw Nana sitting on a chair, in the shade, beneath the domed roof of a weeping willow. Mariam couldn't tell whether Nana saw her or not.

At the stream, Mariam waited by the spot they had agreed on the day before. In the sky, a few gray, cauliflower-shaped clouds drifted by. Jalil had taught her that gray clouds got their color by being so dense that their top parts absorbed the sunlight and cast their own shadow along the base. *That's what you see, Mariam jo*, he had said, *the dark in their underbelly*.

Some time passed.

Mariam went back to the *kolba*. This time, she walked around the west-facing periphery of the clearing so she wouldn't have to pass by Nana. She checked the clock. It was almost one o'clock.

*He's a businessman*, Mariam thought. *Something has come up*.

She went back to the stream and waited awhile longer. Blackbirds circled overhead, dipped into the grass somewhere. She watched a caterpillar inching along the foot of an immature thistle.

She waited until her legs were stiff. This time, she did not go back to the *kolba*. She rolled up the legs of her trousers to the knees, crossed the stream, and, for the first time in her life, headed down the hill for Herat.

Nana was wrong about Herat too. No one pointed. No one laughed. Mariam walked along noisy, crowded, cypress-lined boule-vards, amid a steady stream of pedestrians, bicycle riders, and mule-drawn *garis*, and no one threw a rock at her. No one called her a *harami*. Hardly anyone even looked at her. She was, unexpectedly, marvelously, an ordinary person here.

For a while, Mariam stood by an oval-shaped pool in the center of a big park where pebble paths crisscrossed. With wonder, she ran her fingers over the beautiful marble horses that stood along the edge of the pool and gazed down at the water with opaque eyes. She spied on a cluster of boys who were setting sail to paper ships. Mariam saw flowers everywhere, tulips, lilies, petunias, their petals awash in sunlight. People walked along the paths, sat on benches and sipped tea.

Mariam could hardly believe that she was here. Her heart was battering with excitement. She wished Mullah Faizullah could see her now. How daring he would find her. How brave! She gave herself over to the new life that awaited her in this city, a life with a father, with sisters and brothers, a life in which she would love and be loved back, without reservation or agenda, without shame.

Sprightly, she walked back to the wide thoroughfare near the park. She passed old vendors with leathery faces sitting under the shade of plane trees, gazing at her impassively behind pyramids of cherries and mounds of grapes. Barefoot boys gave chase to cars and buses, waving bags of quinces. Mariam stood at a street corner and watched the passersby, unable to understand how they could be so indifferent to the marvels around them.

After a while, she worked up the nerve to ask the elderly owner of a horse-drawn *gari* if he knew where Jalil, the cinema's owner, lived. The old man had plump cheeks and wore a rainbow-striped *chapan*. 'You're not from Herat, are you?' he said companionably. 'Everyone knows where Jalil Khan lives.'

'Can you point me?'

He opened a foil-wrapped toffee and said, 'Are you alone?'

'Yes.'

'Climb on. I'll take you.'

'I can't pay you. I don't have any money.'

He gave her the toffee. He said he hadn't had a ride in two hours and he was planning on going home anyway. Jalil's house was on the way.

Mariam climbed onto the *gari*. They rode in silence, side by side. On the way there, Mariam saw herb shops, and open-fronted cubbyholes where shoppers bought oranges and pears, books, shawls, even falcons. Children played marbles in circles drawn in dust. Outside teahouses, on carpet-covered wooden platforms, men drank tea and smoked tobacco from hookahs.

The old man turned onto a wide, conifer-lined street. He brought his horse to a stop at the midway point.

'There. Looks like you're in luck, *dokhtar jo*. That's his car.'

Mariam hopped down. He smiled and rode on.

Mariam had never before touched a car. She ran her fingers along the hood of Jalil's car, which was black, shiny, with glittering wheels in which Mariam saw a flattened, widened version of herself. The seats were made of white leather. Behind the steering wheel, Mariam saw round glass panels with needles behind them.

For a moment, Mariam heard Nana's voice in her head, mocking, dousing the deep-seated glow of her hopes. With shaky legs, Mariam approached the front door of the house. She put her hands on the walls. They were so tall, so foreboding, Jalil's walls. She had to crane her neck to see where the tops of cypress trees protruded over them from the other side. The treetops swayed in the breeze, and she imagined they were nodding their welcome

37

to her. Mariam steadied herself against the waves of dismay passing through her.

A barefoot young woman opened the door. She had a tattoo under her lower lip.

'I'm here to see Jalil Khan. I'm Mariam. His daughter.'

A look of confusion crossed the girl's face. Then, a flash of recognition. There was a faint smile on her lips now, and an air of eagerness about her, of anticipation. 'Wait here,' the girl said quickly.

She closed the door.

A few minutes passed. Then a man opened the door. He was tall and square-shouldered, with sleepy-looking eyes and a calm face.

'I'm Jalil Khan's chauffeur,' he said, not unkindly.

'His what?'

'His driver. Jalil Khan is not here.'

'I see his car,' Mariam said.

'He's away on urgent business.'

'When will he be back?'

'He didn't say.'

Mariam said she would wait.

He closed the gates. Mariam sat, and drew her knees to her chest. It was early evening already, and she was getting hungry. She ate the *gari* driver's toffee. A while later, the driver came out again.

'You need to go home now,' he said. 'It'll be dark in less than an hour.'

'I'm used to the dark.'

38

'It'll get cold too. Why don't you let me drive you home? I'll tell him you were here.'

Mariam only looked at him.

'I'll take you to a hotel, then. You can sleep comfortably there. We'll see what we can do in the morning.'

'Let me in the house.'

'I've been instructed not to. Look, no one knows when he's coming back. It could be days.'

Mariam crossed her arms.

The driver sighed and looked at her with gentle reproach.

Over the years, Mariam would have ample occasion to think about how things might have turned out if she had let the driver take her back to the *kolba*. But she didn't. She spent the night outside Jalil's house. She watched the sky darken, the shadows engulf the neighboring housefronts. The tattooed girl brought her some bread and a plate of rice, which Mariam said she didn't want. The girl left it near Mariam. From time to time, Mariam heard footsteps down the street, doors swinging open, muffled greetings. Electric lights came on, and windows glowed dimly. Dogs barked. When she could no longer resist the hunger, Mariam ate the plate of rice and the bread. Then she listened to the crickets chirping from gardens. Overhead, clouds slid past a pale moon.

In the morning, she was shaken awake. Mariam saw that during the night someone had covered her with a blanket.

It was the driver shaking her shoulder.

'This is enough. You've made a scene. *Bas*. It's time to go.'

Mariam sat up and rubbed her eyes. Her back and neck were sore. 'I'm going to wait for him.'

'Look at me,' he said. 'Jalil Khan says that I need to take you back now. Right now. Do you understand? Jalil Khan says so.'

He opened the rear passenger door to the car. '*Bia*. Come on,' he said softly.

'I want to see him,' Mariam said. Her eyes were tearing over.

The driver sighed. 'Let me take you home. Come on, *dokhtar jo*.'

Mariam stood up and walked toward him. But then, at the last moment, she changed direction and ran to the front gates. She felt the driver's fingers fumbling for a grip at her shoulder. She shed him and burst through the open gates.

In the handful of seconds that she was in Jalil's garden, Mariam's eyes registered seeing a gleaming glass structure with plants inside it, grape vines clinging to wooden trellises, a fishpond built with gray blocks of stone, fruit trees, and bushes of brightly colored flowers everywhere. Her gaze skimmed over all of these things before they found a face, across the garden, in an upstairs window. The face was there for only an instant, a flash, but long enough. Long enough for Mariam to see the eyes widen, the mouth open. Then it snapped away from view. A hand appeared and frantically pulled at a cord. The curtains fell shut.

40

Then a pair of hands buried into her armpits and she was lifted off the ground. Mariam kicked. The pebbles spilled from her pocket. Mariam kept kicking and crying as she was carried to the car and lowered onto the cold leather of the backseat.

The driver talked in a muted, consoling tone as he drove. Mariam did not hear him. All during the ride, as she bounced in the backseat, she cried. They were tears of grief, of anger, of disillusionment. But mainly tears of a deep, deep shame at how foolishly she had given herself over to Jalil, how she had fretted over what dress to wear, over the mismatching *hijab*, walking all the way here, refusing to leave, sleeping on the street like a stray dog. And she was ashamed of how she had dismissed her mother's stricken looks, her puffy eyes. Nana, who had warned her, who had been right all along.

Mariam kept thinking of his face in the upstairs window. He let her sleep on the street. *On the street*. Mariam cried lying down. She didn't sit up, didn't want to be seen. She imagined all of Herat knew this morning how she'd disgraced herself. She wished Mullah Faizullah were here so she could put her head on his lap and let him comfort her.

After a while, the road became bumpier and the nose of the car pointed up. They were on the uphill road between Herat and Gul Daman.

What would she say to Nana, Mariam wondered.

41

How would she apologize? How could she even face Nana now?

The car stopped and the driver helped her out. 'I'll walk you,' he said.

She let him guide her across the road and up the track. There was honeysuckle growing along the path, and milkweed too. Bees were buzzing over twinkling wildflowers. The driver took her hand and helped her cross the stream. Then he let go, and he was talking about how Herat's famous one hundred and twenty days' winds would start blowing soon, from midmorning to dusk, and how the sand flies would go on a feeding frenzy, and then suddenly he was standing in front of her, trying to cover her eyes, pushing her back the way they had come and saying, 'Go back! No. Don't look now. Turn around! Go back!'

But he wasn't fast enough. Mariam saw. A gust of wind blew and parted the drooping branches of the weeping willow like a curtain, and Mariam caught a glimpse of what was beneath the tree: the straight-backed chair, overturned. The rope dropping from a high branch. Nana dangling at the end of it.

# CHAPTER 6

They buried Nana in a corner of the cemetery in Gul Daman. Mariam stood beside Bibi jo, with the women, as Mullah Faizullah recited prayers at the graveside and the men lowered Nana's shrouded body into the ground.

Afterward, Jalil walked Mariam to the *kolba*, where, in front of the villagers who accompanied them, he made a great show of tending to Mariam. He collected a few of her things, put them in a suitcase. He sat beside her cot, where she lay down, and fanned her face. He stroked her forehead, and, with a woebegone expression on his face, asked if she needed *anything? anything?* – he said it like that, twice.

'I want Mullah Faizullah,' Mariam said.

'Of course. He's outside. I'll get him for you.'

It was when Mullah Faizullah's slight, stooping figure appeared in the *kolba's* doorway that Mariam cried for the first time that day.

'Oh, Mariam jo.'

He sat next to her and cupped her face in his hands. 'You go on and cry, Mariam jo. Go on.

43

There is no shame in it. But remember, my girl, what the Koran says, 'Blessed is He in Whose hand is the kingdom, and He Who has power over all things, Who created death and life that He may try you.' The Koran speaks the truth, my girl. Behind every trial and every sorrow that He makes us shoulder, God has a reason.'

But Mariam could not hear comfort in God's words. Not that day. Not then. All she could hear was Nana saying, *I'll die if you go. I'll just die.* All she could do was cry and cry and let her tears fall on the spotted, paper-thin skin of Mullah Faizullah's hands.

On the ride to his house, Jalil sat in the backseat of his car with Mariam, his arm draped over her shoulder.

'You can stay with me, Mariam jo,' he said. 'I've asked them already to clean a room for you. It's upstairs. You'll like it, I think. You'll have a view of the garden.'

For the first time, Mariam could hear him with Nana's ears. She could hear so clearly now the insincerity that had always lurked beneath, the hollow, false assurances. She could not bring herself to look at him.

When the car stopped before Jalil's house, the driver opened the door for them and carried Mariam's suitcase. Jalil guided her, one palm cupped around each of her shoulders, through the same gates outside of which, two days before,

Mariam had slept on the sidewalk waiting for him. Two days before – when Mariam could think of nothing in the world she wanted more than to walk in this garden with Jalil – felt like another lifetime. How could her life have turned upside down so quickly, Mariam asked herself. She kept her gaze to the ground, on her feet, stepping on the gray stone path. She was aware of the presence of people in the garden, murmuring, stepping aside, as she and Jalil walked past. She sensed the weight of eyes on her, looking down from the windows upstairs.

Inside the house too, Mariam kept her head down. She walked on a maroon carpet with a repeating blue-and-yellow octagonal pattern, saw out of the corner of her eye the marble bases of statues, the lower halves of vases, the frayed ends of richly colored tapestries hanging from walls. The stairs she and Jalil took were wide and covered with a similar carpet, nailed down at the base of each step. At the top of the stairs, Jalil led her to the left, down another long, carpeted hallway. He stopped by one of the doors, opened it, and let her in.

'Your sisters Niloufar and Atieh play here some-times,' Jalil said, 'but mostly we use this as a guest room. You'll be comfortable here, I think. It's nice, isn't it?'

The room had a bed with a green-flowered blanket knit in a tightly woven, honeycomb design. The curtains, pulled back to reveal the garden

45

below, matched the blanket. Beside the bed was a threedrawer chest with a flower vase on it. There were shelves along the walls, with framed pictures of people Mariam did not recognize. On one of the shelves, Mariam saw a collection of identical wooden dolls, arranged in a line in order of decreasing size.

Jalil saw her looking. '*Matryoshka* dolls. I got them in Moscow. You can play with them, if you want. No one will mind.'

Mariam sat down on the bed.

'Is there anything you want?' Jalil said.

Mariam lay down. Closed her eyes. After a while, she heard him softly shut the door.

Except for when she had to use the bathroom down the hall, Mariam stayed in the room. The girl with the tattoo, the one who had opened the gates to her, brought her meals on a tray: lamb kebab, *sabzi, aush* soup. Most of it went uneaten. Jalil came by several times a day, sat on the bed beside her, asked her if she was all right.

'You could eat downstairs with the rest of us,' he said, but without much conviction. He understood a little too readily when Mariam said she preferred to eat alone.

From the window, Mariam watched impassively what she had wondered about and longed to see for most of her life: the comings and goings of Jalil's daily life. Servants rushed in and out of the front gates. A gardener was always trimming bushes,

46

watering plants in the greenhouse. Cars with long, sleek hoods pulled up on the street. From them emerged men in suits, in *chapans* and caracul hats, women in *hijabs*, children with neatly combed hair. And as Mariam watched Jalil shake these strangers' hands, as she saw him cross his palms on his chest and nod to their wives, she knew that Nana had spoken the truth. She did not belong here.

*But where do I belong? What am I going to do now?*

*I'm all you have in this world, Mariam, and when I'm gone you'll have nothing. You'll have nothing. You are nothing!*

Like the wind through the willows around the *kolba*, gusts of an inexpressible blackness kept passing through Mariam.

On Mariam's second full day at Jalil's house, a little girl came into the room.

'I have to get something,' she said.

Mariam sat up on the bed and crossed her legs, pulled the blanket on her lap.

The girl hurried across the room and opened the closet door. She fetched a square-shaped gray box.

'You know what this is?' she said. She opened the box. 'It's called a gramophone. *Gramo. Phone.* It plays records. You know, music. A gramophone.'

'You're Niloufar. You're eight.'

The little girl smiled. She had Jalil's smile and his dimpled chin. 'How did you know?'

Mariam shrugged. She didn't say to this girl that she'd once named a pebble after her.

47

'Do you want to hear a song?'

Mariam shrugged again.

Niloufar plugged in the gramophone. She fished a small record from a pouch beneath the box's lid. She put it on, lowered the needle. Music began to play.

> *I will use a flower petal for paper,*
> *And write you the sweetest letter,*
> *You are the sultan of my heart,*
> *the sultan of my heart.*

'Do you know it?'

'No.'

'It's from an Iranian film. I saw it at my father's cinema. Hey, do you want to see something?'

Before Mariam could answer, Niloufar had put her palms and forehead to the ground. She pushed with her soles and then she was standing upside down, on her head, in a three-point stance.

'Can you do that?' she said thickly.

'No.'

Niloufar dropped her legs and pulled her blouse back down. 'I could teach you,' she said, pushing hair from her flushed brow. 'So how long will you stay here?'

'I don't know.'

'My mother says you're not really my sister like you say you are.'

'I never said I was,' Mariam lied.

'She says you did. I don't care. What I mean is,

I don't mind if you did say it, or if you are my sister. I don't mind.'

Mariam lay down. 'I'm tired now.'

'My mother says a *jinn* made your mother hang herself.'

'You can stop that now,' Mariam said, turning to her side. 'The music, I mean.'

Bibi jo came to see her that day too. It was raining by the time she came. She lowered her large body onto the chair beside the bed, grimacing.

'This rain, Mariam jo, it's murder on my hips. Just murder, I tell you. I hope . . . Oh, now, come here, child. Come here to Bibi jo. Don't cry. There, now. You poor thing. *Tsk.* You poor, poor thing.'

That night, Mariam couldn't sleep for a long time. She lay in bed looking at the sky, listening to the footsteps below, the voices muffled by walls and the sheets of rain punishing the window. When she did doze off, she was startled awake by shouting. Voices downstairs, sharp and angry. Mariam couldn't make out the words. Someone slammed a door.

The next morning. Mullah Faizullah came to visit her. When she saw her friend at the door, his white beard and his amiable, toothless smile, Mariam felt tears stinging the corners of her eyes again. She swung her feet over the side of the bed and hurried over. She kissed his hand as always and he her brow. She pulled him up a chair.

He showed her the Koran he had brought with

49

him and opened it. 'I figured no sense in skipping our routine, eh?'

'You know I don't need lessons anymore, Mullah sahib. You taught me every *surrah* and *ayat* in the Koran years ago.'

He smiled, and raised his hands in a gesture of surrender. 'I confess, then. I've been found out. But I can think of worse excuses to visit you.'

'You don't need excuses. Not you.'

'You're kind to say that, Mariam jo.'

He passed her his Koran. As he'd taught her, she kissed it three times – touching it to her brow between each kiss – and gave it back to him.

'How are you, my girl?'

'I keep,' Mariam began. She had to stop, feeling like a rock had lodged itself in her throat. 'I keep thinking of what she said to me before I left. She—'

'*Nay, nay, nay.*' Mullah Faizullah put his hand on her knee. 'Your mother, may Allah forgive her, was a troubled and unhappy woman, Mariam jo. She did a terrible thing to herself. To herself, to you, and also to Allah. He will forgive her, for He is all-forgiving, but Allah is saddened by what she did. He does not approve of the taking of life, be it another's or one's own, for He says that life is sacred. You see—' He pulled his chair closer, took Mariam's hand in both of his own. 'You see,' I knew your mother before you were born, when she was a little girl, and I tell you that she was unhappy then. The seed for what she did was

50

planted long ago, I'm afraid. What I mean to say is that this was not your fault. It wasn't your fault, my girl.'

'I shouldn't have left her. I should have—'

'You stop that. These thoughts are no good, Mariam jo. You hear me, child? No good. They will destroy you. It wasn't your fault. It wasn't your fault. No.'

Mariam nodded, but as desperately as she wanted to she could not bring herself to believe him.

One afternoon, a week later, there was a knock on the door, and a tall woman walked in. She was fair-skinned, had reddish hair and long fingers.

'I'm Afsoon,' she said. 'Niloufar's mother. Why don't you wash up, Mariam, and come downstairs?'

Mariam said she would rather stay in her room.

'No, *na fahmidi*, you don't understand. You *need* to come down. We have to talk to you. It's important.'

# CHAPTER 7

They sat across from her, Jalil and his wives, at a long, dark brown table. Between them, in the center of the table, was a crystal vase of fresh marigolds and a sweating pitcher of water. The red-haired woman who had introduced herself as Niloufar's mother, Afsoon, was sitting on Jalil's right. The other two, Khadija and Nargis, were on his left. The wives each had on a flimsy black scarf, which they wore not on their heads but tied loosely around the neck like an afterthought. Mariam, who could not imagine that they would wear black for Nana, pictured one of them suggesting it, or maybe Jalil, just before she'd been summoned.

Afsoon poured water from the pitcher and put the glass before Mariam on a checkered cloth coaster. 'Only spring and it's warm already,' she said. She made a fanning motion with her hand.

'Have you been comfortable?' Nargis, who had a small chin and curly black hair, asked. 'We hope you've been comfortable. This . . . ordeal . . . must be very hard for you. So difficult.'

The other two nodded. Mariam took in their

plucked eyebrows, the thin, tolerant smiles they were giving her. There was an unpleasant hum in Mariam's head. Her throat burned. She drank some of the water.

Through the wide window behind Jalil, Mariam could see a row of flowering apple trees. On the wall beside the window stood a dark wooden cabinet. In it was a clock, and a framed photograph of Jalil and three young boys holding a fish. The sun caught the sparkle in the fish's scales. Jalil and the boys were grinning.

'Well,' Afsoon began. 'I – that is, we – have brought you here because we have some very good news to give you.'

Mariam looked up.

She caught a quick exchange of glances between the women over Jalil, who slouched in his chair looking unseeingly at the pitcher on the table. It was Khadija, the oldest-looking of the three, who turned her gaze to Mariam, and Mariam had the impression that this duty too had been discussed, agreed upon, before they had called for her.

'You have a suitor,' Khadija said.

Mariam's stomach fell. 'A what?' she said through suddenly numb lips.

'A *khastegar*. A suitor. His name is Rasheed,' Khadija went on. 'He is a friend of a business acquaintance of your father's. He's a Pashtun, from Kandahar originally, but he lives in Kabul, in the Deh-Mazang district, in a two-story house that he owns.'

Afsoon was nodding. 'And he does speak Farsi, like us, like you. So you won't have to learn Pashto.'

Mariam's chest was tightening. The room was reeling up and down, the ground shifting beneath her feet.

'He's a shoemaker,' Khadija was saying now. 'But not some kind of ordinary street-side *moochi*, no, no. He has his own shop, and he is one of the most sought-after shoemakers in Kabul. He makes them for diplomats, members of the presidential family – that class of people. So you see, he will have no trouble providing for you.'

Mariam fixed her eyes on Jalil, her heart somersaulting in her chest. 'Is this true? What she's saying, is it true?'

But Jalil wouldn't look at her. He went on chewing the corner of his lower lip and staring at the pitcher.

'Now he *is* a little older than you,' Afsoon chimed in. 'But he can't be more than . . . forty. Forty-five at the most. Wouldn't you say, Nargis?'

'Yes. But I've seen nine-year-old girls given to men twenty years older than your suitor, Mariam. We all have. What are you, fifteen? That's a good, solid marrying age for a girl.' There was enthusiastic nodding at this. It did not escape Mariam that no mention was made of her half sisters Saideh or Naheed, both her own age, both students in the Mehri School in Herat, both with plans to enroll in Kabul University. Fifteen,

54

evidently, was not a good, solid marrying age for them.

'What's more,' Nargis went on, 'he too has had a great loss in his life. His wife, we hear, died during childbirth ten years ago. And then, three years ago, his son drowned in a lake.'

'It's very sad, yes. He's been looking for a bride the last few years but hasn't found anyone suitable.'

'I don't want to,' Mariam said. She looked at Jalil. 'I don't want this. Don't make me.' She hated the sniffling, pleading tone of her voice but could not help it.

'Now, be reasonable, Mariam,' one of the wives said.

Mariam was no longer keeping track of who was saying what. She went on staring at Jalil, waiting for him to speak up, to say that none of this was true.

'You can't spend the rest of your life here.'

'Don't you want a family of your own?'

'Yes. A home, children of your own?'

'You have to move on.'

'True that it would be preferable that you marry a local, a Tajik, but Rasheed is healthy, and interested in you. He has a home and a job. That's all that really matters, isn't it? And Kabul is a beautiful and exciting city. You may not get another opportunity this good.'

Mariam turned her attention to the wives.

'I'll live with Mullah Faizullah,' she said. 'He'll take me in. I know he will.'

'That's no good,' Khadija said. 'He's old and so . . .' She searched for the right word, and Mariam knew then that what she really wanted to say was *He's so close.* She understood what they meant to do. *You may not get another opportunity this good.* And neither would they. They had been disgraced by her birth, and this was their chance to erase, once and for all, the last trace of their husband's scandalous mistake. She was being sent away because she was the walking, breathing embodiment of their shame.

'He's so old and weak,' Khadija eventually said. 'And what will you do when he's gone? You'd be a burden to his family.'

*As you are now to us.* Mariam almost *saw* the unspoken words exit Khadija's mouth, like foggy breath on a cold day.

Mariam pictured herself in Kabul, a big, strange, crowded city that, Jalil had once told her, was some six hundred and fifty kilometers to the east of Herat. *Six hundred and fifty kilometers.* The farthest she'd ever been from the *kolba* was the two-kilometer walk she'd made to Jalil's house. She pictured herself living there, in Kabul, at the other end of that unimaginable distance, living in a stranger's house where she would have to concede to his moods and his issued demands. She would have to clean after this man, Rasheed, cook for him, wash his clothes. And there would be other chores as well – Nana had told her what husbands did to their wives. It was the thought of

56

these intimacies in particular, which she imagined as painful acts of perversity, that filled her with dread and made her break out in a sweat.

She turned to Jalil again. 'Tell them. Tell them you won't let them do this.'

'Actually, your father has already given Rasheed his answer,' Afsoon said. 'Rasheed is here, in Herat; he has come all the way from Kabul. The *nikka* will be tomorrow morning, and then there is a bus leaving for Kabul at noon.'

'Tell them!' Mariam cried.

The women grew quiet now. Mariam sensed that they were watching him too. Waiting. A silence fell over the room. Jalil kept twirling his wedding band, with a bruised, helpless look on his face. From inside the cabinet, the clock ticked on and on.

'Jalil jo?' one of the women said at last.

Jalil's eyes lifted slowly, met Mariam's, lingered for a moment, then dropped. He opened his mouth, but all that came forth was a single, pained groan.

'Say something,' Mariam said.

Then Jalil did, in a thin, threadbare voice. 'Goddamn it, Mariam, don't do this to me,' he said as though he was the one to whom something was being done.

And, with that, Mariam felt the tension vanish from the room.

As Jalil's wives began a new – and more sprightly – round of reassuring, Mariam looked down at the table. Her eyes traced the sleek shape of the table's legs, the sinuous curves of its corners, the gleam of its reflective, dark brown surface. She noticed that every time she breathed out, the surface fogged, and she disappeared from her father's table.

Afsoon escorted her back to the room upstairs. When Afsoon closed the door, Mariam heard the rattling of a key as it turned in the lock.

# CHAPTER 8

In the morning, Mariam was given a long-sleeved, dark green dress to wear over white cotton trousers. Afsoon gave her a green *hijab* and a pair of matching sandals.

She was taken to the room with the long, brown table, except now there was a bowl of sugar-coated almond candy in the middle of the table, a Koran, a green veil, and a mirror. Two men Mariam had never seen before – witnesses, she presumed – and a mullah she did not recognize were already seated at the table.

Jalil showed her to a chair. He was wearing a light brown suit and a red tie. His hair was washed. When he pulled out the chair for her, he tried to smile encouragingly. Khadija and Afsoon sat on Mariam's side of the table this time.

The mullah motioned toward the veil, and Nargis arranged it on Mariam's head before taking a seat. Mariam looked down at her hands.

'You can call him in now,' Jalil said to someone.

Mariam smelled him before she saw him. Cigarette smoke and thick, sweet cologne, not faint like Jalil's. The scent of it flooded Mariam's nostrils. Through the veil, from the corner of her eye, Mariam saw a tall man, thick-bellied and broad-shouldered, stooping in the doorway. The size of him almost made her gasp, and she had to drop her gaze, her heart hammering away. She sensed him lingering in the doorway. Then his slow, heavy-footed movement across the room. The candy bowl on the table clinked in tune with his steps. With a thick grunt, he dropped on a chair beside her. He breathed noisily.

The mullah welcomed them. He said this would not be a traditional *nikka*.

'I understand that Rasheed *agha* has tickets for the bus to Kabul that leaves shortly. So, in the interest of time, we will bypass some of the traditional steps to speed up the proceedings.'

The mullah gave a few blessings, said a few words about the importance of marriage. He asked Jalil if he had any objections to this union, and Jalil shook his head. Then the mullah asked Rasheed if he indeed wished to enter into a marriage contract with Mariam. Rasheed said, 'Yes.' His harsh, raspy voice reminded Mariam of the sound of dry autumn leaves crushed underfoot.

'And do you, Mariam jan, accept this man as your husband?'

Mariam stayed quiet. Throats were cleared.

'She does,' a female voice said from down the table.

'Actually,' the mullah said, 'she herself has to answer. And she should wait until I ask three

60

times. The point is, he's seeking her, not the other way around.'

He asked the question two more times. When Mariam didn't answer, he asked it once more, this time more forcefully. Mariam could feel Jalil beside her shifting on his seat, could sense feet crossing and uncrossing beneath the table. There was more throat clearing. A small, white hand reached out and flicked a bit of dust off the table.

'Mariam,' Jalil whispered.

'Yes,' she said shakily.

A mirror was passed beneath the veil. In it, Mariam saw her own face first, the archless, unshapely eyebrows, the flat hair, the eyes, mirthless green and set so closely together that one might mistake her for being cross-eyed. Her skin was coarse and had a dull, spotty appearance. She thought her brow too wide, the chin too narrow, the lips too thin. The overall impression was of a long face, a triangular face, a bit houndlike. And yet Mariam saw that, oddly enough, the whole of these unmemorable parts made for a face that was not pretty but, somehow, not unpleasant to look at either.

In the mirror, Mariam had her first glimpse of Rasheed: the big, square, ruddy face; the hooked nose; the flushed cheeks that gave the impression of sly cheerfulness; the watery, bloodshot eyes; the crowded teeth, the front two pushed together like a gabled roof; the impossibly low hairline, barely two finger widths above the bushy eyebrows; the wall of thick, coarse, salt-and-pepper hair.

Their gazes met briefly in the glass and slid away. *This is the face of my husband*, Mariam thought.

They exchanged the thin gold bands that Rasheed fished from his coat pocket. His nails were yellow-brown, like the inside of a rotting apple, and some of the tips were curling, lifting. Mariam's hands shook when she tried to slip the band onto his finger, and Rasheed had to help her. Her own band was a little tight, but Rasheed had no trouble forcing it over her knuckles.

'There,' he said.

'It's a pretty ring,' one of the wives said. 'It's lovely, Mariam.'

'All that remains now is the signing of the contract,' the mullah said.

Mariam signed her name – the *meem*, the *reh*, the *ya*, and the *meem* again – conscious of all the eyes on her hand. The next time Mariam signed her name to a document, twenty-seven years later, a mullah would again be present.

'You are now husband and wife,' the mullah said. '*Tabreek*. Congratulations.'

Rasheed waited in the multicolored bus. Mariam could not see him from where she stood with Jalil, by the rear bumper, only the smoke of his cigarette curling up from the open window. Around them, hands shook and farewells were said. Korans were kissed, passed under. Barefoot boys bounced between travelers, their faces invisible behind their trays of chewing gum and cigarettes.

Jalil was busy telling her that Kabul was so beautiful, the Moghul emperor Babur had asked that he be buried there. Next, Mariam knew, he'd go on about Kabul's gardens, and its shops, its trees, and its air, and, before long, she would be on the bus and he would walk alongside it, waving cheerfully, unscathed, spared.

Mariam could not bring herself to allow it.

'I used to worship you,' she said.

Jalil stopped in midsentence. He crossed and uncrossed his arms. A young Hindi couple, the wife cradling a boy, the husband dragging a suitcase, passed between them. Jalil seemed grateful for the interruption. They excused themselves, and he smiled back politely.

'On Thursdays, I sat for hours waiting for you. I worried myself sick that you wouldn't show up.'

'It's a long trip. You should eat something.' He said he could buy her some bread and goat cheese.

'I thought about you all the time. I used to pray that you'd live to be a hundred years old. I didn't know. I didn't know that you were ashamed of me.'

Jalil looked down, and, like an overgrown child, dug at something with the toe of his shoe.

'You were ashamed of me.'

'I'll visit you,' he muttered. 'I'll come to Kabul and see you. We'll—'

'No. No,' she said. 'Don't come. I won't see you.

Don't you come. I don't want to hear from you. Ever. *Ever*.'

He gave her a wounded look.

'It ends here for you and me. Say your good-byes.'

'Don't leave like this,' he said in a thin voice.

'You didn't even have the decency to give me the time to say good-bye to Mullah Faizullah.'

She turned and walked around to the side of the bus. She could hear him following her. When she reached the hydraulic doors, she heard him behind her.

'Mariam jo.'

She climbed the stairs, and though she could spot Jalil out of the corner of her eye walking parallel to her she did not look out the window. She made her way down the aisle to the back, where Rasheed sat with her suitcase between his feet. She did not turn to look when Jalil's palms pressed on the glass, when his knuckles rapped and rapped on it. When the bus jerked forward, she did not turn to see him trotting alongside it. And when the bus pulled away, she did not look back to see him receding, to see him disappear in the cloud of exhaust and dust.

Rasheed, who took up the window and middle seat, put his thick hand on hers.

'There now, girl. There. There,' he said. He was squinting out the window as he said this, as though something more interesting had caught his eye.

# CHAPTER 9

I t was early evening the following day by the time they arrived at Rasheed's house.

'We're in Deh-Mazang,' he said. They were outside, on the sidewalk. He had her suitcase in one hand and was unlocking the wooden front gate with the other. 'In the south and west part of the city. The zoo is nearby, and the university too.'

Mariam nodded. Already she had learned that, though she could understand him, she had to pay close attention when he spoke. She was unaccustomed to the Kabuli dialect of his Farsi, and to the underlying layer of Pashto accent, the language of his native Kandahar. He, on the other hand, seemed to have no trouble understanding her Herati Farsi.

Mariam quickly surveyed the narrow, unpaved road along which Rasheed's house was situated. The houses on this road were crowded together and shared common walls, with small, walled yards in front buffering them from the street. Most of the homes had flat roofs and were made of burned brick, some of mud the same dusty color as the mountains that ringed the city. Gutters separated the sidewalk from the road on both sides and flowed with muddy water. Mariam saw small mounds of flyblown garbage littering the street here and there. Rasheed's house had two stories. Mariam could see that it had once been blue.

When Rasheed opened the front gate, Mariam found herself in a small, unkempt yard where yellow grass struggled up in thin patches. Mariam saw an outhouse on the right, in a side yard, and, on the left, a well with a hand pump, a row of dying saplings. Near the well was a toolshed, and a bicycle leaning against the wall.

'Your father told me you like to fish,' Rasheed said as they were crossing the yard to the house. There was no backyard, Mariam saw. 'There are valleys north of here. Rivers with lots of fish. Maybe I'll take you someday.'

He unlocked the front door and let her into the house.

Rasheed's house was much smaller than Jalil's, but, compared to Mariam and Nana's *kolba*, it was a mansion. There was a hallway, a living room downstairs, and a kitchen in which he showed her pots and pans and a pressure cooker and a kerosene *ishtop*. The living room had a pistachio green leather couch. It had a rip down its side that had been clumsily sewn together. The walls were bare. There was a table, two cane-seat chairs, two folding chairs, and, in the corner, a black, cast-iron stove.

Mariam stood in the middle of the living room, looking around. At the *kolba*, she could touch the ceiling with her fingertips. She could lie in her cot and tell the time of day by the angle of sunlight pouring through the window. She knew how far her door would open before its hinges creaked. She knew every splinter and crack in each of the thirty wooden floorboards. Now all those familiar things were gone. Nana was dead, and she was here, in a strange city, separated from the life she'd known by valleys and chains of snow-capped mountains and entire deserts. She was in a stranger's house, with all its different rooms and its smell of cigarette smoke, with its unfamiliar cupboards full of unfamiliar utensils, its heavy, dark green curtains, and a ceiling she knew she could not reach. The space of it suffocated Mariam. Pangs of longing bore into her, for Nana, for Mullah Faizullah, for her old life.

Then she was crying.

'What's this crying about?' Rasheed said crossly. He reached into the pocket of his pants, uncurled Mariam's fingers, and pushed a handkerchief into her palm. He lit himself a cigarette and leaned against the wall. He watched as Mariam pressed the handkerchief to her eyes.

'Done?'

Mariam nodded.

'Sure?'

'Yes.'

He took her by the elbow then and led her to the living-room window.

'This window looks north,' he said, tapping the

glass with the crooked nail of his index finger. 'That's the Asmai mountain directly in front of us – see? – and, to the left, is the Ali Abad mountain. The university is at the foot of it. Behind us, east, you can't see from here, is the Shir Darwaza mountain. Every day, at noon, they shoot a cannon from it. Stop your crying, now. I mean it.'

Mariam dabbed at her eyes.

'That's one thing I can't stand,' he said, scowling, 'the sound of a woman crying. I'm sorry. I have no patience for it.'

'I want to go home,' Mariam said.

Rasheed sighed irritably. A puff of his smoky breath hit Mariam's face. 'I won't take that personally. This time.'

Again, he took her by the elbow, and led her upstairs.

There was a narrow, dimly lit hallway there and two bedrooms. The door to the bigger one was ajar. Through it Mariam could see that it, like the rest of the house, was sparsely furnished: bed in the corner, with a brown blanket and a pillow, a closet, a dresser. The walls were bare except for a small mirror. Rasheed closed the door.

'This is my room.'

He said she could take the guest room. 'I hope you don't mind. I'm accustomed to sleeping alone.'

Mariam didn't tell him how relieved she was, at least about this.

The room that was to be Mariam's was much

smaller than the room she'd stayed in at Jalil's house. It had a bed, an old, gray-brown dresser, a small closet. The window looked into the yard and, beyond that, the street below. Rasheed put her suitcase in a corner.

Mariam sat on the bed.

'You didn't notice,' he said. He was standing in the doorway, stooping a little to fit. 'Look on the windowsill. You know what kind they are? I put them there before leaving for Herat.'

Only now Mariam saw a basket on the sill. White tuberoses spilled from its sides.

'You like them? They please you?'

'Yes.'

'You can thank me then.'

'Thank you. I'm sorry. *Tashakor*—'

'You're shaking. Maybe I scare you. Do I scare you? Are you frightened of me?'

Mariam was not looking at him, but she could hear something slyly playful in these questions, like a needling. She quickly shook her head in what she recognized as her first lie in their marriage.

'No? That's good, then. Good for you. Well, this is your home now. You're going to like it here. You'll see. Did I tell you we have electricity? Most days and every night?'

He made as if to leave. At the door, he paused, took a long drag, crinkled his eyes against the smoke. Mariam thought he was going to say something. But he didn't. He closed the door, left her alone with her suitcase and her flowers.

69

# CHAPTER 10

The first few days, Mariam hardly left her room. She was awakened every dawn for prayer by the distant cry of *azan*, after which she crawled back into bed. She was still in bed when she heard Rasheed in the bathroom, washing up, when he came into her room to check on her before he went to his shop. From her window, she watched him in the yard, securing his lunch in the rear carrier pack of his bicycle, then walking his bicycle across the yard and into the street. She watched him pedal away, saw his broad, thick-shouldered figure disappear around the turn at the end of the street.

For most of the days, Mariam stayed in bed, feeling adrift and forlorn. Sometimes she went downstairs to the kitchen, ran her hands over the sticky, grease-stained counter, the vinyl, flowered curtains that smelled like burned meals. She looked through the ill-fitting drawers, at the mismatched spoons and knives, the colander and chipped, wooden spatulas, these would-be instruments of her new daily life, all of it reminding her of the havoc that had struck her life, making her feel uprooted, displaced, like an intruder on someone else's life.

At the *kolba*, her appetite had been predictable. Here, her stomach rarely growled for food. Sometimes she took a plate of leftover white rice and a scrap of bread to the living room, by the window. From there, she could see the roofs of the one-story houses on their street. She could see into their yards too, the women working laundry lines and shooing their children, chickens pecking at dirt, the shovels and spades, the cows tethered to trees.

She thought longingly of all the summer nights that she and Nana had slept on the flat roof of the *kolba*, looking at the moon glowing over Gul Daman, the night so hot their shirts would cling to their chests like a wet leaf to a window. She missed the winter afternoons of reading in the *kolba* with Mullah Faizullah, the clink of icicles falling on her roof from the trees, the crows cawing outside from snow-burdened branches.

Alone in the house, Mariam paced restlessly, from the kitchen to the living room, up the steps to her room and down again. She ended up back in her room, doing her prayers or sitting on the bed, missing her mother, feeling nauseated and homesick.

It was with the sun's westward crawl that Mariam's anxiety really ratcheted up. Her teeth rattled when she thought of the night, the time when Rasheed might at last decide to do to her what husbands did to their wives. She lay in bed, wracked with nerves, as he ate alone downstairs.

He always stopped by her room and poked his head in.

'You can't be sleeping already. It's only seven. Are you awake? Answer me. Come, now.'

He pressed on until, from the dark, Mariam said, 'I'm here.'

He slid down and sat in her doorway. From her bed, she could see his large-framed body, his long legs, the smoke swirling around his hook-nosed profile, the amber tip of his cigarette brightening and dimming.

He told her about his day. A pair of loafers he had custom-made for the deputy foreign minister – who, Rasheed said, only bought shoes from him. An order for sandals from a Polish diplomat and his wife. He told her of the superstitions people had about shoes: that putting them on a bed invited death into the family, that a quarrel would follow if one put on the left shoe first.

'Unless it was done unintentionally on a Friday,' he said. 'And did you know it's supposed to be a bad omen to tie shoes together and hang them from a nail?'

Rasheed himself believed none of this. In his opinion, superstitions were largely a female preoccupation.

He passed on to her things he had heard on the streets, like how the American president Richard Nixon had resigned over a scandal.

Mariam, who had never heard of Nixon, or the scandal that had forced him to resign, did not say anything back. She waited anxiously for Rasheed to finish talking, to crush his cigarette, and take his leave. Only when she'd heard him cross the hallway, heard his door open and close, only then would the metal fist gripping her belly let go.

Then one night he crushed his cigarette and instead of saying good night leaned against the doorway.

'Are you ever going to unpack that thing?' he said, motioning with his head toward her suitcase. He crossed his arms. 'I figured you might need some time. But this is absurd. A week's gone and . . . Well, then, as of tomorrow morning I expect you to start behaving like a wife. *Fahmidi?* Is that understood?'

Mariam's teeth began to chatter.

'I need an answer.'

'Yes.'

'Good,' he said. 'What did you think? That this is a hotel? That I'm some kind of hotelkeeper? Well, it . . . Oh. Oh. *La illah u ilillah.* What did I say about the crying? Mariam. What did I say to you about the crying?'

The next morning, after Rasheed left for work, Mariam unpacked her clothes and put them in the dresser. She drew a pail of water from the well and, with a rag, washed the windows of her room and the windows to the living room downstairs.

73

She swept the floors, beat the cobwebs fluttering in the corners of the ceiling. She opened the windows to air the house.

She set three cups of lentils to soak in a pot, found a knife and cut some carrots and a pair of potatoes, left them too to soak. She searched for flour, found it in the back of one of the cabinets behind a row of dirty spice jars, and made fresh dough, kneading it the way Nana had shown her, pushing the dough with the heel of her hand, folding the outer edge, turning it, and pushing it away again. Once she had floured the dough, she wrapped it in a moist cloth, put on a *hijab*, and set out for the communal tandoor.

Rasheed had told her where it was, down the street, a left then a quick right, but all Mariam had to do was follow the flock of women and children who were headed the same way. The children Mariam saw, chasing after their mothers or running ahead of them, wore shirts patched and patched again. They wore trousers that looked too big or too small, sandals with ragged straps that flapped back and forth. They rolled discarded old bicycle tires with sticks.

Their mothers walked in groups of three or four, some in burqas, others not. Mariam could hear their high-pitched chatter, their spiraling laughs. As she walked with her head down, she caught bits of their banter, which seemingly always had to do with sick children or lazy, ungrateful husbands.

*As if the meals cook themselves.*

Wallah o billah, *never a moment's rest!*

*And he says to me, I swear it, it's true, he actually says to me . . .*

This endless conversation, the tone plaintive but oddly cheerful, flew around and around in a circle. On it went, down the street, around the corner, in line at the tandoor. Husbands who gambled. Husbands who doted on their mothers and wouldn't spend a rupiah on them, the wives. Mariam wondered how so many women could suffer the same miserable luck, to have married, all of them, such dreadful men. Or was this a wifely game that she did not know about, a daily ritual, like soaking rice or making dough? Would they expect her soon to join in?

In the tandoor line, Mariam caught sideways glances shot at her, heard whispers. Her hands began to sweat. She imagined they all knew that she'd been born a *harami*, a source of shame to her father and his family. They all knew that she'd betrayed her mother and disgraced herself.

With a corner of her *hijab*, she dabbed at the moisture above her upper lip and tried to gather her nerves.

For a few minutes, everything went well.

Then someone tapped her on the shoulder. Mariam turned around and found a light-skinned, plump woman wearing a *hijab*, like her. She had short, wiry black hair and a good-humored, almost perfectly round face. Her lips were much fuller

75

than Mariam's, the lower one slightly droopy, as though dragged down by the big, dark mole just below the lip line. She had big greenish eyes that shone at Mariam with an inviting glint.

'You're Rasheed jan's new wife, aren't you?' the woman said, smiling widely. 'The one from Herat. You're so young! Mariam jan, isn't it? My name is Fariba. I live on your street, five houses to your left, the one with the green door. This is my son Noor.'

The boy at her side had a smooth, happy face and wiry hair like his mother's. There was a patch of black hairs on the lobe of his left ear. His eyes had a mischievous, reckless light in them. He raised his hand. '*Salaam, Khala* jan.'

'Noor is ten. I have an older boy too, Ahmad.'

'He's thirteen,' Noor said.

'Thirteen going on forty.' The woman Fariba laughed. 'My husband's name is Hakim,' she said. 'He's a teacher here in Deh-Mazang. You should come by sometime, we'll have a cup—'

And then suddenly, as if emboldened, the other women pushed past Fariba and swarmed Mariam, forming a circle around her with alarming speed.

'So you're Rasheed jan's young bride—'

'How do you like Kabul?'

'I've been to Herat. I have a cousin there.'

'Do you want a boy or a girl first?'

'The minarets! Oh, what beauty! What a gorgeous city!'

'Boy is better, Mariam jan, they carry the family name—'

76

'Bah! Boys get married and run off. Girls stay behind and take care of you when you're old.'

'We heard you were coming.'

'Have twins. One of each! Then everyone's happy.'

Mariam backed away. She was hyperventilating. Her ears buzzed, her pulse fluttered, her eyes darted from one face to another. She backed away again, but there was nowhere to go to – she was in the center of a circle. She spotted Fariba, who was frowning, who saw that she was in distress.

'Let her be!' Fariba was saying. 'Move aside, let her be! You're frightening her!'

Mariam clutched the dough close to her chest and pushed through the crowd around her.

'Where are you going, *hamshira*?'

She pushed until somehow she was in the clear and then she ran up the street. It wasn't until she'd reached the intersection that she realized she'd run the wrong way. She turned around and ran back in the other direction, head down, tripping once and scraping her knee badly, then up again and running, bolting past the women.

'What's the matter with you?'

'You're bleeding, *hamshira*!'

Mariam turned one corner, then the other. She found the correct street but suddenly could not remember which was Rasheed's house. She ran up then down the street, panting, near tears now, began trying doors blindly. Some were locked, others opened only to reveal unfamiliar yards, barking dogs, and startled chickens. She pictured Rasheed coming home to find her still searching this way, her knee bleeding, lost on her own street. Now she did start crying. She pushed on doors, muttering panicked prayers, her face moist with tears, until one opened, and she saw, with relief, the outhouse, the well, the toolshed. She slammed the door behind her and turned the bolt. Then she was on all fours, next to the wall, retching. When she was done, she crawled away, sat against the wall, with her legs splayed before her. She had never in her life felt so alone.

When Rasheed came home that night, he brought with him a brown paper bag. Mariam was disappointed that he did not notice the clean windows, the swept floors, the missing cobwebs. But he did look pleased that she had already set his dinner plate, on a clean *sofrah* spread on the living-room floor.

'I made *daal*,' Mariam said.

'Good. I'm starving.'

She poured water for him from the *aftawa* to wash his hands with. As he dried with a towel, she put before him a steaming bowl of *daal* and a plate of fluffy white rice. This was the first meal she had cooked for him, and Mariam wished she had been in a better state when she made it. She'd still been shaken from the incident at the tandoor as she'd cooked, and all day she had fretted about the *daal*'s consistency, its color, worried that he would think she'd stirred in too much ginger or not enough turmeric.

He dipped his spoon into the gold-colored *daal*.

Mariam swayed a bit. What if he was disappointed or angry? What if he pushed his plate away in displeasure?

'Careful,' she managed to say. 'It's hot.'

Rasheed pursed his lips and blew, then put the spoon into his mouth.

'It's good,' he said. 'A little undersalted but good. Maybe better than good, even.'

Relieved, Mariam looked on as he ate. A flare of pride caught her off guard. She had done well – *maybe better than good, even* – and it surprised her, this thrill she felt over his small compliment. The day's earlier unpleasantness receded a bit.

'Tomorrow is Friday,' Rasheed said. 'What do you say I show you around?'

'Around Kabul?'

'No. Calcutta.'

Mariam blinked.

'It's a joke. Of course Kabul. Where else?' He reached into the brown paper bag. 'But first, something I have to tell you.'

He fished a sky blue burqa from the bag. The yards of pleated cloth spilled over his knees when he lifted it. He rolled up the burqa, looked at Mariam.

'I have customers, Mariam, men, who bring their wives to my shop. The women come uncovered, they talk to me directly, look me in the eye without

79

shame. They wear makeup and skirts that show their knees. Sometimes they even put their feet in front of me, the women do, for measurements, and their husbands stand there and watch. They allow it. They think nothing of a stranger touching their wives' bare feet! They think they're being modern men, intellectuals, on account of their education, I suppose. They don't see that they're spoiling their own *nang* and *namoos*, their honor and pride.'

He shook his head.

'Mostly, they live in the richer parts of Kabul. I'll take you there. You'll see. But they're here too, Mariam, in this very neighborhood, these soft men. There's a teacher living down the street, Hakim is his name, and I see his wife Fariba all the time walking the streets alone with nothing on her head but a scarf. It embarrasses me, frankly, to see a man who's lost control of his wife.'

He fixed Mariam with a hard glare.

'But I'm a different breed of man, Mariam. Where I come from, one wrong look, one improper word, and blood is spilled. Where I come from, a woman's face is her husband's business only. I want you to remember that. Do you understand?'

Mariam nodded. When he extended the bag to her, she took it.

The earlier pleasure over his approval of her cooking had evaporated. In its stead, a sensation of shrinking. This man's will felt to Mariam as

80

imposing and immovable as the Safid-koh mountains looming over Gul Daman.

Rasheed passed the paper bag to her. 'We have an understanding, then. Now, let me have some more of that *daal*.'

# CHAPTER 11

Mariam had never before worn a burqa. Rasheed had to help her put it on. The padded headpiece felt tight and heavy on her skull, and it was strange seeing the world through a mesh screen. She practiced walking around her room in it and kept stepping on the hem and stumbling. The loss of peripheral vision was unnerving, and she did not like the suffocating way the pleated cloth kept pressing against her mouth.

'You'll get used to it,' Rasheed said. 'With time, I bet you'll even like it.'

They took a bus to a place Rasheed called the Shar-e-Nau Park, where children pushed each other on swings and slapped volleyballs over ragged nets tied to tree trunks. They strolled together and watched boys fly kites, Mariam walking beside Rasheed, tripping now and then on the burqa's hem. For lunch, Rasheed took her to eat in a small kebab house near a mosque he called the Haji Yaghoub. The floor was sticky and the air smoky. The walls smelled faintly of raw meat and the music, which Rasheed described to her as *logari*, was loud. The cooks were thin boys who fanned skewers with one hand and swatted gnats with the other. Mariam, who had never been inside a restaurant, found it odd at first to sit in a crowded room with so many strangers, to lift her burqa to put morsels of food into her mouth. A hint of the same anxiety as the day at the tandoor stirred in her stomach, but Rasheed's presence was of some comfort, and, after a while, she did not mind so much the music, the smoke, even the people. And the burqa, she learned to her surprise, was also comforting. It was like a one-way window. Inside it, she was an observer, buffered from the scrutinizing eyes of strangers. She no longer worried that people knew, with a single glance, all the shameful secrets of her past.

On the streets, Rasheed named various buildings with authority; this is the American Embassy, he said, that the Foreign Ministry. He pointed to cars, said their names and where they were made: Soviet Volgas, American Chevrolets, German Opels.

'Which is your favorite?' he asked.

Mariam hesitated, pointed to a Volga, and Rasheed laughed.

Kabul was far more crowded than the little that Mariam had seen of Herat. There were fewer trees and fewer *garis* pulled by horses, but more cars, taller buildings, more traffic lights and more paved roads. And everywhere Mariam heard the city's peculiar dialect: 'Dear' was *jan* instead of *jo*, 'sister' became *hamshira* instead of *hamshireh*, and so on.

From a street vendor, Rasheed bought her ice cream. It was the first time she'd eaten ice cream and Mariam had never imagined that such tricks could be played on a palate. She devoured the entire bowl, the crushed-pistachio topping, the tiny rice noodles at the bottom. She marveled at the bewitching texture, the lapping sweetness of it.

They walked on to a place called Kocheh-Morgha, Chicken Street. It was a narrow, crowded bazaar in a neighborhood that Rasheed said was one of Kabul's wealthier ones.

'Around here is where foreign diplomats live, rich businessmen, members of the royal family – that sort of people. Not like you and me.'

'I don't see any chickens,' Mariam said.

'That's the one thing you can't find on Chicken Street.' Rasheed laughed.

The street was lined with shops and little stalls that sold lambskin hats and rainbow-colored *chapans*. Rasheed stopped to look at an engraved silver dagger in one shop, and, in another, at an old rifle that the shopkeeper assured Rasheed was a relic from the first war against the British.

'And I'm Moshe Dayan,' Rasheed muttered. He half smiled, and it seemed to Mariam that this was a smile meant only for her. A private, married smile.

They strolled past carpet shops, handicraft shops, pastry shops, flower shops, and shops that sold suits for men and dresses for women, and, in them, behind lace curtains, Mariam saw young girls sewing buttons and ironing collars. From time to time, Rasheed greeted a shopkeeper he knew, sometimes in Farsi, other times in Pashto. As they shook hands and kissed on the cheek, Mariam stood a few feet away. Rasheed did not wave her over, did not introduce her.

He asked her to wait outside an embroidery shop. 'I know the owner,' he said. 'I'll just go in for a minute, say my *salaam*.'

Mariam waited outside on the crowded sidewalk. She watched the cars crawling up Chicken Street, threading through the horde of hawkers and pedestrians, honking at children and donkeys who wouldn't move. She watched the bored-looking merchants inside their tiny stalls, smoking, or spitting into brass spittoons, their faces emerging from the shadows now and then to peddle textiles and furcollared *poostin* coats to passersby.

But it was the women who drew Mariam's eyes the most.

The women in this part of Kabul were a different breed from the women in the poorer neighborhoods – like the one where she and Rasheed lived, where so many of the women covered fully. These women were – what was the word Rasheed had used? – 'modern.' Yes, modern Afghan women married to modern Afghan men who did not mind that their wives walked among strangers with makeup on their faces and nothing on their heads.

Mariam watched them cantering uninhibited down the street, sometimes with a man, sometimes alone, sometimes with rosy-cheeked children who wore shiny shoes and watches with leather bands, who walked bicycles with high-rise handlebars and gold-colored spokes – unlike the children in Deh-Mazang, who bore sand-fly scars on their cheeks and rolled old bicycle tires with sticks.

These women were all swinging handbags and rustling skirts. Mariam even spotted one smoking behind the wheel of a car. Their nails were long, polished pink or orange, their lips red as tulips. They walked in high heels, and quickly, as if on perpetually urgent business. They wore dark sunglasses, and, when they breezed by, Mariam caught a whiff of their perfume. She imagined that they all had university degrees, that they worked in office buildings, behind desks of their own, where they typed and smoked and made important telephone calls to important people. These women mystified Mariam. They made her aware of her own lowliness, her plain looks, her lack of aspirations, her ignorance of so many things.

Then Rasheed was tapping her on the shoulder and handing her something.

'Here.'

It was a dark maroon silk shawl with beaded fringes and edges embroidered with gold thread.

'Do you like it?'

Mariam looked up. Rasheed did a touching thing then. He blinked and averted her gaze.

Mariam thought of Jalil, of the emphatic, jovial way in which he'd pushed his jewelry at her, the overpowering cheerfulness that left room for no response but meek gratitude. Nana had been right about Jalil's gifts. They had been halfhearted tokens of penance, insincere, corrupt gestures meant more for his own appeasement than hers. This shawl, Mariam saw, was a true gift.

'It's beautiful,' she said.

That night, Rasheed visited her room again. But instead of smoking in the doorway, he crossed the room and sat beside her where she lay on the bed. The springs creaked as the bed tilted to his side.

There was a moment of hesitation, and then his hand was on her neck, his thick fingers slowly pressing the knobs in the back of it. His thumb slid down, and now it was stroking the hollow above her collarbone, then the flesh beneath it. Mariam began shivering. His hand crept lower still, lower, his fingernails catching in the cotton of her blouse.

'I can't,' she croaked, looking at his moonlit profile, his thick shoulders and broad chest, the tufts of gray hair protruding from his open collar.

His hand was on her right breast now, squeezing it hard through the blouse, and she could hear him breathing deeply through the nose.

He slid under the blanket beside her. She could feel his hand working at his belt, at the drawstring of her trouser. Her own hands clenched the sheets in fistfuls. He rolled on top of her, wriggled and shifted, and she let out a whimper. Mariam closed her eyes, gritted her teeth.

The pain was sudden and astonishing. Her eyes sprang open. She sucked air through her teeth and bit on the knuckle of her thumb. She slung her free arm over Rasheed's back and her fingers dug at his shirt.

Rasheed buried his face into her pillow, and Mariam stared, wide-eyed, at the ceiling above his shoulder, shivering, lips pursed, feeling the heat of his quick breaths on her shoulder. The air between them smelled of tobacco, of the onions and grilled lamb they had eaten earlier. Now and then, his ear rubbed against her cheek, and she knew from the scratchy feel that he had shaved it.

When it was done, he rolled off her, panting. He dropped his forearm over his brow. In the dark, she could see the blue hands of his watch. They lay that way for a while, on their backs, not looking at each other.

'There is no shame in this, Mariam,' he said, slurring a little. 'It's what married people do. It's what the Prophet himself and his wives did. There is no shame.'

A few moments later, he pushed back the blanket and left the room, leaving her with the impression of his head on her pillow, leaving her to wait out the pain down below, to look at the frozen stars in the sky and a cloud that draped the face of the moon like a wedding veil.

# CHAPTER 12

Ramadan came in the fall that year, 1974.
For the first time in her life, Mariam saw
how the sighting of the new crescent moon
could transform an entire city, alter its rhythm
and mood. She noticed a drowsy hush overtaking
Kabul. Traffic became languid, scant, even quiet.
Shops emptied. Restaurants turned off their lights,
closed their doors. Mariam saw no smokers on
the streets, no cups of tea steaming from window
ledges. And at *iftar*, when the sun dipped in the
west and the cannon fired from the Shir Darwaza
mountain, the city broke its fast, and so did
Mariam, with bread and a date, tasting for the
first time in her fifteen years the sweetness of
sharing in a communal experience.

Except for a handful of days, Rasheed didn't
observe the fast. The few times he did, he came
home in a sour mood. Hunger made him curt,
irritable, impatient. One night, Mariam was a few
minutes late with dinner, and he started eating
bread with radishes. Even after Mariam put the
rice and the lamb and okra *qurma* in front of him,
he wouldn't touch it. He said nothing, and went

on chewing the bread, his temples working, the vein on his forehead, full and angry. He went on chewing and staring ahead, and when Mariam spoke to him he looked at her without seeing her face and put another piece of bread into his mouth.

Mariam was relieved when Ramadan ended.

Back at the *kolba*, on the first of three days of Eid-ul-Fitr celebration that followed Ramadan, Jalil would visit Mariam and Nana. Dressed in suit and tie, he would come bearing Eid presents. One year, he gave Mariam a wool scarf. The three of them would sit for tea and then Jalil would excuse himself.

'Off to celebrate Eid with his real family,' Nana would say as he crossed the stream and waved.

Mullah Faizullah would come too. He would bring Mariam chocolate candy wrapped in foil, a basketful of dyed boiled eggs, cookies. After he was gone, Mariam would climb one of the willows with her treats. Perched on a high branch, she would eat Mullah Faizullah's chocolates and drop the foil wrappers until they lay scattered about the trunk of the tree like silver blossoms. When the chocolate was gone, she would start in on the cookies, and, with a pencil, she would draw faces on the eggs he had brought her now. But there was little pleasure in this for her. Mariam dreaded Eid, this time of hospitality and ceremony, when families dressed in their best and visited each other. She would imagine the air in Herat crackling with merriness, and high-spirited, bright-eyed people showering each other with endearments and goodwill. A forlornness would descend on her like a shroud then and would lift only when Eid had passed.

This year, for the first time, Mariam saw with her eyes the Eid of her childhood imaginings.

Rasheed and she took to the streets. Mariam had never walked amid such liveliness. Undaunted by the chilly weather, families had flooded the city on their frenetic rounds to visit relatives. On their own street, Mariam saw Fariba and her son Noor, who was dressed in a suit. Fariba, wearing a white scarf, walked beside a small-boned, shy-looking man with eyeglasses. Her older son was there too – Mariam somehow remembered Fariba saying his name, Ahmad, at the tandoor that first time. He had deep-set, brooding eyes, and his face was more thoughtful, more solemn, than his younger brother's, a face as suggestive of early maturity as his brother's was of lingering boyishness. Around Ahmad's neck was a glittering ALLAH pendant.

Fariba must have recognized her, walking in burqa beside Rasheed. She waved, and called out, '*Eid mubarak!*'

From inside the burqa, Mariam gave her a ghost of a nod.

'So you know that woman, the teacher's wife?' Rasheed said.

Mariam said she didn't.

'Best you stay away. She's a nosy gossiper, that

91

one. And the husband fancies himself some kind of educated intellectual. But he's a mouse. Look at him. Doesn't he look like a mouse?'

They went to Shar-e-Nau, where kids romped about in new shirts and beaded, brightly colored vests and compared Eid gifts. Women brandished platters of sweets. Mariam saw festive lanterns hanging from shopwindows, heard music blaring from loudspeakers. Strangers called out '*Eid mubarak*' to her as they passed.

That night they went to *Chaman*, and, standing behind Rasheed, Mariam watched fireworks light up the sky, in flashes of green, pink, and yellow. She missed sitting with Mullah Faizullah outside the *kolba*, watching the fireworks explode over Herat in the distance, the sudden bursts of color reflected in her tutor's soft, cataract-riddled eyes. But, mostly, she missed Nana. Mariam wished her mother were alive to see this. To see *her*, amid all of it. To see at last that contentment and beauty were not unattainable things. Even for the likes of them.

They had Eid visitors at the house. They were all men, friends of Rasheed's. When a knock came, Mariam knew to go upstairs to her room and close the door. She stayed there, as the men sipped tea downstairs with Rasheed, smoked, chatted. Rasheed had told Mariam that she was not to come down until the visitors had left.

Mariam didn't mind. In truth, she was even flattered. Rasheed saw sanctity in what they had together. Her honor, her *namoos*, was something worth guarding to him. She felt prized by his protectiveness. Treasured and significant.

On the third and last day of Eid, Rasheed went to visit some friends. Mariam, who'd had a queasy stomach all night, boiled some water and made herself a cup of green tea sprinkled with crushed cardamom. In the living room, she took in the aftermath of the previous night's Eid visits: the overturned cups, the half-chewed pumpkin seeds stashed between mattresses, the plates crusted with the outline of last night's meal. Mariam set about cleaning up the mess, marveling at how energetically lazy men could be.

She didn't mean to go into Rasheed's room. But the cleaning took her from the living room to the stairs, and then to the hallway upstairs and to his door, and, the next thing she knew, she was in his room for the first time, sitting on his bed, feeling like a trespasser.

She took in the heavy, green drapes, the pairs of polished shoes lined up neatly along the wall, the closet door, where the gray paint had chipped and showed the wood beneath. She spotted a pack of cigarettes atop the dresser beside his bed. She put one between her lips and stood before the small oval mirror on the wall. She puffed air into the mirror and made ash-tapping motions. She put it back. She could never manage the seamless grace with which Kabuli women smoked. On her, it looked coarse, ridiculous.

Guiltily, she slid open the top drawer of his dresser. She saw the gun first. It was black, with a wooden grip and a short muzzle. Mariam made sure to memorize which way it was facing before she picked it up. She turned it over in her hands. It was much heavier than it looked. The grip felt smooth in her hand, and the muzzle was cold. It was disquieting to her that Rasheed owned something whose sole purpose was to kill another person. But surely he kept it for their safety. Her safety.

Beneath the gun were several magazines with curling corners. Mariam opened one. Something inside her dropped. Her mouth gaped of its own will.

On every page were women, beautiful women, who wore no shirts, no trousers, no socks or underpants. They wore nothing at all. They lay in beds amid tumbled sheets and gazed back at Mariam with half-lidded eyes. In most of the pictures, their legs were apart, and Mariam had a full view of the dark place between. In some, the women were prostrated as if – God forbid this thought – in *sujda* for prayer. They looked back over their shoulders with a look of bored contempt.

Mariam quickly put the magazine back where she'd found it. She felt drugged. Who were these women? How could they allow themselves to be photographed this way? Her stomach revolted with distaste. Was this what he did then, those nights that he did not visit her room? Had she been a disappointment to him in this particular regard? And what about all his talk of honor and propriety, his disapproval of the female customers, who, after all, were only showing him their feet to get fitted for shoes? *A woman's face*, he'd said, *is her husband's business only.* Surely the women on these pages had husbands, some of them must. At the least, they had brothers. If so, why did Rasheed insist that *she* cover when he thought nothing of looking at the private areas of other men's wives and sisters?

Mariam sat on his bed, embarrassed and confused. She cupped her face with her hands and closed her eyes. She breathed and breathed until she felt calmer.

Slowly, an explanation presented itself. He was a man, after all, living alone for years before she had moved in. His needs differed from hers. For her, all these months later, their coupling was still an exercise in tolerating pain. His appetite, on the other hand, was fierce, sometimes bordering on the violent. The way he pinned her down, his hard squeezes at her breasts, how furiously his hips worked. He was a man. All those years without a woman. Could she fault him for being the way God had created him?

Mariam knew that she could never talk to him about this. It was unmentionable. But was it unfor-givable? She only had to think of the other man in her life. Jalil, a husband of three and father of nine at the time, having relations with Nana out of wedlock. Which was worse, Rasheed's magazine or what Jalil had done? And what entitled her anyway, a villager, a *harami*, to pass judgment?

Mariam tried the bottom drawer of the dresser. It was there that she found a picture of the boy, Yunus. It was black-and-white. He looked four, maybe five. He was wearing a striped shirt and a bow tie. He was a handsome little boy, with a slender nose, brown hair, and dark, slightly sunken eyes. He looked distracted, as though something had caught his eye just as the camera had flashed.

Beneath that, Mariam found another photo, also black-and-white, this one slightly more grainy. It was of a seated woman and, behind her, a thinner, younger Rasheed, with black hair. The woman was beautiful. Not as beautiful as the women in the magazine, perhaps, but beautiful. Certainly more beautiful than her, Mariam. She had a delicate chin and long, black hair parted in the center. High cheekbones and a gentle forehead. Mariam pictured her own face, her thin lips and long chin, and felt a flicker of jealousy.

She looked at this photo for a long time. There was something vaguely unsettling about the way Rasheed seemed to loom over the woman. His hands on her shoulders. His savoring, tight-lipped smile and her unsmiling, sullen face. The way her body tilted forward subtly, as though she were trying to wriggle free of his hands.

Mariam put everything back where she'd found it.

Later, as she was doing laundry, she regretted

96

that she had sneaked around in his room. For what? What thing of substance had she learned about him? That he owned a gun, that he was a man with the needs of a man? And she shouldn't have stared at the photo of him and his wife for as long as she had. Her eyes had read meaning into what was random body posture captured in a single moment of time.

What Mariam felt now, as the loaded clotheslines bounced heavily before her, was sorrow for Rasheed. He too had had a hard life, a life marked by loss and sad turns of fate. Her thoughts returned to his boy Yunus, who had once built snowmen in this yard, whose feet had pounded these same stairs. The lake had snatched him from Rasheed, swallowed him up, just as a whale had swallowed the boy's namesake prophet in the Koran. It pained Mariam – it pained her considerably – to picture Rasheed panic-stricken and helpless, pacing the banks of the lake and pleading with it to spit his son back onto dry land. And she felt for the first time a kinship with her husband. She told herself that they would make good companions after all.

# CHAPTER 13

O n the bus ride home from the doctor, the strangest thing was happening to Mariam. Everywhere she looked, she saw bright colors: on the drab, gray concrete apartments, on the tin-roofed, open-fronted stores, in the muddy water flowing in the gutters. It was as though a rainbow had melted into her eyes.

Rasheed was drumming his gloved fingers and humming a song. Every time the bus bucked over a pothole and jerked forward, his hand shot protectively over her belly.

'What about Zalmai?' he said. 'It's a good Pashtun name.'

'What if it's a girl?' Mariam said.

'I think it's a boy. Yes. A boy.'

A murmur was passing through the bus. Some passengers were pointing at something and other passengers were leaning across seats to see.

'Look,' said Rasheed, tapping a knuckle on the glass. He was smiling. 'There. See?'

On the streets, Mariam saw people stopping in their tracks. At traffic lights, faces emerged from the windows of cars, turned upward toward the falling softness. What was it about a season's first snow-fall, Mariam wondered, that was so entrancing? Was it the chance to see something as yet unsoiled, untrodden? To catch the fleeting grace of a new season, a lovely beginning, before it was trampled and corrupted?

'If it's a girl,' Rasheed said, 'and it isn't, but, if it *is* a girl, then you can choose whatever name you want.'

Mariam awoke the next morning to the sound of sawing and hammering. She wrapped a shawl around her and went out into the snow-blown yard. The heavy snowfall of the previous night had stopped. Now only a scattering of light, swirling flakes tickled her cheeks. The air was windless and smelled like burning coal. Kabul was eerily silent, quilted in white, tendrils of smoke snaking up here and there.

She found Rasheed in the toolshed, pounding nails into a plank of wood. When he saw her, he removed a nail from the corner of his mouth.

'It was going to be a surprise. He'll need a crib. You weren't supposed to see until it was done.'

Mariam wished he wouldn't do that, hitch his hopes to its being a boy. As happy as she was about this pregnancy, his expectation weighed on her. Yesterday, Rasheed had gone out and come home with a suede winter coat for a boy, lined inside with soft sheepskin, the sleeves embroidered with fine red and yellow silk thread.

Rasheed lifted a long, narrow board. As he began to saw it in half, he said the stairs worried him. 'Something will have to be done about them later, when he's old enough to climb.' The stove worried him too, he said. The knives and forks would have to be stowed somewhere out of reach. 'You can't be too careful. Boys are reckless creatures.'

Mariam pulled the shawl around her against the chill.

The next morning, Rasheed said he wanted to invite his friends for dinner to celebrate. All morning, Mariam cleaned lentils and moistened rice. She sliced eggplants for *borani,* and cooked leeks and ground beef for *aushak.* She swept the floor, beat the curtains, aired the house, despite the snow that had started up again. She arranged mattresses and cushions along the walls of the living room, placed bowls of candy and roasted almonds on the table.

She was in her room by early evening before the first of the men arrived. She lay in bed as the hoots and laughter and bantering voices downstairs began to mushroom. She couldn't keep her hands from drifting to her belly. She thought of what was growing there, and happiness rushed in like a gust of wind blowing a door wide open. Her eyes watered.

Mariam thought of her six-hundred-and-fifty-kilometer bus trip with Rasheed, from Herat in the west, near the border with Iran, to Kabul in the east. They had passed small towns and big towns, and knots of little villages that kept springing up one after another. They had gone over mountains and across raw-burned deserts, from one province to the next. And here she was now, over those boulders and parched hills, with a home of her own, a husband of her own, heading toward one final, cherished province: Motherhood. How delectable it was to think of this baby, *her* baby, *their* baby. How glorious it was to know that her love for it already dwarfed anything she had ever felt as a human being, to know that there was no need any longer for pebble games.

Downstairs, someone was tuning a harmonium. Then the clanging of a hammer tuning a tabla. Someone cleared his throat. And then there was whistling and clapping and yipping and singing.

Mariam stroked the softness of her belly. *No bigger than a fingernail,* the doctor had said.

*I'm going to be a mother,* she thought.

'I'm going to be a mother,' she said. Then she was laughing to herself, and saying it over and over, relishing the words.

When Mariam thought of this baby, her heart swelled inside of her. It swelled and swelled until all the loss, all the grief, all the loneliness and self-abasement of her life washed away. This was why God had brought her here, all the way across the country. She knew this now. She remembered a verse from the Koran that Mullah Faizullah had taught her: *And Allah is the East and the West, there-fore wherever you turn there is Allah's purpose . . .* She laid down her prayer rug and did *namaz.* When she was done, she cupped her hands before her face and asked God not to let all this good fortune slip away from her.

It was Rasheed's idea to go to the *hamam.* Mariam had never been to a bathhouse, but he said there was nothing finer than stepping out and taking that first breath of cold air, to feel the heat rising from the skin.

In the women's *hamam*, shapes moved about in the steam around Mariam, a glimpse of a hip here, the contour of a shoulder there. The squeals of young girls, the grunts of old women, and the trickling of bathwater echoed between the walls as backs were scrubbed and hair soaped. Mariam sat in the far corner by herself, working on her heels with a pumice stone, insulated by a wall of steam from the passing shapes.

Then there was blood and she was screaming.

The sound of feet now, slapping against the wet cobblestones. Faces peering at her through the steam. Tongues clucking.

Later that night, in bed, Fariba told her husband that when she'd heard the cry and rushed over she'd found Rasheed's wife shriveled into a corner, hugging her knees, a pool of blood at her feet.

'You could hear the poor girl's teeth rattling. Hakim, she was shivering so hard.'

When Mariam had seen her, Fariba said, she had asked in a high, supplicating voice, *It's normal, isn't it? Isn't it? Isn't it normal?*

Another bus ride with Rasheed. Snowing again. Falling thick this time. It was piling in heaps on sidewalks, on roofs, gathering in patches on the bark of straggly trees. Mariam watched the merchants plowing snow from their storefronts. A group of boys was chasing a black dog. They waved sportively at the bus. Mariam looked over to Rasheed. His eyes were closed. He wasn't humming. Mariam reclined her head and closed her eyes too. She wanted out of her cold socks, out of the damp wool sweater that was prickly against her skin. She wanted away from this bus.

At the house, Rasheed covered her with a quilt when she lay on the couch, but there was a stiff, perfunctory air about this gesture.

'What kind of answer is that?' he said again. 'That's what a mullah is supposed to say. You pay a doctor his fee, you want a better answer than "God's will."'

Mariam curled up her knees beneath the quilt and said he ought to get some rest.

'God's will,' he simmered.

He sat in his room smoking cigarettes all day.

Mariam lay on the couch, hands tucked between her knees, watched the whirlpool of snow twisting and spinning outside the window. She remembered Nana saying once that each snowflake was a sigh heaved by an aggrieved woman somewhere in the world. That all the sighs drifted up the sky, gathered into clouds, then broke into tiny pieces that fell silently on the people below.

*As a reminder of how women like us suffer,* she'd said. *How quietly we endure all that falls upon us.*

# CHAPTER 14

The grief kept surprising Mariam. All it took to unleash it was her thinking of the unfinished crib in the toolshed or the suede coat in Rasheed's closet. The baby came to life then and she could hear it, could hear its hungry grunts, its gurgles and jabbering. She felt it sniffing at her breasts. The grief washed over her, swept her up, tossed her upside down. Mariam was dumbfounded that she could miss in such a crippling manner a being she had never even seen.

Then there were days when the dreariness didn't seem quite as unrelenting to Mariam. Days when the mere thought of resuming the old patterns of her life did not seem so exhausting, when it did not take enormous efforts of will to get out of bed, to do her prayers, to do the wash, to make meals for Rasheed.

Mariam dreaded going outside. She was envious, suddenly, of the neighborhood women and their wealth of children. Some had seven or eight and didn't understand how fortunate they were, how blessed that their children had flourished in their wombs, lived to squirm in their arms and take the milk from their breasts. Children that they had not bled away with soapy water and the bodily filth of strangers down some bathhouse drain. Mariam resented them when she overheard them complaining about misbehaving sons and lazy daughters.

A voice inside her head tried to soothe her with well-intended but misguided consolation.

*You'll have others,* Inshallah. *You're young. Surely you'll have many other chances.*

But Mariam's grief wasn't aimless or unspecific. Mariam grieved for *this* baby, this particular child, who had made her so happy for a while.

Some days, she believed that the baby had been an undeserved blessing, that she was being punished for what she had done to Nana. Wasn't it true that she might as well have slipped that noose around her mother's neck herself? Treacherous daughters did not deserve to be mothers, and this was just punishment. She had fitful dreams, of Nana's *jinn* sneaking into her room at night, burrowing its claws into her womb, and stealing her baby. In these dreams, Nana cackled with delight and vindication.

Other days, Mariam was besieged with anger. It was Rasheed's fault for his premature celebration. For his foolhardy faith that she was carrying a boy. Naming the baby as he had. Taking God's will for granted. His fault, for making her go to the bathhouse. Something there, the steam, the dirty water, the soap, something there had caused this to happen. No. Not Rasheed. *She* was to blame. She became furious with herself for sleeping in the wrong position, for eating meals that were too spicy, for not eating enough fruit, for drinking too much tea.

It was God's fault, for taunting her as He had. For not granting her what He had granted so many other women. For dangling before her, tantalizingly, what He knew would give her the greatest happiness, then pulling it away.

But it did no good, all this fault laying, all these harangues of accusations bouncing in her head. It was *kofr*, sacrilege, to think these thoughts. Allah was not spiteful. He was not a petty God. Mullah Faizullah's words whispered in her head: *Blessed is He in Whose hand is the kingdom, and He Who has power over all things. Who created death and life that He may try you.*

Ransacked with guilt, Mariam would kneel and pray for forgiveness for these thoughts.

Meanwhile, a change had come over Rasheed ever since the day at the bathhouse. Most nights when he came home, he hardly talked anymore. He ate, smoked, went to bed, sometimes came back in the middle of the night for a brief and, of late, quite rough session of coupling. He was more apt to sulk these days, to fault her cooking, to complain about clutter around the yard or point out even minor uncleanliness in the house. Occasionally, he took her around town on Fridays, like he used to, but on the sidewalks he walked quickly and always a few steps ahead of her, without speaking, unmindful of Mariam who almost had to run to keep up with him. He wasn't so ready with a laugh on these outings anymore. He didn't buy her sweets or gifts, didn't stop and name places to her as he used to. Her questions seemed to irritate him.

One night, they were sitting in the living room listening to the radio. Winter was passing. The stiff winds that plastered snow onto the face and made the eyes water had calmed. Silvery fluffs of snow were melting off the branches of tall elms and would be replaced in a few weeks with stubby, pale green buds. Rasheed was shaking his foot absently to the tabla beat of a Hamahang song, his eyes crinkled against cigarette smoke.

'Are you angry with me?' Mariam asked.

Rasheed said nothing. The song ended and the news came on. A woman's voice reported that President Daoud Khan had sent yet another group of Soviet consultants back to Moscow, to the expected displeasure of the Kremlin.

'I worry that you are angry with me.'

Rasheed sighed.

'Are you?'

His eyes shifted to her. 'Why would I be angry?'

'I don't know, but ever since the baby—'

'Is that the kind of man you take me for, after everything I've done for you?'

'No. Of course not.'

'Then stop pestering me!'

'I'm sorry. *Bebakhsh*, Rasheed. I'm sorry.'

He crushed out his cigarette and lit another. He turned up the volume on the radio.

'I've been thinking, though,' Mariam said, raising her voice so as to be heard over the music.

Rasheed sighed again, more irritably this time, turned down the volume once more. He rubbed his forehead wearily. 'What now?'

'I've been thinking, that maybe we should have a proper burial. For the baby, I mean. Just us, a few prayers, nothing more.'

Mariam had been thinking about it for a while. She didn't want to forget this baby. It didn't seem right, not to mark this loss in some way that was permanent.

'What for? It's idiotic.'

'It would make me feel better, I think.'

'Then *you* do it,' he said sharply. 'I've already buried one son. I won't bury another. Now, if you don't mind, I'm trying to listen.'

He turned up the volume again, leaned his head back and closed his eyes.

One sunny morning that week, Mariam picked a spot in the yard and dug a hole.

'In the name of Allah and with Allah, and in the name of the messenger of Allah upon whom be the blessings and peace of Allah,' she said under her breath as her shovel bit into the ground. She placed the suede coat that Rasheed had bought for the baby in the hole and shoveled dirt over it.

109

'You make the night to pass into the day and You make the day to pass into the night, and You bring forth the living from the dead and You bring forth the dead from the living, and You give sustenance to whom You please without measure.'

She patted the dirt with the back of the shovel. She squatted by the mound, closed her eyes.

*Give sustenance, Allah.*

*Give sustenance to me.*

# CHAPTER 15

## APRIL 1978

On April 17, 1978, the year Mariam turned nineteen, a man named Mir Akbar Khyber was found murdered. Two days later, there was a large demonstration in Kabul. Everyone in the neighborhood was in the streets talking about it. Through the window, Mariam saw neighbors milling about, chatting excitedly, transistor radios pressed to their ears. She saw Fariba leaning against the wall of her house, talking with a woman who was new to Deh-Mazang. Fariba was smiling, and her palms were pressed against the swell of her pregnant belly. The other woman, whose name escaped Mariam, looked older than Fariba, and her hair had an odd purple tint to it. She was holding a little boy's hand. Mariam knew the boy's name was Tariq, because she had heard this woman on the street call after him by that name.

Mariam and Rasheed didn't join the neighbors. They listened in on the radio as some ten thousand people poured into the streets and marched up and

111

down Kabul's government district. Rasheed said that Mir Akbar Khyber had been a prominent communist, and that his supporters were blaming the murder on President Daoud Khan's government. He didn't look at her when he said this. These days, he never did anymore, and Mariam wasn't ever sure if she was being spoken to.

'What's a communist?' she asked.

Rasheed snorted, and raised both eyebrows. 'You don't know what a communist is? Such a simple thing. Everyone knows. It's common knowledge. You don't . . . Bah. I don't know why I'm surprised.' Then he crossed his ankles on the table and mumbled that it was someone who believed in Karl Marxist.

'Who's Karl Marxist?'

Rasheed sighed.

On the radio, a woman's voice was saying that Taraki, the leader of the Khalq branch of the PDPA, the Afghan communist party, was in the streets giving rousing speeches to demonstrators.

'What I meant was, what do they want?' Mariam asked. 'These communists, what is it that they believe?'

Rasheed chortled and shook his head, but Mariam thought she saw uncertainty in the way he crossed his arms, the way his eyes shifted. 'You know nothing, do you? You're like a child. Your brain is empty. There is no information in it.'

'I ask because—'

'*Chup ko.* Shut up.'

112

Mariam did.

It wasn't easy tolerating him talking this way to her, to bear his scorn, his ridicule, his insults, his walking past her like she was nothing but a house cat. But after four years of marriage, Mariam saw clearly how much a woman could tolerate when she was afraid. And Mariam *was* afraid. She lived in fear of his shifting moods, his volatile temperament, his insistence on steering even mundane exchanges down a confrontational path that, on occasion, he would resolve with punches, slaps, kicks, and sometimes try to make amends for with polluted apologies and sometimes not.

In the four years since the day at the bathhouse, there had been six more cycles of hopes raised then dashed, each loss, each collapse, each trip to the doctor more crushing for Mariam than the last. With each disappointment, Rasheed had grown more remote and resentful. Now nothing she did pleased him. She cleaned the house, made sure he always had a supply of clean shirts, cooked him his favorite dishes. Once, disastrously, she even bought makeup and put it on for him. But when he came home, he took one look at her and winced with such distaste that she rushed to the bathroom and washed it all off, tears of shame mixing with soapy water, rouge, and mascara.

Now Mariam dreaded the sound of him coming home in the evening. The key rattling, the creak of the door – these were sounds that set her heart racing. From her bed, she listened to the *click-clack* of his heels, to the muffled shuffling of his feet after he'd shed his shoes. With her ears, she took inventory of his doings: chair legs dragged across the floor, the plaintive squeak of the cane seat when he sat, the clinking of spoon against plate, the flutter of newspaper pages flipped, the slurping of water. And as her heart pounded, her mind wondered what excuse he would use that night to pounce on her. There was always something, some minor thing that would infuriate him, because no matter what she did to please him, no matter how thoroughly she submitted to his wants and demands, it wasn't enough. She could not give him his son back. In this most essential way, she had failed him – seven times she had failed him – and now she was nothing but a burden to him. She could see it in the way he looked at her, *when* he looked at her. She was a burden to him.

'What's going to happen?' she asked him now.

Rasheed shot her a sidelong glance. He made a sound between a sigh and a groan, dropped his legs from the table, and turned off the radio. He took it upstairs to his room. He closed the door.

On April 27, Mariam's question was answered with crackling sounds and intense, sudden roars. She ran barefoot down to the living room and found Rasheed already by the window, in his undershirt, his hair disheveled, palms pressed to the glass. Mariam made her way to the window next to him. Overhead, she could see military planes zooming past, heading north and east. Their deafening shrieks hurt her ears. In the distance, loud booms resonated and sudden plumes of smoke rose to the sky.

'What's going on, Rasheed?' she said. 'What is all this?'

'God knows,' he muttered. He tried the radio and got only static.

'What do we do?'

Impatiently, Rasheed said, 'We wait.'

Later in the day, Rasheed was still trying the radio as Mariam made rice with spinach sauce in the kitchen. Mariam remembered a time when she had enjoyed, even looked forward to, cooking for Rasheed. Now cooking was an exercise in heightened anxiety. The *qurmas* were always too salty or too bland for his taste. The rice was judged either too greasy or too dry, the bread declared too doughy or too crispy. Rasheed's faultfinding left her stricken in the kitchen with self-doubt.

When she brought him his plate, the national anthem was playing on the radio.

'I made *sabzi*,' she said.

'Put it down and be quiet.'

After the music faded, a man's voice came on the radio. He announced himself as Air Force Colonel Abdul Qader. He reported that earlier in the day the rebel Fourth Armored Division had seized the airport and key intersections in the city. Kabul Radio, the ministries of Communication and the Interior, and the Foreign Ministry building had also been captured. Kabul was in the hands of the people now, he said proudly. Rebel MiGs had attacked the Presidential Palace. Tanks had broken into the premises, and a fierce battle was under way there. Daoud's loyalist forces were all but defeated, Abdul Qader said in a reassuring tone.

Days later, when the communists began the summary executions of those connected with Daoud Khan's regime, when rumors began floating about Kabul of eyes gouged and genitals electrocuted in the Pol-e-Charkhi Prison, Mariam would hear of the slaughter that had taken place at the Presidential Palace. Daoud Khan *had* been killed, but not before the communist rebels had killed some twenty members of his family, including women and grandchildren. There would be rumors that he had taken his own life, that he'd been gunned down in the heat of battle; rumors that he'd been saved for last, made to watch the massacre of his family, then shot.

Rasheed turned up the volume and leaned in closer.

'A revolutionary council of the armed forces has been established, and our *watan* will now be known as the Democratic Republic of Afghanistan,' Abdul Qader said. 'The era of aristocracy, nepotism, and inequality is over, fellow *hamwatans*. We have ended decades of tyranny. Power is now in the hands of the masses and freedom-loving people. A glorious new era in the history of our country is afoot. A new Afghanistan is born. We assure you that you have nothing to fear, fellow Afghans. The new regime will maintain the utmost respect for principles, both Islamic and democratic. This is a time of rejoicing and celebration.'

Rasheed turned off the radio.

'So is this good or bad?' Mariam asked.

'Bad for the rich, by the sound of it,' Rasheed said. 'Maybe not so bad for us.'

Mariam's thoughts drifted to Jalil. She wondered if the communists would go after him, then. Would they jail him? Jail his sons? Take his businesses and properties from him?

'Is this warm?' Rasheed said, eyeing the rice.

'I just served it from the pot.'

He grunted, and told her to hand him a plate.

Down the street, as the night lit up in sudden flashes of red and yellow, an exhausted Fariba had propped herself up on her elbows. Her hair was matted with sweat, and droplets of moisture teetered on the edge of her upper lip. At her bedside, the elderly midwife, Wajma, watched as Fariba's husband and sons passed around the infant. They were marveling at the baby's light hair, at her pink cheeks and puckered, rosebud lips, at the slits of jade green eyes moving behind her puffy lids. They smiled at each other when they heard her voice for the first time, a cry that started like the mewl of a cat and exploded into a healthy, full-throated yowl. Noor said her eyes were like gemstones. Ahmad, who was the most religious member of the family, sang the *azan* in his baby sister's ear and blew in her face three times.

'Laila it is, then?' Hakim asked, bouncing his daughter.

'Laila it is,' Fariba said, smiling tiredly. 'Night Beauty. It's perfect.'

Rasheed made a ball of rice with his fingers. He put it in his mouth, chewed once, then twice, before grimacing and spitting it out on the *sofrah*.

'What's the matter?' Mariam asked, hating the apologetic tone of her voice. She could feel her pulse quickening, her skin shrinking.

'What's the matter?' he mewled, mimicking her. 'What's the matter is that you've done it again.'

'But I boiled it five minutes more than usual.'

'That's a bold lie.'

'I swear—'

He shook the rice angrily from his fingers and pushed the plate away, spilling sauce and rice on the *sofrah*. Mariam watched as he stormed out of the living room, then out of the house, slamming the door on his way out.

Mariam kneeled to the ground and tried to pick up the grains of rice and put them back on the plate, but her hands were shaking badly, and she had to wait for them to stop. Dread pressed down on her chest. She tried taking a few deep breaths.

She caught her pale reflection in the darkened living-room window and looked away.

Then she heard the front door opening, and Rasheed was back in the living room.

'Get up,' he said. 'Come here. Get up.'

He snatched her hand, opened it, and dropped a handful of pebbles into it.

'Put these in your mouth.'

'What?'

'Put. These. In your mouth.'

'Stop it, Rasheed, I'm—'

His powerful hands clasped her jaw. He shoved two fingers into her mouth and pried it open, then forced the cold, hard pebbles into it. Mariam struggled against him, mumbling, but he kept pushing the pebbles in, his upper lip curled in a sneer.

'Now chew,' he said.

Through the mouthful of grit and pebbles, Mariam mumbled a plea. Tears were leaking out of the corners of her eyes.

'CHEW!' he bellowed. A gust of his smoky breath slammed against her face.

Mariam chewed. Something in the back of her mouth cracked.

'Good,' Rasheed said. His cheeks were quivering. 'Now you know what your rice tastes like. Now you know what you've given me in this marriage. Bad food, and nothing else.'

Then he was gone, leaving Mariam to spit out pebbles, blood, and the fragments of two broken molars.

# PART II

# CHAPTER 16

## KABUL, SPRING 1987

Nine-year-old Laila rose from bed, as she did most mornings, hungry for the sight of her friend Tariq. This morning, however, she knew there would be no Tariq sighting.

'How long will you be gone?' she'd asked when Tariq had told her that his parents were taking him south, to the city of Ghazni, to visit his paternal uncle.

'Thirteen days.'

'*Thirteen days?*'

'It's not so long. You're making a face, Laila.'

'I am not.'

'You're not going to cry, are you?'

'I am not going to cry! Not over you. Not in a thousand years.'

She'd kicked at his shin, not his artificial but his real one, and he'd playfully whacked the back of her head.

Thirteen days. Almost two weeks. And, just five days in, Laila had learned a fundamental truth about time: Like the accordion on which Tariq's

123

father sometimes played old Pashto songs, time stretched and contracted depending on Tariq's absence or presence.

Downstairs, her parents were fighting. Again. Laila knew the routine: Mammy, ferocious, indomitable, pacing and ranting; Babi, sitting, looking sheepish and dazed, nodding obediently, waiting for the storm to pass. Laila closed her door and changed. But she could still hear them. She could still hear *her*. Finally, a door slammed. Pounding footsteps. Mammy's bed creaked loudly. Babi, it seemed, would survive to see another day.

'Laila!' he called now. 'I'm going to be late for work!'

'One minute!'

Laila put on her shoes and quickly brushed her shoulder-length, blond curls in the mirror. Mammy always told Laila that she had inherited her hair color – as well as her thick-lashed, turquoise green eyes, her dimpled cheeks, her high cheekbones, and the pout of her lower lip, which Mammy shared – from her great-grandmother, Mammy's grandmother. *She was a* pari, *a stunner,* Mammy said. *Her beauty was the talk of the valley. It skipped two generations of women in our family, but it sure didn't bypass you, Laila.* The valley Mammy referred to was the Panjshir, the Farsi-speaking Tajik region one hundred kilometers northeast of Kabul. Both Mammy and Babi, who were first cousins, had been born and raised in Panjshir; they had moved to

Kabul back in 1960 as hopeful, bright-eyed newly-weds when Babi had been admitted to Kabul University.

Laila scrambled downstairs, hoping Mammy wouldn't come out of her room for another round. She found Babi kneeling by the screen door.

'Did you see this, Laila?'

The rip in the screen had been there for weeks. Laila hunkered down beside him. 'No. Must be new.'

'That's what I told Fariba.' He looked shaken, reduced, as he always did after Mammy was through with him. 'She says it's been letting in bees.'

Laila's heart went out to him. Babi was a small man, with narrow shoulders and slim, delicate hands, almost like a woman's. At night, when Laila walked into Babi's room, she always found the downward profile of his face burrowing into a book, his glasses perched on the tip of his nose. Sometimes he didn't even notice that she was there. When he did, he marked his page, smiled a close-lipped, companionable smile. Babi knew most of Rumi's and Hafez's *ghazals* by heart. He could speak at length about the struggle between Britain and czarist Russia over Afghanistan. He knew the difference between a stalactite and a stalagmite, and could tell you that the distance between the earth and the sun was the same as going from Kabul to Ghazni one and a half million times. But if Laila needed the lid of a candy jar

125

forced open, she had to go to Mammy, which felt like a betrayal. Ordinary tools befuddled Babi. On his watch, squeaky door hinges never got oiled. Ceilings went on leaking after he plugged them. Mold thrived defiantly in kitchen cabinets. Mammy said that before he left with Noor to join the jihad against the Soviets, back in 1980, it was Ahmad who had dutifully and competently minded these things.

'But if you have a book that needs urgent reading,' she said, 'then Hakim is your man.'

Still, Laila could not shake the feeling that at one time, before Ahmad and Noor had gone to war against the Soviets – before Babi had *let* them go to war – Mammy too had thought Babi's book-ishness endearing, that, once upon a time, she too had found his forgetfulness and ineptitude charming.

'So what is today?' he said now, smiling coyly. 'Day five? Or is it six?'

'What do I care? I don't keep count,' Laila lied, shrugging, loving him for remembering. Mammy had no idea that Tariq had left.

'Well, his flashlight will be going off before you know it,' Babi said, referring to Laila and Tariq's nightly signaling game. They had played it for so long it had become a bedtime ritual, like brushing teeth.

Babi ran his finger through the rip. 'I'll patch this as soon as I get a chance. We'd better go.' He raised his voice and called over his shoulder, 'We're

126

going now, Fariba! I'm taking Laila to school. Don't forget to pick her up!'

Outside, as she was climbing on the carrier pack of Babi's bicycle, Laila spotted a car parked up the street, across from the house where the shoe-maker, Rasheed, lived with his reclusive wife. It was a Benz, an unusual car in this neighborhood, blue with a thick white stripe bisecting the hood, the roof, and the trunk. Laila could make out two men sitting inside, one behind the wheel, the other in the back.

'Who are they?' she said.

'It's not our business,' Babi said. 'Climb on, you'll be late for class.'

Laila remembered another fight, and, that time, Mammy had stood over Babi and said in a mincing way, *That's your business, isn't it, cousin? To make nothing your business. Even your own sons going to war. How I pleaded with you. But you buried your nose in those cursed books and let our sons go like they were a pair of* haramis.

Babi pedaled up the street, Laila on the back, her arms wrapped around his belly. As they passed the blue Benz, Laila caught a fleeting glimpse of the man in the backseat: thin, white-haired, dressed in a dark brown suit, with a white hand-kerchief triangle in the breast pocket. The only other thing she had time to notice was that the car had Herat license plates.

They rode the rest of the way in silence, except at the turns, where Babi braked cautiously and

127

said, 'Hold on, Laila. Slowing down. Slowing down. There.'

In class that day, Laila found it hard to pay attention, between Tariq's absence and her parents' fight. So when the teacher called on her to name the capitals of Romania and Cuba, Laila was caught off guard.

The teacher's name was Shanzai, but, behind her back, the students called her Khala Rangmaal, Auntie Painter, referring to the motion she favored when she slapped students – palm, then back of the hand, back and forth, like a painter working a brush. Khala Rangmaal was a sharp-faced young woman with heavy eyebrows. On the first day of school, she had proudly told the class that she was the daughter of a poor peasant from Khost. She stood straight, and wore her jet-black hair pulled tightly back and tied in a bun so that, when Khala Rangmaal turned around, Laila could see the dark bristles on her neck. Khala Rangmaal did not wear makeup or jewelry. She did not cover and forbade the female students from doing it. She said women and men were equal in every way and there was no reason women should cover if men didn't.

She said that the Soviet Union was the best nation in the world, along with Afghanistan. It was kind to its workers, and its people were all equal. Everyone in the Soviet Union was happy and friendly, unlike America, where crime made people afraid to leave their homes. And everyone in Afghanistan would be happy too, she said, once the antiprogressives, the backward bandits, were defeated.

'That's why our Soviet comrades came here in 1979. To lend their neighbor a hand. To help us defeat these brutes who want our country to be a backward, primitive nation. And you must lend your own hand, children. You must report anyone who might know about these rebels. It's your duty. You must listen, then report. Even if it's your parents, your uncles or aunts. Because none of them loves you as much as your country does. Your country comes first, remember! I will be proud of you, and so will your country.'

On the wall behind Khala Rangmaal's desk was a map of the Soviet Union, a map of Afghanistan, and a framed photo of the latest communist president, Najibullah, who, Babi said, had once been the head of the dreaded KHAD. the Afghan secret police. There were other photos too, mainly of young Soviet soldiers shaking hands with peasants, planting apple saplings, building homes, always smiling genially.

'Well,' Khala Rangmaal said now, 'have I disturbed your day-dreaming, *Inqilabi* Girl?'

This was her nickname for Laila, Revolutionary Girl, because she'd been born the night of the April coup of 1978 – except Khala Rangmaal became angry if anyone in her class used the word *coup*. What had happened, she insisted, was an *inqilab*, a revolution, an uprising of the working

129

people against inequality. *Jihad* was another forbidden word. According to her, there wasn't even a war out there in the provinces, just skirmishes against troublemakers stirred by people she called foreign provocateurs. And certainly no one, *no one*, dared repeat in her presence the rising rumors that, after eight years of fighting, the Soviets were losing this war. Particularly now that the American president, Reagan, had started shipping the Mujahideen Stinger Missiles to down the Soviet helicopters, now that Muslims from all over the world were joining the cause: Egyptians, Pakistanis, even wealthy Saudis, who left their millions behind and came to Afghanistan to fight the jihad.

'Bucharest. Havana,' Laila managed.

'And are those countries our friends or not?'

'They are, *moalim* sahib. They are friendly countries.'

Khala Rangmaal gave a curt nod.

When school let out, Mammy again didn't show up like she was supposed to. Laila ended up walking home with two of her classmates, Giti and Hasina.

Giti was a tightly wound, bony little girl who wore her hair in twin ponytails held by elastic bands. She was always scowling, and walking with her books pressed to her chest, like a shield. Hasina was twelve, three years older than Laila and Giti, but had failed third grade once and

130

fourth grade twice. What she lacked in smarts Hasina made up for in mischief and a mouth that, Giti said, ran like a sewing machine. It was Hasina who had come up with the Khala Rangmaal nickname.

Today, Hasina was dispensing advice on how to fend off unattractive suitors. 'Foolproof method, guaranteed to work. I give you my word.'

'This is stupid. I'm too young to have a suitor!' Giti said.

'You're not too young.'

'Well, no one's come to ask for *my* hand.'

'That's because you have a beard, my dear.'

Giti's hand shot up to her chin, and she looked with alarm to Laila, who smiled pityingly – Giti was the most humorless person Laila had ever met – and shook her head with reassurance.

'Anyway, you want to know what to do or not, ladies?'

'Go ahead,' Laila said.

'Beans. No less than four cans. On the evening the toothless lizard comes to ask for your hand. But the timing, ladies, the timing is everything. You have to suppress the fireworks 'til it's time to serve him his tea.'

'I'll remember that,' Laila said.

'So will he.'

Laila could have said then that she didn't need this advice because Babi had no intention of giving her away anytime soon. Though Babi worked at Silo, Kabul's gigantic bread factory, where he labored amid the heat and the humming machinery stoking the massive ovens and mill grains all day, he was a university-educated man. He'd been a high school teacher before the communists fired him – this was shortly after the coup of 1978, about a year and a half before the Soviets had invaded. Babi had made it clear to Laila from a young age that the most important thing in his life, after her safety, was her schooling.

*I know you're still young, but I want you to understand and learn this now*, he said. *Marriage can wait, education cannot. You're a very, very bright girl. Truly, you are. You can be anything you want, Laila. I know this about you. And I also know that when this war is over, Afghanistan is going to need you as much as its men, maybe even more. Because a society has no chance of success if its women are uneducated, Laila. No chance.*

But Laila didn't tell Hasina that Babi had said these things, or how glad she was to have a father like him, or how proud she was of his regard for her, or how determined she was to pursue her education just as he had his. For the last two years, Laila had received the *awal numra* certificate, given yearly to the top-ranked student in each grade. She said nothing of these things to Hasina, though, whose own father was an ill-tempered taxi driver who in two or three years would almost certainly give her away. Hasina had told Laila, in one of her infrequent serious moments, that it had already been decided that she would marry a first

132

cousin who was twenty years older than her and owned an auto shop in Lahore. *I've seen him twice,* Hasina had said. *Both times he ate with his mouth open.*

'Beans, girls,' Hasina said. 'You remember that. Unless, of course' – here she flashed an impish grin and nudged Laila with an elbow – 'it's your young handsome, one-legged prince who comes knocking. Then . . .'

Laila slapped the elbow away. She would have taken offense if anyone else had said that about Tariq. But she knew that Hasina wasn't malicious. She mocked – it was what she did – and her mocking spared no one, least of all herself.

'You shouldn't talk that way about people!' Giti said.

'What people is that?'

'People who've been injured because of war,' Giti said earnestly, oblivious to Hasina's toying.

'I think Mullah Giti here has a crush on Tariq. I knew it! Ha! But he's already spoken for, don't you know? Isn't he, Laila?'

'I do not have a crush. On anyone!'

They broke off from Laila, and, still arguing this way, turned in to their street.

Laila walked alone the last three blocks. When she was on her street, she noticed that the blue Benz was still parked there, outside Rasheed and Mariam's house. The elderly man in the brown suit was standing by the hood now, leaning on a cane, looking up at the house.

That was when a voice behind Laila said, 'Hey. Yellow Hair. Look here.'

Laila turned around and was greeted by the barrel of a gun.

# CHAPTER 17

The gun was red, the trigger guard bright green. Behind the gun loomed Khadim's grinning face. Khadim was eleven, like Tariq. He was thick, tall, and had a severe underbite. His father was a butcher in Deh-Mazang, and, from time to time, Khadim was known to fling bits of calf intestine at passersby. Sometimes, if Tariq wasn't nearby, Khadim shadowed Laila in the schoolyard at recess, leering, making little whining noises. One time, he'd tapped her on the shoulder and said, *You're so very pretty, Yellow Hair. I want to marry you.*

Now he waved the gun. 'Don't worry,' he said. 'This won't show. Not on *your* hair.'

'Don't you do it! I'm warning you.'

'What are you going to do?' he said. 'Sic your cripple on me? "Oh, Tariq jan. Oh, won't you come home and save me from the *badmash!*"'

Laila began to backpedal, but Khadim was already pumping the trigger. One after another, thin jets of warm water struck Laila's hair, then her palm when she raised it to shield her face.

Now the other boys came out of their hiding, laughing, cackling.

An insult Laila had heard on the street rose to her lips. She didn't really understand it – couldn't quite picture the logistics of it – but the words packed a fierce potency, and she unleashed them now.

'Your mother eats cock!'

'At least she's not a loony like yours,' Khadim shot back, unruffled. 'At least my father's not a sissy! And, by the way, why don't you smell your hands?'

The other boys took up the chant. 'Smell your hands! Smell your hands!'

Laila did, but she knew even before she did, what he'd meant about it not showing in her hair. She let out a high-pitched yelp. At this, the boys hooted even harder.

Laila turned around and, howling, ran home.

She drew water from the well, and, in the bathroom, filled a basin, tore off her clothes. She soaped her hair, frantically digging fingers into her scalp, whimpering with disgust. She rinsed with a bowl and soaped her hair again. Several times, she thought she might throw up. She kept mewling and shivering, as she rubbed and rubbed the soapy washcloth against her face and neck until they reddened.

This would have never happened if Tariq had been with her, she thought as she put on a clean shirt and fresh trousers. Khadim wouldn't have dared. Of course, it wouldn't have happened if

Mammy had shown up like she was supposed to either. Sometimes Laila wondered why Mammy had even bothered having her. People, she believed now, shouldn't be allowed to have new children if they'd already given away all their love to their old ones. It wasn't fair. A fit of anger claimed her. Laila went to her room, collapsed on her bed.

When the worst of it had passed, she went across the hallway to Mammy's door and knocked. When she was younger, Laila used to sit for hours outside this door. She would tap on it and whisper Mammy's name over and over, like a magic chant meant to break a spell: *Mammy, Mammy, Mammy, Mammy* . . . But Mammy never opened the door. She didn't open it now. Laila turned the knob and walked in.

Sometimes Mammy had good days. She sprang out of bed bright-eyed and playful. The droopy lower lip stretched upward in a smile. She bathed. She put on fresh clothes and wore mascara. She let Laila brush her hair, which Laila loved doing, and pin earrings through her earlobes. They went shopping together to Mandaii Bazaar. Laila got her to play snakes and ladders, and they ate shavings from blocks of dark chocolate, one of the few things they shared a common taste for. Laila's favorite part of Mammy's good days was when Babi came home, when she and Mammy looked up from the board and grinned at him with brown teeth. A gust of contentment puffed through the

137

room then, and Laila caught a momentary glimpse of the tenderness, the romance, that had once bound her parents back when this house had been crowded and noisy and cheerful.

Mammy sometimes baked on her good days and invited neighborhood women over for tea and pastries. Laila got to lick the bowls clean, as Mammy set the table with cups and napkins and the good plates. Later, Laila would take her place at the living-room table and try to break into the conversation, as the women talked boisterously and drank tea and complimented Mammy on her baking. Though there was never much for her to say, Laila liked to sit and listen in because at these gatherings she was treated to a rare pleasure: She got to hear Mammy speaking affectionately about Babi.

'What a first-rate teacher he was,' Mammy said. 'His students loved him. And not only because he wouldn't beat them with rulers, like other teachers did. They respected him, you see, because he respected *them*. He was marvelous.'

Mammy loved to tell the story of how she'd proposed to him.

'I was sixteen, he was nineteen. Our families lived next door to each other in Panjshir. Oh, I had the crush on him, *hamshiras*! I used to climb the wall between our houses, and we'd play in his father's orchard. Hakim was always scared that we'd get caught and that my father would give him a slapping. "Your father's going to give me a slapping," he'd always say. He was so cautions, so serious, even then. And then one day I said to him, I said, "Cousin, what will it be? Are you going to ask for my hand or are you going to make me come *khastegari* to you?" I said it just like that. You should have seen the face on him!'

Mammy would slap her palms together as the women, and Laila, laughed.

Listening to Mammy tell these stories, Laila knew that there had been a time when Mammy always spoke this way about Babi. A time when her parents did not sleep in separate rooms. Laila wished she hadn't missed out on those times.

Inevitably, Mammy's proposal story led to matchmaking schemes. When Afghanistan was free from the Soviets and the boys returned home, they would need brides, and so, one by one, the women paraded the neighborhood girls who might or might not be suitable for Ahmad and Noor. Laila always felt excluded when the talk turned to her brothers, as though the women were discussing a beloved film that only she hadn't seen. She'd been two years old when Ahmad and Noor had left Kabul for Panjshir up north, to join Commander Ahmad Shah Massoud's forces and fight the jihad. Laila hardly remembered anything at all about them. A shiny ALLAH pendant around Ahmad's neck. A patch of black hairs on one of Noor's ears. And that was it.

'What about Azita?'

'The rugmaker's daughter?' Mammy said, slapping her cheek with mock outrage. 'She has a thicker mustache than Hakim!'

'There's Anahita. We hear she's top in her class at Zarghoona.'

'Have you seen the teeth on that girl? Tombstones. She's hiding a graveyard behind those lips.'

'How about the Wahidi sisters?'

'Those two dwarfs? No, no, no. Oh, no. Not for my sons. Not for my sultans. They deserve better.'

As the chatter went on, Laila let her mind drift, and, as always, it found Tariq.

Mammy had pulled the yellowish curtains. In the darkness, the room had a layered smell about it: sleep, unwashed linen, sweat, dirty socks, perfume, the previous night's leftover *qurma*. Laila waited for her eyes to adjust before she crossed the room. Even so, her feet became entangled with items of clothing that littered the floor.

Laila pulled the curtains open. At the foot of the bed was an old metallic folding chair. Laila sat on it and watched the unmoving blanketed mound that was her mother.

The walls of Mammy's room were covered with pictures of Ahmad and Noor. Everywhere Laila looked, two strangers smiled back. Here was Noor mounting a tricycle. Here was Ahmad doing his prayers, posing beside a sundial Babi and he had built when he was twelve. And there they were, her brothers, sitting back to back beneath the old pear tree in the yard.

Beneath Mammy's bed, Laila could see the corner of Ahmad's shoe box protruding. From time to time, Mammy showed her the old, crumpled newspaper clippings in it, and pamphlets that Ahmad had managed to collect from insurgent groups and resistance organizations headquartered in Pakistan. One photo, Laila remembered, showed a man in a long white coat handing a lollipop to a legless little boy. The caption below the photo read: *Children are the intended victims of Soviet land mine campaign.* The article went on to say that the Soviets also liked to hide explosives inside brightly colored toys. If a child picked it up, the toy exploded, tore off fingers or an entire hand. The father could not join the jihad then; he'd have to stay home and care for his child. In another article in Ahmad's box, a young mujahid was saying that the Soviets had dropped gas on his village that burned people's skin and blinded them. He said he had seen his mother and sister running for the stream, coughing up blood.

'Mammy.'

The mound stirred slightly. It emitted a groan.

'Get up, Mammy. It's three o'clock.'

Another groan. A hand emerged, like a submarine periscope breaking surface, and dropped. The mound moved more discernibly this time. Then the rustle of blankets as layers of them shifted over each other. Slowly, in stages, Mammy materialized: first

141

the slovenly hair, then the white, grimacing face, eyes pinched shut against the light, a hand groping for the headboard, the sheets sliding down as she pulled herself up, grunting. Mammy made an effort to look up, flinched against the light, and her head drooped over her chest.

'How was school?' she muttered.

So it would begin. The obligatory questions, the perfunctory answers. Both pretending. Unenthusiastic partners, the two of them, in this tired old dance.

'School was fine,' Laila said.

'Did you learn anything?'

'The usual.'

'Did you eat?'

'I did.'

'Good.'

Mammy raised her head again, toward the window. She winced and her eyelids fluttered. The right side of her face was red, and the hair on that side had flattened. 'I have a headache.'

'Should I fetch you some aspirin?'

Mammy massaged her temples. 'Maybe later. Is your father home?'

'It's only three.'

'Oh. Right. You said that already.' Mammy yawned. 'I was dreaming just now,' she said, her voice only a bit louder than the rustle of her nightgown against the sheets. 'Just now, before you came in. But I can't remember it now. Does that happen to you?'

'It happens to everybody, Mammy.'

'Strangest thing.'

'I should tell you that while you were dreaming, a boy shot piss out of a water gun on my hair.'

'Shot what? What was that? I'm sorry.'

'Piss. Urine.'

'That's . . . that's terrible. God. I'm sorry. Poor you. I'll have a talk with him first thing in the morning. Or maybe with his mother. Yes, that would be better, I think.'

'I haven't told you who it was.'

'Oh. Well, who was it?'

'Never mind.'

'You're angry.'

'You were supposed to pick me up.'

'I was,' Mammy croaked. Laila could not tell whether this was a question. Mammy began picking at her hair. This was one of life's great mysteries to Laila, that Mammy's picking had not made her bald as an egg. 'What about . . . What's his name, your friend, Tariq? Yes, what about him?'

'He's been gone for a week.'

'Oh.' Mammy sighed through her nose. 'Did you wash?'

'Yes.'

'So you're clean, then.' Mammy turned her tired gaze to the window. 'You're clean, and everything is fine.'

Laila stood up. 'I have homework now.'

'Of course you do. Shut the curtains before you go, my love,' Mammy said, her voice fading. She was already sinking beneath the sheets.

As Laila reached for the curtains, she saw a car pass by on the street tailed by a cloud of dust. It was the blue Benz with the Herat license plate finally leaving. She followed it with her eyes until it vanished around a turn, its back window twinkling in the sun.

'I won't forget tomorrow,' Mammy was saying behind her. 'I promise.'

'You said that yesterday.'

'You don't know, Laila.'

'Know what?' Laila wheeled around to face her mother. 'What don't I know?'

Mammy's hand floated up to her chest, tapped there. 'In *here*. What's in *here*.' Then it fell flaccid. 'You just don't know.'

# CHAPTER 18

A week passed, but there was still no sign of Tariq. Then another week came and went. To fill the time, Laila fixed the screen door that Babi still hadn't got around to. She took down Babi's books, dusted and alphabetized them. She went to Chicken Street with Hasina, Giti, and Giti's mother, Nila, who was a seamstress and sometime sewing partner of Mammy's. In that week, Laila came to believe that of all the hardships a person had to face none was more punishing than the simple act of waiting.

Another week passed.

Laila found herself caught in a net of terrible thoughts.

He would never come back. His parents had moved away for good; the trip to Ghazni had been a ruse. An adult scheme to spare the two of them an upsetting farewell.

A land mine had gotten to him again. The way it did in 1981, when he was five, the last time his parents took him south to Ghazni. That was shortly after Laila's third birthday. He'd been lucky that time, losing only a leg; lucky that he'd survived at all.

Her head rang and rang with these thoughts.

Then one night Laila saw a tiny flashing light from down the street. A sound, something between a squeak and a gasp, escaped her lips. She quickly fished her own flashlight from under the bed, but it wouldn't work. Laila banged it against her palm, cursed the dead batteries. But it didn't matter. He was back. Laila sat on the edge of her bed, giddy with relief, and watched that beautiful, yellow eye winking on and off.

On her way to Tariq's house the next day, Laila saw Khadim and a group of his friends across the street. Khadim was squatting, drawing something in the dirt with a stick. When he saw her, he dropped the stick and wiggled his fingers. He said something and there was a round of chuckles. Laila dropped her head and hurried past.

'What did you *do*?' she exclaimed when Tariq opened the door. Only then did she remember that his uncle was a barber.

Tariq ran his hand over his newly shaved scalp and smiled, showing white, slightly uneven teeth.

'Like it?'

'You look like you're enlisting in the army.'

'You want to feel?' He lowered his head.

The tiny bristles scratched Laila's palm pleasantly. Tariq wasn't like some of the other boys, whose hair concealed cone-shaped skulls and unsightly lumps. Tariq's head was perfectly curved and lump-free.

146

When he looked up, Laila saw that his cheeks and brow had sunburned.

'What took you so long?' she said.

'My uncle was sick. Come on. Come inside.'

He led her down the hallway to the family room. Laila loved everything about this house. The shabby old rug in the family room, the patchwork quilt on the couch, the ordinary clutter of Tariq's life: his mother's bolts of fabric, her sewing needles embedded in spools, the old magazines, the accordion case in the corner waiting to be cracked open.

'Who is it?'

It was his mother calling from the kitchen.

'Laila,' he answered.

He pulled her a chair. The family room was brightly lit and had double windows that opened into the yard. On the sill were empty jars in which Tariq's mother pickled eggplant and made carrot marmalade.

'You mean our *aroos*, our daughter-in-law,' his father announced, entering the room. He was a carpenter, a lean, white-haired man in his early sixties. He had gaps between his front teeth, and the squinty eyes of someone who had spent most of his life outdoors. He opened his arms and Laila went into them, greeted by his pleasant and familiar smell of sawdust. They kissed on the cheek three times.

'You keep calling her that and she'll stop coming here,' Tariq's mother said, passing by them. She was carrying a tray with a large bowl, a serving spoon, and four smaller bowls on it. She set the tray on the table. 'Don't mind the old man.' She cupped Laila's face. 'It's good to see you, my dear. Come, sit down. I brought back some water-soaked fruit with me.'

The table was bulky and made of a light, unfinished wood – Tariq's father had built it, as well as the chairs. It was covered with a moss green vinyl tablecloth with little magenta crescents and stars on it. Most of the living-room wall was taken up with pictures of Tariq at various ages. In some of the very early ones, he had two legs.

'I heard your brother was sick,' Laila said to Tariq's father, dipping a spoon into her bowl of soaked raisins, pistachios, and apricots.

He was lighting a cigarette. 'Yes, but he's fine now, *shokr e Khoda*, thanks to God.'

'Heart attack. His second,' Tariq's mother said, giving her husband an admonishing look.

Tariq's father blew smoke and winked at Laila. It struck her again that Tariq's parents could easily pass for his grandparents. His mother hadn't had him until she'd been well into her forties.

'How is your father, my dear?' Tariq's mother said, looking on over her bowl.

As long as Laila had known her, Tariq's mother had worn a wig. It was turning a dull purple with age. It was pulled low on her brow today, and Laila could see the gray hairs of her sideburns. Some days, it rode high on her forehead. But, to Laila, Tariq's mother never looked pitiable in it.

148

What Laila saw was the calm, self-assured face beneath the wig, the clever eyes, the pleasant, unhurried manners.

'He's fine,' Laila said. 'Still at Silo, of course. He's fine.'

'And your mother?'

'Good days. Bad ones too. The same.'

'Yes,' Tariq's mother said thoughtfully, lowering her spoon into the bowl. 'How hard it must be, how terribly hard, for a mother to be away from her sons.'

'You're staying for lunch?' Tariq said.

'You have to,' said his mother. 'I'm making *shorwa*.'

'I don't want to be a *mozahem*.'

'Imposing?' Tariq's mother said. 'We leave for a couple of weeks and you turn polite on us?'

'All right, I'll stay,' Laila said, blushing and smiling.

'It's settled, then.'

The truth was, Laila loved eating meals at Tariq's house as much as she disliked eating them at hers. At Tariq's, there was no eating alone; they always ate as a family. Laila liked the violet plastic drinking glasses they used and the quarter lemon that always floated in the water pitcher. She liked how they started each meal with a bowl of fresh yogurt, how they squeezed sour oranges on everything, even their yogurt, and how they made small, harmless jokes at each other's expense.

Over meals, conversation always flowed. Though

Tariq and his parents were ethnic Pashtuns, they spoke Farsi when Laila was around for her benefit, even though Laila more or less understood their native Pashto, having learned it in school. Babi said that there were tensions between their people – the Tajiks, who were a minority, and Tariq's people, the Pashtuns, who were the largest ethnic group in Afghanistan. *Tajiks have always felt slighted*, Babi had said. *Pashtun kings ruled this country for almost two hundred and fifty years, Laila, and Tajiks for all of nine months, back in 1929.*

*And you*, Laila had asked, *do you feel slighted, Babi?*

Babi had wiped his eyeglasses clean with the hem of his shirt. *To me, it's nonsense – and very dangerous nonsense at that – all this talk of I'm Tajik and you're Pashtun and he's Hazara and she's Uzbek. We're all Afghans, and that's all that should matter. But when one group rules over the others for so long . . . There's contempt. Rivalry. There is. There always has been.*

Maybe so. But Laila never felt it in Tariq's house, where these matters never even came up. Her time with Tariq's family always felt natural to Laila, effortless, uncomplicated by differences in tribe or language, or by the personal spites and grudges that infected the air at her own home.

'How about a game of cards?' Tariq said.

'Yes, go upstairs,' his mother said, swiping disapprovingly at her husband's cloud of smoke. 'I'll get the *shorwa* going.'

150

They lay on their stomachs in the middle of Tariq's room and took turns dealing for *panjpar*. Pedaling air with his foot, Tariq told her about his trip. The peach saplings he had helped his uncle plant. A garden snake he had captured.

This room was where Laila and Tariq did their homework, where they built playing-card towers and drew ridiculous portraits of each other. If it was raining, they leaned on the windowsill, drinking warm, fizzy orange Fanta, and watched the swollen rain droplets trickle down the glass.

'All right, here's one,' Laila said, shuffling. 'What goes around the world but stays in a corner?'

'Wait.' Tariq pushed himself up and swung his artificial left leg around. Wincing, he lay on his side, leaning on his elbow. 'Hand me that pillow.' He placed it under his leg. 'There. That's better.'

Laila remembered the first time he'd shown her his stump. She'd been six. With one finger, she had poked the taut, shiny skin just below his left knee. Her finger had found little hard lumps there, and Tariq had told her they were spurs of bone that sometimes grew after an amputation. She'd asked him if his stump hurt, and he said it got sore at the end of the day, when it swelled and didn't fit the prosthesis like it was supposed to, like a finger in a thimble. *And sometimes it gets rubbed. Especially when it's hot. Then I get rashes and blisters, but my mother has creams that help. It's not so bad.*

Laila had burst into tears.

151

*What are you crying for?* He'd strapped his leg back on. *You asked to see it, you* giryanok, *you crybaby! If I'd known you were going to bawl, I wouldn't have shown you.*

'A stamp,' he said.

'What?'

'The riddle. The answer is a stamp. We should go to the zoo after lunch.'

'You knew that one. Did you?'

'Absolutely not.'

'You're a cheat.'

'And you're envious.'

'Of what?'

'My masculine smarts.'

'Your *masculine* smarts? Really? Tell me, who always wins at chess?'

'I let you win.' He laughed. They both knew that wasn't true.

'And who failed math? Who do you come to for help with your math homework even though you're a grade ahead?'

'I'd be two grades ahead if math didn't bore me.'

'I suppose geography bores you too.'

'How did you know? Now, shut up. So are we going to the zoo or not?'

Laila smiled. 'We're going.'

'Good.'

'I missed you.'

There was a pause. Then Tariq turned to her with a half-grinning, half-grimacing look of distaste. 'What's the *matter* with you?'

How many times had she, Hasina, and Giti said those same three words to each other, Laila wondered, said it without hesitation, after only two or three days of not seeing each other? *I missed you, Hasina. Oh, I missed you too.* In Tariq's grimace, Laila learned that boys differed from girls in this regard. They didn't make a show of friendship. They felt no urge, no need, for this sort of talk. Laila imagined it had been this way for her brothers too. Boys, Laila came to see, treated friendship the way they treated the sun: its existence undisputed; its radiance best enjoyed, not beheld directly.

'I was trying to annoy you,' she said.

He gave her a sidelong glance. 'It worked.'

But she thought his grimace softened. And she thought that maybe the sunburn on his cheeks deepened momentarily.

Laila didn't mean to tell him. She'd, in fact, decided that telling him would be a very bad idea. Someone would get hurt, because Tariq wouldn't be able to let it pass. But when they were on the street later, heading down to the bus stop, she saw Khadim again, leaning against a wall. He was surrounded by his friends, thumbs hooked in his belt loops. He grinned at her defiantly.

And so she told Tariq. The story spilled out of her mouth before she could stop it.

'He did what?'

She told him again.

He pointed to Khadim. 'Him? He's the one? You're sure?'

'I'm sure.'

Tariq clenched his teeth and muttered something to himself in Pashto that Laila didn't catch. 'You wait here,' he said, in Farsi now.

'No, Tariq—'

He was already crossing the street.

Khadim was the first to see him. His grin faded, and he pushed himself off the wall. He unhooked his thumbs from the belt loops and made himself more upright, taking on a self-conscious air of menace. The others followed his gaze.

Laila wished she hadn't said anything. What if they banded together? How many of them were there – ten? eleven? twelve? What if they hurt him?

Then Tariq stopped a few feet from Khadim and his band. There was a moment of consideration, Laila thought, maybe a change of heart, and, when he bent down, she imagined he would pretend his shoelace had come undone and walk back to her. Then his hands went to work, and she understood.

The others understood too when Tariq straightened up, standing on one leg. When he began hopping toward Khadim, then charging him, his unstrapped leg raised high over his shoulder like a sword.

The boys stepped aside in a hurry. They gave him a clear path to Khadim.

Then it was all dust and fists and kicks and yelps.

Khadim never bothered Laila again.

That night, as most nights, Laila set the dinner table for two only. Mammy said she wasn't hungry. On those nights that she was, she made a point of taking a plate to her room before Babi even came home. She was usually asleep or lying awake in bed by the time Laila and Babi sat down to eat.

Babi came out of the bathroom, his hair – peppered white with flour when he'd come home – washed clean now and combed back.

'What are we having, Laila?'

'Leftover *aush* soup.'

'Sounds good,' he said, folding the towel with which he'd dried his hair. 'So what are we working on tonight? Adding fractions?'

'Actually, converting fractions to mixed numbers.'

'Ah. Right.'

Every night after dinner, Babi helped Laila with her homework and gave her some of his own. This was only to keep Laila a step or two ahead of her class, not because he disapproved of the work assigned by the school – the propaganda teaching notwithstanding. In fact, Babi thought that the one thing the communists had done right – or at least intended to – ironically, was in the field of education, the vocation from which they had fired

155

him. More specifically, the education of women. The government had sponsored literacy classes for all women. Almost two-thirds of the students at Kabul University were women now, Babi said, women who were studying law, medicine, engineering.

*Women have always had it hard in this country, Laila, but they're probably more free now, under the communists, and have more rights than they've ever had before,* Babi said, always lowering his voice, aware of how intolerant Mammy was of even remotely positive talk of the communists. *But it's true,* Babi said, *it's good time to be a woman in Afghanistan. And you can take advantage of that, Laila. Of course, women's freedom* – here, he shook his head ruefully – *is also one of the reasons people out there took up arms in the first place.*

By 'out there,' he didn't mean Kabul, which had always been relatively liberal and progressive. Here in Kabul, women taught at the university, ran schools, held office in the government. No, Babi meant the tribal areas, especially the Pashtun regions in the south or in the east near the Pakistani border, where women were rarely seen on the streets and only then in burqa and accompanied by men. He meant those regions where men who lived by ancient tribal laws had rebelled against the communists and their decrees to liberate women, to abolish forced marriage, to raise the minimum marriage age to sixteen for girls. There, men saw it as an insult to their centuries-old tradition, Babi said, to be told by the government – and a godless one at that – that their daughters had to leave home, attend school, and work alongside men.

*God forbid that should happen!* Babi liked to say sarcastically. Then he would sigh, and say, *Laila, my love, the only enemy an Afghan cannot defeat is himself.*

Babi took his seat at the table, dipped bread into his bowl of *aush*.

Laila decided that she would tell him about what Tariq had done to Khadim, over the meal, before they started in on fractions. But she never got the chance. Because, right then, there was a knock at the door, and, on the other side of the door, a stranger with news.

# CHAPTER 19

I need to speak to your parents, *dokhtar jan*,' he said when Laila opened the door. He was a stocky man, with a sharp, weather-roughened face. He wore a potato-colored coat, and a brown wool *pakol* on his head.

'Can I tell them who's here?'

Then Babi's hand was on Laila's shoulder, and he gently pulled her from the door.

'Why don't you go upstairs, Laila. Go on.'

As she moved toward the steps, Laila heard the visitor say to Babi that he had news from Panjshir. Mammy was in the room now too. She had one hand clamped over her mouth, and her eyes were skipping from Babi to the man in the *pakol*.

Laila peeked from the top of the stairs. She watched the stranger sit down with her parents. He leaned toward them. Said a few muted words. Then Babi's face was white, and getting whiter, and he was looking at his hands, and Mammy was screaming, screaming, and tearing at her hair.

The next morning, the day of the *fatiha*, a flock of neighborhood women descended on the house and took charge of preparations for the *khatm* dinner that would take place after the funeral. Mammy sat on the couch the whole morning, her fingers working a handkerchief, her face bloated. She was tended to by a pair of sniffling women who took turns patting Mammy's hand gingerly, like she was the rarest and most fragile doll in the world. Mammy did not seem aware of their presence.

Laila kneeled before her mother and took her hands. 'Mammy.'

Mammy's eyes drifted down. She blinked.

'We'll take care of her, Laila jan,' one of the women said with an air of self-importance. Laila had been to funerals before where she had seen women like this, women who relished all things that had to do with death, official consolers who let no one trespass on their self-appointed duties.

'It's under control. You go on now, girl, and do something else. Leave your mother be.'

Shooed away, Laila felt useless. She bounced from one room to the next. She puttered around the kitchen for a while. An uncharacteristically subdued Hasina and her mother came. So did Giti and her mother. When Giti saw Laila, she hurried over, threw her bony arms around her, and gave Laila a very long, and surprisingly strong, embrace. When she pulled back, tears had pooled in her eyes. 'I am so sorry, Laila,' she said. Laila thanked her. The three girls sat outside in the yard until one of the women assigned them the task of washing glasses and stacking plates on the table.

Babi too kept walking in and out of the house aimlessly, looking, it seemed, for something to do.

'Keep him away from me.' That was the only time Mammy said anything all morning.

Babi ended up sitting alone on a folding chair in the hallway, looking desolate and small. Then one of the women told him he was in the way there. He apologized and disappeared into his study.

That afternoon, the men went to a hall in Karteh-Seh that Babi had rented for the *fatiha*. The women came to the house. Laila took her spot beside Mammy, next to the living-room entrance where it was customary for the family of the deceased to sit. Mourners removed their shoes at the door, nodded at acquaintances as they crossed the room, and sat on folding chairs arranged along the walls. Laila saw Wajma, the elderly midwife who had delivered her. She saw Tariq's mother too, wearing a black scarf over the wig. She gave Laila a nod and a slow, sad, close-lipped smile.

From a cassette player, a man's nasal voice chanted verses from the Koran. In between, the women sighed and shifted and sniffled. There were muted coughs, murmurs, and, periodically, someone let out a theatrical, sorrow-drenched sob.

Rasheed's wife, Mariam, came in. She was wearing a black *hijab*. Strands of her hair strayed from it onto her brow. She took a seat along the wall across from Laila.

Next to Laila, Mammy kept rocking back and forth. Laila drew Mammy's hand into her lap and cradled it with both of hers, but Mammy did not seem to notice.

'Do you want some water, Mammy?' Laila said in her ear. 'Are you thirsty?'

But Mammy said nothing. She did nothing but sway back and forth and stare at the rug with a remote, spiritless look.

Now and then, sitting next to Mammy, seeing the drooping, woebegone looks around the room, the magnitude of the disaster that had struck her family would register with Laila. The possibilities denied. The hopes dashed.

But the feeling didn't last. It was hard to feel, *really* feel, Mammy's loss. Hard to summon sorrow, to grieve the deaths of people Laila had never really thought of as alive in the first place. Ahmad and Noor had always been like lore to her. Like characters in a fable. Kings in a history book.

It was Tariq who was real, flesh and blood. Tariq, who taught her cusswords in Pashto, who liked salted clover leaves, who frowned and made a low, moaning sound when he chewed, who had a light pink birthmark just beneath his left collarbone shaped like an upside-down mandolin.

So she sat beside Mammy and dutifully mourned Ahmad and Noor, but, in Laila's heart, her true brother was alive and well.

# CHAPTER 20

The ailments that would hound Mammy for the rest of her days began. Chest pains and headaches, joint aches and night sweats, paralyzing pains in her ears, lumps no one else could feel. Babi took her to a doctor, who took blood and urine, shot X-rays of Mammy's body, but found no physical illness.

Mammy lay in bed most days. She wore black. She picked at her hair and gnawed on the mole below her lip. When Mammy was awake, Laila found her staggering through the house. She always ended up in Laila's room, as though she would run into the boys sooner or later if she just kept walking into the room where they had once slept and farted and fought with pillows. But all she ran into was their absence. And Laila. Which, Laila believed, had become one and the same to Mammy.

The only task Mammy never neglected was her five daily *namaz* prayers. She ended each *namaz* with her head hung low, hands held before her face, palms up, muttering a prayer for God to bring victory to the Mujahideen. Laila had to shoulder

162

more and more of the chores. If she didn't tend to the house, she was apt to find clothes, shoes, open rice bags, cans of beans, and dirty dishes strewn about everywhere. Laila washed Mammy's dresses and changed her sheets. She coaxed her out of bed for baths and meals. She was the one who ironed Babi's shirts and folded his pants. Increasingly, she was the cook.

Sometimes, after she was done with her chores, Laila crawled into bed next to Mammy. She wrapped her arms around her, laced her fingers with her mother's, buried her face in her hair. Mammy would stir, murmur something. Inevitably, she would start in on a story about the boys.

One day, as they were lying this way, Mammy said, 'Ahmad was going to be a leader. He had the charisma for it. People three times his age listened to him with respect, Laila. It was something to see. And Noor. Oh, my Noor. He was always making sketches of buildings and bridges. He was going to be an architect, you know. He was going to transform Kabul with his designs. And now they're both *shaheed*, my boys, both martyrs.'

Laila lay there and listened, wishing Mammy would notice that *she*, Laila, hadn't become *shaheed*, that she was alive, here, in bed with her, that she had hopes and a future. But Laila knew that her future was no match for her brothers' past. They had overshadowed her in life. They would obliterate her in death. Mammy was now the curator of their lives' museum and she, Laila, a mere visitor. A receptacle for their myths. The parchment on which Mammy meant to ink their legends.

'The messenger who came with the news, he said that when they brought the boys back to camp, Ahmad Shah Massoud personally oversaw the burial. He said a prayer for them at the gravesite. That's the kind of brave young men your brothers were, Laila, that Commander Massoud himself, the Lion of Panjshir, God bless him, would oversee their burial.'

Mammy rolled onto her back. Laila shifted, rested her head on Mammy's chest.

'Some days,' Mammy said in a hoarse voice, 'I listen to that clock ticking in the hallway. Then I think of all the ticks, all the minutes, all the hours and days and weeks and months and years waiting for me. All of it without them. And I can't breathe then, like someone's stepping on my heart, Laila. I get so weak. So weak I just want to collapse somewhere.'

'I wish there was something I could do,' Laila said, meaning it. But it came out sounding broad, perfunctory, like the token consolation of a kind stranger.

'You're a good daughter,' Mammy said, after a deep sigh. 'And I haven't been much of a mother to you.'

'Don't say that.'

'Oh, it's true. I know it and I'm sorry for it, my love.'

'Mammy?'

'Mm.'

Laila sat up, looking down at Mammy. There were gray strands in Mammy's hair now. And it startled Laila how much weight Mammy, who'd always been plump, had lost. Her cheeks had a sallow, drawn look. The blouse she was wearing drooped over her shoulders, and there was a gaping space between her neck and the collar. More than once Laila had seen the wedding band slide off Mammy's finger.

'I've been meaning to ask you something.'

'What is it?'

'You wouldn't . . .' Laila began.

She'd talked about it to Hasina. At Hasina's suggestion, the two of them had emptied the bottle of aspirin in the gutter, hidden the kitchen knives and the sharp kebab skewers beneath the rug under the couch. Hasina had found a rope in the yard. When Babi couldn't find his razors, Laila had to tell him of her fears. He dropped on the edge of the couch, hands between his knees. Laila waited for some kind of reassurance from him. But all she got was a bewildered, hollow-eyed look.

'You wouldn't . . . Mammy I worry that—'

'I thought about it the night we got the news,' Mammy said. 'I won't lie to you, I've thought about it since too. But, no. Don't worry, Laila. I want see my sons' dream come true. I want to see

165

the day the Soviets go home disgraced, the day the Mujahideen come to Kabul in victory. I want to be there when it happens, when Afghanistan is free, so the boys see it too. They'll see it through my eyes.'

Mammy was soon asleep, leaving Laila with dueling emotions: reassured that Mammy meant to live on, stung that *she* was not the reason. *She* would never leave her mark on Mammy's heart the way her brothers had, because Mammy's heart was like a pallid beach where Laila's footprints would forever wash away beneath the waves of sorrow that swelled and crashed, swelled and crashed.

# CHAPTER 21

The driver pulled his taxi over to let pass another long convoy of Soviet jeeps and armored vehicles. Tariq leaned across the front seat, over the driver, and yelled, '*Pajalusta! Pajalusta!*'

A jeep honked and Tariq whistled back, beaming and waving cheerfully. 'Lovely guns!' he yelled. 'Fabulous jeeps! Fabulous army! Too bad you're losing to a bunch of peasants firing slingshots!'

The convoy passed. The driver merged back onto the road.

'How much farther?' Laila asked.

'An hour at the most,' the driver said. 'Barring any more convoys or checkpoints.'

They were taking a day trip, Laila, Babi, and Tariq. Hasina had wanted to come too, had begged her father, but he wouldn't allow it. The trip was Babi's idea. Though he could hardly afford it on his salary, he'd hired a driver for the day. He wouldn't disclose anything to Laila about their destination except to say that, with it, he was contributing to her education.

They had been on the road since five in the

morning. Through Laila's window, the landscape shifted from snowcapped peaks to deserts to canyons and sun-scorched outcroppings of rocks. Along the way, they passed mud houses with thatched roofs and fields dotted with bundles of wheat. Pitched out in the dusty fields, here and there, Laila recognized the black tents of Koochi nomads. And, frequently, the carcasses of burned-out Soviet tanks and wrecked helicopters. This, she thought, was Ahmad and Noor's Afghanistan. This, here in the provinces, was where the war was being fought, after all. Not in Kabul. Kabul was largely at peace. Back in Kabul, if not for the occasional bursts of gunfire, if not for the Soviet soldiers smoking on the sidewalks and the Soviet jeeps always bumping through the streets, war might as well have been a rumor.

It was late morning, after they'd passed two more checkpoints, when they entered a valley. Babi had Laila lean across the seat and pointed to a series of ancient-looking walls of sun-dried red in the distance.

'That's called Shahr-e-Zohak. The Red City. It used to be a fortress. It was built some nine hundred years ago to defend the valley from invaders. Genghis Khan's grandson attacked it in the thirteenth century, but he was killed. It was Genghis Khan himself who then destroyed it.'

'And that, my young friends, is the story of our country, one invader after another,' the driver said, flicking cigarette ash out the window. 'Macedonians.

Sassanians. Arabs. Mongols. Now the Soviets. But we're like those walls up there. Battered, and nothing pretty to look at, but still standing. Isn't that the truth, *badar?*'

'Indeed it is,' said Babi.

Half an hour later, the driver pulled over.

'Come on, you two,' Babi said. 'Come outside and have a look.'

They got out of the taxi. Babi pointed. 'There they are. Look.'

Tariq gasped. Laila did too. And she knew then that she could live to be a hundred and she would never again see a thing as magnificent.

The two Buddhas were enormous, soaring much higher than she had imagined from all the photos she'd seen of them. Chiseled into a sun-bleached rock cliff, they peered down at them, as they had nearly two thousand years before, Laila imagined, at caravans crossing the valley on the Silk Road. On either side of them, along the over-hanging niche, the cliff was pocked with myriad caves.

'I feel so small,' Tariq said.

'You want to climb up?' Babi said

'Up the statues?' Laila asked. 'We can do that?'

Babi smiled and held out his hand. 'Come on.'

The climb was hard for Tariq, who had to hold on to both Laila and Babi as they inched up a winding, narrow, dimly lit staircase. They saw shadowy caves along the way, and tunnels honeycombing the cliff every which way.

'Careful where you step,' Babi said. His voice made a loud echo. 'The ground is treacherous.'

In some parts, the staircase was open to the Buddha's cavity.

'Don't look down, children. Keep looking straight ahead.'

As they climbed, Babi told them that Bamiyan had once been a thriving Buddhist center until it had fallen under Islamic Arab rule in the ninth century. The sandstone cliffs were home to Buddhist monks who carved caves in them to use as living quarters and as sanctuary for weary traveling pilgrims. The monks, Babi said, painted beautiful frescoes along the walls and roofs of their caves.

'At one point,' he said, 'there were five thousand monks living as hermits in these caves.'

Tariq was badly out of breath when they reached the top. Babi was panting too. But his eyes shone with excitement.

'We're standing atop its head,' he said, wiping his brow with a handkerchief. 'There's a niche over here where we can look out.'

They inched over to the craggy overhang and, standing side by side, with Babi in the middle, gazed down on the valley.

'Look at this!' said Laila.

Babi smiled.

The Bamiyan Valley below was carpeted by lush

farming fields. Babi said they were green winter wheat and alfalfa, potatoes too. The fields were bordered by poplars and crisscrossed by streams and irrigation ditches, on the banks of which tiny female figures squatted and washed clothes. Babi pointed to rice paddies and barley fields draping the slopes. It was autumn, and Laila could make out people in bright tunics on the roofs of mud brick dwellings laying out the harvest to dry. The main road going through the town was poplar-lined too. There were small shops and teahouses and street-side barbers on either side of it. Beyond the village, beyond the river and the streams, Laila saw foothills, bare and dusty brown, and, beyond those, as beyond everything else in Afghanistan, the snowcapped Hindu Kush.

The sky above all of this was an immaculate, spotless blue.

'It's so quiet,' Laila breathed. She could see tiny sheep and horses but couldn't hear their bleating and whinnying.

'It's what I always remember about being up here,' Babi said. 'The silence. The peace of it. I wanted you to experience it. But I also wanted you to see your country's heritage, children, to learn of its rich past. You see, some things I can teach you. Some you learn from books. But there are things that, well, you just have to *see* and *feel*.'

'Look,' said Tariq.

They watched a hawk, gliding in circles above the village.

171

'Did you ever bring Mammy up here?' Laila asked.

'Oh, many times. Before the boys were born. After too. Your mother, she used to be adventurous then, and . . . so *alive*. She was just about the liveliest, happiest person I'd ever met.' He smiled at the memory. 'She had this laugh. I swear it's why I married her, Laila, for that laugh. It bull-dozed you. You stood no chance against it.'

A wave of affection overcame Laila. From then on, she would always remember Babi this way: reminiscing about Mammy, with his elbows on the rock, hands cupping his chin, his hair ruffled by the wind, eyes crinkled against the sun.

'I'm going to look at some of those caves,' Tariq said.

'Be careful,' said Babi.

'I will, *Kaka jan*,' Tariq's voice echoed back.

Laila watched a trio of men far below, talking near a cow tethered to a fence. Around them, the trees had started to turn, ochre and orange, scarlet red.

'I miss the boys too, you know,' Babi said. His eyes had welled up a tad. His chin was trem-bling. 'I may not . . . With your mother, both her joy and sadness are extreme. She can't hide either. She never could. Me, I suppose I'm different. I tend to . . . But it broke me too, the boys dying. I miss them too. Not a day passes that I . . . It's very hard, Laila. So very hard.' He squeezed the inner corners of his eyes with his thumb and forefinger. When he tried to talk, his voice broke. He pulled his lips over his teeth and waited. He took a long, deep breath, looked at her. 'But I'm glad I have you. Every day, I thank God for you. Every single day. Sometimes, when your mother's having one of her really dark days, I feel like you're all I have, Laila.'

Laila drew closer to him and rested her cheek up against his chest. He seemed slightly startled – unlike Mammy, he rarely expressed his affection physically. He planted a brisk kiss on the top of her head and hugged her back awkwardly. They stood this way for a while, looking down on the Bamiyan Valley.

'As much as I love this land, some days I think about leaving it,' Babi said.

'Where to?'

'Anyplace where it's easy to forget. Pakistan first, I suppose. For a year, maybe two. Wait for our paperwork to get processed.'

'And then?'

'And then, well, it *is* a big world. Maybe America. Somewhere near the sea. Like California.'

Babi said the Americans were a generous people. They would help them with money and food for a while, until they could get on their feet.

'I would find work, and, in a few years, when we had enough saved up, we'd open a little Afghan restaurant. Nothing fancy, mind you, just a modest little place, a few tables, some rugs. Maybe hang some pictures of Kabul. We'd give the Americans

173

a taste of Afghan food. And with your mother's cooking, they'd line up and down the street.

'And you, you would continue going to school, of course. You know how I feel about that. That would be our absolute top priority, to get you a good education, high school then college. But in your free time, *if* you wanted to, you could help out, take orders, fill water pitchers, that sort of thing.'

Babi said they would hold birthday parties at the restaurant, engagement ceremonies. New Year's get-togethers. It would turn into a gathering place for other Afghans who, like them, had fled the war. And, late at night, after everyone had left and the place was cleaned up, they would sit for tea amid the empty tables, the three of them, tired but thankful for their good fortune.

When Babi was done speaking, he grew quiet. They both did. They knew that Mammy wasn't going anywhere. Leaving Afghanistan had been unthinkable to her while Ahmad and Noor were still alive. Now that they were *shaheed*, packing up and running was an even worse affront, a betrayal, a disavowal of the sacrifice her sons had made.

*How can you think of it?* Laila could hear her saying. *Does their dying mean nothing to you, cousin? The only solace I find is in knowing that I walk the same ground that soaked up their blood. No. Never.*

And Babi would never leave without her, Laila knew, even though Mammy was no more a wife to him now than she was a mother to Laila. For

Mammy, he would brush aside this daydream of his the way he flicked specks of flour from his coat when he got home from work. And so they would stay. They would stay until the war ended. And they would stay for whatever came after war.

Laila remembered Mammy telling Babi once that she had married a man who had no convictions. Mammy didn't understand. She didn't understand that if she looked into a mirror, she would find the one unfailing conviction of his life looking right back at her.

Later, after they'd eaten a lunch of boiled eggs and potatoes with bread, Tariq napped beneath a tree on the banks of a gurgling stream. He slept with his coat neatly folded into a pillow, his hands crossed on his chest. The driver went to the village to buy almonds. Babi sat at the foot of a thick-trunked acacia tree reading a paperback. Laila knew the book; he'd read it to her once. It told the story of an old fisherman named Santiago who catches an enormous fish. But by the time he sails his boat to safety, there is nothing left of his prize fish; the sharks have torn it to pieces.

Laila sat on the edge of the stream, dipping her feet into the cool water. Overhead, mosquitoes hummed and cottonwood seeds danced. A dragonfly whirred nearby. Laila watched its wings catch glints of sunlight as it buzzed from one blade of grass to another. They flashed purple, then green, orange. Across the stream, a group of local Hazara boys were picking patties of dried cow dung from the ground and stowing them into burlap sacks tethered to their backs. Somewhere, a donkey brayed. A generator sputtered to life.

Laila thought again about Babi's little dream. *Somewhere near the sea.*

There was something she hadn't told Babi up there atop the Buddha: that, in one important way, she was glad they couldn't go. She would miss Giti and her pinch-faced earnestness, yes, and Hasina too, with her wicked laugh and reckless clowning around. But, mostly, Laila remembered all too well the inescapable drudgery of those four weeks without Tariq when he had gone to Ghazni. She remembered all too well how time had dragged without him, how she had shuffled about feeling waylaid, out of balance. How could she ever cope with his permanent absence?

Maybe it was senseless to want to be near a person so badly here in a country where bullets had shredded her own brothers to pieces. But all Laila had to do was picture Tariq going at Khadim with his leg and then nothing in the world seemed more sensible to her.

Six months later, in April 1988, Babi came home with big news.

'They signed a treaty!' he said. 'In Geneva. It's official! They're leaving. Within nine months, there won't be any more Soviets in Afghanistan!'

Mammy was sitting up in bed. She shrugged.

176

'But the communist regime is staying,' she said. 'Najibullah is the Soviets' puppet president. He's not going anywhere. No, the war will go on. This is not the end.'

'Najibullah won't last,' said Babi.

'They're leaving, Mammy! They're actually leaving!'

'You two celebrate if you want to. But I won't rest until the Mujahideen hold a victory parade right here in Kabul.'

And, with that, she lay down again and pulled up the blanket.

# CHAPTER 22

## JANUARY 1989

One cold, overcast day in January 1989, three months before Laila turned eleven, she, her parents, and Hasina went to watch one of the last Soviet convoys exit the city. Spectators had gathered on both sides of the thoroughfare outside the Military Club near Wazir Akbar Khan. They stood in muddy snow and watched the line of tanks, armored trucks, and jeeps as light snow flew across the glare of the passing headlights. There were heckles and jeers. Afghan soldiers kept people off the street. Every now and then, they had to fire a warning shot.

Mammy hoisted a photo of Ahmad and Noor high over her head. It was the one of them sitting back-to-back under the pear tree. There were others like her, women with pictures of their *shaheed* husbands, sons, brothers held high.

Someone tapped Laila and Hasina on the shoulder. It was Tariq.

'Where did you get that thing?' Hasina exclaimed.

178

'I thought I'd come dressed for the occasion.' Tariq said. He was wearing an enormous Russian fur hat, complete with earflaps, which he had pulled down. 'How do I look?'

'Ridiculous,' Laila laughed.

'That's the idea.'

'Your parents came here with you dressed like this?'

'They're home, actually,' he said.

The previous fall, Tariq's uncle in Ghazni had died of a heart attack, and, a few weeks later, Tariq's father had suffered a heart attack of his own, leaving him frail and tired, prone to anxiety and bouts of depression that overtook him for weeks at a time. Laila was glad to see Tariq like this, like his old self again. For weeks after his father's illness, Laila had watched him moping around, heavy-faced and sullen.

The three of them stole away while Mammy and Babi stood watching the Soviets. From a street vendor, Tariq bought them each a plate of boiled beans topped with thick cilantro chutney. They ate beneath the awning of a closed rug shop, then Hasina went to find her family.

On the bus ride home, Tariq and Laila sat behind her parents. Mammy was by the window, staring out, clutching the picture against her chest. Beside her, Babi was impassively listening to a man who was arguing that the Soviets might be leaving but that they would send weapons to Najibullah in Kabul.

'He's their puppet. They'll keep the war going through him, you can bet on that.'

Someone in the next aisle voiced his agreement.

Mammy was muttering to herself, long-winded prayers that rolled on and on until she had no breath left and had to eke out the last few words in a tiny, high-pitched squeak.

They went to Cinema Park later that day, Laila and Tariq, and had to settle for a Soviet film that was dubbed, to unintentionally comic effect, in Farsi. There was a merchant ship, and a first mate in love with the captain's daughter. Her name was Alyona. Then came a fierce storm, lightning, rain, the heaving sea tossing the ship. One of the frantic sailors yelled something. An absurdly calm Afghan voice translated: 'My dear sir, would you kindly pass the rope?'

At this, Tariq burst out cackling. And, soon, they both were in the grips of a hopeless attack of laughter. Just when one became fatigued, the other would snort, and off they would go on another round. A man sitting two rows up turned around and shushed them.

There was a wedding scene near the end. The captain had relented and let Alyona marry the first mate. The newlyweds were smiling at each other. Everyone was drinking vodka.

'I'm never getting married,' Tariq whispered.

'Me neither,' said Laila, but not before a moment of nervous hesitation. She worried that her voice had betrayed her disappointment at what he had said. Her heart galloping, she added, more forcefully this time, 'Never.'

'Weddings are stupid.'

'All the fuss.'

'All the money spent.'

'For what?'

'For clothes you'll never wear again.'

'Ha!'

'If I ever *do* get married,' Tariq said, 'they'll have to make room for three on the wedding stage. Me, the bride, and the guy holding the gun to my head.'

The man in the front row gave them another admonishing look.

On the screen, Alyona and her new husband locked lips.

Watching the kiss, Laila felt strangely conspicuous all at once. She became intensely aware of her heart thumping, of the blood thudding in her ears, of the shape of Tariq beside her, tightening up, becoming still. The kiss dragged on. It seemed of utmost urgency to Laila, suddenly, that she not stir or make a noise. She sensed that Tariq was observing her – one eye on the kiss, the other on her – as she was observing *him*. Was he listening to the air whooshing in and out of her nose, she wondered, waiting for a subtle faltering, a revealing irregularity, that would betray her thoughts?

And what would it be like to kiss him, to feel the fuzzy hair above his lip tickling her own lips?

Then Tariq shifted uncomfortably in his seat. In a strained voice, he said, 'Did you know that if you fling snot in Siberia, it's a green icicle before it hits the ground?'

They both laughed, but briefly, nervously, this time. And when the film ended and they stepped outside, Laila was relieved to see that the sky had dimmed, that she wouldn't have to meet Tariq's eyes in the bright daylight.

# CHAPTER 23

## April 1992

Three years passed.

In that time, Tariq's father had a series of strokes. They left him with a clumsy left hand and a slight slur to his speech. When he was agitated, which happened frequently, the slurring got worse.

Tariq outgrew his leg again and was issued a new leg by the Red Cross, though he had to wait six months for it.

As Hasina had feared, her family took her to Lahore, where she was made to marry the cousin who owned the auto shop. The morning that they took her, Laila and Giti went to Hasina's house to say good-bye. Hasina told them that the cousin, her husband-to-be, had already started the process to move them to Germany, where his brothers lived. Within the year, she thought, they would be in Frankfurt. They cried then in a three-way embrace. Giti was inconsolable. The last time Laila ever saw Hasina, she was being helped by her father into the crowded backseat of a taxi.

The Soviet Union crumbled with astonishing swiftness. Every few weeks, it seemed to Laila, Babi was coming home with news of the latest republic to declare independence. Lithuania. Estonia. Ukraine. The Soviet flag was lowered over the Kremlin. The Republic of Russia was born.

In Kabul, Najibullah changed tactics and tried to portray himself as a devout Muslim. 'Too little and far too late,' said Babi. 'You can't be the chief of KHAD one day and the next day pray in a mosque with people whose relatives you tortured and killed.' Feeling the noose tightening around Kabul, Najibullah tried to reach a settlement with the Mujahideen but the Mujahideen balked.

From her bed, Mammy said, 'Good for them.' She kept her vigils for the Mujahideen and waited for her parade. Waited for her sons' enemies to fall.

And, eventually, they did. In April 1992, the year Laila turned fourteen.

Najibullah surrendered at last and was given sanctuary in the UN compound near Darulaman Palace, south of the city.

The jihad was over. The various communist regimes that had held power since the night Laila was born were all defeated. Mammy's heroes, Ahmad's and Noor's brothers-in-war, had won. And now, after more than a decade of sacrificing everything, of leaving behind their families to live in

184

mountains and fight for Afghanistan's sovereignty, the Mujahideen were coming to Kabul, in flesh, blood, and battle-weary bone.

Mammy knew all of their names.

There was Dostum, the flamboyant Uzbek commander, leader of the Junbish-i-Milli faction, who had a reputation for shifting allegiances. The intense, surly Gulbuddin Hekmatyar, leader of the Hezb-e-Islami faction, a Pashtun who had studied engineering and once killed a Maoist student. Rabbani, Tajik leader of the Jamiat-e-Islami faction, who had taught Islam at Kabul University in the days of the monarchy. Sayyaf, a Pashtun from Paghman with Arab connections, a stout Muslim and leader of the Ittehad-i-Islami faction. Abdul Ali Mazari, leader of the Hizb-e-Wahdat faction, known as Baba Mazari among his fellow Hazaras, with strong Shi'a ties to Iran.

And, of course, there was Mammy's hero, Rabbani's ally, the brooding, charismatic Tajik commander Ahmad Shah Massoud, the Lion of Panjshir. Mammy had nailed up a poster of him in her room. Massoud's handsome, thoughtful face, eyebrow cocked and trademark *pakol* tilted, would become ubiquitous in Kabul. His soulful black eyes would gaze back from billboards, walls, storefront windows, from little flags mounted on the antennas of taxicabs.

For Mammy, this was the day she had longed for. This brought to fruition all those years of waiting.

185

At last, she could end her vigils, and her sons could rest in peace.

The day after Najibullah surrendered, Mammy rose from bed a new woman. For the first time in the five years since Ahmad and Noor had become *shaheed*, she didn't wear black. She put on a cobalt blue linen dress with white polka dots. She washed the windows, swept the floor, aired the house, took a long bath. Her voice was shrill with merriment.

'A party is in order,' she declared.

She sent Laila to invite neighbors. 'Tell them we're having a big lunch tomorrow!'

In the kitchen, Mammy stood looking around, hands on her hips, and said, with friendly reproach, 'What have you done to my kitchen, Laila? *Wooy.* Everything is in a different place.'

She began moving pots and pans around, theatrically, as though she were laying claim to them anew, restaking her territory, now that she was back. Laila stayed out of her way. It was best. Mammy could be as indomitable in her fits of euphoria as in her attacks of rage. With unsettling energy, Mammy set about cooking: *aush* soup with kidney beans and dried dill, *kofta*, steaming hot *mantu* drenched with fresh yogurt and topped with mint.

'You're plucking your eyebrows,' Mammy said, as she was opening a large burlap sack of rice by the kitchen counter.

'Only a little.'

Mammy poured rice from the sack into a large black pot of water. She rolled up her sleeves and began stirring.

'How is Tariq?'

'His father's been ill,' Laila said.

'How old is he now anyway?'

'I don't know. Sixties, I guess.'

'I meant Tariq.'

'Oh. Sixteen.'

'He's a nice boy. Don't you think?'

Laila shrugged.

'Not really a boy anymore, though, is he? Sixteen. Almost a man. Don't you think?'

'What are you getting at, Mammy?'

'Nothing,' Mammy said, smiling innocently. 'Nothing. It's just that you . . . Ah, nothing. I'd better not say anyway.'

'I see you want to,' Laila said, irritated by this circuitous, playful accusation.

'Well.' Mammy folded her hands on the rim of the pot. Laila spotted an unnatural, almost rehearsed, quality to the way she said 'Well' and to this folding of hands. She feared a speech was coming.

'It was one thing when you were little kids running around. No harm in that. It was charming. But now. Now. I notice you're wearing a bra, Laila.'

Laila was caught off guard.

'And you could have told me, by the way, about

the bra. I didn't know. I'm disappointed you didn't tell me.' Sensing her advantage, Mammy pressed on. 'Anyway, this isn't about me or the bra. It's about you and Tariq. He's a boy, you see, and, as such, what does he care about reputation? But you? The reputation of a girl, especially one as pretty as you, is a delicate thing, Laila. Like a mynah bird in your hands. Slacken your grip and away it flies.'

'And what about all your wall climbing, the sneaking around with Babi in the orchards?' Laila said, pleased with her quick recovery.

'We were cousins. And we married. Has this boy asked for your hand?'

'He's a friend. A *rafiq*. It's not like that between us,' Laila said, sounding defensive, and not very convincing. 'He's like a brother to me,' she added, misguidedly. And she knew, even before a cloud passed over Mammy's face and her features darkened, that she'd made a mistake.

'*That* he is not,' Mammy said flatly. 'You will not liken that one-legged carpenter's boy to your brothers. There is *no one* like your brothers.'

'I didn't say he . . . That's not how I meant it.'

Mammy sighed through the nose and clenched her teeth.

'Anyway,' she resumed, but without the coy lightheartedness of a few moments ago, 'What I'm trying to say is that if you're not careful, people will talk.'

Laila opened her mouth to say something. It

wasn't that Mammy didn't have a point. Laila knew that the days of innocent, unhindered frolicking in the streets with Tariq had passed. For some time now, Laila had begun to sense a new strangeness when the two of them were out in public. An awareness of being looked at, scrutinized, whispered about, that Laila had never felt before. And *wouldn't* have felt even now but for one fundamental fact: She had fallen for Tariq. Hopelessly and desperately. When he was near, she couldn't help but be consumed with the most scandalous thoughts, of his lean, bare body entangled with hers. Lying in bed at night, she pictured him kissing her belly, wondered at the softness of his lips, at the feel of his hands on her neck, her chest, her back, and lower still. When she thought of him this way, she was overtaken with guilt, but also with a peculiar, warm sensation that spread upward from her belly until it felt as if her face were glowing pink.

No. Mammy had a point. More than she knew, in fact. Laila suspected that some, if not most, of the neighbors were already gossiping about her and Tariq. Laila had noticed the sly grins, was aware of the whispers in the neighborhood that the two of them were a couple. The other day, for instance, she and Tariq were walking up the street together when they'd passed Rasheed, the shoemaker, with his burqa-clad wife, Mariam, in tow. As he'd passed by them, Rasheed had playfully said, 'If it isn't Laili and Majnoon,' referring to the star-crossed lovers of Nezami's popular twelfth-century romantic poem – a Farsi version of *Romeo and Juliet*, Babi said, though he added that Nezami had written his tale of ill-fated lovers four centuries before Shakespeare.

Mammy had a point.

What rankled Laila was that Mammy hadn't earned the right to make it. It would have been one thing if Babi had raised this issue. But Mammy? All those years of aloofness, of cooping herself up and not caring where Laila went and whom she saw and what she thought . . . It was unfair. Laila felt like she was no better than these pots and pans, something that could go neglected, then laid claim to, at will, whenever the mood struck.

But this was a big day, an important day, for all of them. It would be petty to spoil it over this. In the spirit of things, Laila let it pass.

'I get your point,' she said.

'Good!' Mammy said. 'That's resolved, then. Now, where is Hakim? Where, oh where, is that sweet little husband of mine?'

It was a dazzling, cloudless day, perfect for a party. The men sat on rickety folding chairs in the yard. They drank tea and smoked and talked in loud bantering voices about the Mujahideen's plan. From Babi, Laila had learned the outline of it: Afghanistan was now called the Islamic State of Afghanistan. An Islamic Jihad Council, formed in

Peshawar by several of the Mujahideen factions, would oversee things for two months, led by Sibghatullah Mojadidi. This would be followed then by a leadership council led by Rabbani, who would take over for four months. During those six months, a *loya jirga* would be held, a grand council of leaders and elders, who would form an interim government to hold power for two years, leading up to democratic elections.

One of the men was fanning skewers of lamb sizzling over a makeshift grill. Babi and Tariq's father were playing a game of chess in the shade of the old pear tree. Their faces were scrunched up in concentration. Tariq was sitting at the board too, in turns watching the match, then listening in on the political chat at the adjacent table.

The women gathered in the living room, the hallway, and the kitchen. They chatted as they hoisted their babies and expertly dodged, with minute shifts of their hips, the children tearing after each other around the house. An Ustad Sarahang *ghazal* blared from a cassette player.

Laila was in the kitchen, making carafes of *dogh* with Giti. Giti was no longer as shy, or as serious, as before. For several months now, the perpetual severe scowl had cleared from her brow. She laughed openly these days, more frequently, and – it struck Laila – a bit flirtatiously. She had done away with the drab ponytails, let her hair grow, and streaked it with red highlights. Laila learned eventually that the impetus for this transformation was an eighteen-year-old boy whose attention Giti had caught. His name was Sabir, and he was a goalkeeper on Giti's older brother's soccer team.

'Oh, he has the most handsome smile, and this thick, thick black hair!' Giti had told Laila. No one knew about their attraction, of course. Giti had secretly met him twice for tea, fifteen minutes each time, at a small teahouse on the other side of town, in Taimani.

'He's going to ask for my hand, Laila! Maybe as early as this summer. Can you believe it? I swear I can't stop thinking about him.'

'What about school?' Laila had asked. Giti had tilted her head and given her a *We both know better* look.

*By the time we're twenty,* Hasina used to say, *Giti and I, we'll have pushed out four, five kids each. But you, Laila, you'll make us two dummies proud. You're going to be somebody. I know one day I'll pick up a newspaper and find your picture on the front page.*

Giti was beside Laila now, chopping cucumbers, with a dreamy, far-off look on her face.

Mammy was nearby, in her brilliant summer dress, peeling boiled eggs with Wajma, the midwife, and Tariq's mother.

'I'm going to present Commander Massoud with a picture of Ahmad and Noor,' Mammy was saying to Wajma as Wajma nodded and tried to look interested and sincere.

'He personally oversaw the burial. He said a prayer at their grave. It'll be a token of thanks for his decency.' Mammy cracked another boiled egg. 'I hear he's a reflective, honorable man. I think he would appreciate it.'

All around them, women bolted in and out of the kitchen, carried out bowls of *qurma*, platters of *mastawa*, loaves of bread, and arranged it all on the *sofrah* spread on the living-room floor.

Every once in a while, Tariq sauntered in. He picked at this, nibbled on that.

'No men allowed,' said Giti.

'Out, out, out,' cried Wajma.

Tariq smiled at the women's good-humored shooing. He seemed to take pleasure in not being welcome here, in infecting this female atmosphere with his half-grinning, masculine irreverence.

Laila did her best not to look at him, not to give these women any more gossip fodder than they already had. So she kept her eyes down and said nothing to him, but she remembered a dream she'd had a few nights before, of his face and hers, together in a mirror, beneath a soft, green veil. And grains of rice, dropping from his hair, bouncing off the glass with a *tink*.

Tariq reached to sample a morsel of veal cooked with potatoes.

'*Ho bacha!*' Giti slapped the back of his hand. Tariq stole it anyway and laughed.

He stood almost a foot taller than Laila now. He shaved. His face was leaner, more angular. His shoulders had broadened. Tariq liked to wear pleated trousers, black shiny loafers, and short-sleeve shirts

193

that showed off his newly muscular arms – compliments of an old, rusty set of barbells that he lifted daily in his yard. His face had lately adopted an expression of playful contentiousness. He had taken to a self-conscious cocking of his head when he spoke, slightly to the side, and to arching one eyebrow when he laughed. He let his hair grow and had fallen into the habit of tossing the floppy locks often and unnecessarily. The corrupt half grin was a new thing too.

The last time Tariq was shooed out of the kitchen, his mother caught Laila stealing a glance at him. Laila's heart jumped, and her eyes fluttered guiltily. She quickly occupied herself with tossing the chopped cucumber into the pitcher of salted, watered-down yogurt. But she could sense Tariq's mother watching, her knowing, approving half smile.

The men filled their plates and glasses and took their meals to the yard. Once they had taken their share, the women and children settled on the floor around the *sofrah* and ate.

It was after the *sofrah* was cleared and the plates were stacked in the kitchen, when the frenzy of tea making and remembering who took green and who black started, that Tariq motioned with his head and slipped out the door.

Laila waited five minutes, then followed.

She found him three houses down the street, leaning against the wall at the entrance of a narrow-mouthed alley between two adjacent houses. He was humming an old Pashto song, by Ustad Awal Mir:

> *Da ze ma ziba watan,*
> *da ze ma dada watan.*
> *This is our beautiful land,*
> *this is our beloved land.*

And he was smoking, another new habit, which he'd picked up from the guys Laila spotted him hanging around with these days. Laila couldn't stand them, these new friends of Tariq's. They all dressed the same way, pleated trousers, and tight shirts that accentuated their arms and chest. They all wore too much cologne, and they all smoked. They strutted around the neighborhood in groups, joking, laughing loudly, sometimes even calling after girls, with identical stupid, self-satisfied grins on their faces. One of Tariq's friends, on the basis of the most passing of resemblances to Sylvester Stallone, insisted he be called Rambo.

'Your mother would kill you if she knew about your smoking,' Laila said, looking one way, then the other, before slipping into the alley.

'But she doesn't,' he said. He moved aside to make room.

'That could change.'

'Who is going to tell? You?'

Laila tapped her foot. 'Tell your secret to the wind, but don't blame it for telling the trees.'

Tariq smiled, the one eyebrow arched. 'Who said that?'

'Khalil Gibran.'

'You're a show-off.'

'Give me a cigarette.'

He shook his head no and crossed his arms. This was a new entry in his repertoire of poses: back to the wall, arms crossed, cigarette dangling from the corner of his mouth, his good leg casually bent.

'Why not?'

'Bad for you,' he said.

'And it's not bad for you?'

'I do it for the girls.'

'What girls?'

He smirked. 'They think it's sexy.'

'It's not.'

'No?'

'I assure you.'

'Not sexy?'

'You look *khila*, like a half-wit.'

'That hurts,' he said.

'What girls anyway?'

'You're jealous.'

'I'm indifferently curious.'

'You can't be both.' He took another drag and squinted through the smoke. 'I'll bet they're talking about us now.'

In Laila's head, Mammy's voice rang out. *Like a mynah bird in your hands. Slacken your grip and away it flies.* Guilt bore its teeth into her. Then Laila shut off Mammy's voice. Instead, she savored the way Tariq had said *us*. How thrilling, how conspiratorial, it sounded coming from him. And how reassuring to hear him say it like that – casually, naturally. *Us*. It acknowledged their connection, crystallized it.

'And what are they saying?'

'That we're canoeing down the River of Sin,' he said. 'Eating a slice of Impiety Cake.'

'Riding the Rickshaw of Wickedness?' Laila chimed in.

'Making Sacrilege *Qurma*.'

They both laughed. Then Tariq remarked that her hair was getting longer. 'It's nice,' he said.

Laila hoped she wasn't blushing. 'You changed the subject.'

'From what?'

'The empty-headed girls who think you're sexy.'

'You know.'

'Know what?'

'That I only have eyes for you.'

Laila swooned inside. She tried to read his face but was met by a look that was indecipherable: the cheerful, cretinous grin at odds with the narrow, half-desperate look in his eyes. A clever look, calculated to fall precisely at the midpoint between mockery and sincerity.

Tariq crushed his cigarette with the heel of his good foot. 'So what do you think about all this?'

'The party?'

'Who's the half-wit now? I meant the Mujahideen, Laila. Their coming to Kabul.'

'Oh.'

She started to tell him something Babi had said, about the troublesome marriage of guns and ego, when she heard a commotion coming from the house. Loud voices. Screaming.

Laila took off running. Tariq hobbled behind her.

There was a melee in the yard. In the middle of it were two snarling men, rolling on the ground, a knife between them. Laila recognized one of them as a man from the table who had been discussing politics earlier. The other was the man who had been fanning the kebab skewers. Several men were trying to pull them apart. Babi wasn't among them. He stood by the wall, at a safe distance from the fight, with Tariq's father, who was crying.

From the excited voices around her, Laila caught snippets that she put together: The fellow at the politics table, a Pashtun, had called Ahmad Shah Massoud a traitor for 'making a deal' with the Soviets in the 1980s. The kebab man, a Tajik, had taken offense and demanded a retraction. The Pashtun had refused. The Tajik had said that if not for Massoud, the other man's sister would still be 'giving it' to Soviet soldiers. They had come to blows. One of them had then brandished a knife; there was disagreement as to who.

With horror, Laila saw that Tariq had thrown himself into the scuffle. She also saw that some of the peacemakers were now throwing punches of their own. She thought she spotted a second knife.

Later that evening, Laila thought of how the melee had toppled over, with men falling on top of one another, amid yelps and cries and shouts and flying punches, and, in the middle of it, a grimacing Tariq, his hair disheveled, his leg come undone, trying to crawl out.

It was dizzying how quickly everything unraveled.

The leadership council was formed prematurely. It elected Rabbani president. The other factions cried nepotism. Massoud called for peace and patience.

Hekmatyar, who had been excluded, was incensed. The Hazaras, with their long history of being oppressed and neglected, seethed.

Insults were hurled. Fingers pointed. Accusations flew. Meetings were angrily called off and doors slammed. The city held its breath. In the mountains, loaded magazines snapped into Kalashnikovs.

The Mujahideen, armed to the teeth but now lacking a common enemy, had found the enemy in each other.

Kabul's day of reckoning had come at last.

And when the rockets began to rain down on Kabul, people ran for cover. Mammy did too, literally. She changed into black again, went to her room, shut the curtains, and pulled the blanket over her head.

# CHAPTER 24

I t's the whistling,' Laila said to Tariq, 'the damn whistling, I hate more than anything.'

Tariq nodded knowingly.

It wasn't so much the whistling itself, Laila thought later, but the seconds between the start of it and impact. The brief and interminable time of feeling suspended. The not knowing. The waiting. Like a defendant about to hear the verdict.

Often it happened at dinner, when she and Babi were at the table. When it started, their heads snapped up. They listened to the whistling, forks in midair, unchewed food in their mouths. Laila saw the reflection of their half-lit faces in the pitch-black window, their shadows unmoving on the wall. The whistling. Then the blast, blissfully elsewhere, followed by an expulsion of breath and the knowledge that they had been spared for now while somewhere else, amid cries and choking clouds of smoke, there was a scrambling, a bare-handed frenzy of digging, of pulling from the debris, what remained of a sister, a brother, a grandchild.

But the flip side of being spared was the agony of wondering who hadn't. After every rocket blast, Laila raced to the street, stammering a prayer, certain that, this time, surely this time, it was Tariq they would find buried beneath the rubble and smoke.

At night, Laila lay in bed and watched the sudden white flashes reflected in her window. She listened to the rattling of automatic gunfire and counted the rockets whining overhead as the house shook and flakes of plaster rained down on her from the ceiling. Some nights, when the light of rocket fire was so bright a person could read a book by it, sleep never came. And, if it did, Laila's dreams were suffused with fire and detached limbs and the moaning of the wounded.

Morning brought no relief. The muezzin's call for *namaz* rang out, and the Mujahideen set down their guns, faced west, and prayed. Then the rugs were folded, the guns loaded, and the mountains fired on Kabul, and Kabul fired back at the mountains, as Laila and the rest of the city watched as helpless as old Santiago watching the sharks take bites out of his prize fish.

Everywhere Laila went, she saw Massoud's men. She saw them roam the streets and every few hundred yards stop cars for questioning. They sat and smoked atop tanks, dressed in their fatigues and ubiquitous *pakols*. They peeked at passersby from behind stacked sandbags at intersections.

Not that Laila went out much anymore. And, when she did, she was always accompanied by Tariq, who seemed to relish this chivalric duty.

'I bought a gun,' he said one day. They were sitting outside, on the ground beneath the pear tree in Laila's yard. He showed her. He said it was a semiautomatic, a Beretta. To Laila, it merely looked black and deadly.

'I don't like it,' she said. 'Guns scare me.'

Tariq turned the magazine over in his hand.

'They found three bodies in a house in Karteh-Seh last week,' he said. 'Did you hear? Sisters. All three raped. Their throats slashed. Someone had bitten the rings off their fingers. You could tell, they had teeth marks—'

'I don't want to hear this.'

'I don't mean to upset you,' Tariq said. 'But I just . . . I feel better carrying this.'

He was her lifeline to the streets now. He heard the word of mouth and passed it on to her. Tariq was the one who told her, for instance, that militia-men stationed in the mountains sharpened their marksmanship – and settled wagers over said marksmanship – by shooting civilians down below, men, women, children, chosen at random. He told her that they fired rockets at cars but, for some reason, left taxis alone – which explained to Laila the recent rash of people spraying their cars yellow.

Tariq explained to her the treacherous, shifting boundaries within Kabul. Laila learned from him, for instance, that this road, up to the second acacia

202

tree on the left, belonged to one warlord; that the next four blocks, ending with the bakery shop next to the demolished pharmacy, was another warlord's sector; and that if she crossed that street and walked half a mile west, she would find herself in the territory of yet another warlord and, therefore, fair game for sniper fire. And this was what Mammy's heroes were called now. Warlords. Laila heard them called *tofangdar* too. Riflemen. Others still called them Mujahideen, but, when they did, they made a face – a sneering, distasteful face – the word reeking of deep aversion and deep scorn. Like an insult.

Tariq snapped the magazine back into his handgun.

'Do you have it in you?' Laila said.

'To what?'

'To use this thing. To kill with it.'

Tariq tucked the gun into the waist of his denims. Then he said a thing both lovely and terrible. 'For you,' he said. 'I'd kill with it for you, Laila.'

He slid closer to her and their hands brushed, once, then again. When Tariq's fingers tentatively began to slip into hers, Laila let them. And when suddenly he leaned over and pressed his lips to hers, she let him again.

At that moment, all of Mammy's talk of reputations and mynah birds sounded immaterial to Laila. Absurd, even. In the midst of all this killing and looting, all this ugliness, it was a harmless thing to sit here beneath a tree and kiss Tariq. A small thing. An easily forgivable indulgence. So she let him kiss her, and when he pulled back she leaned in and kissed *him*, heart pounding in her throat, her face tingling, a fire burning in the pit of her belly.

In June of that year, 1992, there was heavy fighting in West Kabul between the Pashtun forces of the warlord Sayyaf and the Hazaras of the Wahdat faction. The shelling knocked down power lines, pulverized entire blocks of shops and homes. Laila heard that Pashtun militiamen were attacking Hazara households, breaking in and shooting entire families, execution style, and that Hazaras were retaliating by abducting Pashtun civilians, raping Pashtun girls, shelling Pashtun neighborhoods, and killing indiscriminately. Every day, bodies were found tied to trees, sometimes burned beyond recognition. Often, they'd been shot in the head, had had their eyes gouged out, their tongues cut out.

Babi tried again to convince Mammy to leave Kabul.

'They'll work it out,' Mammy said. 'This fighting is temporary. They'll sit down and figure something out.'

'Fariba, all these people *know* is war,' said Babi. 'They learned to walk with a milk bottle in one hand and a gun in the other.'

'Who are *you* to say?' Mammy shot back. 'Did

204

you fight jihad? Did you abandon everything you had and risk your life? If not for the Mujahideen, we'd still be the Soviets' servants, remember. And now you'd have us betray them!'

'We aren't the ones doing the betraying, Fariba.'

'You go, then. Take your daughter and run away. Send me a postcard. But peace is coming, and I, for one, am going to wait for it.'

The streets became so unsafe that Babi did an unthinkable thing: He had Laila drop out of school.

He took over the teaching duties himself. Laila went into his study every day after sundown, and, as Hekmatyar launched his rockets at Massoud from the southern outskirts of the city, Babi and she discussed the *ghazals* of Hafez and the works of the beloved Afghan poet Ustad Khalilullah Khalili. Babi taught her to derive the quadratic equation, showed her how to factor polynomials and plot parametric curves. When he was teaching, Babi was transformed. In his element, amid his books, he looked taller to Laila. His voice seemed to rise from a calmer, deeper place, and he didn't blink nearly as much. Laila pictured him as he must have been once, erasing his blackboard with graceful swipes, looking over a student's shoulder, fatherly and attentive.

But it wasn't easy to pay attention. Laila kept getting distracted.

'What is the area of a pyramid?' Babi would ask, and all Laila could think of was the fullness of

Tariq's lips, the heat of his breath on her mouth, her own reflection in his hazel eyes. She'd kissed him twice more since the time beneath the tree, longer, more passionately, and, she thought, less clumsily. Both times, she'd met him secretly in the dim alley where he'd smoked a cigarette the day of Mammy's lunch party. The second time, she'd let him touch her breast.

'Laila?'

'Yes, Babi.'

'Pyramid. Area. Where are you?'

'Sorry, Babi. I was, uh . . . Let's see. Pyramid. Pyramid. One-third the area of the base times the height.'

Babi nodded uncertainly, his gaze lingering on her, and Laila thought of Tariq's hands, squeezing her breast, sliding down the small of her back, as the two of them kissed and kissed.

One day that same month of June, Giti was walking home from school with two classmates. Only three blocks from Giti's house, a stray rocket struck the girls. Later that terrible day, Laila learned that Nila, Giti's mother, had run up and down the street where Giti was killed, collecting pieces of her daughter's flesh in an apron, screeching hysterically. Giti's decomposing right foot, still in its nylon sock and purple sneaker, would be found on a rooftop two weeks later.

At Giti's *fatiha*, the day after the killings, Laila sat stunned in a roomful of weeping women. This was the first time that someone whom Laila had known, been close to, loved, had died. She couldn't get around the unfathomable reality that Giti wasn't alive anymore. Giti, with whom Laila had exchanged secret notes in class, whose finger-nails she had polished, whose chin hair she had plucked with tweezers. Giti, who was going to marry Sabir the goalkeeper. Giti was dead. *Dead.* Blown to pieces. At last, Laila began to weep for her friend. And all the tears that she hadn't been able to shed at her brothers' funeral came pouring down.

# CHAPTER 25

Laila could hardly move, as though cement had solidified in every one of her joints. There was a conversation going on, and Laila knew that she was at one end of it, but she felt removed from it, as though she were merely eavesdropping. As Tariq talked, Laila pictured her life as a rotted rope, snapping, unraveling, the fibers detaching, falling away.

It was a hot, muggy afternoon that August of 1992, and they were in the living room of Laila's house. Mammy had had a stomachache all day, and, minutes before, despite the rockets that Hekmatyar was launching from the south, Babi had taken her to see a doctor. And here was Tariq now, seated beside Laila on the couch, looking at the ground, hands between his knees.

Saying that he was leaving.

Not the neighborhood. Not Kabul. But Afghanistan altogether.

Leaving.

Laila was struck blind.

'Where? Where will you go?'

'Pakistan first. Peshawar. Then I don't know. Maybe Hindustan. Iran.'

'How long?'

'I don't know.'

'I mean, how long have you known?'

'A few days. I was going to tell you, Laila, I swear, but I couldn't bring myself to. I knew how upset you'd be.'

'When?'

'Tomorrow.'

'Tomorrow?'

'Laila, look at me.'

'Tomorrow.'

'It's my father. His heart can't take it anymore, all this fighting and killing.'

Laila buried her face in her hands, a bubble of dread filling her chest.

She should have seen this coming, she thought. Almost everyone she knew had packed their things and left. The neighborhood had been all but drained of familiar faces, and now, only four months after fighting had broken out between the Mujahideen factions, Laila hardly recognized anybody on the streets anymore. Hasina's family had fled in May, off to Tehran. Wajma and her clan had gone to Islamabad that same month. Giti's parents and her siblings left in June, shortly after Giti was killed. Laila didn't know where they had gone – she heard a rumor that they had headed for Mashad, in Iran. After people left, their homes sat unoccupied for a few days, then either militiamen took them or strangers moved in.

Everyone was leaving. And now Tariq too.

'And my mother is not a young woman anymore,' he was saying. 'They're so afraid all the time. Laila, look at me.'

'You should have told me.'

'Please look at me.'

A groan came out of Laila. Then a wail. And then she was crying, and when he went to wipe her cheek with the pad of his thumb she swiped his hand away. It was selfish and irrational, but she was furious with him for abandoning her, Tariq, who was like an extension of her, whose shadow sprung beside hers in every memory. How could he leave her? She slapped him. Then she slapped him again and pulled at his hair, and he had to take her by the wrists, and he was saying something she couldn't make out, he was saying it softly, reasonably, and, somehow, they ended up brow to brow, nose to nose, and she could feel the heat of his breath on her lips again.

And when, suddenly, he leaned in, she did too.

In the coming days and weeks, Laila would scramble frantically to commit it all to memory, what happened next. Like an art lover running out of a burning museum, she would grab whatever she could – a look, a whisper, a moan – to salvage from perishing, to preserve. But time is the most unforgiving of fires, and she couldn't, in the end, save it all. Still, she had these: that first, tremendous pang of pain down below. The slant of sunlight on the rug. Her heel grazing the cold hardness of his leg, lying beside them, hastily unstrapped. Her hands cupping his elbows. The upside-down, mandolin-shaped birthmark beneath his collarbone, glowing red. His face hovering over hers. His black curls dangling, tickling her lips, her chin. The terror that they would be discovered. The disbelief at their own boldness, their courage. The strange and indescribable pleasure, interlaced with the pain. And the look, the myriad of *looks*, on Tariq: of apprehension, tenderness, apology, embarrassment, but mostly, mostly, of hunger.

There was frenzy after. Shirts hurriedly buttoned, belts buckled, hair finger-combed. They sat, then, they sat beside each other, smelling of each other, faces flushed pink, both of them stunned, both of them speechless before the enormity of what had just happened. What they had done.

Laila saw three drops of blood on the rug, *her* blood, and pictured her parents sitting on this couch later, oblivious to the sin that she had committed. And now the shame set in, and the guilt, and, upstairs, the clock ticked on, impossibly loud to Laila's ears. Like a judge's gavel pounding again and again, condemning her.

Then Tariq said, 'Come with me.'

For a moment, Laila almost believed that it could be done. She, Tariq, and his parents, setting out together. Packing their bags, climbing aboard a bus, leaving behind all this violence, going to find blessings, or trouble, and whichever came they would face it together. The bleak isolation awaiting her, the murderous loneliness, it didn't have to be.

She could go. They could be together.

They would have more afternoons like this.

'I want to marry you, Laila.'

For the first time since they were on the floor, she raised her eyes to meet his. She searched his face. There was no playfulness this time. His look was one of conviction, of guileless yet ironclad earnestness.

'Tariq—'

'Let me marry you, Laila. Today. We could get married today.'

He began to say more, about going to a mosque, finding a mullah, a pair of witnesses, a quick *nikka*...

But Laila was thinking of Mammy, as obstinate and uncompromising as the Mujahideen, the air around her choked with rancor and despair, and she was thinking of Babi, who had long surrendered, who made such a sad, pathetic opponent to Mammy.

*Sometimes... I feel like you're all I have, Laila.*

These were the circumstances of her life, the inescapable truths of it.

'I'll ask Kaka Hakim for your hand. He'll give us his blessing, Laila, I know it.'

212

He was right. Babi would. But it would shatter him.

Tariq was still speaking, his voice hushed, then high, beseeching, then reasoning; his face hopeful, then stricken.

'I can't,' Laila said.

'Don't say that. I love you.'

'I'm sorry—'

'I love you.'

How long had she waited to hear those words from him? How many times had she dreamed them uttered? There they were, spoken at last, and the irony crushed her.

'It's my father I can't leave,' Laila said. 'I'm all he has left. His heart couldn't take it either.'

Tariq knew this. He knew she could not wipe away the obligations of her life any more than he could his, but it went on, his pleadings and her rebuttals, his proposals and her apologies, his tears and hers.

In the end, Laila had to make him leave.

At the door, she made him promise to go without good-byes. She closed the door on him. Laila leaned her back against it, shaking against his pounding fists, one arm gripping her belly and a hand across her mouth, as he spoke through the door and promised that he would come back, that he would come back for her. She stood there until he tired, until he gave up, and then she listened to his uneven footsteps until they faded, until all was quiet, save for the gunfire cracking in the hills and her own heart thudding in her belly, her eyes, her bones.

# CHAPTER 26

It was, by far, the hottest day of the year. The mountains trapped the bone-scorching heat, stifled the city like smoke. Power had been out for days. All over Kabul, electric fans sat idle, almost mockingly so.

Laila was lying still on the living-room couch, sweating through her blouse. Every exhaled breath burned the tip of her nose. She was aware of her parents talking in Mammy's room. Two nights ago, and again last night, she had awakened and thought she heard their voices downstairs. They were talking every day now, ever since the bullet, ever since the new hole in the gate.

Outside, the far-off *boom* of artillery, then, more closely, the stammering of a long string of gunfire, followed by another.

Inside Laila too a battle was being waged: guilt on one side, partnered with shame, and, on the other, the conviction that what she and Tariq had done was not sinful; that it had been natural, good, beautiful, even inevitable, spurred by the knowledge that they might never see each other again.

Laila rolled to her side on the couch now and

214

tried to remember something: At one point, when they were on the floor, Tariq had lowered his forehead on hers. Then he had panted something, either *Am I hurting you?* or *Is this hurting you?*

Laila couldn't decide which he had said.

*Am I hurting you?*

*Is this hurting you?*

Only two weeks since he had left, and it was already happening. Time, blunting the edges of those sharp memories. Laila bore down mentally. What had he said? It seemed vital, suddenly, that she know.

Laila closed her eyes. Concentrated.

With the passing of time, she would slowly tire of this exercise. She would find it increasingly exhausting to conjure up, to dust off, to resuscitate once again what was long dead. There would come a day, in fact, years later, when Laila would no longer bewail his loss. Or not as relentlessly; not nearly. There would come a day when the details of his face would begin to slip from memory's grip, when overhearing a mother on the street call after her child by Tariq's name would no longer cut her adrift. She would not miss him as she did now, when the ache of his absence was her unremitting companion – like the phantom pain of an amputee.

Except every once in a long while, when Laila was a grown woman, ironing a shirt or pushing her children on a swing set, something trivial, maybe the warmth of a carpet beneath her feet on a hot day or the curve of a stranger's forehead, would set off a memory of that afternoon together. And it would all come rushing back. The spontaneity of it. Their astonishing imprudence. Their clumsiness. The pain of the act, the pleasure of it, the sadness of it. The heat of their entangled bodies.

It would flood her, steal her breath.

But then it would pass. The moment would pass. Leave her deflated, feeling nothing but a vague restlessness.

She decided that he had said *Am I hurting you?* Yes. That was it. Laila was happy that she'd remembered.

Then Babi was in the hallway, calling her name from the top of the stairs, asking her to come up quickly.

'She's agreed!' he said, his voice tremulous with suppressed excitement. 'We're leaving, Laila. All three of us. We're leaving Kabul.'

In Mammy's room, the three of them sat on the bed. Outside, rockets were zipping across the sky as Hekmatyar's and Massoud's forces fought and fought. Laila knew that somewhere in the city someone had just died, and that a pall of black smoke was hovering over some building that had collapsed in a puffing mass of dust. There would be bodies to step around in the morning. Some would be collected. Others not. Then Kabul's dogs, who had developed a taste for human meat, would feast.

All the same, Laila had an urge to run through those streets. She could barely contain her own happiness. It took effort to sit, to not shriek with joy. Babi said they would go to Pakistan first, to apply for visas. Pakistan, where Tariq was! Tariq was only gone seventeen days, Laila calculated excitedly. If only Mammy had made up her mind seventeen days earlier, they could have left together. She would have been with Tariq right now! But that didn't matter now. They were going to Peshawar – she, Mammy, and Babi – and they would find Tariq and his parents there. Surely they would. They would process their paperwork together. Then, who knew? Who knew? Europe? America? Maybe, as Babi was always saying, somewhere near the sea . . .

Mammy was half lying, half sitting against the headboard. Her eyes were puffy. She was picking at her hair.

Three days before, Laila had gone outside for a breath of air. She'd stood by the front gates, leaning against them, when she'd heard a loud crack and something had zipped by her right ear, sending tiny splinters of wood flying before her eyes. After Giti's death, and the thousands of rounds fired and myriad rockets that had fallen on Kabul, it was the sight of that single round hole in the gate, less than three fingers away from where Laila's head had been, that shook Mammy awake. Made her see that one war had cost her two children already; this latest could cost her her remaining one.

From the walls of the room, Ahmad and Noor smiled down. Laila watched Mammy's eyes bouncing now, guiltily, from one photo to the other. As if looking for their consent. Their blessing. As if asking for forgiveness.

'There's nothing left for us here,' Babi said. 'Our sons are gone, but we still have Laila. We still have each other, Fariba. We can make a new life.'

Babi reached across the bed. When he leaned to take her hands, Mammy let him. On her face, a look of concession. Of resignation. They held each other's hands, lightly, and then they were swaying quietly in an embrace. Mammy buried her face in his neck. She grabbed a handful of his shirt.

For hours that night, the excitement robbed Laila of sleep. She lay in bed and watched the horizon light up in garish shades of orange and yellow. At some point, though, despite the exhilaration inside and the crack of artillery fire outside, she fell asleep.

And dreamed.

They are on a ribbon of beach, sitting on a quilt. It's a chilly, overcast day, but it's warm next to Tariq under the blanket draped over their shoulders. She can see cars parked behind a low fence of chipped white paint beneath a row of windswept palm trees. The wind makes her eyes water and buries their shoes in sand, hurls knots of dead grass from the curved ridges of one dune to another. They're watching sailboats bob in the distance. Around them, seagulls squawk and shiver in the wind. The wind whips up another spray of sand off the shallow, windward slopes. There is a noise then like a chant, and she tells him something Babi had taught her years before about singing sand.

He rubs at her eyebrow, wipes grains of sand from it. She catches a flicker of the band on his finger. It's identical to hers – gold with a sort of maze pattern etched all the way around.

*It's true*, she tells him. *It's the friction, of grain against grain. Listen.* He does. He frowns. They wait. They hear it again. A groaning sound, when the wind is soft, when it blows hard, a mewling, high-pitched chorus.

Babi said they should take only what was absolutely necessary. They would sell the rest.

'That should hold us in Peshawar until I find work.'

For the next two days, they gathered items to be sold. They put them in big piles.

In her room, Laila set aside old blouses, old shoes, books, toys. Looking under her bed, she found a tiny yellow glass cow Hasina had passed to her during recess in fifth grade. A miniature-soccer-ball key chain, a gift from Giti. A little wooden zebra on wheels. A ceramic astronaut she and Tariq had found one day in a gutter. She'd been six and he eight. They'd had a minor row,

Laila remembered, over which one of them had found it.

Mammy too gathered her things. There was a reluctance in her movements, and her eyes had a lethargic, faraway look in them. She did away with her good plates, her napkins, all her jewelry – save for her wedding band – and most of her old clothes.

'You're not selling this, are you?' Laila said, lifting Mammy's wedding dress. It cascaded open onto her lap. She touched the lace and ribbon along the neckline, the hand-sewn seed pearls on the sleeves.

Mammy shrugged and took it from her. She tossed it brusquely on a pile of clothes. Like ripping off a Band-Aid in one stroke, Laila thought.

It was Babi who had the most painful task.

Laila found him standing in his study, a rueful expression on his face as he surveyed his shelves. He was wearing a secondhand T-shirt with a picture of San Francisco's red bridge on it. Thick fog rose from the whitecapped waters and engulfed the bridge's towers.

'You know the old bit,' he said. 'You're on a deserted island. You can have five books. Which do you choose? I never thought I'd actually have to.'

'We'll have to start you a new collection, Babi.'

'Mm.' He smiled sadly. 'I can't believe I'm leaving Kabul. I went to school here, got my first job here, became a father in this town. It's strange to think that I'll be sleeping beneath another city's skies soon.'

'It's strange for me too.'

'All day, this poem about Kabul has been bouncing around in my head. Saib-e-Tabrizi wrote it back in the seventeenth century, I think. I used to know the whole poem, but all I can remember now is two lines:

*'One could not count the moons that shimmer on her roofs,*
*Or the thousand splendid suns that hide behind her walls.'*

Laila looked up, saw he was weeping. She put an arm around his waist. 'Oh, Babi. We'll come back. When this war is over. We'll come back to Kabul, *inshallah*. You'll see.'

On the third morning, Laila began moving the piles of things to the yard and depositing them by the front door. They would fetch a taxi then and take it all to a pawnshop.

Laila kept shuffling between the house and the yard, back and forth, carrying stacks of clothes and dishes and box after box of Babi's books. She should have been exhausted by noon, when the mound of belongings by the front door had grown waist high. But, with each trip, she knew that she was that much closer to seeing Tariq again, and, with each trip, her legs became more sprightly, her arms more tireless.

'We're going to need a big taxi.'

Laila looked up. It was Mammy calling down

from her bedroom upstairs. She was leaning out the window, resting her elbows on the sill. The sun, bright and warm, caught in her graying hair, shone on her drawn, thin face. Mammy was wearing the same cobalt blue dress she had worn the day of the lunch party four months earlier, a youthful dress meant for a young woman, but, for a moment, Mammy looked to Laila like an old woman. An old woman with stringy arms and sunken temples and slow eyes rimmed by darkened circles of weariness, an altogether different creature from the plump, round-faced woman beaming radiantly from those grainy wedding photos.

'Two big taxis,' Laila said.

She could see Babi too, in the living room stacking boxes of books atop each other.

'Come up when you're done with those,' Mammy said. 'We'll sit down for lunch. Boiled eggs and leftover beans.'

'My favorite,' Laila said.

She thought suddenly of her dream. She and Tariq on a quilt. The ocean. The wind. The dunes.

What had it sounded like, she wondered now, the singing sands?

Laila stopped. She saw a gray lizard crawl out of a crack in the ground. Its head shot side to side. It blinked. Darted under a rock.

Laila pictured the beach again. Except now the singing was all around. And growing. Louder and louder by the moment, higher and higher. It flooded her ears. Drowned everything else out. The gulls

222

were feathered mimes now, opening and closing their beaks noiselessly, and the waves were crashing with foam and spray but no roar. The sands sang on. Screaming now. A sound like . . . a tinkling?

Not a tinkling. No. A whistling.

Laila dropped the books at her feet. She looked up to the sky. Shielded her eyes with one hand.

Then a giant roar.

Behind her, a flash of white.

The ground lurched beneath her feet.

Something hot and powerful slammed into her from behind. It knocked her out of her sandals. Lifted her up. And now she was flying, twisting and rotating in the air, seeing sky, then earth, then sky, then earth. A big burning chunk of wood whipped by. So did a thousand shards of glass, and it seemed to Laila that she could see each individual one flying all around her, flipping slowly end over end, the sunlight catching in each. Tiny, beautiful rainbows.

Then Laila struck the wall. Crashed to the ground. On her face and arms, a shower of dirt and pebbles and glass. The last thing she was aware of was seeing something thud to the ground nearby. A bloody chunk of something. On it, the tip of a red bridge poking through thick fog.

Shapes moving about. A fluorescent light shines from the ceiling above. A woman's face appears, hovers over hers.

Laila fades back to the dark.

★   ★   ★

Another face. This time a man's. His features seem broad and droopy. His lips move but make no sound. All Laila hears is ringing.

The man waves his hand at her. Frowns. His lips move again.

It hurts. It hurts to breathe. It hurts everywhere.

A glass of water. A pink pill.

Back to the darkness.

The woman again. Long face, narrow-set eyes. She says something. Laila can't hear anything but the ringing. But she can see the words, like thick black syrup, spilling out of the woman's mouth.

Her chest hurts. Her arms and legs hurt.

All around, shapes moving.

Where is Tariq?

Why isn't he here?

Darkness. A flock of stars.

Babi and she, perched somewhere high up. He is pointing to a field of barley. A generator comes to life.

The long-faced woman is standing over her looking down.

It hurts to breathe.

Somewhere, an accordion playing.

Mercifully, the pink pill again. Then a deep hush. A deep hush falls over everything.

# PART III

# CHAPTER 27

# MARIAM

D o you know who I am?'
The girl's eyes fluttered.
'Do you know what has happened?'
The girl's mouth quivered. She closed her eyes. Swallowed. Her hand grazed her left cheek. She mouthed something.

Mariam leaned in closer.

'This ear,' the girl breathed. 'I can't hear.'

For the first week, the girl did little but sleep, with help from the pink pills Rasheed paid for at the hospital. She murmured in her sleep. Sometimes she spoke gibberish, cried out, called out names Mariam did not recognize. She wept in her sleep, grew agitated, kicked the blankets off, and then Mariam had to hold her down. Sometimes she retched and retched, threw up everything Mariam fed her.

When she wasn't agitated, the girl was a sullen pair of eyes staring from under the blanket, breathing out short little answers to Mariam and Rasheed's questions. Some days she was childlike, whipped her head side to side, when Mariam, then Rasheed, tried to feed her. She went rigid when Mariam came at her with a spoon. But she tired easily and submitted eventually to their persistent badgering. Long bouts of weeping followed surrender.

Rasheed had Mariam rub antibiotic ointment on the cuts on the girl's face and neck, and on the sutured gashes on her shoulder, across her forearms and lower legs. Mariam dressed them with bandages, which she washed and recycled. She held the girl's hair back, out of her face, when she had to retch.

'How long is she staying?' she asked Rasheed.

'Until she's better. Look at her. She's in no shape to go. Poor thing.'

It was Rasheed who found the girl, who dug her out from beneath the rubble.

'Lucky I was home,' he said to the girl. He was sitting on a folding chair beside Mariam's bed, where the girl lay. 'Lucky for you, I mean. I dug you out with my own hands. There was a scrap of metal this big—' Here, he spread his thumb and index finger apart to show her, at least doubling, in Mariam's estimation, the actual size of it. 'This big. Sticking right out of your shoulder. It was really embedded in there. I thought I'd have to use a pair of pliers. But you're all right. In no time, you'll be *nau socha*. Good as new.'

It was Rasheed who salvaged a handful of Hakim's books.

'Most of them were ash. The rest were looted, I'm afraid.'

He helped Mariam watch over the girl that first week. One day, he came home from work with a new blanket and pillow. Another day, a bottle of pills.

'Vitamins,' he said.

It was Rasheed who gave Laila the news that her friend Tariq's house was occupied now.

'A gift,' he said. 'From one of Sayyaf's commanders to three of his men. A gift. Ha!'

The three *men* were actually boys with suntanned, youthful faces. Mariam would see them when she passed by, always dressed in their fatigues, squatting by the front door of Tariq's house, playing cards and smoking, their Kalashnikovs leaning against the wall. The brawny one, the one with the self-satisfied, scornful demeanor, was the leader. The youngest was also the quietest, the one who seemed reluctant to wholeheartedly embrace his friends' air of impunity. He had taken to smiling and tipping his head *salaam* when Mariam passed by. When he did, some of his surface smugness dropped away, and Mariam caught a glint of humility as yet uncorrupted.

Then one morning rockets slammed into the house. They were rumored later to have been fired by the Hazaras of Wahdat. For some time, neighbors kept finding bits and pieces of the boys.

'They had it coming,' said Rasheed.

The girl was extraordinarily lucky, Mariam thought, to escape with relatively minor injuries, considering the rocket had turned her house into smoking rubble. And so, slowly, the girl got better. She began to eat more, began to brush her own hair. She took baths on her own. She began taking her meals downstairs, with Mariam and Rasheed.

But then some memory would rise, unbidden, and there would be stony silences or spells of churlishness. Withdrawals and collapses. Wan looks. Nightmares and sudden attacks of grief. Retching.

And sometimes regrets.

'I shouldn't even be here,' she said one day.

Mariam was changing the sheets. The girl watched from the floor, her bruised knees drawn up against her chest.

'My father wanted to take out the boxes. The books. He said they were too heavy for me. But I wouldn't let him. I was so eager. I should have been the one inside the house when it happened.'

Mariam snapped the clean sheet and let it settle on the bed. She looked at the girl, at her blond curls, her slender neck and green eyes, her high cheekbones and plump lips. Mariam remembered seeing her on the streets when she was little, tottering after her mother on the way to the tandoor, riding on the shoulders of her brother, the younger one, with the patch of hair on his ear. Shooting marbles with the carpenter's boy.

The girl was looking back as if waiting for Mariam to pass on some morsel of wisdom, to say something encouraging. But what wisdom did Mariam have to offer? What encouragement?

Mariam remembered the day they'd buried Nana and how little comfort she had found when Mullah Faizullah had quoted the Koran for her. *Blessed is He in Whose hand is the kingdom, and He Who has power over all things, Who created death and life that He may try you.* Or when he'd said of her own guilt, *These thoughts are no good, Mariam jo. They will destroy you. It wasn't your fault. It wasn't your fault.*

What could she say to this girl that would ease her burden?

As it turned out, Mariam didn't have to say anything. Because the girl's face twisted, and she was on all fours then saying she was going to be sick.

'Wait! Hold on. I'll get a pan. Not on the floor. I just cleaned . . . Oh. Oh. *Khodaya*. God.'

Then one day, about a month after the blast that killed the girl's parents, a man came knocking. Mariam opened the door. He stated his business.

'There is a man here to see you,' Mariam said.

The girl raised her head from the pillow.

'He says his name is Abdul Sharif.'

'I don't know any Abdul Sharif.'

'Well, he's here asking for you. You need to come down and talk to him.'

# CHAPTER 28

# LAILA

Laila sat across from Abdul Sharif, who was a thin, small-headed man with a bulbous nose pocked with the same cratered scars that pitted his cheeks. His hair, short and brown, stood on his scalp like needles in a pincushion.

'You'll have to forgive me, *hamshira*,' he said, adjusting his loose collar and dabbing at his brow with a handkerchief. 'I still haven't quite recovered, I fear. Five more days of these, what are they called . . . sulfa pills.'

Laila positioned herself in her seat so that her right ear, the good one, was closest to him. 'Were you a friend of my parents?'

'No, no,' Abdul Sharif said quickly. 'Forgive me.' He raised a finger, took a long sip of the water that Mariam had placed in front of him.

'I should begin at the beginning, I suppose.' He dabbed at his lips, again at his brow. 'I am a businessman. I own clothing stores, mostly men's clothing. *Chapans*, hats, *tumbans*, suits, ties – you name it. Two stores here in Kabul, in Taimani and Shar-e-Nau, though I just sold those. And two in Pakistan, in Peshawar. That's where my warehouse

232

is as well. So I travel a lot, back and forth. Which, these days' – he shook his head and chuckled tiredly – 'let's just say that it's an adventure.

'I was in Peshawar recently, on business, taking orders, going over inventory, that sort of thing. Also to visit my family. We have three daughters, *alhamdulellah*. I moved them and my wife to Peshawar after the Mujahideen began going at each other's throats. I won't have their names added to the *shaheed* list. Nor mine, to be honest. I'll be joining them there very soon, *inshallah*.

'Anyway, I was supposed to be back in Kabul the Wednesday before last. But, as luck would have it, I came down with an illness. I won't bother you with it, *hamshira*, suffice it to say that when I went to do my private business, the simpler of the two, it felt like passing chunks of broken glass. I wouldn't wish it on Hekmatyar himself. My wife, Nadia jan, Allah bless her, she begged me to see a doctor. But I thought I'd beat it with aspirin and a lot of water. Nadia jan insisted and I said no, back and forth we went. You know the saying *A stubborn ass needs a stubborn driver*. This time, I'm afraid, the ass won. That would be me.'

He drank the rest of this water and extended the glass to Mariam. 'If it's not too much *zahmat*.'

Mariam took the glass and went to fill it.

'Needless to say, I should have listened to her. She's always been the more sensible one, God give her a long life. By the time I made it to the hospital, I was burning with a fever and shaking like a *beid*

233

tree in the wind. I could barely stand. The doctor said I had blood poisoning. She said two or three more days and I would have made my wife a widow.

'They put me in a special unit, reserved for really sick people, I suppose. Oh, *tashakor*.' He took the glass from Mariam and from his coat pocket produced a large white pill. 'The *size* of these things.'

Laila watched him swallow his pill. She was aware that her breathing had quickened. Her legs felt heavy, as though weights had been tethered to them. She told herself that he wasn't done, that he hadn't told her anything as yet. But he would go on in a second, and she resisted an urge to get up and leave, leave before he told her things she didn't want to hear.

Abdul Sharif set his glass on the table.

'That's where I met your friend, Mohammad Tariq Walizai.'

Laila's heart sped up. Tariq in a hospital? A special unit? *For really sick people?*

She swallowed dry spit. Shifted on her chair. She had to steel herself. If she didn't, she feared she would come unhinged. She diverted her thoughts from hospitals and special units and thought instead about the fact that she hadn't heard Tariq called by his full name since the two of them had enrolled in a Farsi winter course years back. The teacher would call roll after the bell and say his name like that – Mohammad Tariq Walizai.

It had struck her as comically officious then, hearing his full name uttered.

'What happened to him I heard from one of the nurses,' Abdul Sharif resumed, tapping his chest with a fist as if to ease the passage of the pill. 'With all the time I've spent in Peshawar, I've become pretty proficient in Urdu. Anyway, what I gathered was that your friend was in a lorry full of refugees, twenty-three of them, all headed for Peshawar. Near the border, they were caught in cross fire. A rocket hit the lorry. Probably a stray, but you never know with these people, you never know. There were only six survivors, all of them admitted to the same unit. Three died within twenty-four hours. Two of them lived – sisters, as I understood it – and had been discharged. Your friend Mr Walizai was the last. He'd been there for almost three weeks by the time I arrived.'

So he was alive. But how badly had they hurt him? Laila wondered frantically. How badly? Badly enough to be put in a special unit, evidently. Laila was aware that she had started sweating, that her face felt hot. She tried to think of something else, something pleasant, like the trip to Bamiyan to see the Buddhas with Tariq and Babi. But instead an image of Tariq's parents presented itself: Tariq's mother trapped in the lorry, upside down, screaming for Tariq through the smoke, her arms and chest on fire, the wig melting into her scalp . . .

Laila had to take a series of rapid breaths.

'He was in the bed next to mine. There were no walls, only a curtain between us. So I could see him pretty well.'

Abdul Sharif found a sudden need to toy with his wedding band. He spoke more slowly now.

'Your friend, he was badly – very badly – injured, you understand. He had rubber tubes coming out of him everywhere. At first—' He cleared his throat. 'At first, I thought he'd lost both legs in the attack, but a nurse said no, only the left, the right one was on account of an old injury. There were internal injuries too. They'd operated three times already. Took out sections of intestines, I don't remember what else. And he was burned. Quite badly. That's all I'll say about that. I'm sure you have your fair share of nightmares, *hamshira*. No sense in me adding to them.'

Tariq was legless now. He was a torso with two stumps. *Legless.* Laila thought she might collapse. With deliberate, desperate effort, she sent the tendrils of her mind out of this room, out the window, away from this man, over the street outside, over the city now, and its flat-topped houses and bazaars, its maze of narrow streets turned to sand castles.

'He was drugged up most of the time. For the pain, you understand. But he had moments when the drugs were wearing off when he was clear. In pain but clear of mind. I would talk to him from my bed. I told him who I was, where I was from. He was glad, I think, that there was a *hamwatan* next to him.

236

'I did most of the talking. It was hard for him to. His voice was hoarse, and I think it hurt him to move his lips. So I told him about my daughters, and about our house in Peshawar and the veranda my brother-in-law and I are building out in the back. I told him I had sold the stores in Kabul and that I was going back to finish up the paperwork. It wasn't much. But it occupied him. At least, I like to think it did.

'Sometimes he talked too. Half the time, I couldn't make out what he was saying, but I caught enough. He described where he'd lived. He talked about his uncle in Ghazni. And his mother's cooking and his father's carpentry, him playing the accordion.

'But, mostly, he talked about you, *hamshira*. He said you were – how did he put it – his earliest memory. I think that's right, yes. I could tell he cared a great deal about you. *Balay*, that much was plain to see. But he said he was glad you weren't there. He said he didn't want you seeing him like that.'

Laila's feet felt heavy again, anchored to the floor, as if all her blood had suddenly pooled down there. But her mind was far away, free and fleet, hurtling like a speeding missile beyond Kabul, over craggy brown hills and over deserts ragged with clumps of sage, past canyons of jagged red rock and over snowcapped mountains . . .

'When I told him I was going back to Kabul, he asked me to find you. To tell you that he was thinking of you. That he missed you. I promised him I would. I'd taken quite a liking to him, you see. He was a decent sort of boy, I could tell.'

Abdul Sharif wiped his brow with the handkerchief.

'I woke up one night,' he went on, his interest in the wedding band renewed, 'I think it was night anyway, it's hard to tell in those places. There aren't any windows. Sunrise, sundown, you just don't know. But I woke up, and there was some sort of commotion around the bed next to mine. You have to understand that I was full of drugs myself, always slipping in and out, to the point where it was hard to tell what was real and what you'd dreamed up. All I remember is, doctors huddled around the bed, calling for this and that, alarms bleeping, syringes all over the ground.

'In the morning, the bed was empty. I asked a nurse. She said he fought valiantly.'

Laila was dimly aware that she was nodding. She'd known. Of course she'd known. She'd known the moment she had sat across from this man why he was here, what news he was bringing.

'At first, you see, at first I didn't think you even existed,' he was saying now. 'I thought it was the morphine talking. Maybe I even *hoped* you didn't exist; I've always dreaded bearing bad news. But I promised him. And, like I said, I'd become rather fond of him. So I came by here a few days ago. I asked around for you, talked to some neighbors. They pointed to this house. They also told me what had happened to your parents. When I heard about that, well, I turned around and left. I wasn't going to tell you. I decided it would be too much for you. For anybody.'

Abdul Sharif reached across the table and put a hand on her kneecap. 'But I came back. Because, in the end, I think he would have wanted you to know. I believe that. I'm so sorry. I wish . . .'

Laila wasn't listening anymore. She was remembering the day the man from Panjshir had come to deliver the news of Ahmad's and Noor's deaths. She remembered Babi, white-faced, slumping on the couch, and Mammy, her hand flying to her mouth when she heard. Laila had watched Mammy come undone that day and it had scared her, but she hadn't felt any true sorrow. She hadn't understood the awfulness of her mother's loss. Now another stranger bringing news of another death. Now *she* was the one sitting on the chair. Was this her penalty, then, her punishment for being aloof to her own mother's suffering?

Laila remembered how Mammy had dropped to the ground, how she'd screamed, torn at her hair. But Laila couldn't even manage that. She could hardly move. She could hardly move a muscle.

She sat on the chair instead, hands limp in her lap, eyes staring at nothing, and let her mind fly on. She let it fly on until it found the place, the good and safe place, where the barley fields were green, where the water ran clear and the cotton-wood seeds danced by the thousands in the air;

where Babi was reading a book beneath an acacia and Tariq was napping with his hands laced across his chest, and where she could dip her feet in the stream and dream good dreams beneath the watchful gaze of gods of ancient, sun-bleached rock.

# CHAPTER 29

# MARIAM

'I'm so sorry,' Rasheed said to the girl, taking his bowl of *mastawa* and meatballs from Mariam without looking at her. 'I know you were very close . . . *friends* . . . the two of you. Always together, since you were kids. It's a terrible thing, what's happened. Too many young Afghan men are dying this way.'

He motioned impatiently with his hand, still looking at the girl, and Mariam passed him a napkin.

For years, Mariam had looked on as he ate, the muscles of his temples churning, one hand making compact little rice balls, the back of the other wiping grease, swiping stray grains, from the corners of his mouth. For years, he had eaten without looking up, without speaking, his silence condemning, as though some judgment were being passed, then broken only by an accusatory grunt, a disapproving cluck of his tongue, a one-word command for more bread, more water.

Now he ate with a spoon. Used a napkin. Said *lotfan* when asking for water. And talked. Spiritedly and incessantly.

241

'If you ask me, the Americans armed the wrong man in Hekmatyar. All the guns the CIA handed him in the eighties to fight the Soviets. The Soviets are gone, but he still has the guns, and now he's turning them on innocent people like your parents. And he calls this jihad. What a farce! What does jihad have to do with killing women and children? Better the CIA had armed Commander Massoud.'

Mariam's eyebrows shot up of their own will. *Commander* Massoud? In her head, she could hear Rasheed's rants against Massoud, how he was a traitor and a communist. But, then, Massoud was a Tajik, of course. Like Laila.

'Now, *there* is a reasonable fellow. An honorable Afghan. A man genuinely interested in a peaceful resolution.'

Rasheed shrugged and sighed.

'Not that they give a damn in America, mind you. What do they care that Pashtuns and Hazaras and Tajiks and Uzbeks are killing each other? How many Americans can even tell one from the other? Don't expect help from them, I say. Now that the Soviets have collapsed, we're no use to them. We served our purpose. To them, Afghanistan is a *kenarab*, a shit hole. Excuse my language, but it's true. What do you think, Laila jan?'

The girl mumbled something unintelligible and pushed a meatball around in her bowl.

Rasheed nodded thoughtfully, as though she'd said the most clever thing he'd ever heard. Mariam had to look away.

242

'You know, your father, God give him peace, your father and I used to have discussions like this. This was before you were born, of course. On and on we'd go about politics. About books too. Didn't we, Mariam? You remember.'

Mariam busied herself taking a sip of water.

'Anyway, I hope I am not boring you with all this talk of politics.'

Later, Mariam was in the kitchen, soaking dishes in soapy water, a tightly wound knot in her belly.

It wasn't so much *what* he said, the blatant lies, the contrived empathy, or even the fact that he had not raised a hand to her, Mariam, since he had dug the girl out from under those bricks.

It was the *staged* delivery. Like a performance. An attempt on his part, both sly and pathetic, to impress. To charm.

And suddenly Mariam knew that her suspicions were right. She understood with a dread that was like a blinding whack to the side of her head that what she was witnessing was nothing less than a courtship.

When she'd at last worked up the nerve, Mariam went to his room.

Rasheed lit a cigarette, and said, 'Why not?'

Mariam knew right then that she was defeated. She'd half expected, half hoped, that he would deny everything, feign surprise, maybe even outrage, at what she was implying. She might have had the upper hand then. She might have succeeded in shaming him. But it stole her grit, his calm acknowledgment, his matter-of-fact tone.

'Sit down,' he said. He was lying on his bed, back to the wall, his thick, long legs splayed on the mattress. 'Sit down before you faint and cut your head open.'

Mariam felt herself drop onto the folding chair beside his bed.

'Hand me that ashtray, would you?' he said.

Obediently, she did.

Rasheed had to be sixty or more now – though Mariam, and in fact Rasheed himself did not know his exact age. His hair had gone white, but it was as thick and coarse as ever. There was a sag now to his eyelids and the skin of his neck, which was wrinkled and leathery. His cheeks hung a bit more than they used to. In the mornings, he stooped just a tad. But he still had the stout shoulders, the thick torso, the strong hands, the swollen belly that entered the room before any other part of him did.

On the whole, Mariam thought that he had weathered the years considerably better than she.

'We need to legitimize this situation,' he said now, balancing the ashtray on his belly. His lips scrunched up in a playful pucker. 'People will talk. It looks dishonorable, an unmarried young woman living here. It's bad for my reputation. And hers. And yours, I might add.'

'Eighteen years,' Mariam said. 'And I never asked you for a thing. Not one thing. I'm asking now.'

He inhaled smoke and let it out slowly. 'She can't just *stay* here, if that's what you're suggesting. I can't go on feeding her and clothing her and giving her a place to sleep. I'm not the Red Cross, Mariam.'

'But this?'

'What of it? What? She's too young, you think? She's fourteen. Hardly a child. You were fifteen, remember? My mother was fourteen when she had me. Thirteen when she married.'

'I . . . I don't want this,' Mariam said, numb with contempt and helplessness.

'It's not your decision. It's hers and mine.'

'I'm too old.'

'She's too young, you're too old. This is nonsense.'

'I *am* too old. Too old for you to do this to me,' Mariam said, balling up fistfuls of her dress so tightly her hands shook. 'For you, after all these years, to make me an *ambagh*.'

'Don't be so dramatic. It's a common thing and you know it. I have friends who have two, three, four wives. Your own father had three. Besides, what I'm doing now most men I know would have done long ago. You know it's true.'

'I won't allow it.'

At this, Rasheed smiled sadly.

'There *is* another option,' he said, scratching the sole of one foot with the calloused heel of the other. 'She can leave. I won't stand in her way. But I suspect she won't get far. No food, no water, not a rupiah in her pockets, bullets and rockets flying everywhere. How many days do you suppose she'll last before she's abducted, raped, or tossed into some roadside ditch with her throat slit? Or all three?'

He coughed and adjusted the pillow behind his back.

'The roads out there are unforgiving, Mariam, believe me. Bloodhounds and bandits at every turn. I wouldn't like her chances, not at all. But let's say that by some miracle she gets to Peshawar. What then? Do you have any idea what those camps are like?'

He gazed at her from behind a column of smoke.

'People living under scraps of cardboard. TB, dysentery, famine, crime. And that's before winter. Then it's frostbite season. Pneumonia. People turning to icicles. Those camps become frozen graveyards.'

'Of course,' he made a playful, twirling motion with his hand, 'she could keep warm in one of those Peshawar brothels. Business is booming there, I hear. A beauty like her ought to bring in a small fortune, don't you think?'

He set the ashtray on the nightstand and swung his legs over the side of the bed.

'Look,' he said, sounding more conciliatory now, as a victor could afford to. 'I knew you wouldn't take this well. I don't really blame you. But this is for the best. You'll see. Think of it this way, Mariam. I'm giving *you* help around the house and *her* a sanctuary. A home and a husband. These days, times being what they are, a woman needs a husband. Haven't you noticed all the widows sleeping on the streets? They would kill for this chance. In fact, this is . . . Well, I'd say this is downright charitable of me.'

He smiled.

'The way I see it, I deserve a medal.'

Later, in the dark, Mariam told the girl.

For a long time, the girl said nothing.

'He wants an answer by this morning,' Mariam said.

'He can have it now,' the girl said. 'My answer is yes.'

# CHAPTER 30

# LAILA

The next day, Laila stayed in bed. She was under the blanket in the morning when Rasheed poked his head in and said he was going to the barber. She was still in bed when he came home late in the afternoon, when he showed her his new haircut, his new used suit, blue with cream pinstripes, and the wedding band he'd bought her.

Rasheed sat on the bed beside her, made a great show of slowly undoing the ribbon, of opening the box and plucking out the ring delicately. He let on that he'd traded in Mariam's old wedding ring for it.

'She doesn't care. Believe me. She won't even notice.'

Laila pulled away to the far end of the bed. She could hear Mariam downstairs, the hissing of her iron.

'She never wore it anyway,' Rasheed said.

'I don't want it,' Laila said, weakly. 'Not like this. You have to take it back.'

'Take it back?' An impatient look flashed across his face and was gone. He smiled. 'I had to add some cash too – quite a lot, in fact. This is a better ring, twenty-two-karat gold. Feel how heavy? Go on, feel it. No?' He closed the box. 'How about flowers? That would be nice. You like flowers? Do you have a favorite? Daisies? tulips? lilacs? No flowers? Good! I don't see the point myself. I just thought . . . Now, I know a tailor here in Deh-Mazang. I was thinking we could take you there tomorrow, get you fitted for a proper dress.'

Laila shook her head.

Rasheed raised his eyebrows.

'I'd just as soon—' Laila began.

He put a hand on her neck. Laila couldn't help wincing and recoiling. His touch felt like wearing a prickly old wet wool sweater with no undershirt.

'Yes?'

'I'd just as soon we get it done.'

Rasheed's mouth opened, then spread in a yellow, toothy grin. 'Eager,' he said.

Before Abdul Sharif's visit, Laila had decided to leave for Pakistan. Even after Abdul Sharif came bearing his news, Laila thought now, she might have left. Gone somewhere far from here. Detached herself from this city where every street corner was a trap, where every alley hid a ghost that sprang at her like a jack-in-the-box. She might have taken the risk.

But, suddenly, leaving was no longer an option.

Not with this daily retching.

This new fullness in her breasts.

And the awareness, somehow, amid all of this turmoil, that she had missed a cycle.

Laila pictured herself in a refugee camp, a stark field with thousands of sheets of plastic strung to makeshift poles flapping in the cold, stinging wind. Beneath one of these makeshift tents, she saw her baby, Tariq's baby, its temples wasted, its jaws slack, its skin mottled, bluish gray. She pictured its tiny body washed by strangers, wrapped in a tawny shroud, lowered into a hole dug in a patch of windswept land under the disappointed gaze of vultures.

How could she run now?

Laila took grim inventory of the people in her life. Ahmad and Noor, dead. Hasina, gone. Giti, dead. Mammy, dead. Babi, dead. Now Tariq . . .

But, miraculously, something of her former life remained, her last link to the person that she had been before she had become so utterly alone. A part of Tariq still alive inside her, sprouting tiny arms, growing translucent hands. How could she jeopardize the only thing she had left of him, of her old life?

She made her decision quickly. Six weeks had passed since her time with Tariq. Any longer and Rasheed would grow suspicious.

She knew that what she was doing was dishonorable. Dishonorable, disingenuous, and shameful. And spectacularly unfair to Mariam. But even though the baby inside her was no bigger than a mulberry, Laila already saw the sacrifices a mother had to make. Virtue was only the first.

She put a hand on her belly. Closed her eyes.

Laila would remember the muted ceremony in bits and fragments. The cream-colored stripes of Rasheed's suit. The sharp smell of his hair spray. The small shaving nick just above his Adam's apple. The rough pads of his tobacco-stained fingers when he slid the ring on her. The pen. Its not working. The search for a new pen. The contract. The signing, his sure-handed, hers quavering. The prayers. Noticing, in the mirror, that. Rasheed had trimmed his eyebrows.

And, somewhere in the room, Mariam watching. The air choking with her disapproval. Laila could not bring herself to meet the older woman's gaze.

Lying beneath his cold sheets that night, she watched him pull the curtains shut. She was shaking even before his fingers worked her shirt buttons, tugged at the drawstring of her trousers. He was agitated. His fingers fumbled endlessly with his own shirt, with undoing his belt. Laila had a full view of his sagging breasts, his protruding belly button, the small blue vein in the center of it, the tufts of thick white hair on his chest, his shoulders, and upper arms. She felt his eyes crawling all over her.

'God help me, I think I love you,' he said.

Through chattering teeth, she asked him to turn out the lights.

Later, when she was sure that he was asleep, Laila quietly reached beneath the mattress for the knife she had hidden there earlier. With it, she punctured the pad of her index finger. Then she lifted the blanket and let her finger bleed on the sheets where they had lain together.

# CHAPTER 31

# MARIAM

In the daytime, the girl was no more than a creaking bedspring, a patter of footsteps overhead. She was water splashing in the bathroom, or a teaspoon clinking against glass in the bedroom upstairs. Occasionally, there were sightings: a blur of billowing dress in the periphery of Mariam's vision, scurrying up the steps, arms folded across the chest, sandals slapping the heels.

But it was inevitable that they would run into each other. Mariam passed the girl on the stairs, in the narrow hallway, in the kitchen, or by the door as she was coming in from the yard. When they met like this, an awkward tension rushed into the space between them. The girl gathered her skirt and breathed out a word or two of apology, and, as she hurried past, Mariam would chance a sidelong glance and catch a blush. Sometimes she could smell Rasheed on her. She could smell his sweat on the girl's skin, his tobacco, his appetite. Sex, mercifully, was a closed chapter in her own life. It had been for some time, and now even the thought of those laborious sessions of lying beneath Rasheed made Mariam queasy in the gut.

At night, however, this mutually orchestrated dance of avoidance between her and the girl was not possible. Rasheed said they were a family. He insisted they were, and families had to eat together, he said.

'What is this?' he said, his fingers working the meat off a bone – the spoon-and-fork charade was abandoned a week after he married the girl. 'Have I married a pair of statues? Go on, Mariam, *gap bezan*, say something to her. Where are your manners?'

Sucking marrow from a bone, he said to the girl, 'But you mustn't blame her. She is quiet. A blessing, really, because, *wallah*, if a person hasn't got much to say she might as well be stingy with words. We are city people, you and I, but she is *dehati*. A village girl. Not even a village girl. No. She grew up in a *kolba* made of mud *outside* the village. Her father put her there. Have you told her, Mariam, have you told her that you are a *harami*? Well, she is. But she is not without qualities, all things considered. You will see for yourself, Laila jan. She is sturdy, for one thing, a good worker, and without pretensions. I'll say it this way: If she were a car, she would be a Volga.'

Mariam was a thirty-three-year-old woman now, but that word, *harami* still had sting. Hearing it still made her feel like she was a pest, a cockroach. She remembered Nana pulling her wrists. *You are a clumsy little* harami. *This is my reward for everything I've endured. An heirloom-breaking clumsy little* harami.

254

'You,' Rasheed said to the girl, 'you, on the other hand, would be a Benz. A brand-new, first-class, shiny Benz. *Wah wah*. But. But.' He raised one greasy index finger. 'One must take certain . . . cares . . . with a Benz. As a matter of respect for its beauty and craftsmanship, you see. Oh, you must be thinking that I am crazy, *diwana*, with all this talk of automobiles. I am not saying you are cars. I am merely making a point.'

For what came next, Rasheed put down the ball of rice he'd made back on the plate. His hands dangled idly over his meal, as he looked down with a sober, thoughtful expression.

'One mustn't speak ill of the dead much less the *shaheed*. And I intend no disrespect when I say this, I want you to know, but I have certain . . . reservations . . . about the way your parents – Allah, forgive them and grant them a place in paradise – about their, well, their leniency with you. I'm sorry.'

The cold, hateful look the girl flashed Rasheed at this did not escape Mariam, but he was looking down and did not notice.

'No matter. The point is, I am your husband now, and it falls on me to guard not only *your* honor but *ours*, yes, our *nang* and *namoos*. That is the husband's burden. You let me worry about that. Please. As for you, you are the queen, the *malika*, and this house is your palace. Anything you need done you ask Mariam and she will do it for you. Won't you, Mariam? And if you fancy something, I will get it for you. You see, that is the sort of husband I am.

'All I ask in return, well, it is a simple thing. I ask that you avoid leaving this house without my company. That's all. Simple, no? If I am away and you need something urgently, I mean *absolutely* need it and it cannot wait for me, then you can send Mariam and she will go out and get it for you. You've noticed a discrepancy, surely. Well, one does not drive a Volga and a Benz in the same manner. That would be foolish, wouldn't it? Oh, I also ask that when we are out together, that you wear a burqa. For your own protection, naturally. It is best. So many lewd men in this town now. Such vile intentions, so eager to dishonor even a married woman. So. That's all.'

He coughed.

'I should say that Mariam will be my eyes and ears when I am away.' Here, he shot Mariam a fleeting look that was as hard as a steel-toed kick to the temple. 'Not that I am mistrusting. Quite the contrary. Frankly, you strike me as far wiser than your years. But you are still a young woman, Laila jan, a *dokhtar e jawan*, and young women can make unfortunate choices. They can be prone to mischief. Anyway, Mariam will be accountable. And if there is a slipup . . .'

On and on he went. Mariam sat watching the girl out of the corner of her eye as Rasheed's demands and judgments rained down on them like the rockets on Kabul.

\* \* \*

256

One day, Mariam was in the living room folding some shirts of Rasheed's that she had plucked from the clothesline in the yard. She didn't know how long the girl had been standing there, but, when she picked up a shirt and turned around, she found her standing by the doorway, hands cupped around a glassful of tea.

'I didn't mean to startle you,' the girl said. 'I'm sorry.'

Mariam only looked at her.

The sun fell on the girl's face, on her large green eyes and her smooth brow, on her high cheek-bones and the appealing, thick eyebrows, which were nothing like Mariam's own, thin and feature-less. Her yellow hair, uncombed this morning, was middle-parted.

Mariam could see in the stiff way the girl clutched the cup, the tightened shoulders, that she was nervous. She imagined her sitting on the bed working up the nerve.

'The leaves are turning,' the girl said compan-ionably. 'Have you seen? Autumn is my favorite. I like the smell of it, when people burn leaves in their gardens. My mother, she liked springtime the best. You knew my mother?'

'Not really.'

The girl cupped a hand behind her ear. 'I'm sorry?'

Mariam raised her voice. 'I said no. I didn't know your mother.'

'Oh.'

'Is there something you want?'

'Mariam jan, I want to . . . About the things he said the other night—'

'I have been meaning to talk to you about it.' Mariam broke in.

'Yes, please,' the girl said earnestly, almost eagerly. She took a step forward. She looked relieved.

Outside, an oriole was warbling. Someone was pulling a cart; Mariam could hear the creaking of its hinges, the bouncing and rattling of its iron wheels. There was the sound of gunfire not so far away, a single shot followed by three more, then nothing.

'I won't be your servant,' Mariam said. 'I won't.'

The girl flinched. 'No. Of course not!'

'You may be the palace *malika* and me a *dehati*, but I won't take orders from you. You can complain to him and he can slit my throat, but I won't do it. Do you hear me? I won't be your servant.'

'No! I don't expect—'

'And if you think you can use your looks to get rid of me, you're wrong. I was here first. I won't be thrown out. I won't have you cast me out.'

'It's not what I want,' the girl said weakly.

'And I see you wounds are healed up now. So you can start doing your share of the work in this house—'

The girl was nodding quickly. Some of her tea spilled, but she didn't notice. 'Yes, that's the other

258

reason I came down, to thank you for taking care of me—'

'Well, I wouldn't have,' Mariam snapped. 'I wouldn't have fed you and washed you and nursed you if I'd known you were going to turn around and steal my husband.'

'Steal—'

'I will still cook and wash the dishes. You will do the laundry and the sweeping. The rest we will alternate daily. And one more thing. I have no use for your company. I don't want it. What I want is to be alone. You will leave me be, and I will return the favor. That's how we will get on. Those are the rules.'

When she was done speaking, her heart was hammering and her mouth felt parched. Mariam had never before spoken in this manner, had never stated her will so forcefully. It ought to have felt exhilarating, but the girl's eyes had teared up and her face was drooping, and what satisfaction Mariam found from this outburst felt meager, somehow illicit.

She extended the shirts toward the girl.

'Put them in the *almari*, not the closet. He likes the whites in the top drawer, the rest in the middle, with the socks.'

The girl set the cup on the floor and put her hands out for the shirts, palm up. 'I'm sorry about all of this,' she croaked.

'You should be,' Mariam said. 'You should be sorry.'

# CHAPTER 32

# LAILA

Laila remembered a gathering once, years before at the house, on one of Mammy's good days. The women had been sitting in the garden, eating from a platter of fresh mulberries that Wajma had picked from the tree in her yard. The plump mulberries had been white and pink, and some the same dark purple as the bursts of tiny veins on Wajma's nose.

'You heard how his son died?' Wajma had said, energetically shoveling another handful of mulberries into her sunken mouth.

'He drowned, didn't he?' Nila, Giti's mother, said. 'At Ghargha Lake, wasn't it?'

'But did you know, did you know that Rasheed . . .' Wajma raised a finger, made a show of nodding and chewing and making them wait for her to swallow. 'Did you know that he used to drink *sharab* back then, that he was crying drunk that day? It's true. Crying drunk, is what I heard. And that was midmorning. By noon, he had passed out on a lounge chair. You could have fired the noon cannon next to his ear and he wouldn't have batted an eyelash.'

Laila remembered how Wajma had covered her mouth, burped; how her tongue had gone exploring between her few remaining teeth.

'You can imagine the rest. The boy went into the water unnoticed. They spotted him a while later, floating facedown. People rushed to help, half trying to wake up the boy, the other half the father. Someone bent over the boy, did the . . . the mouth-to-mouth thing you're supposed to do. It was pointless. They could all see that. The boy was gone.'

Laila remembered Wajma raising a finger and her voice quivering with piety. 'This is why the Holy Koran forbids *sharab*. Because it always falls on the sober to pay for the sins of the drunk. So it does.'

It was this story that was circling in Laila's head after she gave Rasheed the news about the baby. He had immediately hopped on his bicycle, ridden to a mosque, and prayed for a boy.

That night, all during the meal, Laila watched Mariam push a cube of meat around her plate. Laila was there when Rasheed sprang the news on Mariam in a high, dramatic voice – Laila had never before witnessed such cheerful cruelty. Mariam's lashes fluttered when she heard. A flush spread across her face. She sat sulking, looking desolate.

After, Rasheed went upstairs to listen to his radio, and Laila helped Mariam clear the *sofrah*.

'I can't imagine what you are now,' Mariam said,

261

picking grains of rice and bread crumbs, 'if you were a Benz before.'

Laila tried a more lighthearted tactic. 'A train? Maybe a big jumbo jet.'

Mariam straightened up. 'I hope you don't think this excuses you from chores.'

Laila opened her mouth, thought better of it. She reminded herself that Mariam was the only innocent party in this arrangement. Mariam and the baby.

Later, in bed, Laila burst into tears.

What was the matter? Rasheed wanted to know, lifting her chin. Was she ill? Was it the baby, was something wrong with the baby? No?

Was Mariam mistreating her?

'That's it, isn't it?'

'No.'

'*Wallah o billah*, I'll go down and teach her a lesson. Who does she think she is, that *harami*, treating you—'

'No!'

He was getting up already, and she had to grab him by the forearm, pull him back down. 'Don't! No! She's been decent to me. I need a minute, that's all. I'll be fine.'

He sat beside her, stroking her neck, murmuring. His hand slowly crept down to her back, then up again. He leaned in, flashed his crowded teeth.

'Let's see, then,' he purred, 'if I can't help you feel better.'

★　★　★

First, the trees – those that hadn't been cut down for firewood – shed their spotty yellow-and-copper leaves. Then came the winds, cold and raw, ripping through the city. They tore off the last of the clinging leaves, and left the trees looking ghostly against the muted brown of the hills. The season's first snowfall was light, the flakes no sooner fallen than melted. Then the roads froze, and snow gathered in heaps on the rooftops, piled halfway up frost-caked windows. With snow came the kites, once the rulers of Kabul's winter skies, now timid trespassers in territory claimed by streaking rockets and fighter jets.

Rasheed kept bringing home news of the war, and Laila was baffled by the allegiances that Rasheed tried to explain to her. Sayyaf was fighting the Hazaras, he said. The Hazaras were fighting Massoud.

'And he's fighting Hekmatyar, of course, who has the support of the Pakistanis. Mortal enemies, those two, Massoud and Hekmatyar. Sayyaf, he's siding with Massoud. And Hekmatyar supports the Hazaras for now.'

As for the unpredictable Uzbek commander Dostum, Rasheed said no one knew where he would stand. Dostum had fought the Soviets in the 1980s alongside the Mujahideen but had defected and joined Najibullah's communist puppet regime after the Soviets had left. He had even earned a medal, presented by Najibullah himself, before defecting once again and returning to the Mujahideen's side. For the time being, Rasheed said, Dostum was supporting Massoud.

In Kabul, particularly in western Kabul, fires raged, and black palls of smoke mushroomed over snow-clad buildings. Embassies closed down. Schools collapsed. In hospital waiting rooms, Rasheed said, the wounded were bleeding to death. In operating rooms, limbs were being amputated without anesthesia.

'But don't worry,' he said. 'You're safe with me, my flower, my *gul*. Anyone tries to harm you, I'll rip out their liver and make them eat it.'

That winter, everywhere Laila turned, walls blocked her way. She thought longingly of the wide-open skies of her childhood, of her days of going to *buzkashi* tournaments with Babi and shopping at Mandaii with Mammy, of her days of running free in the streets and gossiping about boys with Giti and Hasina. Her days of sitting with Tariq in a bed of clover on the banks of a stream somewhere, trading riddles and candy, watching the sun go down.

But thinking of Tariq was treacherous because, before she could stop, she saw him lying on a bed, far from home, tubes piercing his burned body. Like the bile that kept burning her throat these days, a deep, paralyzing grief would come rising up Laila's chest. Her legs would turn to water. She would have to hold on to something.

Laila passed that winter of 1992 sweeping the house, scrubbing the pumpkin-colored walls of the bedroom she shared with Rasheed, washing clothes outside in a big copper *lagaan*. Sometimes she saw herself as if hovering above her own body, saw herself squatting over the rim of the *lagaan*, sleeves rolled up to the elbows, pink hands wringing soapy water from one of Rasheed's undershirts. She felt lost then, casting about, like a shipwreck survivor, no shore in sight, only miles and miles of water.

When it was too cold to go outside, Laila ambled around the house. She walked, dragging a fingernail along the wall, down the hallway, then back, down the steps, then up, her face unwashed, hair uncombed. She walked until she ran into Mariam, who shot her a cheerless glance and went back to slicing the stem off a bell pepper and trimming strips of fat from meat. A hurtful silence would fill the room, and Laila could almost see the wordless hostility radiating from Mariam like waves of heat rising from asphalt. She would retreat back to her room, sit on the bed, and watch the snow falling.

Rasheed took her to his shoe shop one day.

When they were out together, he walked alongside her, one hand gripping her by the elbow. For Laila, being out in the streets had become an exercise in avoiding injury. Her eyes were still adjusting to the limited, gridlike visibility of the burqa, her feet still stumbling over the hem. She walked in perpetual fear of tripping and falling, of breaking an ankle stepping into a pothole. Still, she found some comfort in the anonymity that the burqa provided. She wouldn't be recognized this way if she ran into an old acquaintance of hers. She wouldn't have to watch the surprise in their eyes, or the pity or the glee, at how far she had fallen, at how her lofty aspirations had been dashed.

Rasheed's shop was bigger and more brightly lit than Laila had imagined. He had her sit behind his crowded workbench, the top of which was littered with old soles and scraps of left-over leather. He showed her his hammers, demonstrated how the sandpaper wheel worked, his voice ringing high and proud.

He felt her belly, not through the shirt but under it, his fingertips cold and rough like bark on her distended skin. Laila remembered Tariq's hands, soft but strong, the tortuous, full veins on the backs of them, which she had always found so appealingly masculine.

'Swelling so quickly,' Rasheed said. 'It's going to be a big boy. My son will be a *pahlawan*! Like his father.'

Laila pulled down her shirt. It filled her with fear when he spoke like this.

'How are things with Mariam?'

She said they were fine.

'Good. Good.'

She didn't tell him that they'd had their first true fight.

It had happened a few days earlier. Laila had

266

gone to the kitchen and found Mariam yanking drawers and slamming them shut. She was looking, Mariam said, for the long wooden spoon she used to stir rice.

'Where did you put it?' she said, wheeling around to face Laila.

'Me?' Laila said. 'I didn't take it. I hardly come in here.'

'I've noticed.'

'Is that an accusation? It's how you wanted it, remember. You said you would make the meals. But if you want to switch—'

'So you're saying it grew little legs and walked out. *Teep, teep, teep, teep.* Is that what happened, *degeh*?'

'I'm saying . . .' Laila said, trying to maintain control. Usually, she could will herself to absorb Mariam's derision and finger-pointing. But her ankles had swollen, her head hurt, and the heartburn was vicious that day. 'I am saying that maybe you've misplaced it.'

'Misplaced it?' Mariam pulled a drawer. The spatulas and knives inside it clanked. 'How long have you been here, a few months? I've lived in this house for nineteen years, *dokhtar jo*. I have kept *that* spoon in *this* drawer since you were shitting your diapers.'

'Still,' Laila said, on the brink now, teeth clenched, 'it's possible you put it somewhere and forgot.'

'And it's possible *you* hid it somewhere, to aggravate me.'

'You're a sad, miserable woman,' Laila said.

Mariam flinched, then recovered, pursed her lips. 'And you're a whore. A whore and a *dozd*. A thieving whore, that's what you are!'

Then there was shouting. Pots raised though not hurled. They'd called each other names, names that made Laila blush now. They hadn't spoken since. Laila was still shocked at how easily she'd come unhinged, but, the truth was, part of her had liked it, had liked how it felt to scream at Mariam, to curse at her, to have a target at which to focus all her simmering anger, her grief.

Laila wondered, with something like insight, if it wasn't the same for Mariam.

After, she had run upstairs and thrown herself on Rasheed's bed. Downstairs, Mariam was still yelling, 'Dirt on your head! Dirt on your head!' Laila had lain on the bed, groaning into the pillow, missing her parents suddenly and with an overpowering intensity she hadn't felt since those terrible days just after the attack. She lay there, clutching handfuls of the bedsheet, until, suddenly, her breath caught. She sat up, hands shooting down to her belly.

The baby had just kicked for the first time.

# CHAPTER 33

# MARIAM

Early one morning the next spring, of 1993, Mariam stood by the living-room window and watched Rasheed escort the girl out of the house. The girl was tottering forward, bent at the waist, one arm draped protectively across the taut drum of her belly, the shape of which was visible through her burqa. Rasheed, anxious and overly attentive, was holding her elbow, directing her across the yard like a traffic policeman. He made a *Wait here* gesture, rushed to the front gate, then motioned for the girl to come forward, one foot propping the gate open. When she reached him, he took her by the hand, helped her through the gate. Mariam could almost hear him say, '*Watch your step, now, my flower, my* gul.'

They came back early the next evening.

Mariam saw Rasheed enter the yard first. He let the gate go prematurely, and it almost hit the girl on the face. He crossed the yard in a few, quick steps. Mariam detected a shadow on his face, a darkness underlying the coppery light of dusk. In the house, he took off his coat, threw it on the couch. Brushing past Mariam, he said in a brusque voice, 'I'm hungry. Get supper ready.'

The front door to the house opened. From the hallway, Mariam saw the girl, a swaddled bundle in the hook of her left arm. She had one foot outside, the other inside, against the door, to prevent it from springing shut. She was stooped over and was grunting, trying to reach for the paper bag of belongings that she had put down in order to open the door. Her face was grimacing with effort. She looked up and saw Mariam.

Mariam turned around and went to the kitchen to warm Rasheed's meal.

'It's like someone is ramming a screwdriver into my ear,' Rasheed said, rubbing his eyes. He was standing in Mariam's door, puffy-eyed, wearing only a *tumban* tied with a floppy knot. His white hair was straggly, pointing every which way. 'This crying. I can't stand it.'

Downstairs, the girl was walking the baby across the floor, trying to sing to her.

'I haven't had a decent night's sleep in two months,' Rasheed said. 'And the room smells like a sewer. There's shit cloths lying all over the place. I stepped on one just the other night.'

Mariam smirked inwardly with perverse pleasure.

'Take her outside!' Rasheed yelled over his shoulder. 'Can't you take her outside?'

The singing was suspended briefly. 'She'll catch pneumonia!'

'It's summertime!'

'What?'

Rasheed clenched his teeth and raised his voice. 'I said, It's warm out!'

'I'm not taking her outside!'

The singing resumed.

'Sometimes, I swear, sometimes I want to put that thing in a box and let her float down Kabul River. Like baby Moses.'

Mariam never heard him call his daughter by the name the girl had given her, Aziza, the Cherished One. It was always *the baby*, or, when he was really exasperated, *that thing*.

Some nights, Mariam overheard them arguing. She tiptoed to their door, listened to him complain about the baby – always the baby – the insistent crying, the smells, the toys that made him trip, the way the baby had hijacked Laila's attentions from him with constant demands to be fed, burped, changed, walked, held. The girl, in turn, scolded him for smoking in the room, for not letting the baby sleep with them.

There were other arguments waged in voices pitched low.

'The doctor said six weeks.'

'Not yet, Rasheed. No. Let go. Come on. Don't do that.'

'It's been two months.'

'*Ssht*. There. You woke up the baby.' Then more sharply, '*Khosh shodi?* Happy now?'

Mariam would sneak back to her room.

'Can't you help?' Rasheed said now. 'There must be something you can do.'

'What do I know about babies?' Mariam said.

'Rasheed! Can you bring the bottle? It's sitting on the *almari*. She won't feed. I want to try the bottle again.'

The baby's screeching rose and fell like a cleaver on meat.

Rasheed closed his eyes. 'That thing is a warlord. Hekmatyar. I'm telling you, Laila's given birth to Gulbuddin Hekmatyar.'

Mariam watched as the girl's days became consumed with cycles of feeding, rocking, bouncing, walking. Even when the baby napped, there were soiled diapers to scrub and leave to soak in a pail of the disinfectant that the girl had insisted Rasheed buy for her. There were fingernails to trim with sandpaper, coveralls and pajamas to wash and hang to dry. These clothes, like other things about the baby, became a point of contention.

'What's the matter with them?' Rasheed said.

'They're boy's clothes. For a *bacha*.'

'You think she knows the difference? I paid good money for those clothes. And another thing, I don't care for that tone. Consider that a warning.'

Every week, without fail, the girl heated a black metal brazier over a flame, tossed a pinch of wild rue seeds in it, and wafted the *espandi* smoke in her baby's direction to ward off evil.

Mariam found it exhausting to watch the girl's

lolloping enthusiasm – and had to admit, if only privately, to a degree of admiration. She marveled at how the girl's eyes shone with worship, even in the mornings when her face drooped and her complexion was waxy from a night's worth of walking the baby. The girl had fits of laughter when the baby passed gas. The tiniest changes in the baby enchanted her, and everything it did was declared spectacular.

'Look! She's reaching for the rattle. How clever she is.'

'I'll call the newspapers,' said Rasheed.

Every night, there were demonstrations. When the girl insisted he witness something, Rasheed tipped his chin upward and cast an impatient, sidelong glance down the blue-veined hook of his nose.

'Watch. Watch how she laughs when I snap my fingers. There. See? Did you see?'

Rasheed would grunt, and go back to his plate. Mariam remembered how the girl's mere presence used to overwhelm him. Everything she said used to please him, intrigue him, make him look up from his plate and nod with approval.

The strange thing was, the girl's fall from grace ought to have pleased Mariam, brought her a sense of vindication. But it didn't. It didn't. To her own surprise, Mariam found herself pitying the girl.

It was also over dinner that the girl let loose a steady stream of worries. Topping the list was pneumonia, which was suspected with every minor cough. Then there was dysentery, the specter of which was raised with every loose stool. Every rash was either chicken pox or measles.

'You should not get so attached,' Rasheed said one night.

'What do you mean?'

'I was listening to the radio the other night. Voice of America. I heard an interesting statistic. They said that in Afghanistan one out of four children will die before the age of five. That's what they said. Now, they – What? What? Where are you going? Come back here. Get back here this instant!'

He gave Mariam a bewildered look. 'What's the matter with her?'

That night, Mariam was lying in bed when the bickering started again. It was a hot, dry summer night, typical of the month of *Saratan* in Kabul. Mariam had opened her window, then shut it when no breeze came through to temper the heat, only mosquitoes. She could feel the heat rising from the ground outside, through the wheat brown, splintered planks of the outhouse in the yard, up through the walls and into her room.

Usually, the bickering ran its course after a few minutes, but half an hour passed and not only was it still going on, it was escalating Mariam could hear Rasheed shouting now. The girl's voice, underneath his, was tentative and shrill. Soon the baby was wailing.

Then Mariam heard their door open violently.

In the morning, she would find the doorknob's circular impression in the hallway wall. She was sitting up in bed when her own door slammed open and Rasheed came through.

He was wearing white underpants and a matching undershirt, stained yellow in the under-arms with sweat. On his feet he wore flip-flops. He held a belt in his hand, the brown leather one he'd bought for his *nikka* with the girl, and was wrapping the perforated end around his fist.

'It's your doing. I know it is,' he snarled, advancing on her.

Mariam slid out of her bed and began back-pedaling. Her arms instinctively crossed over her chest, where he often struck her first.

'What are you talking about?' she stammered.

'Her denying me. You're teaching her to.'

Over the years, Mariam had learned to harden herself against his scorn and reproach, his ridi-culing and reprimanding. But this fear she had no control over. All these years and still she shivered with fright when he was like this, sneering, tight-ening the belt around his fist, the creaking of the leather, the glint in his bloodshot eyes. It was the fear of the goat, released in the tiger's cage, when the tiger first looks up from its paws, begins to growl.

Now the girl was in the room, her eyes wide, her face contorted.

'I should have known that you'd corrupt her,' Rasheed spat at Mariam. He swung the belt, testing it against his own thigh. The buckle jingled loudly.

'Stop it, *bas*!' the girl said. 'Rasheed, you can't do this.'

'Go back to the room.'

Mariam backpedaled again.

'No! Don't do this!'

'Now!'

Rasheed raised the belt again and this time came at Mariam.

Then an astonishing thing happened: The girl lunged at him. She grabbed his arm with both hands and tried to drag him down, but she could do no more than dangle from it. She did succeed in slowing Rasheed's progress toward Mariam.

'Let go!' Rasheed cried.

'You win. You win. Don't do this. Please, Rasheed, no beating! Please don't do this.'

They struggled like this, the girl hanging on, pleading, Rasheed trying to shake her off, keeping his eyes on Mariam, who was too stunned to do anything.

In the end, Mariam knew that there would be no beating, not that night. He'd made his point. He stayed that way a few moments longer, arm raised, chest heaving, a fine sheen of sweat filming his brow. Slowly, Rasheed lowered his arm. The girl's feet touched ground and still she wouldn't let go, as if she didn't trust him. He had to yank his arm free of her grip.

'I'm on to you,' he said, slinging the belt over

his shoulder. 'I'm on to you both. I won't be made an *ahmaq*, a fool, in my own house.'

He threw Mariam one last, murderous stare, and gave the girl a shove in the back on the way out.

When she heard their door close, Mariam climbed back into bed, buried her head beneath the pillow, and waited for the shaking to stop.

Three times that night, Mariam was awakened from sleep. The first time, it was the rumble of rockets in the west, coming from the direction of Karteh-Char. The second time, it was the baby crying downstairs, the girl's shushing, the clatter of spoon against milk bottle. Finally, it was thirst that pulled her out of bed.

Downstairs, the living room was dark, save for a bar of moonlight spilling through the window. Mariam could hear the buzzing of a fly some-where, could make out the outline of the cast-iron stove in the corner, its pipe jutting up, then making a sharp angle just below the ceiling.

On her way to the kitchen, Mariam nearly tripped over something. There was a shape at her feet. When her eyes adjusted, she made out the girl and her baby lying on the floor on top of a quilt.

The girl was sleeping on her side, snoring. The baby was awake. Mariam lit the kerosene lamp on the table and hunkered down. In the light, she had her first real close-up look at the baby, the tuft of dark hair, the thick-lashed hazel eyes, the pink cheeks, and lips the color of ripe pomegranate.

Mariam had the impression that the baby too was examining her. She was lying on her back, her head tilted sideways, looking at Mariam intently with a mixture of amusement, confusion, and suspicion. Mariam wondered if her face might frighten her, but then the baby squealed happily and Mariam knew that a favorable judgment had been passed on her behalf.

'*Shh*,' Mariam whispered. 'You'll wake up your mother, half deaf as she is.'

The baby's hand balled into a fist. It rose, fell, found a spastic path to her mouth. Around a mouthful of her own hand, the baby gave Mariam a grin, little bubbles of spittle shining on her lips.

'Look at you. What a sorry sight you are, dressed like a damn boy. And all bundled up in this heat. No wonder you're still awake.'

Mariam pulled the blanket off the baby, was horrified to find a second one beneath, clucked her tongue, and pulled that one off too. The baby giggled with relief. She flapped her arms like a bird.

'Better, *nay*?'

As Mariam was pulling back, the baby grabbed her pinkie. The tiny fingers curled themselves tightly around it. They felt warm and soft, moist with drool.

'*Gunuh*,' the baby said.

'All right, *bas*, let go.'

The baby hung on, kicked her legs again.

Mariam pulled her finger free. The baby smiled

278

and made a series of gurgling sounds. The knuckles went back to the mouth.

'What are you so happy about? Huh? What are you smiling at? You're not so clever as your mother says. You have a brute for a father and a fool for a mother. You wouldn't smile so much if you knew. No you wouldn't. Go to sleep, now. Go on.'

Mariam rose to her feet and walked a few steps before the baby started making the *eh, eh, eh* sounds that Mariam knew signaled the onset of a hearty cry. She retraced her steps.

'What is it? What do you want from me?'

The baby grinned toothlessly.

Mariam sighed. She sat down and let her finger be grabbed, looked on as the baby squeaked, as she flexed her plump legs at the hips and kicked air. Mariam sat there, watching, until the baby stopped moving and began snoring softly.

Outside, mockingbirds were singing blithely, and, once in a while, when the songsters took flight, Mariam could see their wings catching the phosphorescent blue of moonlight beaming through the clouds. And though her throat was parched with thirst and her feet burned with pins and needles, it was a long time before Mariam gently freed her finger from the baby's grip and got up.

# CHAPTER 34

# LAILA

Of all earthly pleasures, Laila's favorite was lying next to Aziza, her baby's face so close that she could watch her big pupils dilate and shrink. Laila loved running her finger over Aziza's pleasing, soft skin, over the dimpled knuckles, the folds of fat at her elbows. Sometimes she lay Aziza down on her chest and whispered into the soft crown of her head things about Tariq, the father who would always be a stranger to Aziza, whose face Aziza would never know. Laila told her of his aptitude for solving riddles, his trickery and mischief, his easy laugh.

'He had the prettiest lashes, thick like yours. A good chin, a fine nose, and a round forehead. Oh, your father was handsome, Aziza. He was perfect. Perfect, like you are.'

But she was careful never to mention him by name.

Sometimes she caught Rasheed looking at Aziza in the most peculiar way. The other night, sitting on the bedroom floor, where he was shaving a corn from his foot, he said quite casually, 'So what was it like between you two?'

280

Laila had given him a puzzled look, as though she didn't understand.

'Laili and Majnoon. You and the *yaklenga*, the cripple. What was it you had, he and you?'

'He was my friend,' she said, careful that her voice not shift too much in key. She busied herself making a bottle. 'You know that.'

'I don't know *what* I know.' Rasheed deposited the shavings on the windowsill and dropped onto the bed. The springs protested with a loud creak. He splayed his legs, picked at his crotch. 'And as . . . *friends*, did the two of you ever do anything out of order?'

'Out of order?'

Rasheed smiled lightheartedly, but Laila could feel his gaze, cold and watchful. 'Let me see, now. Well, did he ever give you a kiss? Maybe put his hand where it didn't belong?'

Laila winced with, she hoped, an indignant air. She could feel her heart drumming in her throat. 'He was like a *brother* to me.'

'So he was a friend or a brother?'

'Both. He—'

'Which was it?'

'He was like both.'

'But brothers and sisters are creatures of curiosity. Yes. Sometimes a brother lets his sister see his pecker, and a sister will—'

'You sicken me,' Laila said.

'So there was nothing.'

'I don't want to talk about this anymore.'

Rasheed tilted his head, pursed his lips, nodded. 'People gossiped, you know. I remember. They said all sorts of things about you two. But you're saying there was nothing.'

She willed herself to glare at him.

He held her eyes for an excruciatingly long time in an unblinking way that made her knuckles go pale around the milk bottle, and it took all that Laila could muster to not falter.

She shuddered at what he would do if he found out that she had been stealing from him. Every week, since Aziza's birth, she pried his wallet open when he was asleep or in the outhouse and took a single bill. Some weeks, if the wallet was light, she took only a five-afghani bill, or nothing at all, for fear that he would notice. When the wallet was plump, she helped herself to a ten or a twenty, once even risking two twenties. She hid the money in a pouch she'd sewn in the lining of her checkered winter coat.

She wondered what he would do if he knew that she was planning to run away next spring. Next summer at the latest. Laila hoped to have a thousand afghanis or more stowed away, half of which would go to the bus fare from Kabul to Peshawar. She would pawn her wedding ring when the time drew close, as well as the other jewelry that Rasheed had given her the year before when she was still the *malika* of his palace.

'Anyway,' he said at last, fingers drumming his

belly, 'I can't be blamed. I am a husband. These are the things a husband wonders. But he's lucky he died the way he did. Because if he was here now, if I got my hands on him . . .' He sucked through his teeth and shook his head.

'What happened to not speaking ill of the dead?'

'I guess some people can't be dead enough,' he said.

Two days later, Laila woke up in the morning and found a stack of baby clothes, neatly folded, outside her bedroom door. There was a twirl dress with little pink fishes sewn around the bodice, a blue floral wool dress with matching socks and mittens, yellow pajamas with carrot-colored polka dots, and green cotton pants with a dotted ruffle on the cuff.

'There is a rumor,' Rasheed said over dinner that night, smacking his lips, taking no notice of Aziza or the pajamas Laila had put on her, 'that Dostum is going to change sides and join Hekmatyar. Massoud will have his hands full then, fighting those two. And we mustn't forget the Hazaras.' He took a pinch of the pickled eggplant Mariam had made that summer. 'Let's hope it's just that, a rumor. Because if that happens, this war,' he waved one greasy hand, 'will seem like a Friday picnic at Paghman.'

Later, he mounted her and relieved himself with wordless haste, fully dressed save for his *tumban*, not removed but pulled down to the ankles. When the frantic rocking was over, he rolled off her and was asleep in minutes.

Laila slipped out of the bedroom and found Mariam in the kitchen squatting, cleaning a pair of trout. A pot of rice was already soaking beside her. The kitchen smelled like cumin and smoke, browned onions and fish.

Laila sat in a corner and draped her knees with the hem of her dress.

'Thank you,' she said.

Mariam took no notice of her. She finished cutting up the first trout and picked up the second. With a serrated knife, she clipped the fins, then turned the fish over, its underbelly facing her, and sliced it expertly from the tail to the gills. Laila watched her put her thumb into its mouth, just over the lower jaw, push it in, and, in one downward stroke, remove the gills and the entrails.

'The clothes are lovely.'

'I had no use for them,' Mariam muttered. She dropped the fish on a newspaper smudged with slimy, gray juice and sliced off its head. 'It was either your daughter or the moths.'

'Where did you learn to clean fish like that?'

'When I was a little girl, I lived by a stream. I used to catch my own fish.'

'I've never fished.'

'Not much to it. It's mostly waiting.'

Laila watched her cut the gutted trout into thirds. 'Did you sew the clothes yourself?'

Mariam nodded.

'When?'

Mariam rinsed sections of fish in a bowl of water. 'When I was pregnant the first time. Or maybe the second time. Eighteen, nineteen years ago. Long time, anyhow. Like I said, I never had any use for them.'

'You're a really good *khayat*. Maybe you can teach me.'

Mariam placed the rinsed chunks of trout into a clean bowl. Drops of water dripping from her fingertips, she raised her head and looked at Laila, looked at her as if for the first time.

'The other night, when he . . . Nobody's ever stood up for me before,' she said.

Laila examined Mariam's drooping cheeks, the eyelids that sagged in tired folds, the deep lines that framed her mouth – she saw these things as though she too were looking at someone for the first time. And, for the first time, it was not an adversary's face Laila saw but a face of grievances unspoken, burdens gone unprotested, a destiny submitted to and endured. If she stayed, would this be her own face, Laila wondered, twenty years from now?

'I couldn't let him,' Laila said. 'I wasn't raised in a household where people did things like that.'

'*This* is your household now. You ought to get used to it.'

'Not to *that*. I won't.'

'He'll turn on you too, you know,' Mariam said,

wiping her hands dry with a rag. 'Soon enough. And you gave him a daughter. So, you see, your sin is even less forgivable than mine.'

Laila rose to her feet. 'I know it's chilly outside, but what do you say we sinners have us a cup of *chai* in the yard?'

Mariam looked surprised. 'I can't. I still have to cut and wash the beans.'

'I'll help you do it in the morning.'

'And I have to clean up here.'

'We'll do it together. If I'm not mistaken, there's some *halwa* left over. Awfully good with *chai*.'

Mariam put the rag on the counter. Laila sensed anxiety in the way she tugged at her sleeves, adjusted her *hijab*, pushed back a curl of hair.

'The Chinese say it's better to be deprived of food for three days than tea for one.'

Mariam gave a half smile. 'It's a good saying.'

'It is.'

'But I can't stay long.'

'One cup.'

They sat on folding chairs outside and ate *halwa* with their fingers from a common bowl. They had a second cup, and when Laila asked her if she wanted a third Mariam said she did. As gunfire cracked in the hills, they watched the clouds slide over the moon and the last of the season's fireflies charting bright yellow arcs in the dark. And when Aziza woke up crying and Rasheed yelled for Laila to come up and shut her up, a look passed between Laila and Mariam. An unguarded, knowing look. And in this fleeting, wordless exchange with Mariam, Laila knew that they were not enemies any longer.

# CHAPTER 35

# MARIAM

From that night on, Mariam and Laila did their chores together. They sat in the kitchen and rolled dough, chopped green onions, minced garlic, offered bits of cucumber to Aziza, who banged spoons nearby and played with carrots. In the yard, Aziza lay in a wicker bassinet, dressed in layers of clothing, a winter muffler wrapped snugly around her neck. Mariam and Laila kept a watchful eye on her as they did the wash, Mariam's knuckles bumping Laila's as they scrubbed shirts and trousers and diapers.

Mariam slowly grew accustomed to this tentative but pleasant companionship. She was eager for the three cups of *chai* she and Laila would share in the yard, a nightly ritual now. In the mornings, Mariam found herself looking forward to the sound of Laila's cracked slippers slapping the steps as she came down for breakfast and to the tinkle of Aziza's shrill laugh, to the sight of her eight little teeth, the milky scent of her skin. If Laila and Aziza slept in, Mariam became anxious waiting. She washed dishes that didn't need washing. She rearranged cushions in the living room. She dusted clean windowsills. She kept herself occupied until Laila entered the kitchen, Aziza hoisted on her hip.

When Aziza first spotted Mariam in the morning, her eyes always sprang open, and she began mewling and squirming in her mother's grip. She thrust her arms toward Mariam, demanding to be held, her tiny hands opening and closing urgently, on her face a look of both adoration and quivering anxiety.

'What a scene you're making,' Laila would say, releasing her to crawl toward Mariam. 'What a scene! Calm down. Khala Mariam isn't going anywhere. There she is, your aunt. See? Go on, now.'

As soon as she was in Mariam's arms, Aziza's thumb shot into her mouth and she buried her face in Mariam's neck.

Mariam bounced her stiffly, a half-bewildered, half-grateful smile on her lips. Mariam had never before been wanted like this. Love had never been declared to her so guilelessly, so unreservedly.

Aziza made Mariam want to weep.

'Why have you pinned your little heart to an old, ugly hag like me?' Mariam would murmur into Aziza's hair. 'Huh? I am nobody, don't you see? A *dehati*. What have I got to give you?'

But Aziza only muttered contentedly and dug her face in deeper. And when she did that, Mariam swooned. Her eyes watered. Her heart took flight. And she marveled at how, after all these years of rattling loose, she had found in this little creature the first true connection in her life of false, failed connections.

Early the following year, in January 1994, Dostum *did* switch sides. He joined Gulbuddin Hekmatyar, and took up position near Bala Hissar, the old citadel walls that loomed over the city from the Koh-e-Shirdawaza mountains. Together, they fired on Massoud and Rabbani forces at the Ministry of Defense and the Presidential Palace. From either side of the Kabul River, they released rounds of artillery at each other. The streets became littered with bodies, glass, and crumpled chunks of metal. There was looting, murder, and, increasingly, rape, which was used to intimidate civilians and reward militiamen. Mariam heard of women who were killing themselves out of fear of being raped, and of men who, in the name of honor, would kill their wives or daughters if they'd been raped by the militia.

Aziza shrieked at the thumping of mortars. To distract her, Mariam arranged grains of rice on the floor, in the shape of a house or a rooster or a star, and let Aziza scatter them. She drew elephants for Aziza the way Jalil had shown her, in one stroke, without ever lifting the tip of the pen.

Rasheed said civilians were getting killed daily, by the dozens. Hospitals and stores holding medical supplies were getting shelled. Vehicles carrying emergency food supplies were being barred from entering the city, he said, raided, shot at. Mariam wondered if there was fighting like this in Herat too, and, if so, how Mullah Faizullah was coping, if he was still alive, and Bibi jo too, with all her sons, brides, and grandchildren. And, of course, Jalil. Was he hiding out, Mariam wondered, as she was? Or had he taken his wives and children and fled the country? She hoped Jalil was somewhere safe, that he'd managed to get away from all of this killing.

For a week, the fighting forced even Rasheed to stay home. He locked the door to the yard, set booby traps, locked the front door too and barricaded it with the couch. He paced the house, smoking, peering out the window, cleaning his gun, loading and loading it again. Twice, he fired his weapon into the street claiming he'd seen someone trying to climb the wall.

'They're forcing young boys to join,' he said. 'The Mujahideen are. In plain daylight, at gunpoint. They drag boys right off the streets. And when soldiers from a rival militia capture these boys, they torture them. I heard they electrocute them – it's what I heard – that they crush their balls with pliers. They make the boys lead them to their homes. Then they break in, kill their fathers, rape their sisters and mothers.'

He waved his gun over his head. 'Let's see them try to break into my house. I'll crush *their* balls! I'll blow their heads off! Do you know how lucky you two are to have a man who's not afraid of Shaitan himself?'

He looked down at the ground, noticed Aziza at his feet. 'Get off my heels!' he snapped, making a shooing motion with his gun. 'Stop following me! And you can stop twirling your wrists like that. I'm not picking you up. Go on! Go on before you get stepped on.'

Aziza flinched. She crawled back to Mariam, looking bruised and confused. In Mariam's lap, she sucked her thumb cheerlessly and watched Rasheed in a sullen, pensive way. Occasionally, she looked up, Mariam imagined, with a look of wanting to be reassured.

But when it came to fathers, Mariam had no assurances to give.

Mariam was relieved when the fighting subsided again, mostly because they no longer had to be cooped up with Rasheed, with his sour temper infecting the household. And he'd frightened her badly waving that loaded gun near Aziza.

One day that winter, Laila asked to braid Mariam's hair.

Mariam sat still and watched Laila's slim fingers in the mirror tighten her plaits, Laila's face scrunched in concentration. Aziza was curled up asleep on the floor. Tucked under her arm was a doll Mariam had hand-stitched for her. Mariam had stuffed it with beans, made it a dress with tea-dyed fabric and a necklace with tiny empty thread spools through which she'd threaded a string.

Then Aziza passed gas in her sleep. Laila began to laugh, and Mariam joined in. They laughed like this, at each other's reflection in the mirror, their eyes tearing, and the moment was so natural, so effortless, that suddenly Mariam started telling her about Jalil, and Nana, and the *jinn*. Laila stood with her hands idle on Mariam's shoulders, eyes locked on Mariam's face in the mirror. Out the words came, like blood gushing from an artery. Mariam told her about Bibi jo, Mullah Faizullah, the humiliating trek to Jalil's house, Nana's suicide. She told about Jalil's wives, and the hurried *nikka* with Rasheed, the trip to Kabul, her pregnancies, the endless cycles of hope and disappointment, Rasheed's turning on her.

After, Laila sat at the foot of Mariam's chair. Absently, she removed a scrap of lint entangled in Aziza's hair. A silence ensued.

'I have something to tell you too,' Laila said.

Mariam did not sleep that night. She sat in bed, watched the snow falling soundlessly.

Seasons had come and gone; presidents in Kabul had been inaugurated and murdered; an empire had been defeated; old wars had ended and new ones had broken out. But Mariam had hardly noticed, hardly cared. She had passed these years in a distant corner of her mind. A dry, barren field, out beyond wish and lament, beyond dream and disillusionment. There, the future did not matter. And the past held only this wisdom: that love was a damaging mistake, and its accomplice, hope, a treacherous illusion. And whenever those twin poisonous flowers began to sprout in the parched land of that field, Mariam uprooted them. She uprooted them and ditched them before they took hold.

But somehow, over these last months, Laila and Aziza – a *harami* like herself, as it turned out – had become extensions of her, and now, without them, the life Mariam had tolerated for so long suddenly seemed intolerable.

*We're leaving this spring, Aziza and I. Come with us, Mariam.*

The years had not been kind to Mariam. But perhaps, she thought, there were kinder years waiting still. A new life, a life in which she would find the blessings that Nana had said a *harami* like her would never see. Two new flowers had unexpectedly sprouted in her life, and, as Mariam watched the snow coming down, she pictured Mullah Faizullah twirling his *tasbeh* beads, leaning in and whispering to her in his soft, tremulous voice, *But it is God Who has planted them, Mariam jo. And it is His will that you tend to them. It is His will, my girl.*

# CHAPTER 36

# LAILA

As daylight steadily bleached darkness from the sky that spring morning of 1994, Laila became certain that Rasheed knew. That, any moment now, he would drag her out of bed and ask whether she'd really taken him for such a khar, such a donkey, that he wouldn't find out. But *azan* rang out, and then the morning sun was falling flat on the rooftops and the roosters were crowing and nothing out of the ordinary happened.

She could hear him now in the bathroom, the tapping of his razor against the edge of the basin. Then downstairs, moving about, heating tea. The keys jingled. Now he was crossing the yard, walking his bicycle.

Laila peered through a crack in the living-room curtains. She watched him pedal away, a big man on a small bicycle, the morning sun glaring off the handlebars.

'Laila?'

Mariam was in the doorway. Laila could tell that she hadn't slept either. She wondered if Mariam too had been seized all night by bouts of euphoria and attacks of mouth-drying anxiety.

'We'll leave in half an hour,' Laila said.

In the backseat of the taxi, they did not speak. Aziza sat on Mariam's lap, clutching her doll, looking with wide-eyed puzzlement at the city speeding by.

'*Ona!*' she cried, pointing to a group of little girls skipping rope. 'Mayam! *Ona.*'

Everywhere she looked, Laila saw Rasheed. She spotted him coming out of barbershops with windows the color of coal dust, from tiny booths that sold partridges, from battered, open-fronted stores packed with old tires piled from floor to ceiling.

She sank lower in her seat.

Beside her, Mariam was muttering a prayer. Laila wished she could see her face, but Mariam was in burqa – they both were – and all she could see was the glitter of her eyes through the grid.

This was Laila's first time out of the house in weeks, discounting the short trip to the pawnshop the day before – where she had pushed her wedding ring across a glass counter, where she'd walked out thrilled by the finality of it, knowing there was no going back.

All around her now, Laila saw the consequences of the recent fighting whose sounds she'd heard from the house. Homes that lay in roofless ruins of brick and jagged stone, gouged buildings with fallen beams poking through the holes, the charred, mangled husks of cars, upended, sometimes stacked on top of each other, walls pocked by holes of every conceivable caliber, shattered glass everywhere. She saw a funeral procession marching toward a mosque, a black-clad old woman at the rear tearing at her hair. They passed a cemetery littered with rock-piled graves and ragged *shaheed* flags fluttering in the breeze.

Laila reached across the suitcase, wrapped her fingers around the softness of her daughter's arm.

At the Lahore Gate bus station, near Pol Mahmood Khan in East Kabul, a row of buses sat idling along the curbside. Men in turbans were busy heaving bundles and crates onto bus tops, securing suitcases down with ropes. Inside the station, men stood in a long line at the ticket booth. Burqa-clad women stood in groups and chatted, their belongings piled at their feet. Babies were bounced, children scolded for straying too far.

Mujahideen militiamen patrolled the station and the curbside, barking curt orders here and there. They wore boots, *pakols*, dusty green fatigues. They all carried Kalashnikovs.

Laila felt watched. She looked no one in the face, but she felt as though every person in this place knew, that they were looking on with disapproval at what she and Mariam were doing.

'Do you see anybody?' Laila asked.

Mariam shifted Aziza in her arms. 'I'm looking.'

This, Laila had known, would be the first risky

part, finding a man suitable to pose with them as a family member. The freedoms and opportunities that women had enjoyed between 1978 and 1992 were a thing of the past now – Laila could still remember Babi saying of those years of communist rule. *It's good time to be a woman in Afghanistan, Laila.* Since the Mujahideen takeover in April 1992, Afghanistan's name had been changed to the Islamic State of Afghanistan. The Supreme Court under Rabbani was filled now with hardliner mullahs who did away with the communist-era decrees that empowered women and instead passed rulings based on Shari'a, strict Islamic laws that ordered women to cover, forbade their travel without a male relative, punished adultery with stoning. Even if the actual enforcement of these laws was sporadic at best. *But they'd enforce them on us more*, Laila had said to Mariam, *if they weren't so busy killing each other. And us.*

The second risky part of this trip would come when they actually arrived in Pakistan. Already burdened with nearly two million Afghan refugees, Pakistan had closed its borders to Afghans in January of that year. Laila had heard that only those with visas would be admitted. But the border was porous – always had been – and Laila knew that thousands of Afghans were still crossing into Pakistan either with bribes or by proving humanitarian grounds – and there were always smugglers who could be hired. *We'll find a way when we get there*, she'd told Mariam.

'How about him?' Mariam said, motioning with her chin.

'He doesn't look trustworthy.'

'And him?'

'Too old. And he's traveling with two other men.'

Eventually, Laila found him sitting outside on a park bench, with a veiled woman at his side and a little boy in a skullcap, roughly Aziza's age, bouncing on his knees. He was tall and slender, bearded, wearing an open-collared shirt and a modest gray coat with missing buttons.

'Wait here,' she said to Mariam. Walking away, she again heard Mariam muttering a prayer.

When Laila approached the young man, he looked up, shielded the sun from his eyes with a hand.

'Forgive me, brother, but are you going to Peshawar?'

'Yes,' he said, squinting.

'I wonder if you can help us. Can you do us a favor?'

He passed the boy to his wife. He and Laila stepped away.

'What is it, *hamshira?*'

She was encouraged to see that he had soft eyes, a kind face.

She told him the story that she and Mariam had agreed on. She was a *biwa*, she said, a widow. She and her mother and daughter had no one left in Kabul. They were going to Peshawar to stay with her uncle.

'You want to come with my family,' the young man said.

'I know it's *zahmat* for you. But you look like a decent brother, and I—'

'Don't worry, *hamshira*. I understand. It's no trouble. Let me go and buy your tickets.'

'Thank you, brother. This is *sawab*, a good deed. God will remember.'

She fished the envelope from her pocket beneath the burqa and passed it to him. In it was eleven hundred afghanis, or about half of the money she'd stashed over the past year plus the sale of the ring. He slipped the envelope in his trouser pocket.

'Wait here.'

She watched him enter the station. He returned half an hour later.

'It's best I hold on to your tickets,' he said. The bus leaves in one hour, at eleven. We'll all board together. My name is Wakil. If they ask – and they shouldn't – I'll tell them you're my cousin.'

Laila gave him their names, and he said he would remember.

'Stay close,' he said.

They sat on the bench adjacent to Wakil and his family's. It was a sunny, warm morning, the sky streaked only by a few wispy clouds hovering in the distance over the hills. Mariam began feeding Aziza a few of the crackers she'd remembered to bring in their rush to pack. She offered one to Laila.

'I'll throw up,' Laila laughed. 'I'm too excited.'

'Me too.'

'Thank you, Mariam.'

'For what?'

'For this. For coming with us,' Laila said. 'I don't think I could do this alone.'

'You won't have to.'

'We're going to be all right, aren't we, Mariam, where we're going?'

Mariam's hand slid across the bench and closed over hers. 'The Koran says Allah is the East and the West, therefore wherever you turn there is Allah's purpose.'

'*Bov!*' Aziza cried, pointing to a bus. 'Mayam, *bov*!'

'I see it, Aziza jo,' Mariam said. 'That's right, *bov*. Soon we're all going to ride on a *bov*. Oh, the things you're going to see.'

Laila smiled. She watched a carpenter in his shop across the street sawing wood, sending chips flying. She watched the cars bolting past, their windows coated with soot and grime. She watched the buses growling idly at the curb, with peacocks, lions, rising suns, and glittery swords painted on their sides.

In the warmth of the morning sun, Laila felt giddy and bold. She had another of those little sparks of euphoria, and when a stray dog with yellow eyes limped by, Laila leaned forward and pet its back.

A few minutes before eleven, a man with a bullhorn called for all passengers to Peshawar to beging boarding. The bus doors opened with

301

a violent hydraulic hiss. A parade of travelers rushed toward it, scampering past each other to squeeze through.

Wakil motioned toward Laila as he picked up his son.

'We're going,' Laila said.

Wakil led the way. As they approached the bus, Laila saw faces appear in the windows, noses and palms pressed to the glass. All around them, farewells were yelled.

A young militia soldier was checking tickets at the bus door.

'*Bov!*' Aziza cried.

Wakil handed tickets to the soldier, who tore them in half and handed them back. Wakil let his wife board first. Laila saw a look pass between Wakil and the militiaman. Wakil, perched on the first step of the bus, leaned down and said something in his ear. The militiaman nodded.

Laila's heart plummeted.

'You two, with the child, step aside,' the soldier said.

Laila pretended not to hear. She went to climb the steps, but he grabbed her by the shoulder and roughly pulled her out of the line.

'You too,' he called to Mariam. 'Hurry up! You're holding up the line.'

'What's the problem, brother?' Laila said through numb lips. 'We have tickets. Didn't my cousin hand them to you?'

He made a *Shh* motion with his finger and spoke

in a low voice to another guard. The second guard, a rotund fellow with a scar down his right cheek, nodded.

'Follow me,' this one said to Laila.

'We have to board this bus,' Laila cried, aware that her voice was shaking. 'We have tickets. Why are you doing this?'

'You're not going to get on this bus. You might as well accept that. You will follow me. Unless you want your little girl to see you dragged.'

As they were led to a truck, Laila looked over her shoulder and spotted Wakil's boy at the rear of the bus. The boy saw her too and waved happily.

At the police station at Torabaz Khan Intersection, they were made to sit apart, on opposite ends of a long, crowded corridor, between them a desk, behind which a man smoked one cigarette after another and clacked occasionally on a typewriter. Three hours passed this way. Aziza tottered from Laila to Mariam, then back. She played with a paper clip that the man at the desk gave her. She finished the crackers. Eventually, she fell asleep in Mariam's lap.

At around three o'clock, Laila was taken to an interview room. Mariam was made to wait with Aziza in the corridor.

The man sitting on the other side of the desk in the interview room was in his thirties and wore civilian clothes – black suit, tie, black loafers. He had a neatly trimmed beard, short hair, and eyebrows that met. He stared at Laila, bouncing a pencil by the eraser end on the desk.

'We know,' he began, clearing his throat and politely covering his mouth with a fist, 'that you have already told one lie today, *hamshira*. The young man at the station was not your cousin. He told us as much himself. The question is whether you will tell more lies today. Personally, I advise you against it.'

'We were going to stay with my uncle,' Laila said. 'That's the truth.'

The policeman nodded. 'The *hamshira* in the corridor, she's your mother?'

'Yes.'

'She has a Herati accent. You don't.'

'She was raised in Herat, I was born here in Kabul.'

'Of course. And you are widowed? You said you were. My condolences. And this uncle, this *kaka*, where does he live?'

'In Peshawar.'

'Yes, you said that.' He licked the point of his pencil and poised it over a blank sheet of paper. 'But where in Peshawar? Which neighborhood, please? Street name, sector number.'

Laila tried to push back the bubble of panic that was coming up her chest. She gave him the name of the only street she knew in Peshawar – she'd heard it mentioned once, at the party Mammy had thrown when the Mujahideen had first come to Kabul – 'Jamrud Road.'

'Oh, yes. Same street as the Pearl Continental Hotel. He might have mentioned it.'

Laila seized this opportunity and said he had. 'That very same street, yes.'

'Except the hotel is on Khyber Road.'

Laila could hear Aziza crying in the corridor. 'My daughter's frightened. May I get her, brother?'

'I prefer "Officer." And you'll be with her shortly. Do you have a telephone number for this uncle?'

'I do. I did. I . . .' Even with the burqa between them, Laila was not buffered from his penetrating eyes. 'I'm so upset, I seem to have forgotten it.'

He sighed through his nose. He asked for the uncle's name, his wife's name. How many children did he have? What were their names? Where did he work? How old was he? His questions left Laila flustered.

He put down his pencil, laced his fingers together, and leaned forward the way parents do when they want to convey something to a toddler. 'You do realize, *hamshira,* that it is a crime for a woman to run away. We see a lot of it. Women traveling alone, claiming their husbands have died. Sometimes they're telling the truth, most times not. You can be imprisoned for running away, I assume you understand that, *nay?*'

'Let us go, Officer . . .' She read the name on his lapel tag. 'Officer Rahman. Honor the meaning of your name and show compassion. What does it matter to you to let a mere two women go? What's the harm in releasing us? We are not criminals.'

'I can't.'

'I beg you, please.'

305

'It's a matter of *qanoon, hamshira*, a matter of law,' Rahman said, injecting his voice with a grave, self-important tone. 'It is my responsibility, you see, to maintain order.'

In spite of her distraught state, Laila almost laughed. She was stunned that he'd used that word in the face of all that the Mujahideen factions had done – the murders, the lootings, the rapes, the tortures, the executions, the bombings, the tens of thousands of rockets they had fired at each other, heedless of all the innocent people who would die in the cross fire. *Order.* But she bit her tongue.

'If you send us back,' she said instead, slowly, 'there is no saying what he will do to us.'

She could see the effort it took him to keep his eyes from shifting. 'What a man does in his home is his business.'

'What about the law, *then*, Officer Rahman?' Tears of rage stung her eyes. 'Will you be there to maintain order?'

'As a matter of policy, we do not interfere with private family matters, *hamshira.*'

'Of course you don't. When it benefits the man. And isn't this a "private family matter," as you say? Isn't it?'

He pushed back from his desk and stood up, straightened his jacket. 'I believe this interview is finished. I must say, *hamshira*, that you have made a very poor case for yourself. Very poor indeed. Now, if you would wait outside I will have a few words with your . . . whoever she is.'

306

Laila began to protest, then to yell, and he had to summon the help of two more men to have her dragged out of his office.

Mariam's interview lasted only a few minutes. When she came out, she looked shaken.

'He asked so many questions,' she said. 'I'm sorry, Laila jo. I am not smart like you. He asked so many questions, I didn't know the answers. I'm sorry.'

'It's not your fault, Mariam,' Laila said weakly. 'It's mine. It's all my fault. Everything is my fault.'

It was past six o'clock when the police car pulled up in front of the house. Laila and Mariam were made to wait in the backseat, guarded by a Mujahid soldier in the passenger seat. The driver was the one who got out of the car, who knocked on the door, who spoke to Rasheed. It was he who motioned for them to come.

'Welcome home,' the man in the front seat said, lighting a cigarette.

'You,' he said to Mariam. 'You wait here.'

Mariam quietly took a seat on the couch.

'You two, upstairs.'

Rasheed grabbed Laila by the elbow and pushed her up the steps. He was still wearing the shoes he wore to work, hadn't yet changed to his flip-flops, taken off his watch, hadn't even shed his coat yet. Laila pictured him as he must have been an hour, or maybe minutes, earlier, rushing from one room to another, slamming doors, furious and incredulous, cursing under his breath.

At the top of the stairs, Laila turned to him.

'She didn't want to do it,' she said. 'I made her do it. She didn't want to go—'

Laila didn't see the punch coming. One moment she was talking and the next she was on all fours, wide-eyed and red-faced, trying to draw a breath. It was as if a car had hit her at full speed, in the tender place between the lower tip of the breast-bone and the belly button. She realized she had dropped Aziza, that Aziza was screaming. She tried to breathe again and could only make a husky, choking sound. Dribble hung from her mouth.

Then she was being dragged by the hair. She saw Aziza lifted, saw her sandals slip off, her tiny feet kicking. Hair was ripped from Laila's scalp, and her eyes watered with pain. She saw his foot kick open the door to Mariam's room, saw Aziza flung onto the bed. He let go of Laila's hair, and she felt the toe of his shoe connect with her left buttock. She howled with pain as he slammed the door shut. A key rattled in the lock.

Aziza was still screaming. Laila lay curled up on the floor, gasping. She pushed herself up on her hands, crawled to where Aziza lay on the bed. She reached for her daughter.

Downstairs, the beating began. To Laila, the sounds she heard were those of a methodical, familiar proceeding. There was no cursing, no screaming, no pleading, no surprised yelps, only the systematic business of beating and being beaten, the *thump, thump* of something solid repeatedly striking flesh, something, someone, hitting a wall with a thud, cloth ripping. Now and then, Laila heard running footsteps, a wordless chase, furniture turning over, glass shattering, then the thumping once more.

Laila took Aziza in her arms. A warmth spread down the front of her dress when Aziza's bladder let go.

Downstairs, the running and chasing finally stopped. There was a sound now like a wooden club repeatedly slapping a side of beef.

Laila rocked Aziza until the sounds stopped, and, when she heard the screen door creak open and slam shut, she lowered Aziza to the ground and peeked out the window. She saw Rasheed leading Mariam across the yard by the nape of her neck. Mariam was barefoot and doubled over. There was blood on his hands, blood on Mariam's face, her hair, down her neck and back. Her shirt had been ripped down the front.

'I'm so sorry, Mariam,' Laila cried into the glass.

She watched him shove Mariam into the toolshed. He went in, came out with a hammer and several long planks of wood. He shut the double doors to the shed, took a key from his pocket, worked the padlock. He tested the doors, then went around the back of the shed and fetched a ladder.

A few minutes later, his face was in Laila's

window, nails tucked in the corner of his mouth. His hair was disheveled. There was a swath of blood on his brow. At the sight of him, Aziza shrieked and buried her face in Laila's armpit.

Rasheed began nailing boards across the window.

The dark was total, impenetrable and constant, without layer or texture. Rasheed had filled the cracks between the boards with something, put a large and immovable object at the foot of the door so no light came from under it. Something had been stuffed in the keyhole.

Laila found it impossible to tell the passage of time with her eyes, so she did it with her good ear. *Azan* and crowing roosters signaled morning. The sounds of plates clanking in the kitchen downstairs, the radio playing, meant evening.

The first day, they groped and fumbled for each other in the dark. Laila couldn't see Aziza when she cried, when she went crawling.

'*Aishee*,' Aziza mewled. '*Aishee*.'

'Soon.' Laila kissed her daughter, aiming for the forehead, finding the crown of her head instead. 'We'll have milk soon. You just be patient. Be a good, patient little girl for Mammy, and I'll get you some *aishee*.'

Laila sang her a few songs.

*Azan* rang out a second time and still Rasheed had not given them any food, and, worse, no water. That day, a thick, suffocating heat fell on them. The room turned into a pressure cooker. Laila dragged a dry tongue over her lips, thinking of the well outside, the water cold and fresh. Aziza kept crying, and Laila noticed with alarm that when she wiped her cheeks her hands came back dry. She stripped the clothes off Aziza, tried to find something to fan her with, settled for blowing on her until she became light-headed. Soon, Aziza stopped crawling around. She slipped in and out of sleep.

Several times that day, Laila banged her fists against the walls, used up her energy screaming for help, hoping that a neighbor would hear. But no one came, and her shrieking only frightened Aziza, who began to cry again, a weak, croaking sound. Laila slid to the ground. She thought guiltily of Mariam, beaten and bloodied, locked in this heat in the toolshed.

Laila fell asleep at some point, her body baking in the heat. She had a dream that she and Aziza had run into Tariq. He was across a crowded street from them, beneath the awning of a tailor's shop. He was sitting on his haunches and sampling from a crate of figs. *That's your father*, Laila said. *That man there, you see him? He's your real* baba. She called his name, but the street noise drowned her voice, and Tariq didn't hear.

She woke up to the whistling of rockets streaking overhead. Somewhere, the sky she couldn't see erupted with blasts and the long, frantic hammering of machine-gun fire. Laila closed her eyes. She woke again to Rasheed's heavy footsteps

311

in the hallway. She dragged herself to the door, slapped her palms against it.

'Just one glass, Rasheed. Not for me. Do it for her. You don't want her blood on your hands.'

He walked past.

She began to plead with him. She begged for forgiveness, made promises. She cursed him.

His door closed. The radio came on.

The muezzin called *azan* a third time. Again the heat. Aziza became even more listless. She stopped crying, stopped moving altogether.

Laila-put her ear over Aziza's mouth, dreading each time that she would not hear the shallow whooshing of breath. Even this simple act of lifting herself made her head swim. She fell asleep, had dreams she could not remember. When she woke up, she checked on Aziza, felt the parched cracks of her lips, the faint pulse at her neck, lay down again. They would die here, of that Laila was sure now, but what she really dreaded was that she would outlast Aziza, who was young and brittle. How much more could Aziza take? Aziza would die in this heat, and Laila would have to lie beside her stiffening little body and wait for her own death. Again she fell asleep. Woke up. Fell asleep. The line between dream and wakefulness blurred.

It wasn't roosters or *azan* that woke her up again but the sound of something heavy being dragged. She heard a rattling. Suddenly, the room was flooded with light. Her eyes screamed in protest. Laila raised her head, winced, and shielded her eyes. Through the cracks between her fingers, she saw a big, blurry silhouette standing in a rectangle of light. The silhouette moved. Now there was a shape crouching beside her, looming over her, and a voice by her ear.

'You try this again and I will find you. I swear on the Prophet's name that I will find you. And, when I do, there isn't a court in this godforsaken country that will hold me accountable for what I will do. To Mariam first, then to her, and you last. I'll make you watch. You understand me? *I'll make you watch.*'

And, with that, he left the room. But not before delivering a kick to the flank that would have Laila pissing blood for days.

# CHAPTER 37

# MARIAM

## SEPTEMBER 1996

T wo and a half years later, Mariam awoke
on the morning of September 27 to the
sounds of shouting and whistling, fire-
crackers and music. She ran to the living room,
found Laila already at the window, Aziza mounted
on her shoulders. Laila turned and smiled.

'The Taliban are here,' she said.

Mariam had first heard of the Taliban two years
before, in October 1994, when Rasheed had
brought home news that they had overthrown the
warlords in Kandahar and taken the city. They
were a guerrilla force, he said, made up of young
Pashtun men whose families had fled to Pakistan
during the war against the Soviets. Most of them
had been raised – some even born – in refugee
camps along the Pakistani border, and in Pakistani
madrasas, where they were schooled in *Shari'a* by
mullahs. Their leader was a mysterious, illiterate,
one-eyed recluse named Mullah Omar, who,
Rasheed said with some amusement, called

himself *Ameer-ul-Mumineen*, Leader of the Faithful.

'It's true that these boys have no *risha*, no roots,' Rasheed said, addressing neither Mariam nor Laila. Ever since the failed escape, two and a half years ago, Mariam knew that she and Laila had become one and the same being to him, equally wretched, equally deserving of his distrust, his disdain and disregard. When he spoke, Mariam had the sense that he was having a conversation with himself, or with some invisible presence in the room, who, unlike her and Laila, was worthy of his opinions.

'They may have no past,' he said, smoking and looking up at the ceiling. 'They may know nothing of the world or this country's history. Yes. And, compared to them, Mariam here might as well be a university professor. Ha! All true. But look around you. What do you see? Corrupt, greedy Mujahideen commanders, armed to the teeth, rich off heroin, declaring jihad on one another and killing everyone in between – that's what. At least the Taliban are pure and incorruptible. At least they're decent Muslim boys. *Wallah*, when they come, they will clean up this place. They'll bring peace and order. People won't get shot anymore going out for milk. No more rockets! Think of it.'

For two years now, the Taliban had been making their way toward Kabul, taking cities from the Mujahideen, ending factional war wherever they'd settled. They had captured the Hazara commander

Abdul Ali Mazari and executed him. For months, they'd settled in the southern outskirts of Kabul, firing on the city, exchanging rockets with Ahmad Shah Massoud. Earlier in that September of 1996, they had captured the cities of Jalalabad and Sarobi.

The Taliban had one thing the Mujahideen did not, Rasheed said. They were united.

'Let them come,' he said. 'I, for one, will shower them with rose petals.'

They went out that day, the four of them, Rasheed leading them from one bus to the next, to greet their new world, their new leaders. In every battered neighborhood, Mariam found people materializing from the rubble and moving into the streets. She saw an old woman wasting handfuls of rice, tossing it at passersby, a drooping, tooth-less smile on her face. Two men were hugging by the remains of a gutted building, in the sky above them the whistle, hiss, and pop of a few fire-crackers set off by boys perched on rooftops. The national anthem played on cassette decks, compet-ing with the honking of cars.

'Look, Mayam!' Aziza pointed to a group of boys running down Jadeh Maywand. They were pounding their fists into the air and dragging rusty cans tied to strings. They were yelling that Massoud and Rabbani had withdrawn from Kabul.

Everywhere, there were shouts: *Allah-u-akbar!*

Mariam saw a bedsheet hanging from a window on Jadeh Maywand. On it, someone had painted three words in big, black letters: ZENDA BAAD TALIBAN! Long live the Taliban!

As they walked the streets, Mariam spotted more signs – painted on windows, nailed to doors, billowing from car antennas – that proclaimed the same.

Mariam saw her first of the Taliban later that day, at Pashtunistan Square, with Rasheed, Laila, and Aziza. A melee of people had gathered there. Mariam saw people craning their necks, people crowded around the blue fountain in the center of the square, people perched on its dry bed. They were trying to get a view of the end of the square, near the old Khyber Restaurant.

Rasheed used his size to push and shove past the onlookers, and led them to where someone was speaking through a loudspeaker.

When Aziza saw, she let out a shriek and buried her face in Mariam's burqa.

The loudspeaker voice belonged to a slender, bearded young man who wore a black turban. He was standing on some sort of makeshift scaffolding. In his free hand, he held a rocket launcher. Beside him, two bloodied men hung from ropes tied to traffic-light posts. Their clothes had been shredded. Their bloated faces had turned purple-blue.

'I know him,' Mariam said, 'the one on the left.'

317

A young woman in front of Mariam turned around and said it was Najibullah. The other man was his brother. Mariam remembered Najibullah's plump, mustachioed face, beaming from billboards and storefront windows during the Soviet years.

She would later hear that the Taliban had dragged Najibullah from his sanctuary at the UN headquarters near Darulaman Palace. That they had tortured him for hours, then tied his legs to a truck and dragged his lifeless body through the streets.

'He killed many, many Muslims!' the young Talib was shouting through the loudspeaker. He spoke Farsi with a Pashto accent, then would switch to Pashto. He punctuated his words by pointing to the corpses with his weapon. 'His crimes are known to everybody. He was a communist and a *kafir*. This is what we do with infidels who commit crimes against Islam!'

Rasheed was smirking.

In Mariam's arms, Aziza began to cry.

The following day, Kabul was overrun by trucks. In Khair khana, in Shar-e-Nau, in Karteh-Parwan, in Wazir Akbar Khan and Taimani, red Toyota trucks weaved through the streets. Armed bearded men in black turbans sat in their beds. From each truck, a loudspeaker blared announcements, first in Farsi, then Pashto. The same message played from loudspeakers perched atop mosques, and on

318

the radio, which was now known as the Voice of *Shari'a*. The message was also written in flyers, tossed into the streets. Mariam found one in the yard.

*Our* watan *is now known as the Islamic Emirate of Afghanistan. These are the laws that we will enforce and you will obey:*

*All citizens must pray five times a day. If it is prayer time and you are caught doing something other, you will be beaten.*

*All men will grow their beards. The correct length is at least one clenched fist beneath the chin. If you do not abide by this, you will be beaten.*

*All boys will wear turbans. Boys in grade one through six will wear black turbans, higher grades will wear white. All boys will wear Islamic clothes. Shirt collars will be buttoned.*

*Singing is forbidden.*

*Dancing is forbidden.*

*Playing cards, playing chess, gambling, and kite flying are forbidden.*

*Writing books, watching films, and painting pictures are forbidden.*

*If you keep parakeets, you will be beaten. Your birds will be killed.*

*If you steal, your hand will be cut off at the wrist. If you steal again, your foot will be cut off.*

*If you are not Muslim, do not worship where*

319

*you can be seen by Muslims. If you do, you will be beaten and imprisoned. If you are caught trying to convert a Muslim to your faith, you will be executed.*

*Attention women:*

*You will stay inside your homes at all times. It is not proper for women to wander aimlessly about the streets. If you go outside, you must be accompanied by a* mahram, *a male relative. If you are caught alone on the street, you will be beaten and sent home.*

*You will not, under any circumstance, show your face. You will cover with burqa when outside. If you do not, you will be severely beaten.*

*Cosmetics are forbidden.*

*Jewelry is forbidden.*

*You will not wear charming clothes.*

*You will not speak unless spoken to.*

*You will not make eye contact with men.*

*You will not laugh in public. If you do, you will be beaten.*

*You will not paint your nails. If you do, you will lose a finger.*

*Girls are forbidden from attending school. All schools for girls will be closed immediately.*

*Women are forbidden from working.*

*If you are found guilty of adultery, you will be stoned to death.*

*Listen. Listen well. Obey.* Allah-u-akbar.

Rasheed turned off the radio. They were sitting on the living-room floor, eating dinner less than a week after they'd seen Najibullah's corpse hanging by a rope.

'They can't make half the population stay home and do nothing,' Laila said.

'Why not?' Rasheed said. For once, Mariam agreed with him. He'd done the same to her and Laila, in effect, had he not? Surely Laila saw that.

'This isn't some village. This is *Kabul*. Women here used to practice law and medicine; they held office in the government—'

Rasheed grinned. 'Spoken like the arrogant daughter of a poetry-reading university man that you are. How urbane, how Tajik, of you. You think this is some new, radical idea the Taliban are bringing? Have you ever lived outside of your precious little shell in Kabul, my *gul*? Ever cared to visit the *real* Afghanistan, the south, the east, along the tribal border with Pakistan? No? I have. And I can tell you that there are many places in this country that have always lived this way, or close enough anyhow. Not that you would know.'

'I refuse to believe it,' Laila said. 'They're not serious.'

'What the Taliban did to Najibullah looked serious to me,' Rasheed said. 'Wouldn't you agree?'

'He was a communist! He was the head of the Secret Police.'

Rasheed laughed.

Mariam heard the answer in his laugh: that in the eyes of the Taliban, being a communist and the leader of the dreaded KHAD made Najibullah only *slightly* more contemptible than a woman.

# CHAPTER 38

## LAILA

Laila was glad, when the Taliban went to work, that Babi wasn't around to witness it. It would have crippled him.

Men wielding pickaxes swarmed the dilapidated Kabul Museum and smashed pre-Islamic statues to rubble – that is, those that hadn't already been looted by the Mujahideen. The university was shut down and its students sent home. Paintings were ripped from walls, shredded with blades. Television screens were kicked in. Books, except the Koran, were burned in heaps, the stores that sold them closed down. The poems of Khalili, Pajwak, Ansari, Haji Dehqan, Ashraqi, Beytaab, Hafez, Jami, Nizami, Rumi, Khayyám, Beydel, and more went up in smoke.

Laila heard of men being dragged from the streets, accused of skipping *namaz*, and shoved into mosques. She learned that Marco Polo Restaurant, near Chicken Street, had been turned into an interrogation center. Sometimes screaming was heard from behind its black-painted windows. Everywhere, the Beard Patrol roamed the streets in Toyota trucks on the lookout for clean-shaven faces to bloody.

They shut down the cinemas too. Cinema Park. Ariana. Aryub. Projection rooms were ransacked and reels of films set to fire. Laila remembered all the times she and Tariq had sat in those theaters and watched Hindi films, all those melodramatic tales of lovers separated by some tragic turn of fate, one adrift in some faraway land, the other forced into marriage, the weeping, the singing in fields of marigolds, the longing for reunions. She remembered how Tariq would laugh at her for crying at those films.

'I wonder what they've done to my father's cinema,' Mariam said to her one day. 'If it's still there, that is. Or if he still owns it.'

Kharabat, Kabul's ancient music ghetto, was silenced. Musicians were beaten and imprisoned, their *rubabs, tambouras*, and harmoniums trampled upon. The Taliban went to the grave of Tariq's favorite singer, Ahmad Zahir, and fired bullets into it.

'He's been dead for almost twenty years,' Laila said to Mariam. 'Isn't dying once enough?'

Rasheed wasn't bothered much by the Taliban. All he had to do was grow a beard, which he did, and visit the mosque, which he also did. Rasheed regarded the Taliban with a forgiving, affectionate kind of bemusement, as one might regard an erratic cousin prone to unpredictable acts of hilarity and scandal.

Every Wednesday night, Rasheed listened to the

Voice of *Shari'a* when the Taliban would announce the names of those scheduled for punishment. Then, on Fridays, he went to Ghazi Stadium, bought a Pepsi, and watched the spectacle. In bed, he made Laila listen as he described with a queer sort of exhilaration the hands he'd seen severed, the lashings, the hangings, the beheadings.

'I saw a man today slit the throat of his brother's murderer,' he said one night, blowing halos of smoke.

'They're savages,' Laila said.

'You think?' he said. 'Compared to what? The Soviets killed a million people. Do you know how many people the Mujahideen killed in Kabul alone these last four years? Fifty thousand. *Fifty thousand!* Is it so insensible, by comparison, to chop the hands off a few thieves? Eye for an eye, tooth for a tooth. It's in the Koran. Besides, tell me this: If someone killed Aziza, wouldn't you want the chance to avenge her?'

Laila shot him a disgusted look.

'I'm making a point,' he said.

'You're just like them.'

'It's an interesting eye color she has, Aziza. Don't you think? It's neither yours nor mine.'

Rasheed rolled over to face her, gently scratched her thigh with the crooked nail of his index finger.

'Let me explain,' he said. 'If the fancy should strike me – and I'm not saying it will, but it could – it could, I would be within my rights to give Aziza away. How would you like that? Or I could go to the Taliban one day, just walk in and say that I have my suspicions about you. That's all it would take. Whose word do you think they would believe? What do you think they'd do to you?'

Laila pulled her thigh from him.

'Not that I would,' he said. 'I wouldn't. *Nay*. Probably not. You know me.'

'You're despicable,' Laila said.

'That's a big word,' Rasheed said. 'I've always disliked that about you. Even when you were little, when you were running around with that cripple, you thought you were so clever, with your books and poems. What good are all your smarts to you now? What's keeping you off the streets, your smarts or me? I'm despicable? Half the women in this city would kill to have a husband like me. They would *kill* for it.'

He rolled back and blew smoke toward the ceiling.

'You like big words? I'll give you one: perspective. That's what I'm doing here, Laila. Making sure you don't lose perspective.'

What turned Laila's stomach the rest of the night was that every word Rasheed had uttered, every last one, was true.

But, in the morning, and for several mornings after that, the queasiness in her gut persisted, then worsened, became something dismayingly familiar.

One cold, overcast afternoon soon after, Laila lay on her back on the bedroom floor. Mariam was napping with Aziza in her room.

In Laila's hands was a metal spoke she had snapped with a pair of pliers from an abandoned bicycle wheel. She'd found it in the same alley where she had kissed Tariq years back. For a long time, Laila lay on the floor, sucking air through her teeth, legs parted.

She'd adored Aziza from the moment when she'd first suspected her existence. There had been none of this self-doubt, this uncertainty. What a terrible thing it was, Laila thought now, for a mother to fear that she could not summon love for her own child. What an unnatural thing. And yet she had to wonder, as she lay on the floor, her sweaty hands poised to guide the spoke, if indeed she could ever love Rasheed's child as she had Tariq's.

In the end, Laila couldn't do it.

It wasn't the fear of bleeding to death that made her drop the spoke, or even the idea that the act was damnable – which she suspected it was. Laila dropped the spoke because she could not accept what the Mujahideen readily had: that sometimes in war innocent life had to be taken. Her war was against Rasheed. The baby was blameless. And there had been enough killing already. Laila had seen enough killing of innocents caught in the cross fire of enemies.

# CHAPTER 39

# MARIAM

## SEPTEMBER 1997

This hospital no longer treats women,' the guard barked. He was standing at the top of the stairs, looking down icily on the crowd gathered in front of Malalai Hospital.

A loud groan rose from the crowd.

'But this is a women's hospital!' a woman shouted behind Mariam. Cries of approval followed this.

Mariam shifted Aziza from one arm to the other. With her free arm, she supported Laila, who was moaning, and had her own arm flung around Rasheed's neck.

'Not anymore,' the Talib said.

'My wife is having a baby!' a heavy-set man yelled. 'Would you have her give birth here on the street, brother?'

Mariam had heard the announcement, in January of that year, that men and women would be seen in different hospitals, that all female staff would be discharged from Kabul's hospitals and sent to work in one central facility. No one had believed it, and the Taliban hadn't enforced the policy. Until now.

'What about Ali Abad Hospital?' another man cried.

The guard shook his head.

'Wazir Akbar Khan?'

'Men only,' he said.

'What are we supposed to do?'

'Go to Rabia Balkhi,' the guard said.

A young woman pushed forward, said she had already been there. They had no clean water, she said, no oxygen, no medications, no electricity. 'There is nothing there.'

'That's where you go,' the guard said.

There were more groans and cries, an insult or two. Someone threw a rock.

The Talib lifted his Kalashnikov and fired rounds into the air. Another Talib behind him brandished a whip.

The crowd dispersed quickly.

The waiting room at Rabia Balkhi was teeming with women in burqas and their children. The air stank of sweat and unwashed bodies, of feet, urine, cigarette smoke, and antiseptic. Beneath the idle ceiling fan, children chased each other, hopping over the stretched-out legs of dozing fathers.

Mariam helped Laila sit against a wall from which patches of plaster shaped like foreign countries had slid off. Laila rocked back and forth, hands pressing against her belly.

'I'll get you seen, Laila jo. I promise.'

'Be quick,' said Rasheed.

Before the registration window was a horde of women, shoving and pushing against each other. Some were still holding their babies. Some broke from the mass and charged the double doors that led to the treatment rooms. An armed Talib guard blocked their way, sent them back.

Mariam waded in. She dug in her heels and burrowed against the elbows, hips, and shoulder blades of strangers. Someone elbowed her in the ribs, and she elbowed back. A hand made a desperate grab at her face. She swatted it away. To propel herself forward, Mariam clawed at necks, at arms and elbows, at hair, and, when a woman nearby hissed, Mariam hissed back.

Mariam saw now the sacrifices a mother made. Decency was but one. She thought ruefully of Nana, of the sacrifices that she too had made. Nana, who could have given her away, or tossed her in a ditch somewhere and run. But she hadn't. Instead, Nana had endured the shame of bearing a *harami*, had shaped her life around the thankless task of raising Mariam and, in her own way, of loving her. And, in the end, Mariam had chosen Jalil over her. As she fought her way with impudent resolve to the front of the melee, Mariam wished she had been a better daughter to Nana. She wished she'd understood then what she understood now about motherhood.

She found herself face-to-face with a nurse, who

330

was covered head to toe in a dirty gray burqa. The nurse was talking to a young woman, whose burqa headpiece had soaked through with a patch of matted blood.

'My daughter's water broke and the baby won't come,' Mariam called.

'*I'm* talking to her!' the bloodied young woman cried. 'Wait your turn!'

The whole mass of them swayed side to side, like the tall grass around the *kolba* when the breeze swept across the clearing. A woman behind Mariam was yelling that her girl had broken her elbow falling from a tree. Another woman cried that she was passing bloody stools.

'Does she have a fever?' the nurse asked. It took Mariam a moment to realize she was being spoken to.

'No,' Mariam said.

'Bleeding?'

'No.'

'Where is she?'

Over the covered heads, Mariam pointed to where Laila was sitting with Rasheed.

'We'll get to her,' the nurse said.

'How long?' Mariam cried. Someone had grabbed her by the shoulders and was pulling her back.

'I don't know,' the nurse said. She said they had only two doctors and both were operating at the moment.

'She's in pain,' Mariam said.

'Me too!' the woman with the bloodied scalp cried. 'Wait your turn!'

Mariam was being dragged back. Her view of the nurse was blocked now by shoulders and the backs of heads. She smelled a baby's milky burp.

'Take her for a walk,' the nurse yelled. 'And wait.'

It was dark outside when a nurse finally called them in. The delivery room had eight beds, on which women moaned and twisted tended to by fully covered nurses. Two of the women were in the act of delivering. There were no curtains between the beds. Laila was given a bed at the far end, beneath a window that someone had painted black. There was a sink nearby, cracked and dry, and a string over the sink from which hung stained surgical gloves. In the middle of the room Mariam saw an aluminum table. The top shelf had a soot-colored blanket on it; the bottom shelf was empty.

One of the women saw Mariam looking.

'They put the live ones on the top,' she said tiredly.

The doctor, in a dark blue burqa, was a small, harried woman with birdlike movements. Everything she said came out sounding impatient, urgent.

'First baby.' She said it like that, not as a question but as a statement.

'Second,' Mariam said.

Laila let out a cry and rolled on her side. Her fingers closed against Mariam's.

'Any problems with the first delivery?'

'No.'

'You're the mother?'

'Yes,' Mariam said.

The doctor lifted the lower half of her burqa and produced a metallic, cone-shaped instrument. She raised Laila's burqa and placed the wide end of the instrument on her belly, the narrow end to her own ear. She listened for almost a minute, switched spots, listened again, switched spots again.

'I have to feel the baby now, *hamshira*.'

She put on one of the gloves hung by a clothespin over the sink. She pushed on Laila's belly with one hand and slid the other inside. Laila whimpered. When the doctor was done, she gave the glove to a nurse, who rinsed it and pinned it back on the string.

'Your daughter needs a caesarian. Do you know what that is? We have to open her womb and take the baby out, because it is in the breech position.'

'I don't understand,' Mariam said.

The doctor said the baby was positioned so it wouldn't come out on its own. 'And too much time has passed as is. We need to go to the operating room now.'

Laila gave a grimacing nod, and her head drooped to one side.

'There *is* something I have to tell you,' the doctor said. She moved closer to Mariam, leaned in, and spoke in a lower, more confidential tone. There was a hint of embarrassment in her voice now.

'What is she saying?' Laila groaned. 'Is something wrong with the baby?'

'But how will she stand it?' Mariam said.

The doctor must have heard accusation in this question, judging by the defensive shift in her tone.

'You think I want it this way?' she said. 'What do you want me to do? They won't give me what I need. I have no X-ray either, no suction, no oxygen, not even simple antibiotics. When NGOs offer money, the Taliban turn them away. Or they funnel the money to the places that cater to men.'

'But, Doctor sahib, isn't there something you can give her?' Mariam asked.

'What's going on?' Laila moaned.

'You can buy the medicine yourself, but—'

'Write the name,' Mariam said. 'You write it down and I'll get it.'

Beneath the burqa, the doctor shook her head curtly. 'There is no time,' she said. 'For one thing, none of the nearby pharmacies have it. So you'd have to fight through traffic from one place to the next, maybe all the way across town, with little likelihood that you'd ever find it. It's almost eight-thirty now, so you'll probably get arrested for breaking curfew. Even if you find the medicine, chances are you can't afford it. Or you'll find yourself in a bidding war with someone just as desperate. There is no time. This baby needs to come out now.'

'Tell me what's going on!' Laila said. She had propped herself up on her elbows.

The doctor took a breath, then told Laila that the hospital had no anesthetic.

'But if we delay, you will lose your baby.'

'Then cut me open,' Laila said. She dropped back on the bed and drew up her knees. 'Cut me open and give me my baby.'

Inside the old, dingy operating room, Laila lay on a gurney bed as the doctor scrubbed her hands in a basin. Laila was shivering. She drew in air through her teeth every time the nurse wiped her belly with a cloth soaked in a yellow-brown liquid. Another nurse stood at the door. She kept cracking it open to take a peek outside.

The doctor was out of her burqa now, and Mariam saw that she had a crest of silvery hair, heavy-lidded eyes, and little pouches of fatigue at the corners of her mouth.

'They want us to operate in burqa,' the doctor explained, motioning with her head to the nurse at the door. 'She keeps watch. She sees them coming; I cover.'

She said this in a pragmatic, almost indifferent, tone, and Mariam understood that this was a woman far past outrage. Here was a woman, she thought, who had understood that she was lucky to even be working, that there was always something, something else, that they could take away.

There were two vertical, metallic rods on either side of Laila's shoulders. With clothespins, the nurse who'd cleansed Laila's belly pinned a sheet to them. It formed a curtain between Laila and the doctor.

Mariam positioned herself behind the crown of Laila's head and lowered her face so their cheeks touched. She could feel Laila's teeth rattling. Their hands locked together.

Through the curtain, Mariam saw the doctor's shadow move to Laila's left, the nurse to the right. Laila's lips had stretched all the way back. Spit bubbles formed and popped on the surface of her clenched teeth. She made quick, little hissing sounds.

The doctor said, 'Take heart, little sister.'

She bent over Laila.

Laila's eyes snapped open. Then her mouth opened. She held like this, held, held, shivering, the cords in her neck stretched, sweat dripping from her face, her fingers crushing Mariam's.

Mariam would always admire Laila for how much time passed before she screamed.

# CHAPTER 40

# LAILA

### FALL 1999

It was Mariam's idea to dig the hole. One morning, she pointed to a patch of soil behind the toolshed. 'We can do it here,' she said. 'This is a good spot.'

They took turns striking the ground with a spade, then shoveling the loose dirt aside. They hadn't planned on a big hole, or a deep one, so the work of digging shouldn't have been as demanding as it turned out. It was the drought, started in 1998, in its second year now, that was wreaking havoc everywhere. It had hardly snowed that past winter and didn't rain at all that spring. All over the country, farmers were leaving behind their parched lands, selling off their goods, roaming from village to village looking for water. They moved to Pakistan or Iran. They settled in Kabul. But water tables were low in the city too, and the shallow wells had dried up. The lines at the deep wells were so long, Laila and Mariam would spend hours waiting their turn. The Kabul River, without its yearly spring floods, had turned bone-dry. It was a public toilet now, nothing in it but human waste and rubble.

So they kept swinging the spade and striking, but the sun-blistered ground had hardened like a rock, the dirt unyielding, compressed, almost petrified.

Mariam was forty now. Her hair, rolled up above her face, had a few stripes of gray in it. Pouches sagged beneath her eyes, brown and crescent-shaped. She'd lost two front teeth. One fell out, the other Rasheed knocked out when she'd accidentally dropped Zalmai. Her skin had coarsened, tanned from all the time they were spending in the yard sitting beneath the brazen sun. They would sit and watch Zalmai chase Aziza.

When it was done, when the hole was dug, they stood over it and looked down.

'It should do,' Mariam said.

Zalmai was two now. He was a plump little boy with curly hair. He had small brownish eyes, and a rosy tint to his cheeks, like Rasheed, no matter the weather. He had his father's hairline too, thick and half-moon-shaped, set low on his brow.

When Laila was alone with him, Zalmai was sweet, good-humored, and playful. He liked to climb Laila's shoulders, play hide-and-seek in the yard with her and Aziza. Sometimes, in his calmer moments, he liked to sit on Laila's lap and have her sing to him. His favorite song was 'Mullah Mohammad Jan.' He swung his meaty little feet as she sang into his curly hair and joined in when she got to the chorus, singing what words he could make with his raspy voice:

*Come and let's go to Mazar, Mullah Mohammad
  jan,
To see the fields of tulips, o beloved companion.*

Laila loved the moist kisses Zalmai planted on her cheeks, loved his dimpled elbows and stout little toes. She loved tickling him, building tunnels with cushions and pillows for him to crawl through, watching him fall asleep in her arms with one of his hands always clutching her ear. Her stomach turned when she thought of that afternoon, lying on the floor with the spoke of a bicycle wheel between her legs. How close she'd come. It was unthinkable to her now that she could have even entertained the idea. Her son was a blessing, and Laila was relieved to discover that her fears had proved baseless, that she loved Zalmai with the marrow of her bones, just as she did Aziza.

But Zalmai worshipped his father, and, because he did, he was transformed when his father was around to dote on him. Zalmai was quick then with a defiant cackle or an impudent grin. In his father's presence, he was easily offended. He held grudges. He persisted in mischief in spite of Laila's scolding, which he never did when Rasheed was away.

Rasheed approved of all of it. 'A sign of intelligence,' he said. He said the same of Zalmai's recklessness – when he swallowed, then pooped, marbles; when he lit matches; when he chewed on Rasheed's cigarettes.

When Zalmai was born, Rasheed had moved him into the bed he shared with Laila. He had bought him a new crib and had lions and crouching leopards painted on the side panels. He'd paid for new clothes, new rattles, new bottles, new diapers, even though they could not afford them and Aziza's old ones were still serviceable. One day, he came home with a battery-run mobile, which he hung over Zalmai's crib. Little yellow-and-black bumblebees dangled from a sunflower, and they crinkled and squeaked when squeezed. A tune played when it was turned on.

'I thought you said business was slow,' Laila said.

'I have friends I can borrow from,' he said dismissively.

'How will you pay them back?'

'Things will turn around. They always do. Look, he likes it. See?'

Most days, Laila was deprived of her son. Rasheed took him to the shop, let him crawl around under his crowded workbench, play with old rubber soles and spare scraps of leather. Rasheed drove in his iron nails and turned the sandpaper wheel, and kept a watchful eye on him. If Zalmai toppled a rack of shoes, Rasheed scolded him gently, in a calm, half-smiling way. If he did it again, Rasheed put down his hammer, sat him up on his desk, and talked to him softly.

His patience with Zalmai was a well that ran deep and never dried.

They came home together in the evening, Zalmai's head bouncing on Rasheed's shoulder, both of them smelling of glue and leather. They grinned the way people who share a secret do, slyly, like they'd sat in that dim shoe shop all day not making shoes at all but devising secret plots. Zalmai liked to sit beside his father at dinner, where they played private games, as Mariam, Laila, and Aziza set plates on the *sofrah*. They took turns poking each other on the chest, giggling, pelting each other with bread crumbs, whispering things the others couldn't hear. If Laila spoke to them, Rasheed looked up with displeasure at the unwelcome intrusion. If she asked to hold Zalmai – or, worse, if Zalmai reached for her – Rasheed glowered at her.

Laila walked away feeling stung.

Then one night, a few weeks after Zalmai turned two, Rasheed came home with a television and a VCR. The day had been warm, almost balmy, but the evening was cooler and already thickening into a starless, chilly night.

He set it down on the living-room table. He said he'd bought it on the black market.

'Another loan?' Laila asked.

'It's a Magnavox.'

Aziza came into the room. When she saw the TV, she ran to it.

'Careful, Aziza jo,' said Mariam. 'Don't touch.'

Aziza's hair had become as light as Laila's. Laila could see her own dimples on her cheeks. Aziza had turned into a calm, pensive little girl, with a demeanor that to Laila seemed beyond her six years. Laila marveled at her daughter's manner of speech, her cadence and rhythm, her thoughtful pauses and intonations, so adult, so at odds with the immature body that housed the voice. It was Aziza who with lighthearted authority had taken it upon herself to wake Zalmai every day, to dress him, feed him his breakfast, comb his hair. She was the one who put him down to nap, who played even-tempered peacemaker to her volatile sibling. Around him, Aziza had taken to giving an exasperated, queerly adult headshake.

Aziza pushed the TV's POWER button. Rasheed scowled, snatched her wrist and set it on the table, not gently at all.

'This is Zalmai's TV,' he said.

Aziza went over to Mariam and climbed in her lap. The two of them were inseparable now. Of late, with Laila's blessing, Mariam had started teaching Aziza verses from the Koran. Aziza could already recite by heart the surah of *ikhlas*, the surah of *fatiha*, and already knew how to perform the four *ruqats* of morning prayer.

*It's all I have to give her*, Mariam had said to

342

Laila, *this knowledge, these prayers. They're the only true possession I've ever had.*

Zalmai came into the room now. As Rasheed watched with anticipation, the way people wait the simple tricks of street magicians, Zalmai pulled on the TV's wire, pushed the buttons, pressed his palms to the blank screen. When he lifted them, the condensed little palms faded from the glass. Rasheed smiled with pride, watched as Zalmai kept pressing his palms and lifting them, over and over.

The Taliban had banned television. Videotapes had been gouged publicly, the tapes ripped out and strung on fence posts. Satellite dishes had been hung from lampposts. But Rasheed said just because things were banned didn't mean you couldn't find them.

'I'll start looking for some cartoon videos tomorrow,' he said. 'It won't be hard. You can buy anything in underground bazaars.'

'Then maybe you'll buy us a new well,' Laila said, and this won her a scornful gaze from him.

It was later, after another dinner of plain white rice had been consumed and tea forgone again on account of the drought, after Rasheed had smoked a cigarette, that he told Laila about his decision.

'No,' Laila said.

He said he wasn't asking.

'I don't care if you are or not.'

'You would if you knew the full story.'

He said he had borrowed from more friends than

he let on, that the money from the shop alone was no longer enough to sustain the five of them. 'I didn't tell you earlier to spare you the worrying.'

'Besides,' he said, 'you'd be surprised how much they can bring in.'

Laila said no again. They were in the living room. Mariam and the children were in the kitchen. Laila could hear the clatter of dishes, Zalmai's high-pitched laugh, Aziza saying something to Mariam in her steady, reasonable voice.

'There will be others like her, younger even,' Rasheed said. 'Everyone in Kabul is doing the same.'

Laila told him she didn't care what other people did with their children.

'I'll keep a close eye on her,' Rasheed said, less patiently now. 'It's a safe corner. There's a mosque across the street.'

'I won't let you turn my daughter into a street beggar!' Laila snapped.

The slap made a loud smacking sound, the palm of his thick-fingered hand connecting squarely with the meat of Laila's cheek. It made her head whip around. It silenced the noises from the kitchen. For a moment, the house was perfectly quiet. Then a flurry of hurried footsteps in the hallway before Mariam and the children were in the living room, their eyes shifting from her to Rasheed and back.

Then Laila punched him.

It was the first time she'd struck anybody, discounting the playful punches she and Tariq used

344

to trade. But those had been open-fisted, more pats than punches, self-consciously friendly, comfortable expressions of anxieties that were both perplexing and thrilling. They would aim for the muscle that Tariq, in a professorial voice, called the *deltoid*.

Laila watched the arch of her closed fist, slicing through the air, felt the crinkle of Rasheed's stubbly, coarse skin under her knuckles. It made a sound like dropping a rice bag to the floor. She hit him hard. The impact actually made him stagger two steps backward.

From the other side of the room, a gasp, a yelp, and a scream. Laila didn't know who had made which noise. At the moment, she was too astounded to notice or care, waiting for her mind to catch up with what her hand had done. When it did, she believed she might have smiled. She might have *grinned* when, to her astonishment, Rasheed calmly walked out of the room.

Suddenly, it seemed to Laila that the collective hardships of their lives – hers, Aziza's, Mariam's – simply dropped away, vaporized like Zalmai's palms from the TV screen. It seemed worthwhile, if absurdly so, to have endured all they'd endured for this one crowning moment, for this act of defiance that would end the suffering of all indignities.

Laila did not notice that Rasheed was back in the room. Until his hand was around her throat. Until she was lifted off her feet and slammed against the wall.

Up close, his sneering face seemed impossibly large. Laila noticed how much puffier it was getting with age, how many more broken vessels charted tiny paths on his nose. Rasheed didn't say anything. And, really, what could be said, what needed saying, when you'd shoved the barrel of your gun into your wife's mouth?

It was the raids, the reason they were in the yard digging. Sometimes monthly raids, sometimes weekly. Of late, almost daily. Mostly, the Taliban confiscated stuff, gave a kick to someone's rear, whacked the back of a head or two. But sometimes there were public beatings, lashings of soles and palms.

'Gently,' Mariam said now, her knees over the edge. They lowered the TV into the hole by each clutching one end of the plastic sheet in which it was wrapped.

'That should do it,' Mariam said.

They patted the dirt when they were done, filling the hole up again. They tossed some of it around so it wouldn't look conspicuous.

'There,' Mariam said, wiping her hands on her dress.

When it was safer, they'd agreed, when the Taliban cut down on their raids, in a month or two or six, or maybe longer, they would dig the TV up.

In Laila's dream, she and Mariam are out behind the toolshed digging again. But, this time, it's Aziza

346

they're lowering into the ground. Aziza's breath fogs the sheet of plastic in which they have wrapped her. Laila sees her panicked eyes, the whiteness of her palms as they slap and push against the sheet. Aziza pleads. Laila can't hear her screams. *Only for a while,* she calls down, *it's only for a while. It's the raids, don't you know, my love? When the raids are over, Mammy and Khala Mariam will dig you out. I promise, my love. Then we can play. We can play all you want.* She fills the shovel. Laila woke up, out of breath, with a taste of soil in her mouth, when the first granular lumps of dirt hit the plastic.

# CHAPTER 41

# MARIAM

In the summer of 2000, the drought reached its third and worst year.

In Helmand, Zabol, Kandahar, villages turned into herds of nomadic communities, always moving, searching for water and green pastures for their livestock. When they found neither, when their goats and sheep and cows died off, they came to Kabul. They took to the Kareh-Ariana hillside, living in makeshift slums, packed in huts, fifteen or twenty at a time.

That was also the summer of *Titanic*, the summer that Mariam and Aziza were a tangle of limbs, rolling and giggling, Aziza insisting *she* get to be Jack.

'Quiet, Aziza jo.'

'Jack! Say my name, Khala Mariam. Say it. Jack!'

'Your father will be angry if you wake him.'

'Jack! And you're Rose.'

It would end with Mariam on her back, surrendering, agreeing again to be Rose. 'Fine, you be Jack,' she relented. 'You die young, and I get to live to a ripe old age.'

'Yes, but I die a hero,' said Aziza, 'while you,

Rose, you spend your entire, miserable life longing for me.' Then, straddling Mariam's chest, she'd announce, 'Now we must kiss!' Mariam whipped her head side to side, and Aziza, delighted with her own scandalous behavior, cackled through puckered lips.

Sometimes Zalmai would saunter in and watch this game. What did *he* get to be, he asked.

'You can be the iceberg,' said Aziza.

That summer, *Titanic* fever gripped Kabul. People smuggled pirated copies of the film from Pakistan – sometimes in their underwear. After curfew, everyone locked their doors, turned out the lights, turned down the volume, and reaped tears for Jack and Rose and the passengers of the doomed ship. If there was electrical power, Mariam, Laila, and the children watched it too. A dozen times or more, they unearthed the TV from behind the toolshed, late at night, with the lights out and quilts pinned over the windows.

At the Kabul River, vendors moved into the parched riverbed. Soon, from the river's sunbaked hollows, it was possible to buy *Titanic* carpets, and *Titanic* cloth, from bolts arranged in wheelbarrows. There was *Titanic* deodorant, *Titanic* toothpaste, *Titanic* perfume, *Titanic pakora*, even *Titanic* burqa. A particularly persistent beggar began calling himself 'Titanic Beggar.'

'Titanic City' was born.

*It's the song*, they said.

*No, the sea. The luxury. The ship.*

*It's the sex*, they whispered.

*Leo*, said Aziza sheepishly. *It's all about Leo*.

'Everybody wants Jack,' Laila said to Mariam. 'That's what it is. Everybody wants Jack to rescue them from disaster. But there is no Jack. Jack is not coming back. Jack is dead.'

Then, late that summer, a fabric merchant fell asleep and forgot to put out his cigarette. He survived the fire, but his store did not. The fire took the adjacent fabric store as well, a second-hand clothing store, a small furniture shop, a bakery.

They told Rasheed later that if the winds had blown east instead of west, his shop, which was at the corner of the block, might have been spared.

They sold everything.

First to go were Mariam's things, then Laila's. Aziza's baby clothes, the few toys Laila had fought Rasheed to buy her. Aziza watched the proceedings with a docile look. Rasheed's watch too was sold, his old transistor radio, his pair of neckties, his shoes, and his wedding ring. The couch, the table, the rug, and the chairs went too. Zalmai threw a wicked tantrum when Rasheed sold the TV.

After the fire, Rasheed was home almost every day. He slapped Aziza. He kicked Mariam. He threw things. He found fault with Laila, the way she smelled, the way she dressed, the way she combed her hair, her yellowing teeth.

'What's happened to you?' he said. 'I married a *pari*, and now I'm saddled with a hag. You're turning into Mariam.'

He got fired from the kebab house near Haji Yaghoub Square because he and a customer got into a scuffle. The customer complained that Rasheed had rudely tossed the bread on his table. Harsh words had passed. Rasheed had called the customer a monkey-faced Uzbek. A gun had been brandished. A skewer pointed in return. In Rasheed's version, he held the skewer. Mariam had her doubts.

Fired from the restaurant in Taimani because customers complained about the long waits, Rasheed said the cook was slow and lazy.

'You were probably out back napping,' said Laila.

'Don't provoke him, Laila jo,' Mariam said.

'I'm warning you, woman,' he said.

'Either that or smoking.'

'I swear to God.'

'You can't help being what you are.'

And then he was on Laila, pummeling her chest, her head, her belly with fists, tearing at her hair, throwing her to the wall. Aziza was shrieking, pulling at his shirt; Zalmai was screaming too, trying to get him off his mother. Rasheed shoved the children aside, pushed Laila to the ground, and began kicking her. Mariam threw herself on Laila. He went on kicking, kicking Mariam now, spittle flying from his mouth, his eyes glittering with

351

murderous intent, kicking until he couldn't anymore.

'I swear you're going to make me kill you, Laila,' he said, panting. Then he stormed out of the house.

When the money ran out, hunger began to cast a pall over their lives. It was stunning to Mariam how quickly alleviating hunger became the crux of their existence.

Rice, boiled plain and white, with no meat or sauce, was a rare treat now. They skipped meals with increasing and alarming regularity. Sometimes Rasheed brought home sardines in a can and brittle, dried bread that tasted like sawdust. Sometimes a stolen bag of apples, at the risk of getting his hand sawed off. In grocery stores, he carefully pocketed canned ravioli, which they split five ways, Zalmai getting the lion's share. They ate raw turnips sprinkled with salt. Limp leaves of lettuce and blackened bananas for dinner.

Death from starvation suddenly became a distinct possibility. Some chose not to wait for it. Mariam heard of a neighborhood widow who had ground some dried bread, laced it with rat poison, and fed it to all seven of her children. She had saved the biggest portion for herself.

Aziza's ribs began to push through the skin, and the fat from her cheeks-vanished. Her calves thinned, and her complexion turned the color of weak tea. When Mariam picked her up, she could feel her hip bone poking through the taut skin. Zalmai lay around the house, eyes dulled and half closed, or in his father's lap limp as a rag. He cried himself to sleep, when he could muster the energy, but his sleep was fitful and sporadic. White dots leaped before Mariam's eyes whenever she got up. Her head spun, and her ears rang all the time. She remembered something Mullah Faizullah used to say about hunger when Ramadan started: *Even the snakebitten man finds sleep, but not the hungry.*

'My children are going to die,' Laila said. 'Right before my eyes.'

'They are not,' Mariam said. 'I won't let them. It's going to be all right, Laila jo. I know what to do.'

One blistering-hot day, Mariam put on her burqa, and she and Rasheed walked to the Intercontinental Hotel. Bus fare was an unaffordable luxury now, and Mariam was exhausted by the time they reached the top of the steep hill. Climbing the slope, she was struck by bouts of dizziness, and twice she had to stop, wait for it to pass.

At the hotel entrance, Rasheed greeted and hugged one of the doormen, who was dressed in a burgundy suit and visor cap. There was some friendly-looking talk between them. Rasheed spoke with his hand on the doorman's elbow. He motioned toward Mariam at one point, and they both looked her way briefly. Mariam thought there was something vaguely familiar about the doorman.

When the doorman went inside, Mariam and Rasheed waited. From this vantage point, Mariam had a view of the Polytechnic Institute, and, beyond that, the old Khair khana district and the road to Mazar. To the south, she could see the bread factory, Silo, long abandoned, its pale yellow facade pocked with yawning holes from all the shelling it had endured. Farther south, she could make out the hollow ruins of Darulaman Palace, where, many years back, Rasheed had taken her for a picnic. The memory of that day was a relic from a past that no longer seemed like her own.

Mariam concentrated on these things, these landmarks. She feared she might lose her nerve if she let her mind wander.

Every few minutes, jeeps and taxis drove up to the hotel entrance. Doormen rushed to greet the passengers, who were all men, armed, bearded, wearing turbans, all of them stepping out with the same self-assured, casual air of menace. Mariam heard bits of their chatter as they vanished through the hotel's doors. She heard Pashto and Farsi, but Urdu and Arabic too.

'Meet our *real* masters,' Rasheed said in a low-pitched voice. 'Pakistani and Arab Islamists. The Taliban are puppets. *These* are the big players and Afghanistan is their playground.'

Rasheed said he'd heard rumors that the Taliban were allowing these people to set up secret camps all over the country, where young men were being trained to become suicide bombers and jihadi fighters.

'What's taking him so long?' Mariam said.

Rasheed spat, and kicked dirt on the spit.

An hour later, they were inside, Mariam and Rasheed, following the doorman. Their heels clicked on the tiled floor as they were led across the pleasantly cool lobby. Mariam saw two men sitting on leather chairs, rifles and a coffee table between them, sipping black tea and eating from a plate of syrup-coated *jelabi*, rings sprinkled with powdered sugar. She thought of Aziza, who loved *jelabi*, and tore her gaze away.

The doorman led them outside to a balcony. From his pocket, he produced a small black cordless phone and a scrap of paper with a number scribbled on it. He told Rasheed it was his supervisor's satellite phone.

'I got you five minutes,' he said. 'No more.'

'*Tashakor*,' Rasheed said. 'I won't forget this.'

The doorman nodded and walked away. Rasheed dialed. He gave Mariam the phone.

As Mariam listened to the scratchy ringing, her mind wandered. It wandered to the last time she'd seen Jalil, thirteen years earlier, back in the spring of 1987. He'd stood on the street outside her house, leaning on a cane, beside the blue Benz with the Herat license plates and the white stripe bisecting the roof, the hood, and trunk. He'd stood there for hours, waiting for her, now and then calling her name, just as she had once called *his* name outside *his* house. Mariam had parted the curtain once, just a bit, and caught a glimpse of him. Only a glimpse, but long enough to see that his hair had turned fluffy white, and that he'd started to stoop. He wore glasses, a red tie, as always, and the usual white handkerchief triangle in his breast pocket. Most striking, he was thinner, much thinner, than she remembered, the coat of his dark brown suit drooping over his shoulders, the trousers pooling at his ankles.

Jalil had seen her too, if only for a moment. Their eyes had met briefly through a part in the curtains, as they had met many years earlier through a part in another pair of curtains. But then Mariam had quickly closed the curtains. She had sat on the bed, waited for him to leave.

She thought now of the letter Jalil had finally left at her door. She had kept it for days, beneath her pillow, picking it up now and then, turning it over in her hands. In the end, she had shredded it unopened.

And now here she was, after all these years, calling him.

Mariam regretted her foolish, youthful pride now. She wished now that she had let him in. What would have been the harm to let him in, sit with him, let him say what he'd come to say? He was her father. He'd not been a good father, it was true, but how ordinary his faults seemed now, how forgivable, when compared to Rasheed's malice, or to the brutality and violence that she had seen men inflict on one another.

She wished she hadn't destroyed his letter.

A man's deep voice spoke in her ear and informed her that she'd reached the mayor's office in Herat.

Mariam cleared her throat. '*Salaam*, brother, I am looking for someone who lives in Herat. Or he did, many years ago. His name is Jalil Khan. He lived in Shar-e-Nau and owned the cinema. Do you have any information as to his where-abouts?'

The irritation was audible in the man's voice. 'This is why you call the mayor's office?'

Mariam said she didn't know who else to call. 'Forgive me, brother. I know you have important things to tend to, but it is life and death, a question of life and death I am calling about.'

'I don't know him. The cinema's been closed for many years.'

'Maybe there's someone there who might know him, someone—'

'There is no one.'

Mariam closed her eyes. 'Please, brother. There are children involved. Small children.'

A long sigh.

'Maybe someone there—'

'There's a groundskeeper here. I think he's lived here all of his life.'

'Yes, ask him, please.'

'Call back tomorrow.'

Mariam said she couldn't. 'I have this phone for five minutes only. I don't—'

There was a click at the other end, and Mariam thought he had hung up. But she could hear footsteps, and voices, a distant car horn, and some mechanical humming punctuated by clicks, maybe an electric fan. She switched the phone to her other ear, closed her eyes.

She pictured Jalil smiling, reaching into his pocket.

*Ah. Of course. Well. Here then. Without further ado . . .*

*A leaf-shaped pendant, tiny coins etched with moons and stars hanging from it.*

*Try it on, Mariam jo.*

*What do you think?*

*I think you look like a queen.*

A few minutes passed. Then footsteps, a creaking sound, and a click. 'He does know him.'

'He does?'

'It's what he says.'

'Where is he?' Mariam said. 'Does this man know where Jalil Khan is?'

There was a pause. 'He says he died years ago, back in 1987.'

Mariam's stomach fell. She'd considered the possibility, of course. Jalil would have been in his mid- to late seventies by now, but . . .

*1987.*

*He was dying then. He had driven all the way from Herat to say good-bye.*

She moved to the edge of the balcony. From up here, she could see the hotel's once-famous swimming pool, empty and grubby now, scarred by bullet holes and decaying tiles. And there was the battered tennis court, the ragged net lying limply in the middle of it like dead skin shed by a snake.

'I have to go now,' the voice at the other end said.

'I'm sorry to have bothered you,' Mariam said, weeping soundlessly into the phone. She saw Jalil waving to her, skipping from stone to stone as he crossed the stream, his pockets swollen with gifts. All the times she had held her breath for him, for God to grant her more time with him. 'Thank you,' Mariam began to say, but the man at the other end had already hung up.

Rasheed was looking at her. Mariam shook her head.

'Useless,' he said, snatching the phone from her. 'Like daughter, like father.'

On their way out of the lobby, Rasheed walked briskly to the coffee table, which was now abandoned, and pocketed the last ring of *jelabi*. He took it home and gave it to Zalmai.

# CHAPTER 42

# LAILA

I n a paper bag, Aziza packed these things: her
flowered shirt and her lone pair of socks, her
mismatched wool gloves, an old, pumpkin-
colored blanket dotted with stars and comets, a
splintered plastic cup, a banana, her set of dice.

It was a cool morning in April 2001, shortly
before Laila's twenty-third birthday. The sky was
a translucent gray, and gusts of a clammy, cold
wind kept rattling the screen door.

This was a few days after Laila heard that Ahmad
Shah Massoud had gone to France and spoken
to the European Parliament. Massoud was now
in his native North, and leading the Northern
Alliance, the sole opposition group still fighting
the Taliban. In Europe, Massoud had warned the
West about terrorist camps in Afghanistan, and
pleaded with the U.S. to help him fight the Taliban.

'If President Bush doesn't help us,' he had said,
'these terrorists will damage the U.S. and Europe
very soon.'

A month before that, Laila had learned that the
Taliban had planted TNT in the crevices of the
giant Buddhas in Bamiyan and blown them apart,

calling them objects of idolatry and sin. There was an outcry around the world, from the U.S. to China. Governments, historians, and archaeologists from all over the globe had written letters, pleaded with the Taliban not to demolish the two greatest historical artifacts in Afghanistan. But the Taliban had gone ahead and detonated their explosives inside the two-thousand-year-old Buddhas. They had chanted *Allah-u-akbar* with each blast, cheered each time the statues lost an arm or a leg in a crumbling cloud of dust. Laila remembered standing atop the bigger of the two Buddhas with Babi and Tariq, back in 1987, a breeze blowing in their sunlit faces, watching a hawk gliding in circles over the sprawling valley below. But when she heard the news of the statues' demise, Laila was numb to it. It hardly seemed to matter. How could she care about statues when her own life was crumbling dust?

Until Rasheed told her it was time to go, Laila sat on the floor in a corner of the living room, not speaking and stone-faced, her hair hanging around her face in straggly curls. No matter how much she breathed in and out, it seemed to Laila that she couldn't fill her lungs with enough air.

On the way to Karteh-Seh, Zalmai bounced in Rasheed's arms, and Aziza held Mariam's hand as she walked quickly beside her. The wind blew the dirty scarf tied under Aziza's chin and rippled the hem of her dress. Aziza was more grim now, as though she'd begun to sense, with each step, that she was being duped. Laila had not found the strength to tell Aziza the truth. She had told her that she was going to a school, a special school where the children ate and slept and didn't come home after class. Now Aziza kept pelting Laila with the same questions she had been asking for days. Did the students sleep in different rooms or all in one great big room? Would she make friends? Was she, Laila, sure that the teachers would be nice?

And, more than once, *How long do I have to stay?*

They stopped two blocks from the squat, barracks-style building.

'Zalmai and I will wait here,' Rasheed said. 'Oh, before I forget . . .'

He fished a stick of gum from his pocket, a parting gift, and held it out to Aziza with a stiff, magnanimous air. Aziza took it and muttered a thank-you. Laila marveled at Aziza's grace, Aziza's vast capacity for forgiveness, and her eyes filled. Her heart squeezed, and she was faint with sorrow at the thought that this afternoon Aziza would not nap beside her, that she would not feel the flimsy weight of Aziza's arm on her chest, the curve of Aziza's head pressing into her ribs, Aziza's breath warming her neck, Aziza's heels poking her belly.

When Aziza was led away, Zalmai began wailing, crying, Ziza! Ziza! He squirmed and kicked in his father's arms, called for his sister, until his attention was diverted by an organ-grinder's monkey across the street.

They walked the last two blocks alone, Mariam, Laila, and Aziza. As they approached the building, Laila could see its splintered façade, the sagging roof, the planks of wood nailed across frames with missing windows, the top of a swing set over a decaying wall.

They stopped by the door, and Laila repeated to Aziza what she had told her earlier.

'And if they ask about your father, what do you say?'

'The Mujahideen killed him,' Aziza said, her mouth set with wariness.

'That's good. Aziza, do you understand?'

'Because this is a special school,' Aziza said. Now that they were here, and the building was a reality, she looked shaken. Her lower lip was quivering and her eyes threatened to well up, and Laila saw how hard she was struggling to be brave. 'If we tell the truth,' Aziza said in a thin, breathless voice, 'they won't take me. It's a special school. I want to go home.'

'I'll visit all the time,' Laila managed to say. 'I promise.'

'Me too,' said Mariam. 'We'll come to see you, Aziza jo, and we'll play together, just like always. It's only for a while, until your father finds work.'

'They have food here,' Laila said shakily. She was glad for the burqa, glad that Aziza couldn't see how she was falling apart inside it. 'Here, you won't go hungry. They have rice and bread and water, and maybe even fruit.'

363

'But *you* won't be here. And Khala Mariam won't be with me.'

'I'll come and see you,' Laila said. 'All the time. Look at me, Aziza. I'll come and see you. I'm your mother. If it kills me, I'll come and see you.'

The orphanage director was a stooping, narrow-chested man with a pleasantly lined face. He was balding, had a shaggy beard, eyes like peas. His name was Zaman. He wore a skullcap. The left lens of his eyeglasses was chipped.

As he led them to his office, he asked Laila and Mariam their names, asked for Aziza's name too, her age. They passed through poorly lit hallways where barefoot children stepped aside and watched. They had disheveled hair or shaved scalps. They wore sweaters with frayed sleeves, ragged jeans whose knees had worn down to strings, coats patched with duct tape. Laila smelled soap and talcum, ammonia and urine, and rising apprehension in Aziza, who had begun whimpering.

Laila had a glimpse of the yard: weedy lot, rickety swing set, old tires, a deflated basketball. The rooms they passed were bare, the windows covered with sheets of plastic. A boy darted from one of the rooms and grabbed Laila's elbow, and tried to climb up into her arms. An attendant, who was cleaning up what looked like a puddle of urine, put down his mop and pried the boy off.

Zaman seemed gently proprietary with the orphans. He patted the heads of some, as he

364

passed by, said a cordial word or two to them, tousled their hair, without condescension. The children welcomed his touch. They all looked at him, Laila thought, in hope of approval.

He showed them into his office, a room with only three folding chairs, and a disorderly desk with piles of paper scattered atop it.

'You're from Herat,' Zaman said to Mariam. 'I can tell from your accent.'

He leaned back in his chair and laced his hands over his belly, and said he had a brother-in-law who used to live there. Even in these ordinary gestures, Laila noted a laborious quality to his movements. And though he was smiling faintly, Laila sensed something troubled and wounded beneath, disappointment and defeat glossed over with a veneer of good humor.

'He was a glassmaker,' Zaman said. 'He made these beautiful, jade green swans. You held them up to sunlight and they glittered inside, like the glass was filled with tiny jewels. Have you been back?'

Mariam said she hadn't.

'I'm from Kandahar myself. Have you ever been to Kandahar, *hamshira*? No? It's lovely. What gardens! And the grapes! Oh, the grapes. They bewitch the palate.'

A few children had gathered by the door and were peeking in. Zaman gently shooed them away, in Pashto.

'Of course I love Herat too. City of artists and

writers, Sufis and mystics. You know the old joke, that you can't stretch a leg in Herat without poking a poet in the rear.'

Next to Laila, Aziza snorted.

Zaman feigned a gasp. 'Ah, there. I've made you laugh, little *hamshira*. That's usually the hard part. I was worried, there, for a while. I thought I'd have to cluck like a chicken or bray like a donkey. But, there you are. And so lovely you are.'

He called in an attendant to look after Aziza for a few moments. Aziza leaped onto Mariam's lap and clung to her.

'We're just going to talk, my love,' Laila said. 'I'll be right here. All right? Right here.'

'Why don't we go outside for a minute, Aziza jo?' Mariam said. 'Your mother needs to talk to Kaka Zaman here. Just for a minute. Now, come on.'

When they were alone, Zaman asked for Aziza's date of birth, history of illnesses, allergies. He asked about Aziza's father, and Laila had the strange experience of telling a lie that was really the truth. Zaman listened, his expression revealing neither belief nor skepticism. He ran the orphanage on the honor system, he said. If a *hamshira* said her husband was dead and she couldn't care for her children, he didn't question it.

Laila began to cry.

Zaman put down his pen.

'I'm ashamed,' Laila croaked, her palm pressed to her mouth.

'Look at me, *hamshira*.'

366

'What kind of mother abandons her own child?'

'Look at me.'

Laila raised her gaze.

'It isn't your fault. Do you hear me? Not you. It's those *savages*, those *wahshis*, who are to blame. They bring shame on me as a Pashtun. They've disgraced the name of my people. And you're not alone, *hamshira*. We get mothers like you all the time – all the time – mothers who come here who can't feed their children because the Taliban won't let them go out and make a living. So you don't blame yourself. No one here blames you. I understand.' He leaned forward. '*Hamshira*. I understand.'

Laila wiped her eyes with the cloth of her burqa.

'As for this place,' Zaman sighed, motioning with his hand, 'you can see that it's in dire state. We're always underfunded, always scrambling, improvising. We get little or no support from the Taliban. But we manage. Like you, we do what we have to do. Allah is good and kind, and Allah provides, and, as long He provides, I will see to it that Aziza is fed and clothed. That much I promise you.'

Laila nodded.

'All right?'

He was smiling companionably. 'But don't cry, *hamshira*. Don't let her see you cry.'

Laila wiped her eyes again. 'God bless you,' she said thickly. 'God bless you, brother.'

But when the time for good-byes came, the scene erupted precisely as Laila had dreaded.

Aziza panicked.

All the way home, leaning on Mariam, Laila heard Aziza's shrill cries. In her head, she saw Zaman's thick, calloused hands close around Aziza's arms; she saw them pull, gently at first, then harder, then with force to pry Aziza loose from her. She saw Aziza kicking in Zaman's arms as he hurriedly turned the corner, heard Aziza screaming as though she were about to vanish from the face of the earth. And Laila saw herself running down the hallway, head down, a howl rising up her throat.

'I smell her,' she told Mariam at home. Her eyes swam unseeingly past Mariam's shoulder, past the yard, the walls, to the mountains, brown as smoker's spit. 'I smell her sleep smell. Do you? Do you smell it?'

'Oh, Laila jo,' said Mariam. 'Don't. What good is this? What good?'

At first, Rasheed humored Laila, and accompanied them – her, Mariam, and Zalmai – to the orphanage, though he made sure, as they walked, that she had an eyeful of his grievous looks, an earful of his rants over what a hardship she was putting him through, how badly his legs and back and feet ached walking to and from the orphanage. He made sure she knew how awfully put out he was.

'I'm not a young man anymore,' he said. 'Not that you care. You'd run me to the ground, if you had your way. But you don't, Laila. You don't have your way.'

They parted ways two blocks from the orphanage, and he never spared them more than fifteen minutes. 'A minute late,' he said, 'and I start walking. I mean it.'

Laila had to pester him, plead with him, in order to spin out the allotted minutes with Aziza a bit longer. For herself, and for Mariam, who was disconsolate over Aziza's absence, though, as always, Mariam chose to cradle her own suffering privately and quietly. And for Zalmai too, who asked for his sister every day, and threw tantrums that sometimes dissolved into inconsolable fits of crying.

Sometimes, on the way to the orphanage, Rasheed stopped and complained that his leg was sore. Then he turned around and started walking home in long, steady strides, without so much as a limp. Or he clucked his tongue and said, 'It's my lungs, Laila. I'm short of breath. Maybe tomorrow I'll feel better, or the day after. We'll see.' He never bothered to feign a single raspy breath. Often, as he turned back and marched home, he lit a cigarette. Laila would have to tail him home, helpless, trembling with resentment and impotent rage.

Then one day he told Laila he wouldn't take her anymore. 'I'm too tired from walking the streets all day,' he said, 'looking for work.'

'Then I'll go by myself,' Laila said. 'You can't

369

stop me, Rasheed. Do you hear me? You can hit me all you want, but I'll keep going there.'

'Do as you wish. But you won't get past the Taliban. Don't say I didn't warn you.'

'I'm coming with you,' Mariam said.

Laila wouldn't allow it. 'You have to stay home with Zalmai. If we get stopped . . . I don't want him to see.'

And so Laila's life suddenly revolved around finding ways to see Aziza. Half the time, she never made it to the orphanage. Crossing the street, she was spotted by the Taliban and riddled with questions – *What is your name? Where are you going? Why are you alone? Where is your* mahram? – before she was sent home. If she was lucky, she was given a tongue-lashing or a single kick to the rear, a shove in the back. Other times, she met with assortments of wooden clubs, fresh tree branches, short whips, slaps, often fists.

One day, a young Talib beat Laila with a radio antenna. When he was done, he gave a final whack to the back of her neck and said, 'I see you again, I'll beat you until your mother's milk leaks out of your bones.'

That time, Laila went home. She lay on her stomach, feeling like a stupid, pitiable animal, and hissed as Mariam arranged damp cloths across her bloodied back and thighs. But, usually, Laila refused to cave in. She made as if she were going home, then took a different route down side streets. Sometimes she was caught, questioned, scolded – two, three, even four times in a single day. Then the whips came down and the antennas sliced through the air, and she trudged home, bloodied, without so much as a glimpse of Aziza. Soon Laila took to wearing extra layers, even in the heat, two, three sweaters beneath the burqa, for padding against the beatings.

But for Laila, the reward, if she made it past the Taliban, was worth it. She could spend as much time as she liked then – *hours*, even – with Aziza. They sat in the courtyard, near the swing set, among other children and visiting mothers, and talked about what Aziza had learned that week.

Aziza said Kaka Zaman made it a point to teach them something every day, reading and writing most days, sometimes geography, a bit of history or science, something about plants, animals.

'But we have to pull the curtains,' Aziza said, 'so the Taliban don't see us.' Kaka Zaman had knitting needles and balls of yarn ready, she said, in case of a Taliban inspection. 'We put the books away and pretend to knit.'

One day, during a visit with Aziza, Laila saw a middle-aged woman, her burqa pushed back, visiting with three boys and a girl. Laila recognized the sharp face, the heavy eyebrows, if not the sunken mouth and gray hair. She remembered the shawls, the black skirts, the curt voice, how she used to wear her jet-black hair tied in a bun so that you could see the dark bristles on the back of her neck. Laila remembered this woman once forbidding the female students from covering, saying women and men were equal, that there was no reason women should cover if men didn't.

At one point, Khala Rangmaal looked up and caught her gaze, but Laila saw no lingering, no light of recognition, in her old teacher's eyes.

'They're fractures along the earth's crust,' said Aziza. 'They're called faults.'

It was a warm afternoon, a Friday, in June of 2001. They were sitting in the orphanage's back lot, the four of them, Laila, Zalmai, Mariam, and Aziza. Rashced had relented this time – as he infrequently did – and accompanied the four of them. He was waiting down the street, by the bus stop.

Barefoot kids scampered about around them. A flat soccer ball was kicked around, chased after listlessly.

'And, on either side of the faults, there are these sheets of rock that make up the earth's crust,' Aziza was saying.

Someone had pulled the hair back from Aziza's face, braided it, and pinned it neatly on top of her head. Laila begrudged whoever had gotten to sit behind her daughter, to flip sections of her hair one over the other, had asked her to sit still.

Aziza was demonstrating by opening her hands, palms up, and rubbing them against each other. Zalmai watched this with intense interest.

'Kectonic plates, they're called?'

'*Tectonic*,' Laila said. It hurt to talk. Her jaw was

still sore, her back and neck ached. Her lip was swollen, and her tongue kept poking the empty pocket of the lower incisor Rasheed had knocked loose two days before. Before Mammy and Babi had died and her life turned upside down, Laila never would have believed that a human body could withstand this much beating, this viciously, this regularly, and keep functioning.

'Right. And when they slide past each other, they catch and slip – see, Mammy? – and it releases energy, which travels to the earth's surface and makes it shake.'

'You're getting so smart,' Mariam said. 'So much smarter than your dumb *khala*.'

Aziza's face glowed, broadened. 'You're not dumb, Khala Mariam. And Kaka Zaman says that, sometimes, the shifting of rocks is deep, deep below, and it's powerful and scary down there, but all we feel on the surface is a slight tremor. Only a slight tremor.'

The visit before this one, it was oxygen atoms in the atmosphere scattering the bluc light from the sun. *If the earth had no atmosphere*, Aziza had said a little breathlessly, *the sky wouldn't be blue at all but a pitch-black sea and the sun a big bright star in the dark.*

'Is Aziza coming home with us this time?' Zalmai said.

'Soon, my love,' Laila said. 'Soon.'

Laila watched him wander away, walking like his father, stooping forward, toes turned in. He walked to the swing set, pushed an empty seat, ended up sitting on the concrete, ripping weeds from a crack.

*Water evaporates from the leaves – Mammy, did you know? – the way it does from laundry hanging from a line. And that drives the flow of water up the tree. From the ground and through the roots, then all the way up the tree trunk, through the branches and into the leaves. It's called transpiration.*

More than once, Laila had wondered what the Taliban would do about Kaka Zaman's clandestine lessons if they found out.

During visits, Aziza didn't allow for much silence. She filled all the spaces with effusive speech, delivered in a high, ringing voice. She was tangential with her topics, and her hands gesticulated wildly, flying up with a nervousness that wasn't like her at all. She had a new laugh, Aziza did. Not so much a laugh, really, as nervous punctuation, meant, Laila suspected, to reassure.

And there were other changes. Laila would notice the dirt under Aziza's fingernails, and Aziza would notice her noticing and bury her hands under her thighs. Whenever a kid cried in their vicinity, snot oozing from his nose, or if a kid walked by bare-assed, hair clumped with dirt, Aziza's eyelids fluttered and she was quick to explain it away. She was like a hostess embarrassed in front of her guests by the squalor of her home, the untidiness of her children.

Questions of how she was coping were met with vague but cheerful replies.

*Doing fine, Khala. I'm fine.*
Do kids pick on you?
*They don't, Mammy. Everyone is nice.*
Are you eating? Sleeping all right?
*Eating. Sleeping too. Yes. We had lamb last night.
Maybe it was last week.*
When Aziza spoke like this, Laila saw more than
a little of Mariam in her.

Aziza stammered now. Mariam noticed it first. It
was subtle but perceptible, and more pronounced
with words that began with *t*. Laila asked Zaman
about it. He frowned and said, 'I thought she'd
always done that.'

They left the orphanage with Aziza that Friday
afternoon for a short outing and met Rasheed,
who was waiting for them by the bus stop. When
Zalmai spotted his father, he uttered an excited
squeak and impatiently wriggled from Laila's
arms. Aziza's greeting to Rasheed was rigid but
not hostile.

Rasheed said they should hurry, he had only two
hours before he had to report back to work. This
was his first week as a doorman for the Intercontinental. From noon to eight, six days a week,
Rasheed opened car doors, carried luggage,
mopped up the occasional spill. Sometimes, at
day's end, the cook at the buffet-style restaurant
let Rasheed bring home a few leftovers – as long
as he was discreet about it – cold meatballs
sloshing in oil; fried chicken wings, the crust gone
hard and dry; stuffed pasta shells turned chewy;

stiff, gravelly rice. Rasheed had promised Laila that once he had some money saved up, Aziza could move back home.

Rasheed was wearing his uniform, a burgundy red polyester suit, white shirt, clip-on tie, visor cap pressing down on his white hair. In this uniform, Rasheed was transformed. He looked vulnerable, pitiably bewildered, almost harmless. Like someone who had accepted without a sigh of protest the indignities life had doled out to him. Someone both pathetic and admirable in his docility.

They rode the bus to Titanic City. They walked into the riverbed, flanked on either side by makeshift stalls clinging to the dry banks. Near the bridge, as they were descending the steps, a barefoot man dangled dead from a crane, his ears cut off, his neck bent at the end of a rope. In the river, they melted into the horde of shoppers milling about, the money changers and bored-looking NGO workers, the cigarette vendors, the covered women who thrust fake antibiotic prescriptions at people and begged for money to fill them. Whip-toting, *naswar*-chewing Talibs patrolled Titanic City on the lookout for the indiscreet laugh, the unveiled face.

From a toy kiosk, between a *poosteen* coat vendor and a fake-flower stand, Zalmai picked out a rubber basketball with yellow and blue swirls.

'Pick something,' Rasheed said to Aziza.

Aziza hedged, stiffened with embarrassment.

'Hurry. I have to be at work in an hour.'

Aziza chose a gum-ball machine – the same coin could be inserted to get candy, then retrieved from the flap-door coin return below.

Rasheed's eyebrows shot up when the seller quoted him the price. A round of haggling ensued, at the end of which Rasheed said to Aziza contentiously, as if it were *she* who'd haggled him, 'Give it back. I can't afford both.'

On the way back, Aziza's high-spirited façade waned the closer they got to the orphanage. The hands stopped flying up. Her face turned heavy. It happened every time. It was Laila's turn now, with Mariam pitching in, to take up the chattering, to laugh nervously, to fill the melancholy quiet with breathless, aimless banter.

Later, after Rasheed had dropped them off and taken a bus to work, Laila watched Aziza wave good-bye and scuff along the wall in the orphanage back lot. She thought of Aziza's stutter, and of what Aziza had said earlier about fractures and powerful collisions deep down and how sometimes all we see on the surface is a slight tremor.

'Get away, you!' Zalmai cried.

'Hush,' Mariam said. 'Who are you yelling at?'

He pointed. 'There. That man.'

Laila followed his finger. There *was* a man at the front door of the house, leaning against it. His head turned when he saw them approaching. He uncrossed his arms. Limped a few steps toward them.

Laila stopped.

A choking noise came up her throat. Her knees weakened. Laila suddenly wanted, *needed*, to grope for Mariam's arm, her shoulder, her wrist, something, anything, to lean on. But she didn't. She didn't dare. She didn't dare move a muscle. She didn't dare breathe, or blink even, for fear that he was nothing but a mirage shimmering in the distance, a brittle illusion that would vanish at the slightest provocation. Laila stood perfectly still and looked at Tariq until her chest screamed for air and her eyes burned to blink. And, somehow, miraculously, after she took a breath, closed and opened her eyes, he was still standing there. Tariq was still standing there.

Laila allowed herself to take a step toward him. Then another. And another. And then she was running.

# CHAPTER 43

# MARIAM

Upstairs, in Mariam's room, Zalmai was wound up. He bounced his new rubber basketball around for a while, on the floor, against the walls. Mariam asked him not to, but he knew that she had no authority to exert over him and so he went on bouncing his ball, his eyes holding hers defiantly. For a while, they pushed his toy car, an ambulance with bold red lettering on the sides, sending it back and forth between them across the room.

Earlier, when they had met Tariq at the door, Zalmai had clutched the basketball close to his chest and stuck a thumb in his mouth – something he didn't do anymore except when he was apprehensive. He had eyed Tariq with suspicion.

'Who is that man?' he said now. 'I don't like him.'

Mariam was going to explain, say something about him and Laila growing up together, but Zalmai cut her off and said to turn the ambulance around, so the front grill faced him, and, when she did, he said he wanted his basketball again.

'Where is it?' he said, 'Where is the ball Baba

jan got me? Where is it? I want it! I want it!' his voice rising and becoming more shrill with each word.

'It was just here,' Mariam said, and he cried, 'No, it's lost, I know it. I just know it's lost! Where is it? Where is it?'

'Here,' she said, fetching the ball from the closet where it had rolled to. But Zalmai was bawling now and pounding his fists, crying that it wasn't the same ball, it couldn't be, because his ball was lost, and this was a fake one, where had his real ball gone? Where? Where where where?

He screamed until Laila had to come upstairs to hold him, to rock him and run her fingers through his tight, dark curls, to dry his moist cheeks and cluck her tongue in his ear.

Mariam waited outside the room. From atop the staircase, all she could see of Tariq were his long legs, the real one and the artificial one, in khaki pants, stretched out on the uncarpeted living-room floor. It was then that she realized why the doorman at the Continental had looked familiar the day she and Rasheed had gone there to place the call to Jalil. He'd been wearing a cap and sunglasses, that was why it hadn't come to her earlier. But Mariam remembered now, from nine years before, remembered him sitting downstairs, patting his brow with a handkerchief and asking for water. Now all manner of questions raced through her mind: Had the sulfa pills too been part of the ruse? Which one of them had plotted

380

the lie, provided the convincing details? And how much had Rasheed paid Abdul Sharif – if that was even his name – to come and crush Laila with the story of Tariq's death?

# CHAPTER 44

# LAILA

Tariq said that one of the men who shared his cell had a cousin who'd been publicly flogged once for painting flamingos. He, the cousin, had a seemingly incurable thing for them.

'Entire sketchbooks,' Tariq said. 'Dozens of oil paintings of them, wading in lagoons, sunbathing in marshlands. Flying into sunsets too, I'm afraid.'

'Flamingos,' Laila said. She looked at him sitting against the wall, his good leg bent at the knee. She had an urge to touch him again, as she had earlier by the front gate when she'd run to him. It embarrassed her now to think of how she'd thrown her arms around his neck and wept into his chest, how she'd said his name over and over in a slurring, thick voice. Had she acted too eagerly, she wondered, too desperately? Maybe so. But she hadn't been able to help it. And now she longed to touch him again, to prove to herself again that he was really here, that he was not a dream, an apparition.

'Indeed,' he said. 'Flamingos.'

When the Taliban had found the paintings, Tariq

said, they'd taken offense at the birds' long, bare legs. After they'd tied the cousin's feet and flogged his soles bloody, they had presented him with a choice: Either destroy the paintings or make the flamingos decent. So the cousin had picked up his brush and painted trousers on every last bird.

'And there you have it. Islamic flamingos,' Tariq said.

Laughter came up, but Laila pushed it back down. She was ashamed of her yellowing teeth, the missing incisor. Ashamed of her withered looks and swollen lip. She wished she'd had the chance to wash her face, at least comb her hair.

'But he'll have the last laugh, the cousin,' Tariq said. 'He painted those trousers with watercolor. When the Taliban are gone, he'll just wash them off.' He smiled – Laila noticed that he had a missing tooth of his own – and looked down at his hands. 'Indeed.'

He was wearing a *pakol* on his head, hiking boots, and a black wool sweater tucked into the waist of khaki pants. He was half smiling, nodding slowly. Laila didn't remember him saying this before, this word *indeed*, and this pensive gesture, the fingers making a tent in his lap, the nodding, it was new too. Such an adult word, such an adult gesture, and why should it be so startling? He *was* an adult now, Tariq, a twenty-five-year-old man with slow movements and a tiredness to his smile. Tall, bearded, slimmer than in her dreams of him, but with strong-looking hands, workman's hands, with tortuous, full veins. His face was still lean and handsome but not fair-skinned any longer; his brow had a weathered look to it, sunburned, like his neck, the brow of a traveler at the end of a long and wearying journey. His *pakol* was pushed back on his head, and she could see that he'd started to lose his hair. The hazel of his eyes was duller than she remembered, paler, or perhaps it was merely the light in the room.

Laila thought of Tariq's mother, her unhurried manners, the clever smiles, the dull purple wig. And his father, with his squinty gaze, his wry humor. Earlier, at the door, with a voice full of tears, tripping over her own words, she'd told Tariq what she thought had happened to him and his parents, and he had shaken his head. So now she asked him how they were doing, his parents. But she regretted the question when Tariq looked down and said, a bit distractedly, 'Passed on.'

'I'm so sorry.'

'Well. Yes. Me too. Here.' He fished a small paper bag from his pocket and passed it to her. 'Compliments of Alyona.' Inside was a block of cheese in plastic wrap.

'Alyona. It's a pretty name.' Laila tried to say this next without wavering. 'Your wife?'

'My goat.' He was smiling at her expectantly, as though waiting for her to retrieve a memory.

Then Laila remembered. The Soviet film. Alyona had been the captain's daughter, the girl in love with the first mate. That was the day that she,

384

Tariq, and Hasina had watched Soviet tanks and jeeps leave Kabul, the day Tariq had worn that ridiculous Russian fur hat.

'I had to tie her to a stake in the ground,' Tariq was saying. 'And build a fence. Because of the wolves. In the foothills where I live, there's a wooded area nearby, maybe a quarter of a mile away, pine trees mostly, some fir, deodars. They mostly stick to the woods, the wolves do, but a bleating goat, one that likes to go wandering, that can draw them out. So the fence. The stake.'

Laila asked him which foothills.

'Pir Panjal, Pakistan,' he said. 'Where I live is called Murree; it's a summer retreat, an hour from Islamabad. It's hilly and green, lots of trees, high above sea level. So it's cool in the summer. Perfect for tourists.'

The British had built it as a hill station near their military headquarters in Rawalpindi, he said, for the Victorians to escape the heat. You could still spot a few relics of the colonial times, Tariq said, the occasional tearoom, tin-roofed bungalows, called cottages, that sort of thing. The town itself was small and pleasant. The main street was called the Mall, where there was a post office, a bazaar, a few restaurants, shops that overcharged tourists for painted glass and hand-knotted carpets. Curiously, the Mall's one-way traffic flowed in one direction one week, the opposite direction the next week.

'The locals say that Ireland's traffic is like that

too in places,' Tariq said. 'I wouldn't know. Anyway, it's nice. It's a plain life, but I like it. I like living there.'

'With your goat. With Alyona.'

Laila meant this less as a joke than as a surreptitious entry into another line of talk, such as who else was there with him worrying about wolves eating goats. But Tariq only went on nodding.

'I'm sorry about your parents too,' he said.

'You heard.'

'I spoke to some neighbors earlier,' he said. A pause, during which Laila wondered what else the neighbors had told him. 'I don't recognize anybody. From the old days, I mean.'

'They're all gone. There's no one left you'd know.'

'I don't recognize Kabul.'

'Neither do I,' Laila said. 'And I never left.'

'Mammy has a new friend,' Zalmai said after dinner later that same night, after Tariq had left. 'A man.'

Rasheed looked up. '*Does* she, now?'

Tariq asked if he could smoke.

They had stayed awhile at the Nasir Bagh refugee camp near Peshawar, Tariq said, tapping ash into a saucer. There were sixty thousand Afghans living there already when he and his parents arrived.

'It wasn't as bad as some of the other camps

like, God forbid, Jalozai,' he said. 'I guess at one point it was even some kind of model camp, back during the Cold War, a place the West could point to and prove to the world they weren't just funneling arms into Afghanistan.'

But that had been during the Soviet war, Tariq said, the days of jihad and worldwide interest and generous funding and visits from Margaret Thatcher.

'You know the rest, Laila. After the war, the Soviets fell apart, and the West moved on. There was nothing at stake for them in Afghanistan anymore and the money dried up. Now Nasir Bagh is tents, dust, and open sewers. When we got there, they handed us a stick and a sheet of canvas and told us to build ourselves a tent.'

Tariq said what he remembered most about Nasir Bagh, where they had stayed for a year, was the color brown. 'Brown tents. Brown people. Brown dogs. Brown porridge.'

There was a leafless tree he climbed every day, where he straddled a branch and watched the refugees lying about in the sun, their sores and stumps in plain view. He watched little emaciated boys carrying water in their jerry cans, gathering dog droppings to make fire, carving toy AK-47s out of wood with dull knives, lugging the sacks of wheat flour that no one could make bread from that held together. All around the refugee town, the wind made the tents flap. It hurled stubbles of weed everywhere, lifted kites flown from the roofs of mud hovels.

'A lot of kids died. Dysentery, TB, hunger – you name it. Mostly, that damn dysentery. God, Laila. I saw so many kids buried. There's nothing worse a person can see.'

He crossed his legs. It grew quiet again between them for a while.

'My father didn't survive that first winter,' he said. 'He died in his sleep. I don't think there was any pain.'

That same winter, he said, his mother caught pneumonia and almost died, would have died, if not for a camp doctor who worked out of a station wagon made into a mobile clinic. She would wake up all night long, feverish, coughing out thick, rust-colored phlegm. The queues were long to see the doctor, Tariq said. Everyone was shivering in line, moaning, coughing, some with shit running down their legs, others too tired or hungry or sick to make words.

'But he was a decent man, the doctor. He treated my mother, gave her some pills, saved her life that winter.'

That same winter, Tariq had cornered a kid.

'Twelve, maybe thirteen years old,' he said evenly. 'I held a shard of glass to his throat and took his blanket from him. I gave it to my mother.'

He made a vow to himself, Tariq said, after his mother's illness, that they would not spend another winter in camp. He'd work, save, move them to an apartment in Peshawar with heating and clean water. When spring came, he looked for work. From time to time, a truck came to camp early in the morning and rounded up a couple of dozen boys, took them to a field to move stones or an orchard to pick apples in exchange for a little money, sometimes a blanket, a pair of shoes. But they never wanted him, Tariq said.

'One look at my leg and it was over.'

There were other jobs. Ditches to dig, hovels to build, water to carry, feces to shovel from outhouses. But young men fought over these jobs, and Tariq never stood a chance.

Then he met a shopkeeper one day, that fall of 1993.

'He offered me money to take a leather coat to Lahore. Not a lot but enough, enough for one or maybe two months' apartment rent.'

The shopkeeper gave him a bus ticket, Tariq said, and the address of a street corner near the Lahore Rail Station where he was to deliver the coat to a friend of the shopkeeper's.

'I knew already. Of course I knew,' Tariq said. 'He said that if I got caught, I was on my own, that I should remember that he knew where my mother lived. But the money was too good to pass up. And winter was coming again.'

'How far did you get?' Laila asked.

'Not far,' he said and laughed, sounding apologetic, ashamed. 'Never even got on the bus. But I thought I was immune, you know, safe. As though there was some accountant up there somewhere, a guy with a pencil tucked behind his ear who kept track of these things, who tallied things

389

up, and he'd look down and say, "Yes, yes, he can have this, we'll let it go. He's paid some dues already, this one.'"

It was in the seams, the hashish, and it spilled all over the street when the police took a knife to the coat.

Tariq laughed again when he said this, a climbing, shaky kind of laugh, and Laila remembered how he used to laugh like this when they were little, to cloak embarrassment, to make light of things he'd done that were foolhardy or scandalous.

'He has a limp,' Zalmai said.

'Is this who I *think* it is?'

'He was only visiting,' Mariam said.

'Shut up, you,' Rasheed snapped, raising a finger. He turned back to Laila. 'Well, what do you know? Laili and Majnoon reunited. Just like old times.' His face turned stony. 'So you let him in. Here. In my house. You let him in. He was in here with my son.'

'You duped me. You lied to me,' Laila said, gritting her teeth. 'You had that man sit across from me and . . . You knew I would leave if I thought he was alive.'

'AND YOU DIDN'T LIE TO ME?' Rasheed roared. 'You think I didn't figure it out? About your *harami*? You take me for a fool, you whore?'

The more Tariq talked, the more Laila dreaded the moment when he would stop. The silence that would follow, the signal that it was her turn to give account, to provide the why and how and when, to make official what he surely already knew. She felt a faint nausea whenever he paused. She averted his eyes. She looked down at his hands, at the coarse, dark hairs that had sprouted on the back of them in the intervening years.

Tariq wouldn't say much about his years in prison save that he'd learned to speak Urdu there. When Laila asked, he gave an impatient shake of his head. In this gesture, Laila saw rusty bars and unwashed bodies, violent men and crowded halls, and ceilings rotting with moldy deposits. She read in his face that it had been a place of abasement, of degradation and despair.

Tariq said his mother tried to visit him after his arrest.

'Three times she came. But I never got to see her,' he said.

He wrote her a letter, and a few more after that, even though he doubted that she would receive them.

'And I wrote you.'

'You did?'

'Oh, *volumes*,' he said. 'Your friend Rumi would have envied my production.' Then he laughed again, uproariously this time, as though he was both startled at his own boldness and embarrassed by what he had let on.

Zalmai began bawling upstairs.

★    ★    ★

'Just like old times, then,' Rasheed said. 'The two of you. I suppose you let him see your face.'

'She did,' said Zalmai. Then, to Laila, 'You did, Mammy. I saw you.'

'Your son doesn't care for me much,' Tariq said when Laila returned downstairs.

'I'm sorry,' she said. 'It's not that. He just . . . Don't mind him.' Then quickly she changed the subject because it made her feel perverse and guilty to feel that about Zalmai, who was a child, a little boy who loved his father, whose instinctive aversion to this stranger was understandable and legitimate.

*And I wrote you.*

*Volumes.*

*Volumes.*

'How long have you been in Murree?'

'Less than a year,' Tariq said.

He befriended an older man in prison, he said, a fellow named Salim, a Pakistani, a former field hockey player who had been in and out of prison for years and who was serving ten years for stabbing an undercover policeman. Every prison has a man like Salim, Tariq said. There was always someone who was cunning and connected, who worked the system and found you things, someone around whom the air buzzed with both opportunity and danger. It was Salim who had sent out Tariq's queries about his mother, Salim who had sat him down and told him, in a soft, fatherly voice, that she had died of exposure.

392

Tariq spent seven years in the Pakistani prison. 'I got off easy,' he said. 'I was lucky. The judge sitting on my case, it turned out, had a brother who'd married an Afghan woman. Maybe he showed mercy. I don't know.'

When Tariq's sentence was up, early in the winter of 2000, Salim gave him his brother's address and phone number. The brother's name was Sayeed.

'He said Sayeed owned a small hotel in Murree,' Tariq said. 'Twenty rooms and a lounge, a little place to cater to tourists. He said tell him I sent you.'

Tariq had liked Murree as soon as he'd stepped off the bus: the snow-laden pines; the cold, crisp air; the shuttered wooden cottages, smoke curling up from chimneys.

Here was a place, Tariq had thought, knocking on Sayeed's door, a place not only worlds removed from the wretchedness he'd known but one that made even the notion of hardship and sorrow somehow obscene, unimaginable.

'I said to myself, here is a place where a man can get on.'

Tariq was hired as a janitor and handyman. He did well, he said, during the one-month trial period, at half pay, that Sayeed granted him. As Tariq spoke, Laila saw Sayeed, whom she imagined narrow-eyed and ruddy-faced, standing at the reception office window watching Tariq chop wood and shovel snow off the driveway. She saw him stooping over Tariq's legs, observing, as Tariq lay beneath the sink fixing a leaky pipe. She pictured him checking the register for missing cash.

Tariq's shack was beside the cook's little bungalow, he said. The cook was a matronly old widow named Adiba. Both shacks were detached from the hotel itself, separated from the main building by a scattering of almond trees, a park bench, and a pyramid-shaped stone fountain that, in the summer, gurgled water all day. Laila pictured Tariq in his shack, sitting up in bed, watching the leafy world outside his window.

At the end of the grace period, Sayeed raised Tariq's pay to full, told him his lunches were free, gave him a wool coat, and fitted him for a new leg. Tariq said he'd wept at the man's kindness.

With his first month's full salary in his pocket, Tariq had gone to town and bought Alyona.

'Her fur is perfectly white,' Tariq said, smiling. 'Some mornings, when it's snowed all night, you look out the window and all you see of her is two eyes and a muzzle.'

Laila nodded. Another silence ensued. Upstairs, Zalmai had begun bouncing his ball again against the wall.

'I thought you were dead,' Laila said.

'I know. You told me.'

Laila's voice broke. She had to clear her throat, collect herself. 'The man who came to give the news, he was so earnest. . . I believed him, Tariq. I wish I hadn't, but I did. And then I felt so alone

394

and scared. Otherwise, I wouldn't have agreed to marry Rasheed. I wouldn't have . . .'

'You don't have to do this,' he said softly, avoiding her eyes. There was no hidden reproach, no recrimination, in the way he had said this. No suggestion of blame.

'But I do. Because there was a bigger reason why I married him. There's something you don't know, Tariq. *Someone*. I have to tell you.'

'Did you sit and talk with him too?' Rasheed asked Zalmai.

Zalmai said nothing. Laila saw hesitation and uncertainty in his eyes now, as if he had just realized that what he'd disclosed had turned out to be far bigger than he'd thought.

'I asked you a question, boy.'

Zalmai swallowed. His gaze kept shifting. 'I was upstairs, playing with Mariam.'

'And your mother?'

Zalmai looked at Laila apologetically, on the verge of tears.

'It's all right, Zalmai,' Laila said. 'Tell the truth.'

'She was . . . She was downstairs, talking to that man,' he said in a thin voice hardly louder than a whisper.

'I see,' said Rasheed. 'Teamwork.'

As he was leaving, Tariq said, 'I want to meet her. I want to see her.'

'I'll arrange it,' Laila said.

'Aziza. Aziza.' He smiled, tasting the word. Whenever Rasheed uttered her daughter's name, it came out sounding unwholesome to Laila, almost vulgar. 'Aziza. It's lovely.'

'So is she. You'll see.'

'I'll count the minutes.'

Almost ten years had passed since they had last seen each other. Laila's mind flashed to all the times they'd met in the alley, kissing in secret. She wondered how she must seem to him now. Did he still find her pretty? Or did she seem withered to him, reduced, pitiable, like a fearful, shuffling old woman? Almost ten years. But, for a moment, standing there with Tariq in the sunlight, it was as though those years had never happened. Her parents' deaths, her marriage to Rasheed, the killings, the rockets, the Taliban, the beatings, the hunger, even her children, all of it seemed like a dream, a bizarre detour, a mere interlude between that last afternoon together and this moment.

Then Tariq's face changed, turned grave. She knew this expression. It was the same look he'd had on his face that day, all those years ago when they'd both been children, when he'd unstrapped his leg and gone after Khadim. He reached with one hand now and touched the corner of her lower lip.

'He did this to you,' he said coldly.

At his touch, Laila remembered the frenzy of that afternoon again when they'd conceived Aziza. His breath on her neck, the muscles of his hips flexing, his chest pressing against her breasts, their hands interlocked.

'I wish I'd taken you with me,' Tariq nearly whispered.

Laila had to lower her gaze, try not to cry.

'I know you're a married woman and a mother now. And here I am, after all these years, after all that's happened, showing up at your doorstep. Probably, it isn't proper, or fair, but I've come such a long way to see you, and . . . Oh, Laila, I wish I'd never left you.'

'Don't,' she croaked.

'I should have tried harder. I should have married you when I had the chance. Everything would have been different, then.'

'Don't talk this way. Please. It hurts.'

He nodded, started to take a step toward her, then stopped himself. 'I don't want to assume anything. And I don't mean to turn your life upside down, appearing like this out of nowhere. If you want me to leave, if you want me to go back to Pakistan, say the word, Laila. I mean it. Say it and I'll go. I'll never trouble you again. I'll—'

'No!' Laila said more sharply than she'd intended to. She saw that she'd reached for his arm, that she was clutching it. She dropped her hand. 'No. Don't leave, Tariq. No. Please stay.'

Tariq nodded.

'He works from noon to eight. Come back tomorrow afternoon. I'll take you to Aziza.'

'I'm not afraid of him, you know.'

'I know. Come back tomorrow afternoon.'

'And then?'

'And then. . . I don't know. I have to think. This is . . .'

'I know it is,' he said. 'I understand. I'm sorry. I'm sorry for a lot of things.'

'Don't be. You promised you'd come back. And you did.'

His eyes watered. 'It's good to see you, Laila.'

She watched him walk away, shivering where she stood. She thought, *Volumes*, and another shudder passed through her, a current of something sad and forlorn, but also something eager and recklessly hopeful.

# CHAPTER 45

# MARIAM

'I was upstairs, playing with Mariam,' Zalmai said.

'And your mother?'

'She was . . . She was downstairs, talking to that man.'

'I see,' said Rasheed. 'Teamwork.'

Mariam watched his face relax, loosen. She watched the folds clear from his brow. Suspicion and misgiving winked out of his eyes. He sat up straight, and, for a few brief moments, he appeared merely thoughtful, like a ship captain informed of imminent mutiny taking his time to ponder his next move.

He looked up.

Mariam began to say something, but he raised a hand, and, without looking at her, said, 'It's too late, Mariam.'

To Zalmai he said coldly, 'You're going upstairs, boy.'

On Zalmai's face, Mariam saw alarm. Nervously, he looked around at the three of them. He sensed now that his tattletale game had let something serious – adult serious – into the room. He cast a despondent, contrite glance toward Mariam, then his mother.

In a challenging voice, Rasheed said, '*Now!*'

He took Zalmai by the elbow. Zalmai meekly let himself be led upstairs.

They stood frozen, Mariam and Laila, eyes to the ground, as though looking at each other would give credence to the way Rasheed saw things, that while he was opening doors and lugging baggage for people who wouldn't spare him a glance a lewd conspiracy was shaping behind his back, in his home, in his beloved son's presence. Neither one of them said a word. They listened to the footsteps in the hallway above, one heavy and foreboding, the other the pattering of a skittish little animal. They listened to muted words passed, a squeaky plea, a curt retort, a door shut, the rattle of a key as it turned. Then one set of footsteps returning, more impatiently now.

Mariam saw his feet pounding the steps as he came down. She saw him pocketing the key, saw his belt, the perforated end wrapped tightly around his knuckles. The fake brass buckle dragged behind him, bouncing on the steps.

She went to stop him, but he shoved her back and blew by her. Without saying a word, he swung the belt at Laila. He did it with such speed that she had no time to retreat or duck, or even raise a protective arm. Laila touched her fingers to her temple, looked at the blood, looked at Rasheed, with astonishment. It lasted only a moment or

400

two, this look of disbelief, before it was replaced by something hateful.

Rasheed swung the belt again.

This time, Laila shielded herself with a forearm and made a grab at the belt. She missed, and Rasheed brought the belt down again. Laila caught it briefly before Rasheed yanked it free and lashed at her again. Then Laila was dashing around the room, and Mariam was screaming words that ran together and imploring Rasheed, as he chased Laila, as he blocked her way and cracked his belt at her. At one point, Laila ducked and managed to land a punch across his ear, which made him spit a curse and pursue her even more relentlessly. He caught her, threw her up against the wall, and struck her with the belt again and again, the buckle slamming against her chest, her shoulder, her raised arms, her fingers, drawing blood wherever it struck.

Mariam lost count of how many times the belt cracked, how many pleading words she cried out to Rasheed, how many times she circled around the incoherent tangle of teeth and fists and belt, before she saw fingers clawing at Rasheed's face, chipped nails digging into his jowls and pulling at his hair and scratching his forehead. How long before she realized, with both shock and relish, that the fingers were hers.

He let go of Laila and turned on her. At first, he looked at her without seeing her, then his eyes narrowed, appraised Mariam with interest. The look in them shifted from puzzlement to shock, then disapproval, disappointment even, lingering there a moment.

Mariam remembered the first time she had seen his eyes, under the wedding veil, in the mirror, with Jalil looking on, how their gazes had slid across the glass and met, his indifferent, hers docile, conceding, almost apologetic.

*Apologetic.*

Mariam saw now in those same eyes what a fool she had been.

Had she been a deceitful wife? she asked herself. A complacent wife? A dishonorable woman? Discreditable? Vulgar? What harmful thing had she willfully done to this man to warrant his malice, his continual assaults, the relish with which he tormented her? Had she not looked after him when he was ill? Fed him, and his friends, cleaned up after him dutifully?

Had she not given this man her youth?

Had she ever justly deserved his meanness?

The belt made a thump when Rasheed dropped it to the ground and came for her. Some jobs, that *thump* said, were meant to be done with bare hands.

But just as he was bearing down on her, Mariam saw Laila behind him pick something up from the ground. She watched Laila's hand rise overhead, hold, then come swooping down against the side of his face. Glass shattered. The jagged remains of the drinking glass rained down to the ground.

There was blood on Laila's hands, blood flowing from the open gash on Rasheed's cheek, blood down his neck, on his shirt. He turned around, all snarling teeth and blazing eyes.

They crashed to the ground, Rasheed and Laila, thrashing about. He ended up on top, his hands already wrapped around Laila's neck.

Mariam clawed at him. She beat at his chest. She hurled herself against him. She struggled to uncurl his fingers from Laila's neck. She bit them. But they remained tightly clamped around Laila's windpipe, and Mariam saw that he meant to carry this through.

He meant to suffocate her, and there was nothing either of them could do about it.

Mariam backed away and left the room. She was aware of a thumping sound from upstairs, aware that tiny palms were slapping against a locked door. She ran down the hallway. She burst through the front door. Crossed the yard.

In the toolshed, Mariam grabbed the shovel.

Rasheed didn't notice her coming back into the room. He was still on top of Laila, his eyes wide and crazy, his hands wrapped around her neck. Laila's face was turning blue now, and her eyes had rolled back. Mariam saw that she was no longer struggling. *He's going to kill her*, she thought. *He really means to*. And Mariam could not, would not, allow that happen. He'd taken so much from her in twenty-seven years of marriage. She would not watch him take Laila too.

Mariam steadied her feet and tightened her grip around the shovel's handle. She raised it. She said his name. She wanted him to see.

'Rasheed.'

He looked up.

Mariam swung.

She hit him across the temple. The blow knocked him off Laila.

Rasheed touched his head with the palm of his hand. He looked at the blood on his fingertips, then at Mariam. She thought she saw his face soften. She imagined that something had passed between them, that maybe she had quite literally knocked some understanding into his head. Maybe he saw something in her face too, Mariam thought, something that made him hedge. Maybe he saw some trace of all the self-denial, all the sacrifice, all the sheer exertion it had taken her to live with him for all these years, live with his continual condescension and violence, his fault-finding and meanness. Was that respect she saw in his eyes? Regret?

But then his upper lip curled back into a spiteful sneer, and Mariam knew then the futility, maybe even the irresponsibility, of not finishing this. If she let him walk now, how long before he fetched the key from his pocket and went for that gun of his upstairs in the room where he'd locked Zalmai? Had Mariam been certain that he would be satisfied with shooting only her, that there was a chance he would spare Laila, she might have dropped the shovel. But in Rasheed's eyes she saw murder for them both.

And so Mariam raised the shovel high, raised it as high as she could, arching it so it touched the small of her back. She turned it so the sharp edge was vertical, and, as she did, it occurred to her that this was the first time that *she* was deciding the course of her own life.

And, with that, Mariam brought down the shovel. This time, she gave it everything she had.

# CHAPTER 46

# LAILA

Laila was aware of the face over her, all teeth and tobacco and foreboding eyes. She was dimly aware, too, of Mariam, a presence beyond the face, of her fists raining down. Above them was the ceiling, and it was the ceiling Laila was drawn to, the dark markings of mold spreading across it like ink on a dress, the crack in the plaster that was a stolid smile or a frown, depending on which end of the room you looked at it from. Laila thought of all the times she had tied a rag around the end of a broom and cleaned cobwebs from this ceiling. The three times she and Mariam had put coats of white paint on it. The crack wasn't a smile any longer now but a mocking leer. And it was receding. The ceiling was shrinking, lifting, rising away from her and toward some hazy dimness beyond. It rose until it shrank to the size of a postage stamp, white and bright, everything around it blotted out by the shuttered darkness. In the dark, Rasheed's face was like a sunspot.

Brief little bursts of blinding light before her eyes now, like silver stars exploding. Bizarre geometric forms in the light, worms, egg-shaped things, moving up and down, sideways, melting into each other, breaking apart, morphing into something else, then fading, giving way to blackness.

Voices muffled and distant.

Behind the lids of her eyes, her children's faces flared and fizzled. Aziza, alert and burdened, knowing, secretive. Zalmai, looking up at his father with quivering eagerness.

It would end like this, then, Laila thought. What a pitiable end.

But then the darkness began to lift. She had a sensation of rising up, of being hoisted up. The ceiling slowly came back, expanded, and now Laila could make out the crack again, and it was the same old dull smile.

She was being shaken. *Are you all right? Answer me, are you all right?* Mariam's face, engraved with scratches, heavy with worry, hovered over Laila.

Laila tried a breath. It burned her throat. She tried another. It burned even more this time, and not just her throat but her chest too. And then she was coughing, and wheezing. Gasping. But breathing. Her good ear rang.

The first thing she saw when she sat up was Rasheed. He was lying on his back, staring at nothing with an unblinking, fish-mouthed expression. A bit of foam, lightly pink, had dribbled from

407

his mouth down his cheek. The front of his pants was wet. She saw his forehead.

Then she saw the shovel.

A groan came out of her. 'Oh,' she said, tremulously, barely able to make a voice, 'Oh, Mariam.'

Laila paced, moaning and banging her hands together, as Mariam sat near Rasheed, her hands in her lap, calm and motionless. Mariam didn't say anything for a long time.

Laila's mouth was dry, and she was stammering her words, trembling all over. She willed herself not to look at Rasheed, at the rictus of his mouth, his open eyes, at the blood congealing in the hollow of his collarbone.

Outside, the light was fading, the shadows deepening. Mariam's face looked thin and drawn in this light, but she did not appear agitated or frightened, merely preoccupied, thoughtful, so self-possessed that when a fly landed on her chin she paid it no attention. She just sat there with her bottom lip stuck out, the way she did when she was absorbed in thought.

At last, she said, 'Sit down, Laila jo.'

Laila did, obediently.

'We have to move him. Zalmai can't see this.'

Mariam fished the bedroom key from Rasheed's pocket before they wrapped him in a bedsheet. Laila took him by the legs, behind the knees, and Mariam grabbed him under the arms. They tried lifting him, but he was too heavy, and they ended up dragging him. As they were passing through the front door and into the yard, Rasheed's foot caught against the doorframe and his leg bent sideways. They had to back up and try again, and then something thumped upstairs and Laila's legs gave out. She dropped Rasheed. She slumped to the ground, sobbing and shaking, and Mariam had to stand over her, hands on hips, and say that she had to get herself together. That what was done was done.

After a time, Laila got up and wiped her face, and they carried Rasheed to the yard without further incident. They took him into the toolshed. They left him behind the workbench, on which sat his saw, some nails, a chisel, a hammer, and a cylindrical block of wood that Rasheed had been meaning to carve into something for Zalmai but had never gotten around to doing.

Then they went back inside. Mariam washed her hands, ran them through her hair, took a deep breath and let it out. 'Let me tend to your wounds now. You're all cut up, Laila jo.'

Mariam said she needed the night to think things over. To get her thoughts together and devise a plan.

'There is a way,' she said, 'and I just have to find it.'

'We have to leave! We can't stay here,' Laila said in a broken, husky voice. She thought suddenly of the sound the shovel must have made striking Rasheed's head, and her body pitched forward. Bile surged up her chest.

Mariam waited patiently until Laila felt better. Then she had Laila lie down, and, as she stroked Laila's hair in her lap, Mariam said not to worry, that everything would be fine. She said that they would leave – she, Laila, the children, and Tariq too. They would leave this house, and this unforgiving city. They would leave this despondent country altogether, Mariam said, running her hands through Laila's hair, and go someplace remote and safe where no one would find them, where they could disown their past and find shelter.

'Somewhere with trees,' she said. 'Yes. Lots of trees.'

They would live in a small house on the edge of some town they'd never heard of, Mariam said, or in a remote village where the road was narrow and unpaved but lined with all manner of plants and shrubs. Maybe there would be a path to take, a path that led to a grass field where the children could play, or maybe a graveled road that would take them to a clear blue lake where trout swam and reeds poked through the surface. They would raise sheep and chickens, and they would make bread together and teach the children to read. They would make new lives for themselves – peaceful, solitary lives – and there the weight of all that they'd endured would lift from them, and they would be deserving of all the happiness and simple prosperity they would find.

Laila murmured encouragingly. It would be an existence rife with difficulties, she saw, but of a pleasurable kind, difficulties they could take pride in, possess, value, as one would a family heirloom. Mariam's soft maternal voice went on, brought a degree of comfort to her. *There is a way*, she'd said, and, in the morning, Mariam would tell her what needed to be done and they would do it, and maybe by tomorrow this time they would be on their way to this new life, a life luxuriant with possibility and joy and welcomed difficulties. Laila was grateful that Mariam was in charge, unclouded and sober, able to think this through for both of them. Her own mind was a jittery, muddled mess.

Mariam got up. 'You should tend to your son now.' On her was the most stricken expression Laila had ever seen on a human face.

Laila found him in the dark, curled up on Rasheed's side of the mattress. She slipped beneath the covers beside him and pulled the blanket over them.

'Are you asleep?'

Without turning around to face her, he said, 'Can't sleep yet. Baba jan hasn't said the *Babaloo* prayers with me.'

'Maybe I can say them with you tonight.'

'You can't say them like he can.'

She squeezed his little shoulder. Kissed the nape of his neck. 'I can try.'

'Where is Baba jan?'

'Baba jan has gone away,' Laila said, her throat closing up again.

And there it was, spoken for the first time, the great, damning lie. How many more times would this lie have to be told? Laila wondered miserably. How many more times would Zalmai have to be deceived? She pictured Zalmai, his jubilant, running welcomes when Rasheed came home and Rasheed picking him up by the elbows and swinging him round and round until Zalmai's legs flew straight out, the two of them giggling afterward when Zalmai stumbled around like a drunk. She thought of their disorderly games and their boisterous laughs, their secretive glances.

A pall of shame and grief for her son fell over Laila.

'Where did he go?'

'I don't know, my love.'

When was he coming back? Would Baba jan bring a present with him when he returned?

She did the prayers with Zalmai. Twenty-one *Bismallah-e-rahman-e-rahims* — one for each knuckle of seven fingers. She watched him cup his hands before his face and blow into them, then place the back of both hands on his forehead and make a casting-away motion, whispering, Babaloo, *be gone, do not come to Zalmai, he has no business with you.* Babaloo, *be gone.* Then, to finish off, they said *Allah-u-akbar* three times. And later, much later that night, Laila was startled by a muted voice: *Did Baba jan leave because of me? Because of what I said, about you and the man downstairs?*

She leaned over him, meaning to reassure, meaning to say *It had nothing to do with you, Zalmai. No. Nothing is your fault.* But he was asleep, his small chest rising and sinking.

When Laila went to bed, her mind was muffled up, clouded, incapable of sustained rational thought. But when she woke up, to the muezzin's call for morning prayer, much of the dullness had lifted.

She sat up and watched Zalmai sleep for a while, the ball of his fist under his chin. Laila pictured Mariam sneaking into the room in the middle of the night as she and Zalmai had slept, watching them, making plans in her head.

Laila slipped out of bed. It took effort to stand. She ached everywhere. Her neck, her shoulders, her back, her arms, her thighs, all engraved with the cuts of Rasheed's belt buckle. Wincing, she quietly left the bedroom.

In Mariam's room, the light was a shade darker than gray, the kind of light Laila had always associated with crowing roosters and dew rolling off blades of grass. Mariam was sitting in a corner, on a prayer rug facing the window. Slowly, Laila

413

lowered herself to the ground, sitting down across from her.

'You should go and visit Aziza this morning,' Mariam said.

'I know what you mean to do.'

'Don't walk. Take the bus, you'll blend in. Taxis are too conspicuous. You're sure to get stopped for riding alone.'

'What you promised last night . . .'

Laila could not finish. The trees, the lake, the nameless village. A delusion, she saw. A lovely lie meant to soothe. Like cooing to a distressed child.

'I meant it,' Mariam said. 'I meant it for *you*, Laila jo.'

'I don't want any of it without you,' Laila croaked.

Mariam smiled wanly.

'I want it to be just like you said, Mariam, all of us going together, you, me, the children. Tariq has a place in Pakistan. We can hide out there for a while, wait for things to calm down—'

'That's not possible,' Mariam said patiently, like a parent to a well-meaning but misguided child.

'We'll take care of each other,' Laila said, choking on the words, her eyes wet with tears. 'Like you said. No. I'll take care of *you* for a change.'

'Oh, Laila jo.'

Laila went on a stammering rant. She bargained. She promised. She would do all the cleaning, she said, and all the cooking. 'You won't have to do a thing. Ever again. You rest, sleep in, plant a

414

garden. Whatever you want, you ask and I'll get it for you. Don't do this, Mariam. Don't leave me. Don't break Aziza's heart.'

'They chop off hands for stealing bread,' Mariam said. 'What do you think they'll do when they find a dead husband and two missing wives?'

'No one will know,' Laila breathed. 'No one will find us.'

'They will. Sooner or later. They're blood-hounds.' Mariam's voice was low, cautioning; it made Laila's promises sound fantastical, trumped-up, foolish.

'Mariam, please—'

'When they do, they'll find you as guilty as me. Tariq too. I won't have the two of you living on the run, like fugitives. What will happen to your children if you're caught?'

Laila's eyes brimming, stinging.

'Who will take care of them then? The Taliban? Think like a mother, Laila jo. Think like a mother. I am.'

'I can't.'

'You have to.'

'It isn't fair,' Laila croaked.

'But it *is*. Come here. Come lie here.'

Laila crawled to her and again put her head on Mariam's lap. She remembered all the after-noons they'd spent together, braiding each other's hair, Mariam listening patiently to her random thoughts and ordinary stories with an air of gratitude, with the expression of a person to whom a unique and coveted privilege had been extended.

'It *is* fair,' Mariam said. 'I've killed our husband. I've deprived your son of his father. It isn't right that I run. I *can't*. Even if they never catch us, I'll never...' Her lips trembled. 'I'll never escape your son's grief. How do I look at him? How do I ever bring myself to look at him, Laila jo?'

Mariam twiddled a strand of Laila's hair, untangled a stubborn curl.

'For me, it ends here. There's nothing more I want. Everything I'd ever wished for as a little girl you've already given me. You and your children have made me so very happy. It's all right, Laila jo. This is all right. Don't be sad.'

Laila could find no reasonable answer for anything Mariam said. But she rambled on anyway, incoherently, childishly, about fruit trees that awaited planting and chickens that awaited raising. She went on about small houses in unnamed towns, and walks to trout-filled lakes. And, in the end, when the words dried up, the tears did not, and all Laila could do was surrender and sob like a child overwhelmed by an adult's unassailable logic. All she could do was roll herself up and bury her face one last time in the welcoming warmth of Mariam's lap.

Later that morning, Mariam packed Zalmai a small lunch of bread and dried figs. For Aziza too she packed some figs, and a few cookies shaped like animals. She put it all in a paper bag and gave it to Laila.

'Kiss Aziza for me,' she said. 'Tell her she is the *noor* of my eyes and the sultan of my heart. Will you do that for me?'

Laila nodded, her lips pursed together.

'Take the bus, like I said, and keep your head low.'

'When will I see you, Mariam? I want to see you before I testify. I'll tell them how it happened. I'll explain that it wasn't your fault. That you had to do it. They'll understand, won't they, Mariam? They'll understand.'

Mariam gave her a soft look.

She hunkered down to eye level with Zalmai. He was wearing a red T-shirt, ragged khakis, and a used pair of cowboy boots Rasheed had bought him from Mandaii. He was holding his new basketball with both hands. Mariam planted a kiss on his cheek.

'You be a good, strong boy, now,' she said. 'You treat your mother well.' She cupped his face. He pulled back but she held on. 'I am so sorry, Zalmai jo. Believe me that I'm so very sorry for all your pain and sadness.'

Laila held Zalmai's hand as they walked down the road together. Just before they turned the corner, Laila looked back and saw Mariam at the door. Mariam was wearing a white scarf over her head, a dark blue sweater buttoned in the front, and white cotton trousers. A crest of gray hair had fallen loose over her brow. Bars of sunlight slashed across her face and shoulders. Mariam waved amiably.

They turned the corner, and Laila never saw Mariam again.

# CHAPTER 47

# MARIAM

Back in a *kolba*, it seemed, after all these years.

The Walayat women's prison was a drab, square-shaped building in Shar-e-Nau near Chicken Street. It sat in the center of a larger complex that housed male inmates. A padlocked door separated Mariam and the other women from the surrounding men. Mariam counted five working cells. They were unfurnished rooms, with dirty, peeling walls, and small windows that looked into the courtyard. The windows were barred, even though the doors to the cells were unlocked and the women were free to come and go to the courtyard as they pleased. The windows had no glass. There were no curtains either, which meant the Talib guards who roamed the courtyard had an eyeful of the interior of the cells. Some of the women complained that the guards smoked outside the window and leered in, with their inflamed eyes and wolfish smiles, that they muttered indecent jokes to each other about them. Because of this, most of the women wore burqas all day and lifted them only after sundown, after

419

the main gate was locked and the guards had gone to their posts.

At night, the cell Mariam shared with five women and four children was dark. On those nights when there was electrical power, they hoisted Naghma, a short, flat-chested girl with black frizzy hair, up to the ceiling. There was a wire there from which the coating had been stripped. Naghma would hand-wrap the live wire around the base of the lightbulb then to make a circuit.

The toilets were closet-sized, the cement floor cracked. There was a small, rectangular hole in the ground, at the bottom of which was a heap of feces. Flies buzzed in and out of the hole.

In the middle of the prison was an open, rectangular courtyard, and, in the middle of that, a well. The well had no drainage, meaning the courtyard was often a swamp and the water tasted rotten. Laundry lines, loaded with hand-washed socks and diapers, slashed across each other in the courtyard. This was where inmates met visitors, where they boiled the rice their families brought them – the prison provided no food. The court-yard was also the children's playground – Mariam had learned that many of the children had been born in Walayat, had never seen the world outside these walls. Mariam watched them chase each other around, watched their shoeless feet sling mud. All day, they ran around, making up lively games, unaware of the stench of feces and urine that permeated Walayat and their own bodies, unmindful of the Talib guards until one smacked them.

Mariam had no visitors. That was the first and only thing she had asked the Talib officials here. No visitors.

None of the women in Mariam's cell were serving time for violent crime – they were all there for the common offense of 'running away from home.' As a result, Mariam gained some notoriety among them, became a kind of celebrity. The women eyed her with a reverent, almost awestruck, expression. They offered her their blankets. They competed to share their food with her.

The most avid was Naghma, who was always hugging her elbows and following Mariam everywhere she went. Naghma was the sort of person who found it entertaining to dispense news of misfortune, whether others' or her own. She said her father had promised her to a tailor some thirty years older than her.

'He smells like *goh*, and has fewer teeth than fingers,' Naghma said of the tailor.

She'd tried to elope to Gardez with a young man she'd fallen in love with, the son of a local mullah. They'd barely made it out of Kabul. When they were caught and sent back, the mullah's son was flogged before he repented and said that Naghma had seduced him with her feminine charms. She'd cast a spell on him, he said. He promised he would rededicate himself to the study of Koran. The mullah's son was freed. Naghma was sentenced to five years.

It was just as well, she said, her being here in prison. Her father had sworn that the day she was released he would take a knife to her throat.

Listening to Naghma, Mariam remembered the dim glimmer of cold stars and the stringy pink clouds streaking over the Safid-koh mountains that long-ago morning when Nana had said to her, *Like a compass needle that points north, a man's accusing finger always finds a woman. Always. You remember that, Mariam.*

Mariam's trial had taken place the week before. There was no legal council, no public hearing, no cross-examining of evidence, no appeals. Mariam declined her right to witnesses. The entire thing lasted less than fifteen minutes.

The middle judge, a brittle-looking Talib, was the leader. He was strikingly gaunt, with yellow, leathery skin and a curly red beard. He wore eyeglasses that magnified his eyes and revealed how yellow the whites were. His neck looked too thin to support the intricately wrapped turban on his head.

'You admit to this, *hamshira*?' he asked again in a tired voice

'I do,' Mariam said.

The man nodded. Or maybe he didn't. It was hard to tell; he had a pronounced shaking of his

422

hands and head that reminded Mariam of Mullah Faizullah's tremor. When he sipped tea, he did not reach for his cup. He motioned to the square-shouldered man to his left, who respectfully brought it to his lips. After, the Talib closed his eyes gently, a muted and elegant gesture of gratitude.

Mariam found a disarming quality about him. When he spoke, it was with a tinge of guile and tenderness. His smile was patient. He did not look at Mariam despisingly. He did not address her with spite or accusation but with a soft tone of apology.

'Do you fully understand what you're saying?' the bony-faced Talib to the judge's right, not the tea giver, said. This one was the youngest of the three. He spoke quickly and with emphatic, arrogant confidence. He'd been irritated that Mariam could not speak Pashto. He struck Mariam as the sort of quarrelsome young man who relished his authority, who saw offenses everywhere, thought it his birthright to pass judgment.

'I do understand,' Mariam said.

'I wonder,' the young Talib said. 'God has made us differently, you women and us men. Our brains are different. You are not able to think like we can. Western doctors and their science have proven this. This is why we require only one male witness but two female ones.'

'I admit to what I did, brother,' Mariam said. 'But, if I hadn't, he would have killed her. He was strangling her.'

423

'So you say. But, then, women swear to all sorts of things all the time.'

'It's the truth.'

'Do you have witnesses? Other than your *ambagh*?'

'I do not,' said Mariam.

'Well, then.' He threw up his hands and snickered.

It was the sickly Talib who spoke next.

'I have a doctor in Peshawar,' he said. 'A fine, young Pakistani fellow. I saw him a month ago, and then again last week. I said, tell me the truth, friend, and he said to me, three months, Mullah sahib, maybe six at most – all God's will, of course.'

He nodded discreetly at the square-shouldered man on his left and took another sip of the tea he was offered. He wiped his mouth with the back of his tremulous hand. 'It does not frighten me to leave this life that my only son left five years ago, this life that insists we bear sorrow upon sorrow long after we can bear no more. No, I believe I shall gladly take my leave when the time comes.

'What frightens me, *hamshira,* is the day God summons me before Him and asks, *Why did you not do as I said, Mullah? Why did you not obey my laws?* How shall I explain myself to Him, *hamshira?* What will be my defense for not heeding His commands? All I can do, all any of us can do, in the time we are granted, is to go on abiding by the laws He has set for us. The clearer I see my

424

end, *hamshira,* the nearer I am to my day of reckoning, the more determined I grow to carry out His word. However painful it may prove.'

He shifted on his cushion and winced.

'I believe you when you say that your husband was a man of disagreeable temperament,' he resumed, fixing Mariam with his bespectacled eyes, his gaze both stern and compassionate. 'But I cannot help but be disturbed by the brutality of your action, *hamshira.* I am troubled by what you have done; I am troubled that his little boy was crying for him upstairs when you did it.

'I am tired and dying, and I want to be merciful. I want to forgive you. But when God summons me and says, *But it wasn't for you to forgive, Mullah,* what shall I say?'

His companions nodded and looked at him with admiration.

'Something tells me you are not a wicked woman, *hamshira.* But you have done a wicked thing. And you must pay for this thing you have done. *Shari'a* is not vague on this matter. It says I must send you where I will soon join you myself.

'Do you understand, *hamshira?*'

Mariam looked down at her hands. She said she did.

'May Allah forgive you.'

Before they led her out, Mariam was given a document, told to sign beneath her statement and the mullah's sentence. As the three Taliban watched, Mariam wrote it out, her name – the

425

*meem,* the *reh,* the *yah,* and the *meem* – remembering the last time she'd signed her name to a document, twenty-seven years before, at Jalil's table, beneath the watchful gaze of another mullah.

Mariam spent ten days in prison. She sat by the window of the cell, watched the prison life in the courtyard. When the summer winds blew, she watched bits of scrap paper ride the currents in a frenzied, corkscrew motion, as they were hurled this way and that, high above the prison walls. She watched the winds stir mutiny in the dust, whipping it into violent spirals that ripped through the courtyard. Everyone – the guards, the inmates, the children, Mariam – burrowed their faces in the hook of their elbows, but the dust would not be denied. It made homes of ear canals and nostrils, of eyelashes and skin folds, of the space between molars. Only at dusk did the winds die down. And then if a night breeze blew, it did so timidly, as if to atone for the excesses of its daytime sibling.

On Mariam's last day at Walayat, Naghma gave her a tangerine. She put it in Mariam's palm and closed her fingers around it. Then she burst into tears.

'You're the best friend I ever had,' she said.

Mariam spent the rest of the day by the barred window watching the inmates below. Someone was cooking a meal, and a stream of cumin-scented smoke and warm air wafted through the window. Mariam could see the children playing a blindfolded

426

game. Two little girls were singing a rhyme, and Mariam remembered it from her childhood, remembered Jalil singing it to her as they'd sat on a rock, fishing in the stream:

> *Lili lili birdbath,*
> *Sitting on a dirt path,*
> *Minnow sat on the rim and drank,*
> *Slipped, and in the water she sank.*

Mariam had disjointed dreams that last night. She dreamed of pebbles, eleven of them, arranged vertically. Jalil, young again, all winning smiles and dimpled chins and sweat patches, coat flung over his shoulder, come at last to take his daughter away for a ride in his shiny black Buick Roadmaster. Mullah Faizullah twirling his rosary beads, walking with her along the stream, their twin shadows gliding on the water and on the grassy banks sprinkled with a blue-lavender wild iris that, in this dream, smelled like cloves. She dreamed of Nana in the doorway of the *kolba,* her voice dim and distant, calling her to dinner, as Mariam played in cool, tangled grass where ants crawled and beetles scurried and grasshoppers skipped amid all the different shades of green. The squeak of a wheelbarrow laboring up a dusty path. Cowbells clanging. Sheep baaing on a hill.

On the way to Ghazi Stadium, Mariam bounced in the bed of the truck as it skidded around potholes and its wheels spat pebbles. The bouncing hurt her tailbone. A young, armed Talib sat across from her looking at her.

Mariam wondered if he would be the one, this amiable-looking young man with the deep-set bright eyes and slightly pointed face, with the black-nailed index finger drumming the side of the truck.

'Are you hungry, mother?' he said.

Mariam shook her head.

'I have a biscuit. It's good. You can have it if you're hungry. I don't mind.'

'No. *Tashakor*, brother.'

He nodded, looked at her benignly. 'Are you afraid, mother?'

A lump closed off her throat. In a quivering voice, Mariam told him the truth. 'Yes. I'm very afraid.'

'I have a picture of my father,' he said. 'I don't remember him. He was a bicycle repairman once, I know that much. But I don't remember how he moved, you know, how he laughed or the sound of his voice.' He looked away, then back at Mariam. 'My mother used to say that he was the bravest man she knew. Like a lion, she'd say. But she told me he was crying like a child the morning the communists took him. I'm telling you so you know that it's normal to be scared. It's nothing to be ashamed of, mother.'

For the first time that day, Mariam cried a little.

★    ★    ★

428

Thousands of eyes bore down on her. In the crowded bleachers, necks were craned for the benefit of a better view. Tongues clucked. A murmuring sound rippled through the stadium when Mariam was helped down from the truck. Mariam imagined heads shaking when the loudspeaker announced her crime. But she did not look up to see whether they were shaking with disapproval or charity, with reproach or pity. Mariam blinded herself to them all.

Earlier that morning, she had been afraid that she would make a fool of herself, that she would turn into a pleading, weeping spectacle. She had feared that she might scream or vomit or even wet herself, that, in her last moments, she would be betrayed by animal instinct or bodily disgrace. But when she was made to descend from the truck, Mariam's legs did not buckle. Her arms did not flail. She did not have to be dragged. And when she did feel herself faltering, she thought of Zalmai, from whom she had taken the love of his life, whose days now would be shaped by the sorrow of his father's disappearance. And then Mariam's stride steadied and she could walk without protest.

An armed man approached her and told her to walk toward the southern goalpost. Mariam could sense the crowd tightening up with anticipation. She did not look up. She kept her eyes to the ground, on her shadow, on her executioner's shadow trailing hers.

Though there had been moments of beauty in it, Mariam knew that life for the most part had been unkind to her. But as she walked the final twenty paces, she could not help but wish for more of it. She wished she could see Laila again, wished to hear the clangor of her laugh, to sit with her once more for a pot of *chaai* and leftover *halwa* under a starlit sky. She mourned that she would never see Aziza grow up, would not see the beautiful young woman that she would one day become, would not get to paint her hands with henna and toss *noqul* candy at her wedding. She would never play with Aziza's children. She would have liked that very much, to be old and play with Aziza's children.

Near the goalpost, the man behind her asked her to stop. Mariam did. Through the crisscrossing grid of the burqa, she saw his shadow arms lift his shadow Kalashnikov.

Mariam wished for so much in those final moments. Yet as she closed her eyes, it was not regret any longer but a sensation of abundant peace that washed over her. She thought of her entry into this world, the *harami* child of a lowly villager, an unintended thing, a pitiable, regrettable accident. A weed. And yet she was leaving the world as a woman who had loved and been loved back. She was leaving it as a friend, a companion, a guardian. A mother. A person of consequence at last. No. It was not so bad, Mariam thought, that she should die this way. Not so bad.

This was a legitimate end to a life of illegitimate beginnings.

Mariam's final thoughts were a few words from the Koran, which she muttered under her breath.

*He has created the heavens and the earth with the truth; He makes the night cover the day and makes the day overtake the night, and He has made the sun and the moon subservient; each one runs on to an assigned term; now surely He is the Mighty, the Great Forgiver.*

'Kneel,' the Talib said.

*O my Lord! Forgive and have mercy, for you are the best of the merciful ones.*

'Kneel here, *hamshira*. And look down.'

One last time, Mariam did as she was told.

# PART IV

# CHAPTER 48

Tariq has headaches now.

Some nights, Laila awakens and finds him on the edge of their bed, rocking, his undershirt pulled over his head. The headaches began in Nasir Bagh, he says, then worsened in prison. Sometimes they make him vomit, blind him in one eye. He says it feels like a butcher's knife burrowing in one temple, twisting slowly through his brain, then poking out the other side.

'I can taste the metal, even, when they begin.'

Sometimes Laila wets a cloth and lays it on his forehead and that helps a little. The little round white pills Sayeed's doctor gave Tariq help too. But some nights, all Tariq can do is hold his head and moan, his eyes bloodshot, his nose dripping. Laila sits with him when he's in the grip of it like that, rubs the back of his neck, takes his hand in hers, the metal of his wedding band cold against her palm.

They married the day that they arrived in Murree. Sayeed looked relieved when Tariq told him they would. He would not have to broach with Tariq the delicate matter of an unmarried couple living in his hotel. Sayeed is not at all as Laila had pictured him, ruddy-faced and pea-eyed. He has a salt-and-pepper mustache whose ends he rolls to a sharp tip, and a shock of long gray hair combed back from the brow. He is a soft-spoken, mannerly man, with measured speech and graceful movements.

It was Sayeed who summoned a friend and a mullah for the *nikka* that day, Sayeed who pulled Tariq aside and gave him money. Tariq wouldn't take it, but Sayeed insisted. Tariq went to the Mall then and came back with two simple, thin wedding bands. They married later that night, after the children had gone to bed.

In the mirror, beneath the green veil that the mullah draped over their heads, Laila's eyes met Tariq's. There were no tears, no wedding-day smiles, no whispered oaths of long-lasting love. In silence, Laila looked at their reflection, at faces that had aged beyond their years, at the pouches and lines and sags that now marked their once-scrubbed, youthful faces. Tariq opened his mouth and began to say something, but, just as he did, someone pulled the veil, and Laila missed what it was that he was going to say.

That night, they lay in bed as husband and wife, as the children snored below them on sleeping cots. Laila remembered the ease with which they would crowd the air between them with words, she and Tariq, when they were younger, the haywire, brisk flow of their speech, always interrupting each other, tugging each other's collar to emphasize a point, the quickness to laugh, the eagerness to delight. So much had happened since those childhood days, so much that needed to be said. But that first night the enormity of it all stole the words from her. That night, it was blessing enough to be beside him. It was blessing enough to know that he was here, to feel the warmth of him next to her, to lie with him, their heads touching, his right hand laced in her left.

In the middle of the night, when Laila woke up thirsty, she found their hands still clamped together, in the white-knuckle, anxious way of children clutching balloon strings.

Laila likes Murree's cool, foggy mornings and its dazzling twilights, the dark brilliance of the sky at night; the green of the pines and the soft brown of the squirrels darting up and down the sturdy tree trunks; the sudden downpours that send shoppers in the Mall scrambling for awning cover. She likes the souvenir shops, and the various hotels that house tourists, even as the locals bemoan the constant construction, the expansion of infrastructure that they say is eating away at Murree's natural beauty. Laila finds it odd that people should lament the *building* of buildings. In Kabul, they would celebrate it.

She likes that they have a bathroom, not an outhouse but an actual bathroom, with a toilet that flushes, a shower, and a sink too, with twin faucets from which she can draw, with a flick of her wrist, water, either hot or cold. She likes waking up to the sound of Alyona bleating in the morning, and the harmlessly cantankerous cook, Adiba, who works marvels in the kitchen.

Sometimes, as Laila watches Tariq sleep, as her children mutter and stir in their own sleep, a great big lump of gratitude catches in her throat, makes her eyes water.

In the mornings, Laila follows Tariq from room to room. Keys jingle from a ring clipped to his waist and a spray bottle of window cleaner dangles from the belt loops of his jeans. Laila brings a pail filled with rags, disinfectant, a toilet brush, and spray wax for the dressers. Aziza tags along, a mop in one hand, the bean-stuffed doll Mariam had made for her in the other. Zalmai trails them reluctantly, sulkily, always a few steps behind.

Laila vacuums, makes the bed, and dusts. Tariq washes the bathroom sink and tub, scrubs the toilet and mops the linoleum floor. He stocks the shelves with clean towels, miniature shampoo bottles, and bars of almond-scented soap. Aziza has laid claim to the task of spraying and wiping the windows. The doll is never far from where she works.

Laila told Aziza about Tariq a few days after the *nikka*.

It is strange, Laila thinks, almost unsettling, the thing between Aziza and Tariq. Already, Aziza is finishing his sentences and he hers. She hands him things before he asks for them. Private smiles shoot between them across the dinner table as if they are not strangers at all but companions reunited after a lengthy separation.

Aziza looked down thoughtfully at her hands when Laila told her.

'I like him,' she said, after a long pause.

'He loves *you*.'

'He said that?'

'He doesn't have to, Aziza.'

'Tell me the rest, Mammy. Tell me so I know.'

And Laila did.

'Your father is a good man. He is the best man I've ever known.'

'What if he leaves?' Aziza said.

'He will never leave. Look at me, Aziza. Your father will never hurt you, and he will never leave.'

The relief on Aziza's face broke Laila's heart.

Tariq has bought Zalmai a rocking horse, built him a wagon. From a prison inmate, he learned to make paper animals, and so he has folded, cut, and tucked countless sheets of paper into lions and kangaroos for Zalmai, into horses and brightly plumed birds. But these overtures are dismissed by Zalmai unceremoniously, sometimes venomously.

'You're a donkey!' he cries. 'I don't want your toys!'

'Zalmai!' Laila gasps.

'It's all right,' Tariq says. 'Laila, it's all right. Let him.'

'You're not my Baba jan! My real Baba jan is away on a trip, and when he gets back he's going to beat you up! And you won't be able to run away, because he has two legs and you only have one!'

At night, Laila holds Zalmai against her chest and recites the *Babaloo* prayers with him. When he asks, she tells him the lie again, tells him his Baba jan has gone away and she doesn't know when he would come back. She abhors this task, abhors herself for lying like this to a child.

Laila knows that this shameful lie will have to be told again and again. It will have to because Zalmai will ask, hopping down from a swing, waking from an afternoon nap, and, later, when he's old enough to tie his own shoes, to walk to school by himself, the lie will have to be delivered again.

At some point, Laila knows, the questions will dry up. Slowly, Zalmai will cease wondering why his father has abandoned him. He will not spot his father any longer at traffic lights, in stooping old men shuffling down the street or sipping tea in open-fronted samovar houses. And one day it will hit him, walking along some meandering river, or gazing out at an untracked snowfield, that his father's disappearance is no longer an open, raw wound. That it has become something else altogether, something more soft-edged and indolent. Like a lore. Something to be revered, mystified by.

Laila is happy here in Murree. But it is not an easy happiness. It is not a happiness without cost.

On his days off, Tariq takes Laila and the children to the Mall, along which are shops that sell trinkets and next to which is an Anglican church built in the mid-nineteenth century. Tariq buys them spicy *chapli* kebabs from street vendors. They stroll amid the crowds of locals, the Europeans and their cellular phones and digital cameras, the Punjabis who come here to escape the heat of the plains.

Occasionally, they board a bus to Kashmir Point. From there, Tariq shows them the valley of the Jhelum River, the pine-carpeted slopes, and the lush, densely wooded hills, where he says monkeys can still be spotted hopping from branch to branch. They go to the maple-clad Nathia Gali too, some thirty kilometers from Murree, where Tariq holds Laila's hand as they walk the tree-shaded road to the Governor's House. They stop by the old British cemetery, or take a taxi up a mountain peak for a view of the verdant, fog-shrouded valley below.

Sometimes on these outings, when they pass by a store window, Laila catches their reflections in it. Man, wife, daughter, son. To strangers, she knows, they must appear like the most ordinary of families, free of secrets, lies, and regrets.

Aziza has nightmares from which she wakes up shrieking. Laila has to lie beside her on the cot, dry her cheeks with her sleeve, soothe her back to sleep.

Laila has her own dreams. In them, she's always back at the house in Kabul, walking the hall, climbing the stairs. She is alone, but behind the doors she hears the rhythmic hiss of an iron, bedsheets snapped, then folded. Sometimes she hears a woman's low-pitched humming of an old Herati song. But when she walks in, the room is empty. There is no one there.

The dreams leave Laila shaken. She wakes from them coated in sweat, her eyes prickling with tears. It is devastating. Every time, it is devastating.

# CHAPTER 49

One Sunday that September, Laila is putting Zalmai, who has a cold, down for a nap when Tariq bursts into their bungalow.

'Did you hear?' he says, panting a little. 'They killed him. Ahmad Shah Massoud. He's dead.'

'What?'

From the doorway, Tariq tells her what he knows.

'They say he gave an interview to a pair of journalists who claimed they were Belgians originally from Morocco. As they're talking, a bomb hidden in the video camera goes off. Kills Massoud and one of the journalists. They shoot the other one as he tries to run. They're saying now the journalists were probably Al-Qaeda men.'

Laila remembers the poster of Ahmad Shah Massoud that Mammy had nailed to the wall of her bedroom. Massoud leaning forward, one eyebrow cocked, his face furrowed in concentration, as though he was respectfully listening to someone. Laila remembers how grateful Mammy was that Massoud had said a graveside prayer at her sons' burial, how she told everyone about it. Even after war broke out between his faction and the others, Mammy had refused to blame him. *He's a good man,* she used to say. *He wants peace. He wants to rebuild Afghanistan. But they won't let him. They just won't let him.* For Mammy, even in the end, even after everything went so terribly wrong and Kabul lay in ruins, Massoud was still the Lion of Panjshir.

Laila is not as forgiving. Massoud's violent end brings her no joy, but she remembers too well the neighborhoods razed under his watch, the bodies dragged from the rubble, the hands and feet of children discovered on rooftops or the high branch of some tree days after their funeral. She remembers too clearly the look on Mammy's own face moments before the rocket slammed in and, much as she has tried to forget, Babi's headless torso landing nearby, the bridge tower printed on his T-shirt poking through thick fog and blood.

'There is going to be a funeral,' Tariq is saying. 'I'm sure of it. Probably in Rawalpindi. It'll be huge.'

Zalmai, who was almost asleep, is sitting up now, rubbing his eyes with balled fists.

Two days later, they are cleaning a room when they hear a commotion. Tariq drops the mop and hurries out. Laila tails him.

The noise is coming from the hotel lobby. There is a lounge area to the right of the reception desk, with several chairs and two couches upholstered in beige suede. In the corner, facing the couches, is a television, and Sayeed, the concierge, and several guests are gathered in front of.

444

Laila and Tariq work their way in.

The TV is tuned to BBC. On the screen is a building, a tower, black smoke billowing from its top floors. Tariq says something to Sayeed and Sayeed is in midreply when a plane appears from the corner of the screen. It crashes into the adjacent tower, exploding into a fireball that dwarfs any ball of fire that Laila has ever seen. A collective yelp rises from everyone in the lobby.

In less than two hours, both towers have collapsed.

Soon all the TV stations are talking about Afghanistan and the Taliban and Osama bin Laden.

'Did you hear what the Taliban said?' Tariq asks. 'About bin Laden?'

Aziza is sitting across from him on the bed, considering the board. Tariq has taught her to play chess. She is frowning and tapping her lower lip now, mimicking the body language her father assumes when he's deciding on a move.

Zalmai's cold is a little better. He is asleep, and Laila is rubbing Vicks on his chest.

'I heard,' she says.

The Taliban have announced that they won't relinquish bin Laden because he is a *mehman*, a guest, who has found sanctuary in Afghanistan and it is against the *Pashtunwali* code of ethics to turn over a guest. Tariq chuckles bitterly, and Laila hears in his chuckle that he is revolted by this distortion of an honorable Pashtun custom, this misrepresentation of his people's ways.

A few days after the attacks, Laila and Tariq are in the hotel lobby again. On the TV screen, George W. Bush is speaking. There is a big American flag behind him. At one point, his voice wavers, and Laila thinks he is going to weep.

Sayeed, who speaks English, explains to them that Bush has just declared war.

'On whom?' says Tariq.

'On your country, to begin with.'

'It may not be such a bad thing,' Tariq says.

They have finished making love. He's lying beside her, his head on her chest, his arm draped over her belly. The first few times they tried, there was difficulty. Tariq was all apologies, Laila all reassurances. There are still difficulties, not physical now but logistical. The shack they share with the children is small. The children sleep on cots below them and so there is little privacy. Most times, Laila and Tariq make love in silence, with controlled, muted passion, fully clothed beneath the blanket as a precaution against interruptions by the children. They are forever wary of the rustling sheets, the creaking bedsprings. But for Laila, being with Tariq is worth weathering these apprehensions. When they make love, Laila feels anchored, she feels

446

sheltered. Her anxieties, that their life together is a temporary blessing, that soon it will come loose again in strips and tatters, are allayed. Her fears of separation vanish.

'What do you mean?' she says now.

'What's going on back home. It may not be so bad in the end.'

Back home, bombs are falling once again, this time American bombs – Laila has been watching images of the war every day on the television as she changes sheets and vacuums. The Americans have armed the warlords once more, and enlisted the help of the Northern Alliance to drive out the Taliban and find bin Laden.

But it rankles Laila, what Tariq is saying. She pushes his head roughly off her chest.

'Not so bad? People dying? Women, children, old people? Homes destroyed again? Not so bad?'

'*Shh*. You'll wake the children.'

'How can you say that, Tariq?' she snaps. 'After the so-called blunder in Karam? A hundred innocent people! You saw the bodies for yourself!'

'No,' Tariq says. He props himself up on his elbow, looks down at Laila. 'You misunderstand. What I meant was—'

'You wouldn't know,' Laila says. She is aware that her voice is rising, that they are having their first fight as husband and wife. 'You left when the Mujahideen began fighting, remember? I'm the one who stayed behind. Me. I *know* war. I lost my parents to war. My *parents*, Tariq. And now to hear you say that war is not so bad?'

'I'm sorry, Laila. I'm sorry.' He cups her face in his hands. 'You're right. I'm sorry. Forgive me. What I meant was that maybe there will be hope at the other end of this war, that maybe for the first time in a long time—'

'I don't want to talk about this anymore,' Laila says, surprised at how she has lashed out at him. It's unfair, she knows, what she said to him – hadn't war taken his parents too? – and whatever flared in her is softening already. Tariq continues to speak gently, and, when he pulls her to him, she lets him. When he kisses her hand, then her brow, she lets him. She knows that he is probably right. She knows how his comment was intended. Maybe this *is* necessary. Maybe there *will* be hope when Bush's bombs stop falling. But she cannot bring herself to say it, not when what happened to Babi and Mammy is happening to someone now in Afghanistan, not when some unsuspecting girl or a boy back home has just been orphaned by a rocket as she was. Laila cannot bring herself to say it. It's hard to rejoice. It seems hypocritical, perverse.

That night, Zalmai wakes up coughing. Before Laila can move, Tariq swings his legs over the side of the bed. He straps on his prosthesis and walks over to Zalmai, lifts him up into his arms. From the bed, Laila watches Tariq's shape moving back and forth in the darkness. She sees the outline of

448

Zalmai's head on his shoulder, the knot of his hands at Tariq's neck, his small feet bouncing by Tariq's hip.

When Tariq comes back to bed, neither of them says anything. Laila reaches over and touches his face. Tariq's cheeks are wet.

# CHAPTER 50

For Laila, life in Murree is one of comfort and tranquillity. The work is not cumbersome, and, on their days off, she and Tariq take the children to ride the chairlift to Patriata hill, or go to Pindi Point, where, on a clear day, you can see as far as Islamabad and downtown Rawalpindi. There, they spread a blanket on the grass and eat meatball sandwiches with cucumbers and drink cold ginger ale.

It is a good life, Laila tells herself, a life to be thankful for. It is, in fact, precisely the sort of life she used to dream for herself in her darkest days with Rasheed. Every day, Laila reminds herself of this.

Then one warm night in July 2002, she and Tariq are lying in bed talking in hushed voices about all the changes back home. There have been so many. The coalition forces have driven the Taliban out of every major city, pushed them across the border to Pakistan and to the mountains in the south and east of Afghanistan. ISAF, an international peace-keeping force, has been sent to Kabul. The country has an interim president now, Hamid Karzai.

Laila decides that now is the time to tell Tariq.

A year ago, she would have gladly given an arm to get out of Kabul. But in the last few months, she has found herself missing the city of her childhood. She misses the bustle of Shor Bazaar, the Gardens of Babur, the call of the water carriers lugging their goatskin bags. She misses the garment hagglers at Chicken Street and the melon hawkers in Karteh-Parwan.

But it isn't mere homesickness or nostalgia that has Laila thinking of Kabul so much these days. She has become plagued by restlessness. She hears of schools built in Kabul, roads repaved, women returning to work, and her life here, pleasant as it is, grateful as she is for it, seems . . . insufficient to her. Inconsequential. Worse yet, wasteful. Of late, she has started hearing Babi's voice in her head. *You can be anything you want, Laila,* he says. *I know this about you. And I also know that when this war is over, Afghanistan is going to need you.*

Laila hears Mammy's voice too. She remembers Mammy's response to Babi when he would suggest that they leave Afghanistan. *I want to see my sons' dream come true. I want to be there when it happens, when Afghanistan is free, so the boys see it too. They'll see it through my eyes.* There is a part of Laila now that wants to return to Kabul, for Mammy and Babi, for them to see it through *her* eyes.

And then, most compellingly for Laila, there is Mariam. Did Mariam die for this? Laila asks herself. Did she sacrifice herself so she, Laila, could be a maid in a foreign land? Maybe it wouldn't matter to Mariam what Laila did as long as she and the children were safe and happy. But it matters to Laila. Suddenly, it matters very much.

'I want to go back,' she says.

Tariq sits up in bed and looks down at her.

Laila is struck again by how beautiful he is, the perfect curve of his forehead, the slender muscles of his arms, his brooding, intelligent eyes. A year has passed, and still there are times, at moments like this, when Laila cannot believe that they have found each other again, that he is really here, with her, that he is her husband.

'Back? To Kabul?' he asks.

'Only if you want it too.'

'Are you unhappy here? You seem happy. The children too.'

Laila sits up. Tariq shifts on the bed, makes room for her.

'I *am* happy,' Laila says. 'Of course I am. But . . . where do we go from here, Tariq? How long do we stay? This isn't home. Kabul is, and back there so much is happening, a lot of it good. I want to be a part of it all. I want to *do* something. I want to contribute. Do you understand?'

Tariq nods slowly. 'This is what you want, then? You're sure?'

'I want it, yes, I'm sure. But it's more than that. I feel like I *have* to go back. Staying here, it doesn't feel right anymore.'

Tariq looks at his hands, then back up at her.

'But only – only – if you want to go too.'

Tariq smiles. The furrows from his brow clear, and for a brief moment he is the old Tariq again, the Tariq who did not get headaches, who had once said that in Siberia snot turned to ice before it hit the ground. It may be her imagination, but Laila believes there are more frequent sightings of this old Tariq these days.

'Me?' he says. 'I'll follow you to the end of the world, Laila.'

She pulls him close and kisses his lips. She believes she has never loved him more than at this moment. 'Thank you,' she says, her forehead resting against his.

'Let's go home.'

'But first, I want to go to Herat,' she says.

'Herat?'

Laila explains.

The children need reassuring, each in their own way. Laila has to sit down with an agitated Aziza, who still has nightmares, who'd been startled to tears the week before when someone had shot rounds into the sky at a wedding nearby. Laila has to explain to Aziza that when they return to Kabul the Taliban won't be there, that there will not be any fighting, and that she will not be sent back to the orphanage. 'We'll all live together. Your father, me, Zalmai. And you, Aziza. You'll never, ever, have to be apart from me again. I promise.'

She smiles at her daughter. 'Until the day *you* want to, that is. When you fall in love with some young man and want to marry him.'

On the day they leave Murree, Zalmai is inconsolable. He has wrapped his arms around Alyona's neck and will not let go.

'I can't pry him off of her, Mammy,' says Aziza.

'Zalmai. We can't take a goat on the bus,' Laila explains again.

It isn't until Tariq kneels down beside him, until he promises Zalmai that he will buy him a goat just like Alyona in Kabul, that Zalmai reluctantly lets go.

There are tearful farewells with Sayeed as well. For good luck, he holds a Koran by the doorway for Tariq, Laila, and the children to kiss three times, then holds it high so they can pass under it. He helps Tariq load the two suitcases into the trunk of his car. It is Sayeed who drives them to the station, who stands on the curb waving goodbye as the bus sputters and pulls away.

As she leans back and watches Sayeed receding in the rear window of the bus, Laila hears the voice of doubt whispering in her head. Are they being foolish, she wonders, leaving behind the safety of Murree? Going back to the land where her parents and brothers perished, where the smoke of bombs is only now settling?

And then, from the darkened spirals of her memory, rise two lines of poetry, Babi's farewell ode to Kabul:

*One could not count the moons that shimmer on her roofs,*
*Or the thousand splendid suns that hide behind her walls.*

Laila settles back in her seat, blinking the wetness from her eyes. Kabul is waiting. Needing. This journey home is the right thing to do.

But first there is one last farewell to be said.

The wars in Afghanistan have ravaged the roads connecting Kabul, Herat, and Kandahar. The easiest way to Herat now is through Mashad, in Iran. Laila and her family are there only overnight. They spend the night at a hotel, and, the next morning, they board another bus.

Mashad is a crowded, bustling city. Laila watches as parks, mosques, and *chelo kebab* restaurants pass by. When the bus passes the shrine to Imam Reza, the eighth Shi'a imam, Laila cranes her neck to get a better view of its glistening tiles, the minarets, the magnificent golden dome, all of it immaculately and lovingly preserved. She thinks of the Buddhas in her own country. They are grains of dust now, blowing about the Bamiyan Valley in the wind.

The bus ride to the Iranian-Afghan border takes almost ten hours. The terrain grows more desolate, more barren, as they near Afghanistan. Shortly before they cross the border into Herat, they pass an Afghan refugee camp. To Laila, it is a blur of yellow dust and black tents and scanty structures made of corrugated-steel sheets. She reaches across the seat and takes Tariq's hand.

In Herat, most of the streets are paved, lined with fragrant pines. There are municipal parks and libraries in midconstruction, manicured court-yards, freshly painted buildings. The traffic lights work, and, most surprisingly to Laila, electricity is steady. Laila has heard that Herat's feudal-style warlord, Ismail Khan, has helped rebuild the city with the considerable customs revenue that he collects at the Afghan-Iranian border, money that Kabul says belongs not to him but to the central government. There is both a reverential and fearful tone when the taxi driver who takes them to Muwaffaq Hotel mentions Ismail Khan's name.

The two-night stay at the Muwaffaq will cost them nearly a fifth of their savings, but the trip from Mashad has been long and wearying, and the children are exhausted. The elderly clerk at the desk tells Tariq, as he fetches the room key, that the Muwaffaq is popular with journalists and NGO workers.

'Bin Laden slept here once,' he boasts.

The room has two beds, and a bathroom with running cold water. There is a painting of the poet Khaja Abdullah Ansary on the wall between the beds. From the window, Laila has a view of the busy street below, and of a park across the street with pastel-colored-brick paths cutting through

456

thick clusters of flowers. The children, who have grown accustomed to television, are disappointed that there isn't one in the room. Soon enough, though, they are asleep. Soon enough, Tariq and Laila too have collapsed. Laila sleeps soundly in Tariq's arms, except for once in the middle of the night when she wakes from a dream she cannot remember.

The next morning, after a breakfast of tea with fresh bread, quince marmalade, and boiled eggs, Tariq finds her a taxi.

'Are you sure you don't want me to come along?' Tariq says. Aziza is holding his hand. Zalmai isn't, but he is standing close to Tariq, leaning one shoulder on Tariq's hip.

'I'm sure.'

'I worry.'

'I'll be fine,' Laila says. 'I promise. Take the children to a market. Buy them something.'

Zalmai begins to cry when the taxi pulls away, and, when Laila looks back, she sees that he is reaching for Tariq. That he is beginning to accept Tariq both eases and breaks Laila's heart.

'You're not from Herat,' the driver says.

He has dark, shoulder-length hair – a common thumbing of the nose at the departed Taliban, Laila has discovered – and some kind of scar interrupting his mustache on the left side. There is a photo taped to the windshield, on his side. It's of

457

a young girl with pink cheeks and hair parted down the middle into twin braids.

Laila tells him that she has been in Pakistan for the last year, that she is returning to Kabul. 'Deh-Mazang.'

Through the windshield, she sees coppersmiths welding brass handles to jugs, saddlemakers laying out cuts of rawhide to dry in the sun.

'Have you lived here long, brother?' she asks.

'Oh, my whole life. I was born here. I've seen everything. You remember the uprising?'

Laila says she does, but he goes on.

'This was back in March 1979, about nine months before the Soviets invaded. Some angry Heratis killed a few Soviet advisers, so the Soviets sent in tanks and helicopters and pounded this place. For three days, *hamshira*, they fired on the city. They collapsed buildings, destroyed one of the minarets, killed thousands of people. *Thousands*. I lost two sisters in those three days. One of them was twelve years old.' He taps the photo on his windshield. 'That's her.'

'I'm sorry,' Laila says, marveling at how every Afghan story is marked by death and loss and unimaginable grief. And yet, she sees, people find a way to survive, to go on. Laila thinks of her own life and all that has happened to her, and she is astonished that she too has survived, that she is alive and sitting in this taxi listening to this man's story.

★   ★   ★

458

Gul Daman is a village of a few walled houses rising among flat *kolbas* built with mud and straw. Outside the *kolbas*, Laila sees sunburned women cooking, their faces sweating in steam rising from big blackened pots set on makeshift firewood grills. Mules eat from troughs. Children giving chase to chickens begin chasing the taxi. Laila sees men pushing wheelbarrows filled with stones. They stop and watch the car pass by. The driver takes a turn, and they pass a cemetery with a weather-worn mausoleum in the center of it. The driver tells her that a village Sufi is buried there.

There is a windmill too. In the shadow of its idle, rust-colored vanes, three little boys are squatting, playing with mud. The driver pulls over and leans out of the window. The oldest-looking of the three boys is the one to answer. He points to a house farther up the road. The driver thanks him, puts the car back in gear.

He parks outside the walled, one-story house. Laila sees the tops of fig trees above the walls, some of the branches spilling over the side.

'I won't be long,' she says to the driver.

The middle-aged man who opens the door is short, thin, russet-haired. His beard is streaked with parallel stripes of gray. He is wearing a *chapan* over his *pirhan-tumban.*

They exchange *salaam alaykums.*

'Is this Mullah Faizullah's house?' Laila asks.

459

'Yes. I am his son, Hamza. Is there something I can do for you, *hamshireh?*'

'I've come here about an old friend of your father's, Mariam.'

Hamza blinks. A puzzled look passes across his face. 'Mariam . . .'

'Jalil Khan's daughter.'

He blinks again. Then he puts a palm to his cheek and his face lights up with a smile that reveals missing and rotting teeth. 'Oh!' he says. It comes out sounding like *Ohhhhh,* like an expelled breath. 'Oh! Mariam! Are you her daughter? Is she—' He is twisting his neck now, looking behind her eagerly, searching. 'Is she here? It's been so long! Is Mariam here?'

'She has passed on, I'm afraid.'

The smile fades from Hamza's face.

For a moment, they stand there, at the doorway, Hamza looking at the ground. A donkey brays somewhere.

'Come in,' Hamza says. He swings the door open. 'Please come in.'

They sit on the floor in a sparsely furnished room. There is a Herati rug on the floor, beaded cushions to sit on, and a framed photo of Mecca on the wall. They sit by the open window, on either side of an oblong patch of sunlight. Laila hears women's voices whispering from another room. A little barefoot boy places before them a platter of green tea and pistachio *gaaz* nougats. Hamza nods at him.

460

'My son.'

The boy leaves soundlessly.

'So tell me,' Hamza says tiredly.

Laila does. She tells him everything. It takes longer than she'd imagined. Toward the end, she struggles to maintain composure. It still isn't easy, one year later, talking about Mariam.

When she's done, Hamza doesn't say anything for a long time. He slowly turns his teacup on its saucer, one way, then the other.

'My father, may he rest in peace, was so very fond of her,' he says at last. 'He was the one who sang *azan* in her ear when she was born, you know. He visited her every week, never missed. Sometimes he took me with him. He was her tutor, yes, but he was a friend too. He was a charitable man, my father. It nearly broke him when Jalil Khan gave her away.'

'I'm sorry to hear about your father. May God forgive him.'

Hamza nods his thanks. 'He lived to be a very old man. He out-lived Jalil Khan, in fact. We buried him in the village cemetery, not far from where Mariam's mother is buried. My father was a dear, dear man, surely heaven-bound.'

Laila lowers her cup.

'May I ask you something?'

'Of course.'

'Can you show me?' she says. 'Where Mariam lived. Can you take me there?'

★　★　★

The driver agrees to wait awhile longer.

Hamza and Laila exit the village and walk downhill on the road that connects Gul Daman to Herat. After fifteen minutes or so, he points to a narrow gap in the tall grass that flanks the road on both sides.

'That's how you get there,' he says. 'There is a path there.'

The path is rough, winding, and dim, beneath the vegetation and undergrowth. The wind makes the tall grass slam against Laila's calves as she and Hamza climb the path, take the turns. On either side of them is a kaleidoscope of wildflowers swaying in the wind, some tall with curved petals, others low, fan-leafed. Here and there a few ragged buttercups peep through the low bushes. Laila hears the twitter of swallows overhead and the busy chatter of grasshoppers underfoot.

They walk uphill this way for two hundred yards or more. Then the path levels, and opens into a flatter patch of land. They stop, catch their breath. Laila dabs at her brow with her sleeve and bats at a swarm of mosquitoes hovering in front of her face. Here she sees the low-slung mountains in the horizon, a few cottonwoods, some poplars, various wild bushes that she cannot name.

'There used to be a stream here,' Hamza says, a little out of breath. 'But it's long dried up now.'

He says he will wait here. He tells her to cross the dry streambed, walk toward the mountains.

'I'll wait here,' he says, sitting on a rock beneath a poplar. 'You go on.'

'I won't—'

'Don't worry. Take your time. Go on, *hamshireh.*'

Laila thanks him. She crosses the streambed, stepping from one stone to another. She spots broken soda bottles amid the rocks, rusted cans, and a mold-coated metallic container with a zinc lid half buried in the ground.

She heads toward the mountains, toward the weeping willows, which she can see now, the long drooping branches shaking with each gust of wind. In her chest, her heart is drumming. She sees that the willows are arranged as Mariam had said, in a circular grove with a clearing in the middle. Laila walks faster, almost running now. She looks back over her shoulder and sees that Hamza is a tiny figure, his *chapan* a burst of color against the brown of the trees' bark. She trips over a stone and almost falls, then regains her footing. She hurries the rest of the way with the legs of her trousers pulled up. She is panting by the time she reaches the willows.

Mariam's *kolba* is still here.

When she approaches it, Laila sees that the lone windowpane is empty and that the door is gone. Mariam had described a chicken coop and a tandoor, a wooden outhouse too, but Laila sees no sign of them. She pauses at the entrance to the *kolba.* She can hear flies buzzing inside.

To get in, she has to sidestep a large fluttering

463

spiderweb. It's dim inside. Laila has to give her eyes a few moments to adjust. When they do, she sees that the interior is even smaller than she'd imagined. Only half of a single rotting, splintered board remains of the floorboards. The rest, she imagines, have been ripped up for burning as firewood. The floor is carpeted now with dry-edged leaves, broken bottles, discarded chewing gum wrappers, wild mushrooms, old yellowed cigarette butts. But mostly with weeds, some stunted, some springing impudently halfway up the walls.

Fifteen years, Laila thinks. Fifteen years in this place.

Laila sits down, her back to the wall. She listens to the wind filtering through the willows. There are more spiderwebs stretched across the ceiling. Someone has spray-painted something on one of the walls, but much of it has sloughed off, and Laila cannot decipher what it says. Then she realizes the letters are Russian. There is a deserted bird's nest in one corner and a bat hanging upside down in another corner, where the wall meets the low ceiling.

Laila closes her eyes and sits there awhile.

In Pakistan, it was difficult sometimes to remember the details of Mariam's face. There were times when, like a word on the tip of her tongue, Mariam's face eluded her. But now, here in this place, it's easy to summon Mariam behind the lids of her eyes: the soft radiance of her gaze, the long chin, the coarsened skin of her neck, the tight-lipped smile. Here,

Laila can lay her cheek on the softness of Mariam's lap again, can feel Mariam swaying back and forth, reciting verses from the Koran, can feel the words vibrating down Mariam's body, to her knees, and into her own ears.

Then, suddenly, the weeds begin to recede, as if something is pulling them by the roots from beneath the ground. They sink lower and lower until the earth in the *kolba* has swallowed the last of their spiny leaves. The spiderwebs magically unspin themselves. The bird's nest self-disassembles, the twigs snapping loose one by one, flying out of the *kolba* end over end. An invisible eraser wipes the Russian graffiti off the wall.

The floorboards are back. Laila sees a pair of sleeping cots now, a wooden table, two chairs, a cast-iron stove in the corner, shelves along the walls, on which sit clay pots and pans, a blackened teakettle, cups and spoons. She hears chickens clucking outside, the distant gurgling of the stream.

A young Mariam is sitting at the table making a doll by the glow of an oil lamp. She's humming something. Her face is smooth and youthful, her hair washed, combed back. She has all her teeth.

Laila watches Mariam glue strands of yarn onto her doll's head. In a few years, this little girl will be a woman who will make small demands on life, who will never burden others, who will never let on that she too has had sorrows, disappointments, dreams that have been ridiculed. A woman who will be like a rock in a riverbed, enduring without complaint, her grace not sullied but *shaped* by the turbulence that washes over her. Already Laila sees something behind this young girl's eyes, something deep in her core, that neither Rasheed nor the Taliban will be able to break. Something as hard and unyielding as a block of limestone. Something that, in the end, will be *her* undoing and Laila's salvation.

The little girl looks up. Puts down the doll. Smiles.

*Laila jo?*

Laila's eyes snap open. She gasps, and her body pitches forward. She startles the bat, which zips from one end of the *kolba* to the other, its beating wings like the fluttering pages of a book, before it flies out the window.

Laila gets to her feet, beats the dead leaves from the seat of her trousers. She steps out of the *kolba*. Outside, the light has shifted slightly. A wind is blowing, making the grass ripple and the willow branches click.

Before she leaves the clearing, Laila takes one last look at the *kolba* where Mariam had slept, eaten, dreamed, held her breath for Jalil. On sagging walls, the willows cast crooked patterns that shift with each gust of wind. A crow has landed on the flat roof. It pecks at something, squawks, flies off.

'Good-bye, Mariam.'

And, with that, unaware that she is weeping, Laila begins to run through the grass.

She finds Hamza still sitting on the rock. When he spots her, he stands up.

'Let's go back,' he says. Then, 'I have something to give you.'

Laila waits for Hamza in the garden by the front door. The boy who had served them tea earlier is standing beneath one of the fig trees holding a chicken, watching her impassively. Laila spies two faces, an old woman and a young girl in *hijabs*, observing her demurely from a window.

The door to the house opens and Hamza emerges. He is carrying a box.

He gives it to Laila.

'Jalil Khan gave this to my father a month or so before he died,' Hamza says. 'He asked my father to safeguard it for Mariam until she came to claim it. My father kept it for two years. Then, just before he passed away, he gave it to me, and asked me to save it for Mariam. But she . . . you know, she never came.'

Laila looks down at the oval-shaped tin box. It looks like an old chocolate box. It's olive green, with fading gilt scrolls all around the hinged lid. There is a little rust on the sides, and two tiny dents on the front rim of the lid. Laila tries to open the box, but the latch is locked.

'What's in it?' she asks.

Hamza puts a key in her palm. 'My father never unlocked it. Neither did I. I suppose it was God's will that it be you.'

★   ★   ★

Back at the hotel, Tariq and the children are not back yet.

Laila sits on the bed, the box on her lap. Part other wants to leave it unopened, let whatever Jalil had intended remain a secret. But, in the end, the curiosity proves too strong. She slides in the key. It takes some rattling and shaking, but she opens the box.

In it, she finds three things: an envelope, a burlap sack, and a video cassette.

Laila takes the tape and goes down to the reception desk. She learns from the elderly clerk who had greeted them the day before that the hotel has only one VCR, in its biggest suite. The suite is vacant at the moment, and he agrees to take her. He leaves the desk to a mustachioed young man in a suit who is talking on a cellular phone.

The old clerk leads Laila to the second floor, to a door at the end of a long hallway. He works the lock, lets her in. Laila's eyes find the TV in the corner. They register nothing else about the suite.

She turns on the TV, turns on the VCR. Puts the tape in and pushes the PLAY button. The screen is blank for a few moments, and Laila begins to wonder why Jalil had gone to the trouble of passing a blank tape to Mariam. But then there is music, and images begin to play on the screen.

Laila frowns. She keeps watching for a minute or two. Then she pushes STOP, fast-forwards the tape, and pushes PLAY again. It's the same film.

The old man is looking at her quizzically.

The film playing on the screen is Walt Disney's *Pinocchio*. Laila does not understand.

Tariq and the children come back to the hotel just after six o'clock. Aziza runs to Laila and shows her the earrings Tariq has bought for her, silver with an enamel butterfly on each. Zalmai is clutching an inflatable dolphin that squeaks when its snout is squeezed.

'How are you?' Tariq asks, putting his arm around her shoulder.

'I'm fine,' Laila says. 'I'll tell you later.'

They walk to a nearby kebab house to eat. It's a small place, with sticky, vinyl tablecloths, smoky and loud. But the lamb is tender and moist and the bread hot. They walk the streets for a while after. Tariq buys the children rosewater ice cream from a street-side kiosk. They eat, sitting on a bench, the mountains behind them silhouetted against the scarlet red of dusk. The air is warm, rich with the fragrance of cedar.

Laila had opened the envelope earlier when she'd come back to the room after viewing the video-tape. In it was a letter, handwritten in blue ink on a yellow, lined sheet of paper.

It read:

May 13, 1987

My dear Mariam:

I pray that this letter finds you in good health.

As you know, I came to Kabul a month ago to speak with you. But you would not see me. I was disappointed but could not blame you. In your place, I might have done the same. I lost the privilege of your good graces a long time ago and for that I only have myself to blame. But if you are reading this letter, then you have read the letter that I left at your door. You have read it and you have come to see Mullah Faizullah, as I had asked that you do. I am grateful that you did, Mariam jo. I am grateful for this chance to say a few words to you.

Where do I begin?

Your father has known so much sorrow since we last spoke, Mariam jo. Your stepmother Afsoon was killed on the first day of the 1979 uprising. A stray bullet killed your sister Niloufar that same day. I can still see her, my little Niloufar, doing headstands to impress guests. Your brother Farhad joined the jihad in 1980. The Soviets killed him in 1982, just outside of Helmand. I never got to see his body. I don't know if you have children of your own, Mariam jo, but if you do I pray that God look after them and spare you the grief that I have known. I still dream of them. I still dream of my dead children.

I have dreams of you too, Mariam jo. I miss you. I miss the sound of your voice, your laughter. I miss reading to you, and all those times we fished together. Do you remember all those times we fished together? You were a good daughter, Mariam jo, and I cannot ever think of you without feeling shame and regret. Regret . . . When it comes to you, Mariam jo, I have oceans of it. I regret that I did not see you the day you came to Herat. I regret that I did not open the door and take you in. I regret that I did not make you a daughter to me, that I let you live in that place for all those years. And for what? Fear of losing face? Of staining my so-called good name? How little those things matter to me now after all the loss, all the terrible things I have seen in this cursed war. But now, of course, it is too late. Perhaps this is just punishment for those who have been heartless, to understand only when nothing can be undone. Now all I can do is say that you were a good daughter, Mariam jo, and that I never deserved you. Now all I can do is ask for your forgiveness. So forgive me, Mariam jo. Forgive me. Forgive me. Forgive me.

I am not the wealthy man you once knew. The communists confiscated so much of my land, and all of my stores as well. But it is petty to complain, for God – for reasons that I do not understand – has still blessed me with far more than most people. Since my return from Kabul, I have managed to sell what little remained of my land. I have enclosed for you your share of the inheritance. You can see that it is far from a fortune, but it is something. It is something. (You will also notice that I have taken the liberty of exchanging the money into dollars. I think it is for the best. God alone knows the fate of our own beleaguered currency.)

I hope you do not think that I am trying to buy your forgiveness. I hope you will credit me with knowing that your forgiveness is not for sale. It never was. I am merely giving you, if belatedly, what was rightfully yours all along. I was not a dutiful father to you in life. Perhaps in death I can be.

Ah, death. I won't burden you with details, but death is within sight for me now. Weak heart, the doctors say. It is a fitting manner of death, I think, for a weak man.

Mariam jo,

I dare, I dare allow myself the hope that, after you read this, you will be more charitable to me than I ever was to you. That you might find it in your heart to come and see your father. That you will knock on my door one more time and give me the chance to open it this time, to welcome you, to take you in my arms, my daughter, as I should have all those years ago. It is a hope as weak as my heart. This I know. But I will be waiting. I will be listening for your knock. I will be hoping.

May God grant you a long and prosperous life, my daughter. May God give you many healthy and beautiful children. May you find the happiness, peace, and acceptance that I did not give you. Be well. I leave you in the loving hands of God.

Your undeserving father,
Jalil

That night, after they return to the hotel, after the children have played and gone to bed, Laila tells Tariq about the letter. She shows him the money in the burlap sack. When she begins to cry, he kisses her face and holds her in his arms.

# CHAPTER 51

## APRIL 2003

T he drought has ended. It snowed at last this past winter, knee-deep, and now it has been raining for days. The Kabul River is flowing once again. Its spring floods have washed away Titanic City.

There is mud on the streets now. Shoes squish. Cars get trapped. Donkeys loaded with apples slog heavily, their hooves splattering muck from rain puddles. But no one is complaining about the mud, no one is mourning Titanic City. *We need Kabul to be green again*, people say.

Yesterday, Laila watched her children play in the downpour, hopping from one puddle to another in their backyard beneath a lead-colored sky. She was watching from the kitchen window of the small two-bedroom house that they are renting in Deh-Mazang. There is a pomegranate tree in the yard and a thicket of sweetbriar bushes. Tariq has patched the walls and built the children a slide, a swing set, a little fenced area for Zalmai's new goat. Laila watched the rain slide

474

off Zalmai's scalp – he has asked that he be shaved, like Tariq, who is in charge now of saying the *Babaloo* prayers. The rain flattened Aziza's long hair, turned it into sodden tendrils that sprayed Zalmai when she snapped her head.

Zalmai is almost six. Aziza is ten. They celebrated her birthday last week, took her to Cinema Park, where, at last, *Titanic* was openly screened for the people of Kabul.

'Come on, children, we're going to be late,' Laila calls, putting their lunches in a paper bag.

It's eight o'clock in the morning. Laila was up at five. As always, it was Aziza who shook her awake for morning *namaz*. The prayers, Laila knows, are Aziza's way of clinging to Mariam, her way of keeping Mariam close awhile yet before time has its way, before it snatches Mariam from the garden of her memory like a weed pulled by its roots.

After *namaz*, Laila had gone back to bed, and was still asleep when Tariq left the house. She vaguely remembers him kissing her cheek. Tariq has found work with a French NGO that fits land mine survivors and amputees with prosthetic limbs.

Zalmai comes chasing Aziza into the kitchen.

'You have your notebooks, you two? Pencils? Textbooks?'

'Right here,' Aziza says, lifting her backpack. Again, Laila notices how her stutter is lessening.

475

'Let's go, then.'

Laila lets the children out of the house, locks the door. They step out into the cool morning. It isn't raining today. The sky is blue, and Laila sees no clumps of clouds in the horizon. Holding hands, the three of them make their way to the bus stop. The streets are busy already, teeming with a steady stream of rickshaws, taxicabs, UN trucks, buses, ISAF jeeps. Sleepy-eyed merchants are unlocking store gates that had been rolled down for the night. Vendors sit behind towers of chewing gum and cigarette packs. Already the widows have claimed their spots at street corners, asking the passersby for coins.

Laila finds it strange to be back in Kabul. The city has changed. Every day now she sees people planting saplings, painting old houses, carrying bricks for new ones. They dig gutters and wells. On windowsills, Laila spots flowers potted in the empty shells of old Mujahideen rockets – rocket flowers, Kabulis call them. Recently, Tariq took Laila and the children to the Gardens of Babur, which are being renovated. For the first time in years, Laila hears music at Kabul's street corners, *rubab* and tabla, *dootar*, harmonium and tamboura, old Ahmad Zahir songs.

Laila wishes Mammy and Babi were alive to see these changes. But, like Jalil's letter, Kabul's penance has arrived too late.

Laila and the children are about to cross the street to the bus stop when suddenly a black Land

Cruiser with tinted windows blows by. It swerves at the last instant and misses Laila by less than an arm's length. It splatters tea-colored rainwater all over the children's shirts.

Laila yanks her children back onto the sidewalk, heart somersaulting in her throat.

The Land Cruiser speeds down the street, honks twice, and makes a sharp left.

Laila stands there, trying to catch her breath, her fingers gripped tightly around her children's wrists.

It slays Laila. It slays her that the warlords have been allowed back to Kabul. That her parents' murderers live in posh homes with walled gardens, that they have been appointed minister of this and deputy minister of that, that they ride with impunity in shiny, bulletproof SUVs through neighborhoods that they demolished. It slays her.

But Laila has decided that she will not be crippled by resentment. Mariam wouldn't want it that way. *What's the sense?* she would say with a smile both innocent and wise. *What good is it, Laila jo?* And so Laila has resigned herself to moving on. For her own sake, for Tariq's, for her children's. And for Mariam, who still visits Laila in her dreams, who is never more than a breath or two below her consciousness. Laila has moved on. Because in the end she knows that's all she can do. That and hope.

Zaman is standing at the free throw line, his knees bent, bouncing a basketball. He is instructing a

477

group of boys in matching jerseys sitting in a semi-circle on the court. Zaman spots Laila, tucks the ball under his arm, and waves. He says something to the boys, who then wave and cry out, '*Salaam, moalim sahib!*'

Laila waves back.

The orphanage playground has a row of apple saplings now along the east-facing wall. Laila is planning to plant some on the south wall as well as soon as it is rebuilt. There is a new swing set, new monkey bars, and a jungle gym.

Laila walks back inside through the screen door.

They have repainted both the exterior and the interior of the orphanage. Tariq and Zaman have repaired all the roof leaks, patched the walls, replaced the windows, carpeted the rooms where the children sleep and play. This past winter, Laila bought a few beds for the children's sleeping quarters, pillows too, and proper wool blankets. She had cast-iron stoves installed for the winter.

*Anis*, one of Kabul's newspapers, had run a story the month before on the renovation of the orphanage. They'd taken a photo too, of Zaman, Tariq, Laila, and one of the attendants, standing in a row behind the children. When Laila saw the article, she'd thought of her childhood friends Giti and Hasina, and Hasina saying, *By the time we're twenty, Giti and I, we'll have pushed out four, five kids each. But you, Laila, you'll make us two dummies proud. You're going to be somebody. I know one day I'll pick up a newspaper and find your picture on the front page.* The photo hadn't made the front page, but there it was nevertheless, as Hasina had predicted.

Laila takes a turn and makes her way down the same hallway where, two years before, she and Mariam had delivered Aziza to Zaman. Laila still remembers how they had to pry Aziza's fingers from her wrist. She remembers running down this hallway, holding back a howl, Mariam calling after her, Aziza screaming with panic. The hallway's walls are covered now with posters, of dinosaurs, cartoon characters, the Buddhas of Bamiyan, and displays of artwork by the orphans. Many of the drawings depict tanks running over huts, men brandishing AK-47s, refugee camp tents, scenes of jihad.

Laila turns a corner in the hallway and sees the children now, waiting outside the classroom. She is greeted by their scarves, their shaved scalps covered by skullcaps, their small, lean figures, the beauty of their drabness.

When the children spot Laila, they come running. They come running at full tilt. Laila is swarmed. There is a flurry of high-pitched greetings, of shrill voices, of patting, clutching, tugging, groping, of jostling with one another to climb into her arms. There are outstretched little hands and appeals for attention. Some of them call her *Mother.* Laila does not correct them.

It takes Laila some work this morning to calm the children down, to get them to form a proper queue, to usher them into the classroom.

It was Tariq and Zaman who built the classroom by knocking down the wall between two adjacent rooms. The floor is still badly cracked and has missing tiles. For the time being, it is covered with tarpaulin, but Tariq has promised to cement some new tiles and lay down carpeting soon.

Nailed above the classroom doorway is a rectangular board, which Zaman has sanded and painted in gleaming white. On it, with a brush, Zaman has written four lines of poetry, his answer, Laila knows, to those who grumble that the promised aid money to Afghanistan isn't coming, that the rebuilding is going too slowly, that there is corruption, that the Taliban are regrouping already and will come back with a vengeance, that the world will forget once again about Afghanistan. The lines are from his favorite of Hafez's *ghazals*:

*Joseph shall return to Canaan, grieve not,*
*Hovels shall turn to rose gardens, grieve not.*
*If a flood should arrive, to drown all that's alive,*
*Noah is your guide in the typhoon's eye, grieve not.*

Laila passes beneath the sign and enters the classroom. The children are taking their seats, flipping notebooks open, chattering. Aziza is talking to a girl in the adjacent row. A paper airplane floats across the room in a high arc. Someone tosses it back.

'Open your Farsi books, children,' Laila says, dropping her own books on her desk.

To a chorus of flipping pages, Laila makes her way to the curtainless window. Through the glass, she can see the boys in the playground lining up to practice their free throws. Above them, over the mountains, the morning sun is rising. It catches the metallic rim of the basketball hoop, the chain link of the tire swings, the whistle hanging around Zaman's neck, his new, unchipped spectacles. Laila flattens her palms against the warm glass panes. Closes her eyes. She lets the sunlight fall on her cheeks, her eyelids, her brow.

When they first came back to Kabul, it distressed Laila that she didn't know where the Taliban had buried Mariam. She wished she could visit Mariam's grave, to sit with her awhile, leave a flower or two. But Laila sees now that it doesn't matter. Mariam is never very far. She is here, in these walls they've repainted, in the trees they've planted, in the blankets that keep the children warm, in these pillows and books and pencils. She is in the children's laughter. She is in the verses Aziza recites and in the prayers she mutters when she bows westward. But, mostly, Mariam is in Laila's own heart, where she shines with the bursting radiance of a thousand suns.

Someone has been calling her name, Laila realizes. She turns around, instinctively tilts her head, lifting her good ear just a tad. It's Aziza.

'Mammy? Are you all right?'

The room has become quiet. The children are watching her.

Laila is about to answer when her breath suddenly catches. Her hands shoot down. They pat the spot where, a moment before, she'd felt a wave go through her. She waits. But there is no more movement.

'Mammy?'

'Yes, my love.' Laila smiles. 'I'm all right. Yes. Very much.'

As she walks to her desk at the front of the class, Laila thinks of the naming game they'd played again over dinner the night before. It has become a nightly ritual ever since Laila gave Tariq and the children the news. Back and forth they go, making a case for their own choice. Tariq likes Mohammad. Zalmai, who has recently watched *Superman* on tape, is puzzled as to why an Afghan boy cannot be named Clark. Aziza is campaigning hard for Aman. Laila likes Omar.

But the game involves only male names.

Because, if it's a girl, Laila has already named her.

# AFTERWORD

For almost three decades now, the Afghan refugee crisis has been one of the most severe around the globe. War, hunger, anarchy, and oppression forced millions of people – like Tariq and his family in this tale – to abandon their homes and flee Afghanistan to settle in neighboring Pakistan and Iran. At the height of the exodus, as many as eight million Afghans were living abroad as refugees. Today, more than two million Afghan refugees remain in Pakistan.

Over the past year, I have had the privilege of working as a U.S. envoy for UNHCR, the UN refugee agency, one of the world's foremost humanitarian agencies. UNHCR's mandate is to protect the basic human rights of refugees, provide emergency relief, and to help refugees restart their lives in a safe environment. UNHCR provides assistance to more than twenty million displaced people around the world, not only in Afghanistan but also in places such as Colombia, Burundi, the Congo, Chad, and the Darfur region of Sudan. Working with UNHCR to help refugees has been one of the most rewarding and meaningful experiences of my life.

To help, or simply to learn more about UNHCR, its work, or the plight of refugees in general, please visit: www.UNrefugees.org.
Thank you.

Khaled Hosseini
January 31, 2007

# ACKNOWLEDGMENTS

A few clarifications before I give thanks. The village of Gul Daman is a fictional place – as far as I know. Those who are familiar with the city of Herat will notice that I have taken minor liberties describing the geography around it. Last, the title of this novel comes from a poem composed by Saeb-e-Tabrizi, a seventeenth-century Persian poet. Those who know the original Farsi poem will doubtless note that the English translation of the line containing the title of this novel is not a literal one. But it is the generally accepted translation, by Dr Josephine Davis, and I found it lovely. I am grateful to her.

I would like to thank Qayoum Sarwar, Hekmat Sadat, Elyse Hathaway, Rosemary Stasek, Lawrence Quill, and Haleema Jazmin Quill for their assistance and support.

Very special thanks to my father, Baba, for reading this manuscript, for his feedback, and, as ever, for his love and support. And to my mother, whose selfless, gentle spirit permeates this tale. You are my reason, Mother jo. My thanks go to my in-laws for their generosity and many kindnesses. To the rest of my wonderful family, I remain indebted and grateful to each and every one of you.

I wish to thank my agent, Elaine Koster, for always, always believing, Jody Hotchkiss (Onward!), David Grossman, Helen Heller, and the tireless Chandler Crawford. I am grateful and indebted to every single person at Riverhead Books. In particular, I want to thank Susan Petersen Kennedy and Geoffrey Kloske for their faith in this story. My heartfelt thanks also go to Marilyn Ducksworth, Mih-Ho Cha, Catharine Lynch, Craig D. Burke, Leslie Schwartz, Honi Werner, and Wendy Pearl. Special thanks to my sharp-eyed copy editor, Tony Davis, who misses nothing, and, lastly, to my talented editor, Sarah McGrath, for her patience, foresight, and guidance.

Finally, thank you, Roya. For reading this story, again and again, for weathering my minor crises of confidence (and a couple of major ones), for never doubting. This book would not be without you. I love you.